Eternal Knight

Matt Heppe

I hope you enjoy
Eternal Knight!

Matt H

Published by Matt Heppe
2011

ISBN:
978-1461009832

Contact:
MattHeppe+EternalKnight@gmail.com

Cover by Ken Hendrix
Kenhendrix24@gmail.com

Map by Steve Sandford

For my wife, Helen

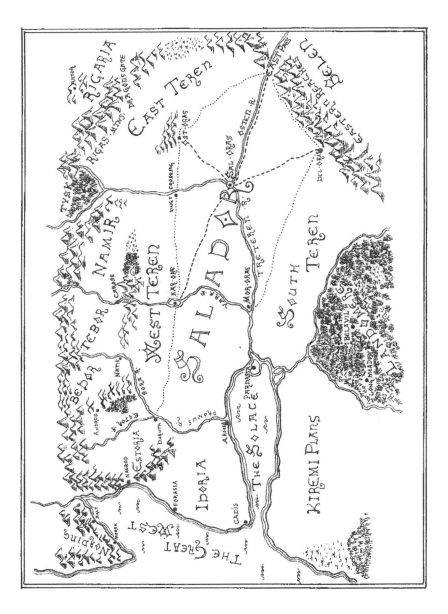

Chapter One

Hadde crouched behind the rotting trunk of a fallen tree. Ahead of her the Kiremi raiding party crept deeper into the forest. She counted a score of them—more than enough to destroy Long Meadow. And the Kiremi weren't alone. Strange warriors in fur cloaks marched with them.

She flexed her fingers against the cold wind and gripped her bow tighter. *Dromost take them! Isn't the Wasting enough?*

Dry leaves crunched behind her. Startled, she ducked and turned, but it was only Belor and Calen. *"Danger,"* she hunter-signed. *"Stay down."*

Belor nodded and the two hunters crouched lower as they made their way toward her. Hadde was about to turn back to the raiders when a gust of wind sent a wave of dead leaves washing over them. Nearby, a Wasting-weakened tree branch cracked and fell crashing to the forest floor.

Three arrows whipped into the forest, one embedding itself into a tree just strides from Hadde. Belor and Calen snatched arrows from their quivers as Hadde drew her bow. Shoot and flee, she thought as she took aim.

She ducked back without loosing her arrow as one of the strange warriors struck a Kiremi a hard blow with a javelin shaft. The Kiremi cowered as the warrior berated him. "Fool," she heard, and other words she couldn't make out. With a contemptuous glare, the bear-cloaked warrior strode into the forest.

Hadde gave Belor and Calen a warning sign. Both pulled the hoods of their mottled green and brown cloaks over their heads and lay still against the leaf-littered ground. Hadde pressed against the log, willing herself not to be seen. The falling branch must have startled them, she thought. They don't know we're here.

Leaves crunched underfoot as the warrior walked past Hadde's hiding place. Her heart pounded in her chest—she was certain she'd be seen. *Kill him and escape into the forest. It's our only hope.*

But the warrior didn't spare them a glance as he jammed his javelin into the ground and stepped over the freshly fallen branch. "This?" he called back to the Kiremi. "This is what you fear?" He easily lifted the heavy branch over his head and tossed it in the direction of the raiding party. "Cowards!"

His eyes swept the forest as he retrieved his javelin. Hadde clenched her jaws as his gaze passed over her and her companions. *Silver eyes.* She stifled a gasp.

She froze as his eyes flicked back in her direction, but then he turned and strode out of sight. Hadde raised herself to look over the log, sighing in relief as the raiders moved on. But the image of his silver eyes stuck in her mind. It must have been a chance reflection or her imagination playing tricks on her. No one had silver eyes.

She gave a low whistle and Belor and Calen joined her. "They're still heading for Long Meadow," she said. "Any more following behind?"

"We backtracked five arrow-flights," Belor said, his breath misting in the cold air. "I think this is all of them."

"Where are the rest of their horses?" Calen asked. "They only have four." His voice wavered as he spoke. At fourteen he was the youngest among them.

Hadde squeezed Calen's shoulder. "The Wasting is as bad on the plains as it is in the forest. They're desperate. But don't fear. We'll warn the village." She hoped she sounded more confident than she felt.

"Enough," Belor said. "We should attack. It'll spoil their raid."

Calen's eyes bulged and he clutched his bow tighter.

"There are a score of them at least," Hadde said. "We can't attack them alone." She motioned Calen closer. "Run for the village. Tell them raiders are coming. Kiremi and strangers." Hadde ignored the disapproving glance Belor shot her.

"But I should stay, " Calen said. "I want to——"

"Go now, Calen," Hadde said. "I need you to do this. You have to warn Long Meadow."

"Yes, Huntress."

He turned to leave, but Belor caught him by the arm. "We need him here. We——"

"No. He goes." She ignored the flash of anger that crossed his face. She loved him, but he was always too rash. "You both chose me as hunt leader. "

"This is different. This is important. I'll——"

"Don't be an akinos. " Belor flinched at the insult. She silenced him with a glare before he could reply. "Go ahead, Calen, " she said.

Calen, with one last glance at the raiders, slipped into the forest.

Hadde sighed with relief at his departure. "The village has to be warned," she said to Belor. "And he'll be better off fighting at the side of our people. "

Belor grunted his assent as he peered after the raiders. "The Kiremi have no sense in the woods. They make too much noise."

He was right, Hadde thought. They didn't even have scouts. But they were still a terrible threat. She blew warm air into her cupped hands. "We'll stash our packs here and follow them. Stay to my left—I'll watch the right. We'll only attack if Calen fails to warn Long Meadow."

"Let's show the Kiremi who owns the forest, " he said as he took off his pack and placed it next to hers.

Hadde caught the excited gleam in his eyes. "Be safe. Don't risk too much."

He chuckled and, leaning close, gave her a quick kiss on the cheek. "You too, Hadde." Before she could reply he nocked an arrow and left the cover of the fallen tree. Belor, despite his height, moved like a shadow as he slipped off. She hoped he wouldn't betray their presence with his eagerness to come to grips with the raiders.

Hadde nocked her own arrow—not a light flight arrow, but a heavy broadhead. With one last deep breath, she set off after the raiders. Following them was easy—the column was slow and stopped often. She observed the lone Kiremi rear-guard as he paused to inspect the forest behind the column. Not much of a guard, she thought. He barely spared the forest a glance. The Kiremi had little hope of spotting the two stealthy Landomeri. But still, she held her bow ready each time his gaze strayed in her direction.

The shadows lengthened on the forest floor. Where were Long Meadow's hunters? Calen couldn't have become lost; they were too close to home. And she was certain they would have heard something if he had been caught.

The raiders stopped. The village was only a few arrow-flights off. Time had run out.

Hadde froze behind the tree that hid her. The raiders picketed their few horses and saw to their weapons. She looked for Belor and spotted him staring at her. *"Now?"* he hunter-signed with a quick gesture.

If they attacked the raiders and drew them off, it would spoil the raid. The shouts and the sound of the pursuit might even carry far enough to warn Long Meadow. But she and Belor wouldn't likely survive the pursuit. *"Wait, "* she replied.

"When?"

"Not yet. "

Belor flexed his bowstring impatiently as the raiding party crept

3

toward the village. There was no putting it off. *"Now,"* she signed. *"That one."*

"No clear shot. You take him."

She took a deep breath, hooked her thumb ring against her bowstring, and drew the arrow to her ear. The Kiremi stood motionless a stone's throw away. As she took aim her left hand shook uncontrollably. She let the tension out of the string and rubbed her forearm across her brow.

She glanced to her left.

"Take him!" Belor signed with a quick slash.

She had to do it. The man was a raider. He was there to attack the village.

Hadde took another breath. The raider's back was to her. He wore a leather aketon, but it wouldn't stop an arrow at this range. The warrior peered into the forest where his companions had just disappeared.

She had killed a man before. And she would have to again.

In one smooth motion Hadde pulled the bowstring taut, took aim, and let the arrow fly. The broad-head tip punched through the man's armor just below his right shoulder blade. The startled raider let out a short cry, arching his back in pain. He dropped his bow and clutched at the shaft in his back.

Hadde kept her eyes on the raider as she nocked another arrow. He had somehow kept his feet and staggered to his right. She saw his face. Just a boy. For a moment, she stood frozen.

The young raider's mouth gaped, but the agony of the arrow prevented him from calling out. He gasped and choked as he struggled for a breath. Hadde stepped out from behind the tree and took aim. Her second arrow toppled the Kiremi to the ground. To her left she heard the snorting and shuffling of the horses. There were shouts in the distance.

"Good," Belor signed.

Good? She glanced back at the body. What good was there in a boy's death? Why did it have to be like this? With an arrow held ready, Hadde padded silently toward the downed raider. His dead eyes stared up at her—the round eyes of a Kiremi. Even the tattoos covering his face couldn't mask his anguish. Just a boy. She turned away.

"Follow me," Belor signed as he started after the other raiders.

"Wait." Hadde waved to get his attention, but he had disappeared. "Just wait a moment," she muttered to herself. *Always too hasty.*

More shouts, and then a hunting horn. Her people. Hadde jogged forward, eyes searching the forest for more raiders. And for any sign of Belor. She took a deep breath to calm herself.

Footsteps crashed through the underbrush as one of the strangers burst into view, his silver eyes blazing. Hadde loosed her arrow at the same moment he cast his javelin. The javelin buried itself in a tree next to her. Her arrow flew past his head into the forest canopy.

"Belor!" she shouted and pulled another arrow from her quiver.

Grasping a second javelin, the raider rushed her. Hadde half-drew her bow and loosed the arrow.

She tried to spin away but he crashed into her, sending her tumbling. Gasping for breath, she struggled to her feet. The raider was on his knees, almost in reach of her. He clutched the arrow lodged in the leather armor protecting his right arm.

Dazed, Hadde staggered away from him. Blood trickled into her eye as she scanned the ground for her bow. Grinning, the warrior stood and stepped over it. "You die now, forest girl," he said, his accent thick.

Hadde flinched from his cold, metallic gaze. What had done this to him? What kind of beast was he? But the blood dripping down his arm was red, and his wounds were real. She drew her long hunting knife and backed toward the horses.

"Belor!" she called out again. She could hear commotion to her left but dared not look.

"Keep away from horse," the raider snarled as he advanced. He drew his short-hafted axe from his belt with his good left hand.

Hadde heard the distant sounds of men yelling and running. Time to retreat—one man twice her size would be dangerous enough.

He rushed her just as she turned to flee.

She leaped to her right, but her foot caught on a root and she fell. As she rose the raider swung his axe in a wicked arc. She rolled aside, the blade whistling past her face.

He jumped after her and she slashed at his stomach with her knife, gashing his armor. He snorted and kicked her in the ribs. Crying out in pain, she crawled from him.

"Not so strong without bow?" He spat on her. "You like?" He aimed a heavy kick at her, but she rolled toward him, taking some of the force out of the blow.

She wouldn't get another chance. His armor protected his legs from blows coming from above, but not below. As the raider attacked she thrust her knife under his aketon's skirt. He bellowed in rage and reeled away from her.

Hadde staggered to her feet, her head pounding out a drumbeat of pain. The raider's blood covered her blade and ran down onto her fist.

And then she saw her bow only a stride away. She flung her knife at the raider. As he ducked it, she snatched up her bow and dodged away. His axe whirled past her face as she drew an arrow and turned to face him. He lurched after her, sliding a knife from his belt.

5

Her arrow took him in the chest. With a grunt, he lurched back, and fell hard. Hadde drew a deep breath and wiped away the blood that ran down her face. Horns blared nearby, followed by the shouts of men.

The raider grunted and rolled to his side. Hadde stood frozen at the sight. Her arrow was still in him, sunk all the way to the fletching. How was it possible he was alive? As he struggled to his knees, she drew another arrow and shot him. He staggered and fell to his back, the second arrow protruding just a hand span from the first.

Icy fear gripped her stomach as he rolled onto his side choking and coughing up blood. *Not dead. Still not dead.* His silver eyes stared at her as he attempted to rise.

Hadde drew another arrow. He seemed to stare at it—it was hard to tell—and then he collapsed. She stood frozen, bow ready, as his eyes faded to dull gray and then to black.

More shouts—closer this time. The fight wasn't over.

Chapter Two

"Careful now, Mother!" Hadde raised her arms as her mother pulled the woolen hunting tunic over Hadde's head. She sat on the bench near the fireplace. It was good to be back in the warmth of the family cottage—a well-built structure, the lower half river stone and mortar and the top logs with a thatch roof.

"Lean back and let me see what those bastards have done to my daughter," Enna said, her usually pretty face locked in a scowl. Hadde obliged, not that she had any choice with her mother in this mood.

"There's a cut right at your hairline. It's bled a lot, but it isn't deep. Sit still and I'll clean it."

"Were there many wounded?" Hadde asked.

"Lanwe was knocked cold and cousin Thad took a bad cut to his arm. They'll be fine as long as Thad's wound doesn't go bad. A few other cuts and bruises." Enna's mouth curled down. "They got Old Gaw."

"I know," Hadde replied. "He put two arrows into one of the strange warriors, but it didn't put him down."

"He's with Helna now," Enna said as she limped to the cottage fireplace. It provided the only light in the room. Evening had fallen and the windows were shuttered against the winter wind. "He was never the same after the children died."

She returned with a small pottery bowl of hot water, a linen towel, and some herbs. "You killed the filth who did this to you?"

"I stabbed him in the leg and——"

"I hope it was his middle leg."

"Mother!"

"I'm serious." There was no hint of humor in her mother's tone. "I hope you cut——"

"Yes, I killed him."

"Good for you. And the others?"

"Belor and a few other hunters are tracking them down. I don't think any will get away." She smiled. "Belor sent me home to clean up before Father could see me. Poor Belor thinks Father will blame him for letting me get wounded."

"Good thinking," Enna said as she took Hadde's face in her hands. "The boy didn't find the time to pledge himself to you, did he?"

"Not now, Mother."

"Taking his time," Enna muttered. And then louder, she said, "This poultice will help. The herbs will take the pain out." Enna cleaned the blood from Hadde's face and neck. "They've wounded both of us now, those Kiremi vultures. But you've made them pay both times. Don't move—I'm going to tend the wound."

Hadde tried not to flinch as her mother washed out the cut. "They weren't all Kiremi. There were... strangers. They had silver eyes and wore bear furs. They were terribly strong."

"Thad mentioned the silver eyes when I tended to his arm. But I've never heard of such a thing."

"Their eyes were silver. And when they died their eyes turned black."

Enna gave her a cautious look. "Maybe they're creatures of the Wasting." She pressed a clean cloth to Hadde's forehead.

"I don't think so," Hadde said. "The Wasting is weakness. It's illness and death. But these men were strong. I'm just glad Calen reached our village in time."

"The poor child screamed like the veden were after him." Enna paused. "Maybe that's what they are—veden."

"Mother, please, those stories are ancient myth. These men were strange, but they weren't veden."

"Well, Calen made it in time. We all had bows in hand in just moments. Your father took a few hunters into the woods to find the raiders while the rest of the village lay in ambush. I wanted to take part, but he wouldn't let me."

"He was right not to, Mother. Not with your leg."

"Hold this to your head, dear. I'm going to make the compress." Enna mashed some dried silver root and birch bark powder with a mortar and pestle she fetched from the hearth. Adding warm water, she stirred the ingredients into a paste she kneaded under her chapped hands. She chanted a prayer to Helna as she wrapped the paste inside a linen bandage.

Hadde couldn't help herself. "The words don't do anything. The gods are gone."

"Shush, you listen to your father too much. Helna's spirit is still with us. Now hold still." Enna bound the compress to Hadde's head with a strip of cloth. "Too tight?"

"It's fine." Hadde reached out and touched the three small, rayed orbs tattooed on her mother's cheekbone. "Thank you, Mother."

Enna traced her finger across Hadde's cheek, where her own marks rested. "Anything for my daughter." She paused and smiled. "I'm sure you're hungry. I'll put on some split peas."

"Thank you. I'll wash up."

"The cauldrons are hot. Leave the little one for peas."

"Thank you. I'll refill it later." Hadde stood and stretched. Her ribs were sore from being kicked. She looked longingly at the deep tub hanging high on the wall. A long soak would have done wonderfully, but the tub had sprung a leak months ago and there hadn't been time to repair it.

Hadde grabbed a spare linen shirt and a washrag and knelt by the fire. She stripped off her linen shirt and set to scrubbing off a week's worth of grime. "This is good. It's good to be home." She sighed with pleasure as the heat warmed her body. It had been a cold, frustrating hunt.

"It's good to have you back. And your timing was perfect." Enna grimaced as she knelt beside her daughter, and placed a half empty sack on a shelf beside her.

Hadde paused at washing her face. "It's hurting you?" she asked, her eyes going to her mother's knee.

"The cold got into it this past week," Enna replied as she poured a few measures of peas into a pot.

"Are those all the peas we have left?"

"Just this sack." She brushed a stray lock of graying black hair from her face.

"Not enough—not for the rest of the winter." Hadde said. An image of the raiders and their skinny horses entered Hadde's mind. Everyone was desperate. Everyone was hungry. And then she imagined the first raider reeling with an arrow in his back. She shook her head. "Mother?"

"Yes?"

"Remember the day the Kiremi attacked Forest Edge?"

"Of course, how could I not? You were my hero. That vile Kiremi would've had me if not for you."

Hadde stared into the fire without talking. She soaked her washrag and absently ran it down her arm. "Back then, when the first man loosed his arrow at me, I never felt any fear. And the second man...when I killed him I felt nothing at all." She paused, remembering her arrow's flight as it struck the Kiremi from his horse. The memory was cold, as if she hadn't even been the one who had loosed the arrow.

"But this time it was different," Hadde continued. "I almost couldn't shoot him. And when the arrow did hit him, and he turned to face me, he was just a boy."

Enna pushed the pot of peas further over the fire, and then sat on a low stool by the fireplace. "Before, it was desperation. There was no

9

time to be afraid, to worry about life and death or consequences. Your village and people were threatened, and you did what had to be done."

"But the village was threatened today. And I love Long Meadow just as much as I loved Forest Edge. I kept waiting and waiting, hoping father and the other hunters would attack. I didn't want to have to fight." Hadde toweled off and, kneeling next to the fire, pulled a linen shirt over her head.

"It troubled you because you had time to think. You were only a child then—only a thirteen-year-old apprentice. You're eight years older now and a full huntress. You know the Way of the Forest. You try to make clean kills to prevent suffering. It's all part of a cycle. Some suffer so others can live. The men attacking our village today had to be killed so others could live. They suffered pain, but you prevented further pain. You saved us." Enna reached out and pulled Hadde close to her.

Hadde gave her mother a weak smile. "I wish there didn't have to be suffering."

"Helna created a world without suffering. Her brothers ruined it. Now, back to work." Enna kissed Hadde's brow, stood, and limped from the fire. "I'm proud of you, Hadde. Belor and Calen too."

Hadde turned as the door flew open and her father strode into the cottage. Arno was tall and sturdily built, with the black hair and gray eyes of many Landomere folk. Hadde had her father's hair and eyes, but was small and slender like her mother.

"Ah, there you are, Hadde," he said, his voice grave. "How are you? How's your head?"

"Good, Father."

"She's fine," her mother added. "A cut to her scalp. It bled like head injuries do, but looked worse than it was."

He grunted as he peered at Hadde's bandage. "So I send you out with young Calen to teach him how to hunt, and you lead a bunch of berserk raiders to us?"

"The village is lucky we happened upon them."

"I'll give you that much," he replied. "I don't know what they were, but Dromost take them, they were tough. Four arrows to kill a single one! Calen got too brave and was nearly skewered when one of them refused to die."

"He wasn't hurt, was he?" Hadde hadn't seen her apprentice in the midst of the fighting.

"Nah, the boy is quick."

"Did you see their eyes?" Hadde asked.

"I did. Dromost take me if I knew what they were."

"Stop uttering that name!" Enna scolded. "Don't anger the gods."

10

He shrugged. "Did you see any game out there, Hadde?"

She shook her head. "It wasn't much of a hunt. We were out for a week and didn't see a single animal. That's twice this season. The Wasting is getting worse. Far worse."

Arno prodded the fire. "I think you're right. In thirty years I've not seen it this bad. And all the game taken this year has been thin and mean."

"And no harvest to speak of," Enna added. "We won't make spring unless we——"

"We will now," Arno said.

"What do you mean?" Hadde asked.

He peered at her for a moment without speaking.

"What is it, Father?"

"Come with me. I want to show you something." Hadde wanted to object; she was finally getting warm and didn't relish the idea of going out again. Something in her father's eyes told her it wasn't a good idea. "What's going on?" she asked.

"At the stable. Just come with me."

"Stay warm, Hadde," Enna urged. "Don't want you catching——"

"I'll be warm. Don't worry." Hadde wrapped her green cloak around her shoulders, pulled on her boots, and followed her father out the door, all the time wondering at her father's words. A few villagers were out, all armed with bow or spear and moving purposefully. Long Meadow was still turned out for the fight.

She glanced around the village as they walked, happy it was safe. Eight years ago she and her family had arrived in Long Meadow with the other refugees from the Kiremi War. Her last memories of Forest Edge were of burning cottages and her wounded mother sprawled on the ground.

Long Meadow had welcomed them warmly. It was deep in the Great Forest of Landomere, safe from the Kiremi, or so they thought back then. The village had been half deserted, the population cut down by the Wasting. With the help of the Forest Edge refugees they had rebuilt the village, and for a time almost prospered. Neat cottages of stone, log, and thatch were scattered haphazardly along the southern edge of their meadows and farm fields. Great Landomeri oaks surrounded them in every other direction.

But the Wasting was too strong for them. The village was in decline again and many of the cottages stood abandoned with cold hearths and sagging roofs. And now the Kiremi had found them. The Kiremi and the silver-eyes.

"What's going on, Father?" she asked again.

11

For several strides he didn't speak. "Hadde… the elders have decided to slaughter the horses. Not all at once, but one at a time."

"Of course. It's a shame, but those Kiremi nags are half dead. I smelled the sores on them before I even caught sight of them."

"No, Hadde, Not just the Kiremi horses. All of them."

Hadde halted abruptly and grabbed him by the arm, spinning him around. "What? Not our horses, too? Not Lightfoot." Her heart sank into her stomach as he looked away. "You wouldn't."

"I'll make sure that Lightfoot is last. Maybe things will improve before we get to—"

"No! It doesn't make sense." Blood rushed to her face as she spoke. Her head pounded. "We need the horses for hunting."

"We aren't plains people anymore. We're forest people now. There isn't any more forage for them in the meadows. And we can't spare the grain. They just aren't worth the weight of the grain they eat."

"How can you say that about Lightfoot? I raised her from a foal. She was the last—there've been no more born since her."

"Stop it, Hadde! Remember your place—you're a huntress."

"I know my place." Anger boiled up in her. Anger at her father's rebuke, and even more at what they proposed to do.

"Then you should know there's nothing to be done for it. The horses eat food that we need to survive. Even with the Kiremi horses we might not make summer."

Hadde looked around in desperation. "I'll take Lightfoot onto the plains. We'll take an auroch. She'll prove herself."

"You'll do no such thing!" he shouted. A few villagers turned at the anger in his voice. "The Kiremi own the plains now. You are forbidden from going there. You understand?"

"I'm not a child."

"Then don't behave like one!"

Hadde stormed off toward the stable, Arno following behind.

"We never should have given up the plains," Hadde yelled over her shoulder.

Arno jogged to catch up. "We didn't give them up. We lost them." As they entered the stable Arno gestured to a stash of weapons and gear. "Look what the Kiremi and those silver-eyes left us." Axes, spears, and bows stood propped against the stable wall. Leather aketons and even a few mail coats lay on the ground next to them. Saddlebags and backpacks sat piled nearby. Hadde wasn't interested in what he had to show her. She went straight to Lightfoot.

As Hadde stroked Lightfoot's nose, Belor strode in from outside. He carried three barbed javelins and a decorated Kiremi bow. His face broke into a smile when he spotted her. Despite her anger at her father, she couldn't help but smile in return.

Belor tossed the raider weapons with the others and embraced her. "I was just coming to see you," he said. "How's your head?"

"I'll be fine. I'm glad you're safe."

"The raiders?" Arno asked.

"We think we took the last of them," Belor said, motioning to the weapons. "The last hunters will be back before full dark."

"We're safe for now, then," Hadde said. "Belor, Father said they're going to slaughter the horses. Not just the Kiremi, but Lightfoot and Windwalker, all of them."

"It has to be done," Arno said.

Belor looked from Arno to Hadde and then past them. After a few moments he nodded his head. "I think your father is right."

Hadde pushed away from him. "What? How can you say that? You're the one who's always saying we'll survive the Wasting. You're the one who sees a better future."

"I do, Hadde. But maybe this is necessary to get us there. The horses have to be sacrificed in order for us to make it to that future."

"No," Hadde started, "It doesn't—"

"Look at this, Hadde," Arno ordered. He opened a Kiremi saddlebag and pulled out a greasy leather pouch. He dumped the contents onto the ground. "What do you see?"

Hadde knelt and stared at the bits of bone and strips of flesh. She reached out to pick up one of the bones and then recoiled before she touched it.

"You think you'll find any aurochs on the plains, Hadde? The Kiremi are eating—"

"I see what they're eating! But look around you, Father. Look at our village. Where are the people?" She motioned toward the open door. "How long until we are all gone? How long until all the homes are empty and all the hearths are cold?"

"We'll last longer if we slaughter the horses."

"But we'll die for sure without them! You're not killing Lightfoot. I'll take her away."

"And abandon your people? Is that the Way of the Forest? Is that the way of a huntress?"

She looked away from him. She couldn't bear the thought of what he was suggesting. It was too awful.

"There's nothing to be done, Hadde."

"Then let me take her out once more." She met her father's eyes. "We'll prove our value, and then you won't kill her."

13

"You'll accomplish nothing."

Smiling, she said, "You can't stop me."

"I know." His shoulders sagged. "But, Hadde, promise me this. Promise me you'll stay safe. Promise me you won't go to the plains."

"I promise." She gestured to the half-eaten hand lying in the dirt. "This won't be my future."

Chapter Three

The late afternoon sun cast long shadows as Hadde halted Lightfoot near the log where she and Belor had stashed their packs. Her hand drifted to the bowcase by her thigh as she scanned the forest for any sign of danger.

The Great Forest had suddenly become a more ominous place. It wasn't enough that the forest was dying; now she had to fear the silver-eyes and the Kiremi. A nearby oak wept sap from long cracks in its trunk. Brown leaves rattled on dead branches. Nothing resisted the Wasting.

"There's no hope, Lightfoot. Everything is dying."

The words brought her back to Old Gaw's funeral that morning. At sunrise they had placed the last stone on his cairn. He rested next to his wife and children. And others. There were too many graves. Too many moss-free stones. Who would build the last cairn?

A shadowy movement caught Hadde's eye and brought her back. She reached for her bow, fearful that her lapse had let the silver-eyes creep up on her. But it was no raider that had caught her attention. It was a deer— a stag! She took a deep breath to calm herself.

It wasn't just any stag, but a magnificent beast. Tall, well muscled, with a lustrous coat. She couldn't believe he was real. Lightfoot snorted and pawed the ground.

Hadde drew her bow from its sheath as the stag moved into a clear space between the trees. His rack was huge. She counted twelve points. Forcing herself to move slowly, she nocked an arrow. The stag snorted and put its nose to the ground.

Hadde froze. Lightfoot stood silently under her.

Patience rewards the hunter, she remembered her father's words. But she couldn't afford to let the stag get away. It would be a bounty for her village. And it would save Lightfoot by proving how well hunter and horse worked together.

The stag raised its head and stared at Hadde. She froze—her heart pounding out the moments in time. All thought of taking the stag fled her mind as she sat rock-still under the animal's gaze. The stag knew her,

15

Hadde thought. It knew what she intended. She dared not move—for a moment she didn't even think she *could.*

The stag sprang forward and dashed off the trail. "Go! On, Lightfoot!" Clods of dirt flew into the air as the horse surged forward. A dead branch shattered as Hadde knocked it aside with her arm. Horse and rider moved as one as they dashed through the forest in pursuit.

Standing in her stirrups, Hadde flexed her legs and let them even out the rough ride. Lightfoot was trained for horse archery and ran with smooth short strides, but all of her training couldn't make up for the uneven forest floor and the fact she had to avoid trees and logs.

The stag leaped and dodged as it raced through the woods. There were so many obstacles, Hadde thought. Wasting-weakened trees dropped limbs so easily with any gust of wind. She timed the motion of her horse as it jumped a rotten log and let fly with an arrow. It pierced a branch with a *thunk.*

Hadde drew another arrow to her ear and let loose. But at the very moment she released her thumb the stag leapt aside and the arrow flew harmlessly into the forest.

She would hold her next arrow for a closer shot. One that wouldn't miss. Branches swiped at her, but she managed to keep her bow low and prevent it from getting snagged. As the vegetation became denser, she realized she must take the stag soon or risk him getting away.

Hadde scowled. The deer should have flagged long ago. He didn't have Lightfoot's stamina. The stag drew her deeper and deeper into the forest. Despite the best efforts of both horse and rider, they couldn't close the gap.

Dark shadows spread over the forest floor. Time was short. "Go, Lightfoot, go!" Hadde yelled. Her thighs burned from trying to hold her body steady and her breath rasped from the exertion.

Despite the pain, a fierce smile crossed her face. She would take this stag. Lightfoot would prove herself. The buck jumped over a bush and disappeared from view. Hadde crouched in her saddle in preparation for the jump. But instead of leaping, Lightfoot skidded to a halt and threw Hadde over her head.

Helpless, Hadde closed her eyes and tucked her body in expectation of a bruising landing on the forest floor. With a tremendous splash, she landed in a pool of water. Cold, shocking cold. Gasping, she sucked in a lungful of water.

She fought her way to the surface. Coughing, gagging, she tried to stand and was surprised to find she could. The pool was small and in a few strides she made shallower water. Her lungs burned as she choked up water. Finally she looked up and saw Lightfoot watching

16

reproachfully from the water's edge.

"Ugh, you could have warned me," Hadde said between coughs. She saw her bow and arrow floating in the deeper water and waded back to retrieve them. After dragging herself from the water, she glanced around for signs of her quarry, but the stag had disappeared. And the cold was not as bad as she had thought. Or maybe the heat of the ride was still in her.

She frowned. Something was different with the forest here. Something odd. She drew a breath. The forest appeared untouched by the blight of the Wasting. Dark green fern beds interspersed with wildflowers encircled the pond. Beyond the fern, tall trees grew, their leaves still green. How could this be? The Wasting was merciless.

Taking Lightfoot's reins, Hadde walked to the water's edge. A brilliant cascade of water tumbled down a rock wall into the pond. Moss grew thick on the round stones. From between them sprang a multitude of tiny white flowers. Everbloom—they were usually so rare. Their scent always brought a smile to her face when she came upon them. Hadde had lived in the forest her entire life and remembered seeing large patches of beauty before the Wasting had worsened. From time to time she still came across pockets of still-vibrant forest. And while each year she saw fewer of these sights, it made the remaining ones more precious.

But this was different—it was eerily beautiful. Every rock, tree, and even the water plants at the edge of the pond conveyed pristine serenity.

The last slanting rays of sunlight shone upon the top of the rock outcropping. She saw a flash of white at its summit. The waterfall emerged from the peak of the rocks, and unlike most springs, it flowed with the urgency of a small stream. Where was the water coming from? The rocks were not a part of a cliff face. They simply emerged from the forest floor. Hadde shivered with a sudden chill as the breeze picked up.

She thought for a moment of riding home, but decided better of it. It would be a cold and hungry night, but at least she could build a fire and dry out. She wished she had picked up the two hunting packs. They would have made the night easy. Riding through the night, chilled and wet, she risked illness. With the Wasting, even a cold could mean death.

"You're tired too, Lightfoot. It was a long chase." Hadde tended to her mount as best she could. Some grain remained in her feedbag. Hadde took off the horse's light saddle and bridle and rubbed her down with her saddle blanket. When she finished, she draped Lightfoot's blanket across her back. The horse happily munched a patch of everbloom.

Hadde opened her belt pouch and took out her fire kit. She cursed as she unwrapped the oiled leather. It was soaked. The pouch could withstand a rainstorm, but not immersion in a pond. Her charcloth and tinder were ruined. She strode to a birch tree and stripped some of the thin bark. Hadde took it and some kindling to her campsite by the pool. Her flint and steel were damp, but still sparked.

Hadde cleared a place in the leaves and prepared the bark and kindling. She struck sparks into the pile of bark until she was short of breath and sweating. The bark wouldn't catch. She rearranged the pile and tried again. It wasn't working. She cursed under her breath and wished she were on her way home. The sky had grown dark. Lightfoot snorted and pawed the ground. Hadde glanced over her shoulder. The horse looked at her with what could only be described as reproach. "I'm usually good at this. Now I'm in for a miserable night."

Hadde turned at a crackling noise to see a small flame growing in the pile of bark. She hadn't seen a spark catch, but it must have. She smiled at her great luck. "Or was it skill, Lightfoot?" She added kindling to the flames. They too caught fire and soon the fire burned well enough to resist even a strong gust of wind.

Once certain of her fire, Hadde gathered a pile of dry wood for the night. "We'll be all right," she said to Lightfoot as she brought a final load in. "Except for an empty stomach. But I've been hungry before. At least you have the everbloom." Hadde harvested armloads of fern for a bed and piled them near the fire. She propped some sturdy sticks in the ground and made a small frame to hang her clothes on to dry. She stripped off her tunic and leggings and placed them on the frame and propped her cloak up as a windbreak.

The cold wind cut through her wet linen shirt, but it was all she had between her and the elements. The linen would dry quickly enough. She kept her hair in its long braid, as she had no comb or cloth to dry it with if she were to undo it. Before lying down on her bed of ferns, she unstrung her bow and put the string on the rack to dry as well.

Ignoring her hunger, she lay down. The fire burned well, the orange light flickering off of the surrounding trees. Embers cracked and floated into the sky. She thought of the silver-eyes. Could they be near? Would the fire bring them to her?

She glanced into the darkness. Her fire was invisible to anyone more than a stone's throw away. And the smoke rose nearly straight up. No one would smell it. She hoped. Regretting her decision to stay, Hadde moved as close to the fire as she could bear. It would be a fitful night of waking to put more wood on the fire and rotating as first one side of her body and then the other became cold.

She looked up into the sky. Stars shone in the crisp air. She was close enough to the pond that the forest canopy didn't obstruct her view. Only the steep slope of the rocky outcropping blocked part of the night sky.

Bright white light peeked over the top of the hill. *The moon must be rising.*

It took a moment to realize her error.

The wrong part of the sky, she thought. She sat up, keeping her eyes on the top of the outcropping. She shivered as a cold breeze blew through the camp and threw a few more sticks on the fire. She didn't want to leave its warmth, but her curiosity was too strong.

Hadde walked to the base of the hill. The breeze calmed and the bite had gone out of the air. Leaving the fire wasn't as bad as she had expected. She started up the slope. As she climbed higher the falling water to her right took on a musical quality. The everbloom growing amongst the rocks scented the air with a beautiful honey fragrance. She paused and plucked one of the blossoms. The flower glowed in the starlight, and when she put it to her nose the scent took her breath away. Sudden warmth coursed through her. Before she could catch herself she giggled.

The flower smelled like hope.

She couldn't help the smile that crossed her face. *What is going on?* The thought flitted through her mind and disappeared. Glancing up the hill, she again saw the flash of light.

Unable to stop herself, she scampered to the top of the hill. The peak, about five strides across, was shaped like a bowl. Water gushed from the bottom of the bowl in a fountain and filled a small pool before flowing through a gap in the rocks to the pond below. Moss-covered stones and innumerable white flowers surrounded her.

In the center of the fountain stood a flat-topped table of stone. Water flowed smoothly over its surface before falling into the pool at the hill's peak. A golden chain lay at the center of the stone.

Hadde caught her breath. She had seen gold only once, a worn coin Father brought back to the village years before. Landomeri had little use for the trinket, but they had still been curious. It was the rarity, the exotic nature of it, that got their attention. They had all heard stories about the riches of distant lords and kings.

Hadde knelt at the pool's edge and took a closer look at the chain. In the starlight she could see that the chain held a pendant, but she couldn't make out any details. She reached for the chain but drew back, glancing around as if someone was watching. She laughed at her own foolishness.

Did the chain belong to someone? Who had left it in such an unusual place? She extended her hand and took the chain from the stone. The heavy links were as wide as her finger. The pendant filled her palm. She drew it close and starlight flashed across the pendant's face. There she saw a wavy-rayed Orb. Hadde knew what it was at once—the sun-symbol of the goddess Helna.

Hadde frowned. How long had it been there? Was it lost? Or was it a gift from Helna?

The older villagers gave the gods respect, but Hadde had never been devout. Why thank the gods? They were banished long ago. The gods did nothing for the Landomeri and there was no reason to give thanks. What help had they provided against the Wasting?

Hadde hefted the chain. It was probably worth a fortune. "Well, Helna, maybe now I've some reason to give thanks. Your chain will save my village from great want."

Hadde sat down at the table in her family's cottage, a mug of bark tea cupped in her hands. "Tell us your story," Enna said as she and Arno sat down at the plank table.

"Yes, what has your tail on fire?" Arno asked. "We were worried to death about you."

Hadde dug her spoon into a small bowl of split pea soup. "I'm sorry, but I couldn't help it. I was hunting a very large stag, twelve points, I think." Arno laughed and she glared at him. "It was ten points or more!"

"Yes, dear," he laughed again. "Do go on."

Between mouthfuls, Hadde told them her story. As she finished she opened her collar and pulled the golden chain over her head. Her parents gasped as she laid it on the table. "It's beautiful," Enna said. "It was just lying there?"

Hadde nodded. "It was so strange. After I found it I went down to my little fire and before I knew it, I was asleep. I slept through the night and never once awoke to put more wood on the fire. I woke well after light had come, but the fire was still blazing."

"Sounds like magic to me," Arno said in a serious tone. He picked up the chain and stared at the medallion.

"Really?"

"Ooooh, and the spiridus fairies came out and made a bonfire and had a feast and we made love the entire night," he said in a high-pitched voice.

"Arno, be nice to her." Enna said as Arno laughed. "Something really special has happened. You cannot ignore this necklace."

The door flew open and Belor barged into the room. "Hadde," he said, out of breath, "are you hurt?"

Arno glared at the younger man. "Did you pledge yourself to Hadde while you were out hunting?" he snapped. "No? Then you're not part of the family yet! Try knocking."

20

"Arno! Stop it," Enna said.

Belor looked down at his feet. "I apologize. I was just worried for Hadde."

"But not worried enough to pledge yourself to her..." Arno winked at his wife.

Enna laughed. "Come in, Belor. Arno's just harassing you. See what Hadde found."

"Helna's light," Belor said. He strode up to the table and stared at the chain in Hadde's father's hands. "You found it?"

"Yes, in an un-wasted part of the forest. A beautiful place."

"It's magic," he declared. "Landomere called you to that place."

Hadde sighed as her father snorted. "It's probably been there for ages," Arno said.

"It couldn't have been," Belor said. His face was full of enthusiasm as he looked from the pendant to Hadde. "Elder Themon would say—"

"Oh, no," Arno said. "You spend too much time listening to the elder's stories." He waved Belor silent and turned to Hadde. "What do you want to do with it?"

"We could trade it, couldn't we?" Hadde asked. "If it's valuable enough it could feed the village for some time."

"There's not been a tinker or trader in this area for many years," Enna said. "And no Landomeri would have any use for it."

"You would have to take it to the border of the South Teren," Arno said, placing the chain in front of her. "To a large Landomeri village there or even to a Saladoran town."

"Would the trek be worth it?" Hadde asked.

He shrugged. "The Saladorans value gold greatly. But if things are as bad everywhere else as they're here, food will be expensive. If you do go, you should break the chain and trade it one link at a time. Wealth like this could be dangerous. Saladorans will do evil things for this much gold. I've dealt with them before."

"You can't do that," Belor said. "It's a gift from Landomere. A sign. How long have we been cursed with the Wasting? Twenty years?"

"About that," Arno said. "Right around when Hadde was born. But it's much worse now."

"And even with the raiders' horses we captured, how much longer can we survive?"

Hadde's father shook his head. "We can survive this winter."

"What are you getting at, Belor?" Enna asked as she picked up the chain.

"There used to be magic in Landomere. Before the veden came and slew the spiridus," Belor said.

21

"Of course," Arno replied. "But that was five hundred years ago. The Spirit of Landomere died with the spiridus. She couldn't live without them."

Hadde watched the exchange. There was something infectious about Belor's excitement. She found herself leaning forward as she listened to him.

"But there were also human elementars, weren't there?" Belor asked. "Like Handrin the Great. He came to Landomere and slew the veden."

"There are no more elementars," Hadde said. "Handrin was the last."

"How do you know? Hmm?" He stared at her with brows raised.

She stared right back at him. "The legends don't mention any others. I've listened to Elder Themon's stories too. Handrin was the only elementar to survive the War for the Orb. And Akinos murdered him and stole the Orb. There were no elementars after him."

"Maybe his children grew up to be elementars, and we don't know of them because they never came to Landomere. Maybe there is someone out there who could save us from the Wasting." He ticked the facts off on his fingers. "And not just save us for weeks or months, but forever. This chain is a sign. It will lead us to help!"

"But... I don't know..." Hadde tailed off. "How can a necklace lead us to help?"

Belor smacked the table. "I don't know. But I can't stand by and do nothing as the Wasting takes us all. I have to do something."

"There's no more magic, Belor." Arno's voice was final.

"I'm not sure the magic is *all* gone," Hadde said quietly. "When I found the chain, well, it wasn't natural."

"You see!" Belor said.

"I don't," Arno said. "You would run off on a fool's errand to find an elementar to save us all? The kings of Salador lived in the city of Sal-Oras, not on the border. You would waste months on a journey that has no hope of success."

"So we just give up?" Belor asked.

"No! We sell the necklace. We live and fight and do the best we can a little longer."

"Our best isn't enough, Father," Hadde said. "The Wasting will take us."

Arno's normal gruff happiness faded from his face and his age showed in his sad expression. "Don't get your hopes up about any elementar or magical salvation from the Wasting. There isn't one."

"I'm not saying I believe all that Belor does. But I know that we must try." Hadde glanced at Belor and then at her father. "I don't think we'll find an elementar, but at least I could go to Salador and sell the chain. It will sell there as well as anywhere. The supplies it will purchase will keep us going a little longer."

Enna gently placed the necklace on the table in front of Hadde. "I know you and your father aren't convinced, but I believe Helna is still with us. The spirit of Landomere will live again." She traced the pendant with her finger as she spoke. "This is a message—a message to you, Hadde. You must seek aid."

Belor smiled his agreement. "All the way to Sal-Oras."

"No," Enna said. She lifted her hand from the pendant and touched Hadde's cheek. "You should go to the Saladoran border and sell the chain there—no further. We... I need you here." Enna took Hadde's hand in her own. "You're our protector. The necklace is a sign, not an invitation to folly."

Arno exchanged a look with his wife and nodded slowly.

"I have to do more for the village, Mother. I'm a huntress, but soon there will be nothing left to hunt. And maybe, just maybe, Belor is right and we'll find an answer to the Wasting in Sal-Oras."

"But what of the silver-eyed raiders?" Enna asked. "What if they return?"

"The village is warned. It won't be caught at unawares. Two bows won't make a great difference." Hadde took the golden chain and put it on.

"It made a difference to me... before." Enna's voice was quiet.

There were tears on her mother's cheeks. Hadde brushed them away with her thumb. "The Wasting is winning, Mother. It's killing us and there's nothing I can do about it. I'm supposed to protect and provide for the village, but I'm failing. I have to do something that will make a difference. Killing a skinny boar will feed us for a few days, but what if there is something greater I can do?"

"It's hard enough when you go hunting for weeks at a time." More tears fell from Enna's eyes. "You're my only child."

"I'll only go as far as I have to," Hadde said. She wiped her mother's tears away as best she could. It was hard for Hadde to fight off her own tears. "But if there's hope... if there's any chance an elementar still rules in Salador, I must go farther. I'll go to Sal-Oras."

Belor smiled at her. "We'll go to Sal-Oras," he said. "And we'll find you an elementar-king."

Chapter Four

Hadde and Arno walked through the misty morning light toward the smithy. Smoke rose from less than half the village's chimneys. The remaining cottages stood empty and dark. The thatched roofs on more than one home had collapsed.

"It gets worse and worse," Arno said. "These cottages were all filled after we moved here from Forest's Edge. It hasn't been that long."

"I remember," Hadde said. "It's too quiet now." They passed the smithy's cold furnace and entered the workspace. Two lanterns barely lit the room. Belor had already arrived. He wore a red Kiremi aketon. A mail coif covered his head. To Hadde he looked striking and proud. Next to him, uncle Segreg checked the fit of the armor.

"Hello, Hadde," Segreg said. He gave her a hug. He turned to Arno and clasped forearms with him. "Brother."

"Did you find anything that will fit Hadde?" Arno asked.

"I did." He motioned her toward a table. "What would you think of a mail shirt?"

"A mail shirt?" She couldn't help but laugh at the thought of wearing one. "I've never seen one up close."

"There it is. One of the raiders wore it under his aketon. It's a little worse for wear, but I've fixed it up some."

Hadde nodded appreciatively as she ran her hand over the armor. She had only ever seen mail from a distance. The armor was tarnished, and a rent had been wired together, but it still looked magnificent and foreign.

"Put this on first," Segreg said, holding up a padded aketon. "Linen boiled in wax, seven layers thick, and stuffed with tow."

Arno helped her pull the thick quilted armor on and then tied the laces tight. She grimaced at the smell of old sweat and mildew. "Ugh, it stinks," she said.

"Better than a sword in the ribs," Arno replied.

"Not bad," her uncle announced. The armor covered her from neck to mid thigh and had sleeves to her elbows.

She tried to move her arms and bend at her waist. The armor was stiff, but manageable. "You think this is really necessary?" she asked.

"You have to wear an aketon under your mail," Segreg said. "The mail stops blades but the concussion will break your bones without an aketon underneath."

"No, I mean the armor itself."

"Saladorans are not like us," Arno said. "They're very conscious of wealth and rank. You've heard the old tales. Nobles, kings and queens, knights and ladies, are held above all others. And only those of great rank wear armor and carry weapons."

"It will be to your advantage to be well fitted out," her uncle said. "The Saladorans will give you more respect."

Hadde sighed. "What's next?"

"The mail corselet," Segreg said.

Hadde obediently raised her arms as he slipped the mail over her head.

"Buckle this around your waist." Segreg handed her a wide belt. "It will take some of the weight off your shoulders." Hadde nodded in thanks.

"And finally, your helm." He placed a padded leather cap on her head and tied it under her chin. It covered the top of her head and had flaps that went over her ears. On top of the arming cap he placed a conical iron helm with a mail aventail that covered the back of her neck.

"You're joking, right?" Hadde asked when he finished.

He smiled and shook his head. "Just like a heroic Saladoran knight."

"A short, skinny, heroic Saldoran knight," added Belor. He laughed at Hadde's glare.

"You'll have your bows, of course," Segreg said. "But Saladorans don't think them proper weapons. I have two battle axes and the raiders' swords, but here is something special."

From behind the table he pulled a sheathed sword. Its blade gleamed in the lantern light as he drew it.

"It's been years since I last saw it," Hadde said. She remembered it only as a prop when the elders told ancient tales of Salador. It saddened her that it might be used for its original intended purpose.

"This is no Kiremi sabre," Segreg said. "It's a Saladoran broadsword. It has been in our village for a hundred years. I never had the heart to re-forge it into something useful. Take it up, Hadde. It's well balanced and not as heavy as it looks."

The sword's light weight surprised her as she took it from him. "Still, it seems too large for me." She held it with two hands so that it was easier to handle.

"It isn't a matter of wielding it," Arno said. "You'll rely on your bows and your speed to escape danger. For Saladorans, the sword is a symbol

25

of status."

"May I see it?" Belor asked.

Hadde handed it to him and smiled at the excitement in his eyes as he swept the sword up in a salute. "It will look good on you, Belor. You wear it."

"Really? Thank you!"

"Put you in mail and you'll truly look the part of a knight."

Segreg shook his head. "None of the mail will fit him. He'll have to do with the aketon. It's a good one—we took it off one of the silver-eyes."

"I'll wear his helm as well." Belor held up a black steel helm chased in bronze. A bronze bear's head roared from atop the nasal. Hadde laughed as he imitated the bear's fierce scowl.

"This isn't a game," Arno snapped. "Get to Salador, sell the necklace, and come back with food."

"Yesterday we agreed that Hadde and I would go to Sal-Oras and find the king," Belor said.

"I never agreed to it. And every day you're gone will be a torment for Enna."

"The Goddess Helna will guide them, Brother," Segreg said. "And the Spirit of Landomere will sustain them. Enna knows as well as anyone that something has to be done. We all play our part." He turned to Hadde and Belor. "We'll all pray that you'll have no need for these arms and armor. We'll all pray for your success."

Hadde mounted Lightfoot and waved to the villagers gathered around her. All fifty-eight of Long Meadow's residents were present. Beside her, Belor sat impatiently on Quickstep.

"Thank you for your kind farewell," Hadde said. "I promise we'll return soon. I promise to bring aid."

"You'll save us, Hadde!" Calen called out. Applause followed his words, although there were more than a few glum faces in the crowd. Not everyone was happy to see the two hunters ride off with three horses.

"We'll try," she replied, but too quietly to be heard. Her father appeared beside her and offered her the lead to their third horse. She tied it to her saddle.

"Windwalker is ready," he said. "You brought your spare bow?"

"Yes, Father."

"And how many arrows?"

"A score in my bowcase and another two score in my saddle quiver."

26

"I should get more."

"Stop it, Father," Hadde said as he turned to leave. "Belor has more. And we aren't riding off to war."

"I know. But... I'm worried for you." He paused as if considering his words. "You know where to go? You know the way to Silver Spring?"

"Father!" There were chuckles from the crowd behind her father. Hadde rolled her eyes.

"From Belavil you ride...."

"Four days north and east. I keep the high ground to my right and go downstream at every opportunity. I know the way."

Arno took her elbow and pulled her down close. In a hushed voice he said, "Hadde, you and I are of the same mind. Don't trust to some supernatural guidance. Don't trust to luck. Sell the——"

He paused as Enna stepped up to them. "Don't tarry, Hadde," she said. "Come home as soon as you can. Helna is with you."

"I promise. As soon as my task is complete."

Tears welled in Enna's eyes. "I'll miss you. Take care of each other." She squeezed Hadde's hand one last time and turned away.

"I'll miss you, too," Hadde replied. With a final glance at her father, she and Belor turned their horses and rode from Long Meadow.

For the rest of the day they guided their horses across familiar hunting grounds. They rode hard but spared their horses by switching mounts, or walking, every few hundred arrow-flights. Even in the forest they made good time.

Seven days until Belavil, the ancient capital of the spiridus. Every Landomeri went there at least once. Hadde had gone four years before. She wished she could explore the ruins again. But there was no time to spare. The Wasting made her journey too urgent.

Belor had been there several times——he always managed some excuse. He claimed the hunting was better there, but had never brought home the game to prove it. His arrows always *just barely* missed, or *just barely* nicked an intervening branch. But even he hadn't been there in over a year.

It would be nice to visit the ruins with him——although she wished the times could be different. That she could visit the ruins for pleasure, and not in passing while on a desperate task. The constant struggle to find food made for little time to be together. She loved the fleeting moments they shared. She smiled. They would——

"Stop, Hadde!" Belor called out too late.

Splashing hooves and flying mud startled her from her reverie. "Whoa! Stop!" she shouted as she pulled back on the reins.

Belor laughed from behind her. "You haven't been listening to a thing

I've been saying, have you?"

Hadde frowned and scanned the forest around them. Blackened, dead trees tilted precariously from the sodden ground. Swaths of mud and muck divided fetid pools of black water. "Ummm...." She reddened. "You were talking?" Belor had stopped strides ago, at the edge of the pool.

"Yes, I was talking. I was mentioning that there shouldn't be a bog here." He laughed again. "What were you so deep in thought about?"

Hadde didn't reply, how could she? She scanned their surroundings instead. Except for the small sounds the horses made, she was surrounded by silence. No birds sang, no creatures moved amongst the trees, no insect disturbed the surface of a single murky puddle.

"I—ah, wasn't thinking of anything in particular," she replied. "What's going on here? I hunted here just a month ago. "

"Landomere is dead here," Belor replied. "Completely dead. I can feel it."

Hadde shivered. "I know what you mean. It's like when someone stands between you and a bright fire. There is no life here. No warmth. Let's go, Belor. We have to get through this." She tapped her heels against Lightfoot's flanks.

For hours they trudged through the swamp. The oppressive weight of the dead landscape crushed her happiness at their earlier progress. The swamp seemed endless—as if she rode into the heart of the Wasting. The muck deepened and her hopes of ever reaching the other side faded. If she weren't careful night would fall with them still deep in the mire.

"We have to turn aside," she said. "There's higher ground to the southeast. It will cost us a day, but I don't want to spend a night in this swamp."

"A little farther," Belor said.

Hadde peered into the gloomy forest ahead. Shaking her head, she said, "There isn't enough time."

"This isn't just your choice, " Belor said. "I know we just have to go a little further. I know it."

"We don't want to end up sleeping in this..."

"Just a little further."

They rode another arrow-flight when Hadde pulled Lightfoot up short. A scent caught her attention and an image of sunshine and growing trees flashed in her mind. She breathed deeper. The smell was familiar to her. She closed her eyes and saw the glade where she had discovered the golden chain.

Everbloom.

"Do you smell that?" she asked.

"I do." Belor smiled. "It isn't this dreadful marsh."

Hadde surveyed her surroundings. Nothing but dead trees and sodden ground. But the scent of the flowers still lingered. The faintest of breezes blew from the northeast, and Hadde rode in that direction. Soon the ground became solid and she found herself on a path through the forest.

The narrow track ran almost straight, here and there widening to a stride or so. Green grass, bordered with swaths of white flowers, covered the path. Hadde smiled at the sweet smell. She glanced into the forest and saw that it hadn't changed. Dead trees and marsh began at the path's edge. Only those trees actually touching the trail showed any sign of life.

Dismounting, she knelt and touched the grass. Unlike the thin stalks that grew near Long Meadow, it was thick and full of life. Belor splashed up behind her.

"Look at this," she said. "In the middle of the Wasting."

"Just as I said."

Hadde rolled her eyes. "Luck. We would have smelled the everbloom even if we had turned aside."

"If you say so, mighty leader. You know what this is? A Spiridus Road—a path created by Landomere to guide the spiridus on their journeys."

"You listen to too many elder's tales."

"Didn't you follow a path like this to Belavil when you went there before?"

Hadde glanced at the trail. "No. I saw patches of flowers, but no trail like this."

"Well, it's a sign. Landomere is guiding us."

She laughed as she changed her horses' leads and mounted Windwalker. "I said it before—luck."

"You were guided to that golden chain."

She thought for a moment of the glade where she had discovered the pendant. Had the stag led her there on purpose? Or had it just been chance? "I don't know. Spiridus magic is a little hard to believe in."

"But—"

"Come on, Belor. There is still time left in the day."

They slogged on, until finally the marsh broke, and they found themselves in living forest again. For four more days they pushed their horses toward Belavil. From time to time the dead bogs returned, but none was so great as the first. Landomere still resisted the Wasting, but the forest's time was short.

The crag of Belavil jutted from the forest floor. Terraces and paths wandered up its slopes and everywhere Hadde looked there were piles of stones that had once been the walls of houses and towers. Belavil was both magnificent and sad. She sighed as her eyes followed the broad avenue leading to the plateau and the greatest of the city's ruins.

"We could spend the night in the ruins," Belor suggested.

Hadde saw the hope in his eyes. She stared up at the ancient stones and longed to perch atop them and see the broad expanse of Landomere below her. "We don't have time to tarry. We'd lose half a day." She tapped Lightfoot and started for the road that would take them around the city.

Later, they set up camp in the shadow of Belavil. A gurgling stream let them clean the bog mud from their bodies. After eating and caring for their horses, they curled together next to the fire. "It will be cold tonight," Hadde said. "This is a hard winter." She stared into the flames. Belor held her close.

"There are ways of fending off the cold," he said.

"Is that right?" she asked, smiling into the fire.

"It is. And I can't imagine a nicer place."

Hadde gazed up into the star-filled sky. "Except maybe up there, in Belavil."

"I was thinking that earlier, but you wouldn't let us go." He traced his hand across her cheek.

She turned to look at him. "Were you, now? For three days you've not seemed to think much of me."

"For three days you've been covered with bog mud."

Hadde laughed and twisted into his arms. "You look better now, too."

They were well on their way before first light. Beyond Belavil the forest was new to Hadde. It was as ancient as in the west, but rougher, with undulating hills and deep gullies hiding rushing streams.

For four days they continued northeast. The dead marshes persisted, but the flower-lined paths disappeared. These dead zones were worse than those they had seen before, some with mud so thick as to be impassible. Their trek would have ended if not for the high ridges paralleling their route.

Descending one of the hills, Hadde smelled smoke. She paused and peered into the forest. Belor stopped beside her. A white haze wafted through the trees. Lightfoot whinnied and Hadde stroked the horse's neck.

"Forest fire?" Belor asked.

"I don't know. The smoke is widespread, but not thick. The wind is calm. If it's a forest fire, it won't move fast enough to trap us." Riding forward, she undid the straps that held her bowcase closed. Fires were unusual in Landomere. Her people were much too careful. Strangers, however...

She glanced at Belor and saw him loosen his bow in its case.

The smoke thinned as the forest opened in front of them. Through the light haze she saw the outline of a village. Hadde rode to its edge and halted. Her heart lurched at the destruction in front of her.

"Was this Silver Spring?" Belor asked.

"I don't know. Whatever Landomeri village it was, it's destroyed now." She thought of her parents. Was this what the raiders would have done to her home? Worry gnawed at her. "We shouldn't have left."

Belor edged up closer to her. "We're a long way from Long Meadow. And our people are wary now."

Half of the dozen cottages had burned to the ground. Smoke still rose from them and drifted toward the woods. Broken furniture, discarded tools, and shattered pottery lay scattered between the dwellings. She looked for any sign of life, but there was none.

Hadde saw a javelin embedded in the door of a cottage. She drew her bow from its case and nocked an arrow. "This didn't happen long ago. Yesterday, maybe."

"Where are the bodies?" Belor asked as he started into the village. He held his bow at the ready.

"Wait, Belor," Hadde said. "We don't know if anyone is still here."

"It's empty," he said and continued forward.

Hadde followed a few strides behind. Pools of dried blood stained the ground. Bodies had been cleared and heavy objects dragged across the dirt. Riding past one cottage, she leaned low and peered inside. Empty. Belor paused to glance into a home. Hadde rode past him toward the village green.

She stopped Lightfoot short as she emerged from between two buildings. On the ground before her rested a helm. She dismounted and fetched it.

"What is it?" Belor asked.

"Like yours, but wolf this time." She held up the helm. "A different group of silver-eyes?"

He grimaced. "How many are there?"

She felt a knot of worry in her stomach. "Belor, what if they're Saladorans? None of us have been to Salador for many years. What if this is what they have become?"

"No, they couldn't... I don't think so."

Hadde stared at the helm. "In the stories they wear great helms and shining armor. They aren't silver-eyed monsters."

"We'll find out soon enough, I suppose," Belor said.

"I wanted to speak with the eastern Landomeri before we went on to Salador," Hadde said.

"There will be other villages nearby," Belor said, pulling his gaze from the helm and glancing uncertainly into the forest. "But we could lose days searching for them. I want to be on our way to Sal-Oras."

"I don't know. Maybe we should find the nearest Saladorans and trade the gold for supplies. I want to get home to Long Meadow. We need to be there to protect them."

"That isn't our task," Belor said, full of certainty. "Landomere wants more from us. That's why she gave you the pendant."

"Landomere didn't ask anything of me," Hadde replied. "Let's do what we have to and go home." She tossed the helm on the ground. "Before it's too late."

Chapter Five

"So, this is Salador," Hadde said. Before her stood a huge two-story structure built of river stone and mortar. It was by far the largest house she had ever seen. But it, like most of the surrounding cottages, had partially collapsed years before. "I wonder if a king lived here."

"A noble, maybe," Belor corrected. "There's only one king."

"I suppose you're right. I wonder if his house is so large."

"Much larger, I imagine."

Hadde took in the ruined structure and the fallen cottages. "Maybe the Wasting is worse here. Maybe there are no more Saladorans. Only those silver-eyes."

"No, I don't think so," he said as his gaze wandered over the surroundings.

Hadde glanced at him. He sounded less than confident. "How would you know if there were no more Saladorans?"

"We would've heard it. We just need to go on a little farther."

"We hardly hear from other Landomeri any more. Only Fallingbrook. The Saladorans could be long gone and we would have no way of knowing it." They rode to the back of the huge house.

"Most of the roof is there, but I don't want to sleep under it," Belor said.

The two hunters quickly established a camp in the shelter of a collapsed cottage. Hadde cared for their mounts while Belor set up their lean-to. "Do you think you should do that?" Hadde asked as Belor unlaced his aketon.

"What? Take off my armor?"

"We should sleep in it. And we should keep no fire tonight. There could be more of those men about."

He sighed as he glanced around. "Hadde, this is no different than last night. It is no more dangerous now that we are in Salador."

"I would rather be prepared."

"I'd like to get some real sleep, and I can't do that in armor."

"I'm wearing my armor." She gave him a pointed stare.

He shrugged and gave her a smile. "And I'm not."

The distant howls of wolves kept Hadde awake long into the night. That and the discomfort of sleeping in aketon and mail. She shifted under her blanket and glared at the contentedly sleeping Belor. Taking off her mail would certainly wake him. She'd never hear the end of it.

Hadde tried to will herself to sleep, but doubts crept into her mind as she thought about the decaying manor house. The ruined structure didn't bode well for their mission. What if there truly were no more Saladorans? Or just a few scraping by against the Wasting? A king who couldn't even keep his own kingdom from falling would have little charity for Landomere. And little value for a gold chain.

A fool's errand, she thought.

They rode four days deeper into Salador. With each day, Hadde grew more restless, fearful that their task was hopeless. They had passed two villages, one abandoned, and one recently destroyed.

The first had been long deserted. Several years or more. But the second showed signs of having been attacked within the past month or so. Nothing of value remained in the village. At first Hadde thought the attackers had looted everything. But even things of no value to raiders had been taken. She imagined the villagers had driven off the attackers and then abandoned their homes, taking the meager belongings with them.

Or had they been defeated and taken off into captivity? She looked across the muddy fields surrounding the village and understood why they had left in either case. There wasn't anything to stay for. The Wasting had taken everything.

On the fifth day Hadde and Belor came upon a wide road paved in stone. Hadde stared off into the distance. The road ran unbroken, perfectly straight as far as she could see. "This is amazing," she said, staring at the flawless construction.

"It must be the road from Del-Oras to Mor-Oras. Look over there." Belor pointed. Four arrow-flights away stood a walled fort. "It's a real town, I think. At the very worst I think we'll be able to buy shelter with a link of gold."

"If it isn't abandoned."

"We'll find people there."

"Belor, if we don't find anyone, I think we should return to Landomere."

"Don't give up yet. We're still a long way from the big cities. Come on." Hadde followed Belor as he led her up the road. The fort stood on a flat plain with little cover nearby. A few patches of forest grew less than a mile from its walls.

"It looks abandoned," Hadde said. "Not a wisp of smoke from the cottages or from behind the wall." She examined the fort as they approached. Wooden walls sat on a stone foundation that led into a dry moat. Offset on one side was a short square tower, its bottom half stone. Next to the tower a wooden gate rested half open. They rode to within twenty strides of the tower.

"Hello! Is anyone there?" Belor called out. There was no response.

A wooden bridge spanned the moat. Thick ropes lay strewn across the heavy timbers. Someone had cut the heavy cables, leaving the drawbridge useless for defense.

"No one here," Belor said.

"Hold the horses. I'll take a look," Hadde said. She dismounted, and with her bow ready, crossed the bridge and peered inside the gate. Beyond, she saw an open square with wattle and daub buildings built into the outer walls. Along one wall rested a line of wagons and carts. All had been heavily laden. And all had been burned to the ground.

A scrawny rabbit nibbled at a patch of weeds near a broken wagon wheel. Hadde drew and loosed her arrow, but the rabbit sprang away at the last moment. It disappeared under a wagon before she could draw again.

"What is it?" Belor called to her.

"A rabbit." She entered the fort. There was nobody living there. If it hadn't *felt* abandoned, the rabbit was proof of it.

Hadde glanced over the wagons. Why had they been burned? She saw no sign of attack. And then she thought back to the abandoned village. The villagers had come here in hopes of succor. But when they arrived, they found an empty fort.

And then they abandoned hope.

"This is the best I've felt since we started the journey," Hadde said. "Such a relief to wash off all that dirt and sweat." She knelt before their fire and ran her comb through her still-wet hair. The fire's warmth felt wonderful against her naked body.

She and Belor had set up camp in the upper floor of the fort's gatehouse tower. Debris filled the room, but at least it was secure. The iron-shod door barred entry. A ladder in the corner led to a trapdoor that gave access to the roof. The horses were safely stabled on the ground floor. Hadde heard them shuffling below.

They hadn't only secured the tower but also managed to close and bar the fort's main gate. For the first time since leaving the sanctuary of

Landomere, Hadde felt safe.

"It's great to be clean again," Belor said as he wrung out his wet leggings. "And it's great to see you all clean again as well."

Hadde didn't have to look at him to know that he was ogling her. "I knew I should have locked you out of the tower when I had the chance."

He laughed. "You've had that mail suit on four days straight now. You can't blame me for appreciating that you've taken it off. That and more."

"You've seen me like this before."

"And I never tire of it."

"To my eternal suffering."

"Ha, funny. You never complained before."

Hadde smiled and stirred the pot of split peas she had placed on the fire. "It seems so strange. An entire town abandoned. Why would they leave such a place?"

Belor joined her by the fire. He wore only a breechcloth, but she pretended not to notice. He brushed a loose strand of hair back from her face. "Your wound is nearly healed. You're lucky the Wasting didn't get into it."

"Mother is a good herbalist. It didn't bother me after the first few days."

Belor glanced around the room. "I'm certain some held on as long as they could. But when the travelers stopped coming down the road, and the residents were too few to hold the fort, they probably departed for Mor-Oras."

"Maybe the cities are just as empty."

"They can't be. I'm sure we'll find someone soon."

"We should go back." She glanced at him to see his reaction.

Belor shook his head. "Not yet."

"Belor... "

"We can't give up hope! There must be someone who can help us."

"And if there isn't?"

"We'll go home."

"When? Because... well, I'm giving up hope."

For a time they both stared into the fire.

"Hadde... do you know why I want so much for this task of ours to succeed?"

"You want the Wasting to end." She said the obvious answer, but she knew he had more to say. "I know how much you hate the Wasting."

"More than just that. I want us to succeed for *us*. I know I've dodged your questions before—"

"Not just my questions. You dodge me. I never know which Belor I will happen into."

"I know. And I'm sorry for it."

"You know I love you, Belor." She looked into his eyes as she said it. "I've loved you ever since I first arrived in Long Meadow."

"It didn't stop you from befriending Geros."

"What was I supposed to do?" A flush of anger crossed her cheeks. "There was always..."

Her words died as Belor looked away from her and into the fire. "There was always Ina," he finished for her. "But the Wasting took Ina and the baby from me. I won't have it happen again. I won't go through it again."

Hadde reached out and touched his arm. "I know, Belor. And I accept the way we are. Don't mind my parents. I don't mind that we don't share a hearth. We spend as much time——"

"It does matter," he said, cutting her off. "It matters to me. And that's why we'll succeed. We'll find the elementar and end the Wasting. And when we do we'll pledge ourselves, build a cottage, and have children together."

She turned away from him and stared into the fire as he spoke the last words. "It sounds wonderful."

"But..."

But I'll only truly have your love if the Wasting is ended, she wanted to say. And I don't think it will end. "You know... you know I don't think I can have children," she said instead.

His hand touched her jaw and he gently turned her face toward his. "Only because of the Wasting. You will when it is gone." He paused a moment. "We will do this, Hadde. We won't fail."

The following day they came upon a small village sheltered in a valley. Smoke issued from the manor's two chimneys and from holes in the peaks of half a dozen cottage roofs. Hadde's heart pounded at the sight. Hope and fear grew in her. She had come so close to giving up.

"This is it. I told you so," Belor said.

"You're never wrong, are you?" Hadde replied.

"Never."

Hadde laughed. Belor's face glowed with joy. As they rode closer she spotted several people moving around the village, women and children amongst them. It surprised Hadde at how long it took them to notice approaching riders. She and Belor were two arrow-flights away when the alarm went up.

A horn sounded and people scrambled every which way. A few ran out of the manor shouting, while others in the village fled toward its safety. Those running to the manor carried bundles of possessions in their arms. The two masses collided in confusion on the ramp leading into the structure.

Hadde waved toward them. She hoped it was a friendly gesture.

"They must think we're raiders," Belor said. "Or silver-eyes." The village went silent as the last refugees crowded into the manor.

The filth amazed Hadde as they rode closer. It was far worse than the abandoned villages they had seen. Mud and refuse were everywhere. She and Belor halted their horses at the far edge of the village. A circle of cleared ground surrounded the manor. A ramp over a dry ditch led into the second story entrance. The first floor had no windows at all, while the second and third had evenly-spaced tall narrow windows. Hadde spotted movement behind some of them.

They waited for some kind of greeting, but none came. "We don't look dangerous, do we?" Hadde asked. "Two riders and a spare horse?"

"I wouldn't think so," Belor said. "We're not wearing our helms or holding weapons. Maybe they have been raided recently." He paused a moment. "I'll approach and tell them we're friendly."
Before Hadde could object, he started forward.

"Hail Salador!" he called out. "We are travelers from Landomere. We come in peace. Will you give us sanctuary for the night?"

There was no response. Hadde could still see people moving behind the narrow windows and her hand crept to her bow.

"Ur yo nibla lirds?" someone shouted from a window.

Belor turned and looked back at Hadde. She shrugged. The words had made no sense. She rode up to him.

"We're travelers from Landomere," Belor replied to the Saladoran.

"Speredos from firrast?"

"Spiridus," Hadde said. "He wants to know if we're spiridus."

"No, not spiridus," Belor said to the man. "Just travelers. People like you. We're going to Sal-Oras to see the king."

Again there was silence from the manor. A few moments later the heavy door creaked open, groaning in protest as it was pushed wide. Five men stepped from the darkness. All were dirty and disheveled, with matted hair and unkempt clothing. Two had spears and shields but wore no armor. The others carried strange bows mounted sideways on shafts. The Saladorans shuffled forward, none seeming to want to stand in front.

"Should we approach them?" Hadde asked.

"Slowly," Belor said. But as soon as they started forward the men retreated a few paces and raised their weapons. Hadde and Belor stopped. "They're afraid," Belor said. "I'll dismount and go alone."

Hands held open before him, he led his horse toward the men on the ramp. He towered over the villagers, his red aketon adding to his stature. Hadde watched as the villagers nervously retreated.

Raising his hands, Belor spoke to the men. Hadde couldn't keep up with what they were saying, but the Saladorans became more relaxed. A few of the men nodded in agreement to something Belor said. He led them toward Hadde.

"This is Hadde," he said when he arrived, introducing her to the men.

The five men each spoke in turn, but Hadde couldn't make out what they said. "The villagers have invited us to stay for the night," Belor said. "The manor house is full, but they will give us an empty cottage at the edge of the village."

"How do you understand them?" Hadde asked.

Belor smiled. "They're speaking Landomeri. It's just the way they pronounce the words that's different. I'm getting most of it."

Hadde noticed two of the Saladorans staring at her and talking to one another. One turned to Belor and asked, *"Is he wimun?"* to Belor.

"Am I a woman?" She looked from Belor, who nodded, to the man. "Of course I am!"

The men looked aghast. *"Woman in urmir? With wapin?"*

"Why not?" Hadde asked, glancing at her mail.

All five villagers stared openly at her. There were hurried whispers between them.

"Belor, what are they talking about?" Hadde asked.

"I don't know. They're talking too fast and whispering. Something about your being a woman." He looked at one of the yeomen. "What's wrong?"

The man half-bowed and looked embarrassed. "Nothing, Lord. Let *os* show you the stable." Hadde nodded. Their accent was heavy, and the vowels were different, but she understood them.

Hadde and Belor dismounted as two of the men led them to the only other stone structure in the village. Looking over her shoulder, she saw a crowd of people at the top of the ramp.

The stench from the stable forced Hadde to step back from its entrance. It hadn't been mucked out in ages. But it wasn't just the smell of old manure that turned her away; she smelled the rot of some dead carcass. Belor refused the use of it, sending the villagers into a hurried huddle of conversation. They showed Hadde and Belor to a cottage, offering to let them keep their horses with them. The cottage had a decent thatched roof, but that was the only good thing that could be said for it. Old threshes covered the dirt floor.

"Should we take it?" Hadde asked.

"Better than staying out of doors."

"Are you sure?"

Belor smiled and shrugged and they led their three horses into the cottage. Hadde cared for their mounts while Belor spoke with the men. By the time she finished, the villagers were heading back to the manor.

"Yeoman Edo told me their lord left them a year ago," Belor said as he entered. "A short time later his wife, their squire, and their soldiers departed as well. Someone named Bailiff was left to manage things, but bandits killed him. Since that time nobody has returned."

"Have they seen the silver-eyes?"

"No. I think they thought me crazy when I described them."

"What a mess," Hadde said, looking around the room.

"At least we can get out of this armor and get some rest." As Hadde helped Belor out of his aketon she asked if the villagers could help supply them. "I don't think so. I think they have barely enough for themselves." He draped his hauberk over a plow handle.

"Is there another manor nearby we can go to? Some place that isn't so disgusting. Somewhere we can purchase supplies?"

Belor shrugged as he closed the door. "I didn't talk to them that long." He helped Hadde from her armor, and they made their preparations for the night. It wasn't long before Hadde had a fire going in the center of the floor. The smoke filled the peaked roof and hid the rafters from sight before exiting through a ragged hole cut in the ceiling. Hadde set a travel pot over the fire and started some split pea soup.

While the peas cooked, Hadde spread her weapons on a blanket in front of her. Everything would get a going-over with her sharpening stone. Belor followed her example. "What's a yeoman?" she asked as she went to work on the axe uncle Segreg had armed her with.

"Some sort of title, I think. Like calling you a huntress," he replied. "In the stories, Saladorans all have ranks and titles." He ran a sharpening stone over his sword. "A squire is a young noble who isn't yet a knight."

"I wonder how you get to be a noble."

Belor looked perplexed. "I don't know. I don't think you get to choose."

"Maybe the king tells you."

He shrugged.

"They seemed to think I was strange," Hadde said.

"I think their warriors are all men. They—" There was a knock at the door and Belor stood to open it. One of the yeomen stepped into the room, his eyes widening at the sight of Belor, sword in hand, and Hadde with her axe across her lap.

"Come in," Belor said. "You are welcome." He leaned his sword against the wall to make his words more convincing.

The yeoman was filthy and reeked in the confined space of the cottage. He glanced nervously back and forth from Belor to Hadde. Behind the villager another face peered through the door. "Will you feast with us in the manor?" the man asked.

Belor glanced at Hadde. Another whiff of the yeoman's stench and a glance at his dirt-encrusted hands convinced Hadde she wouldn't eat with him. She motioned toward the bubbling pot of pea porridge and said, "We have already cooked our meal, thank you. I think we'll stay here and rest."

"I thank you as well," Belor said. "But we're tired from our long journey."

The man wrung his hands as if he didn't know what to do. Hadde thought he hadn't understood them. After a moment he nodded, apologized, and backed out of the hut.

"I don't like it here," Hadde said after Belor closed the door. "These people make me uncomfortable. I hope all Saladorans aren't like them."

Belor latched the door and sat down next to the fire. "I know. There is something wrong with this manor. I think it's because they don't have a lord. I think they're used to being told what to do."

Hadde looked at the closed door. "Do you think we should bar it as well?"

"We don't have much to fear from this ragged bunch. That last one was terrified at the sight of our weapons."

"They seem desperate."

"They are just miserable."

Hadde looked around the room at the broken tools and after a moment selected a few stout poles. She propped them against the cottage door and braced them against the floor.

"You don't have to do that," Belor said.

"It doesn't hurt."

"As you wish." He nodded at the small pile of wood in the corner of the cottage. "They didn't leave us much."

"We shouldn't be too cold in here out of the wind." Hadde placed her axe next to her cased bow and served up two small bowls of porridge.

Belor looked past her at a pile of broken tools. "We could always burn some of those if we wanted to."

"Do you think we should? They may want to repair them for the spring."

"This group? They'll be lucky if they make spring. They're hopeless."

Hadde woke, startled. For a moment she thought it was the cold, but it wasn't that uncomfortable in the cottage. She lay still, listening for any noise. Dull red embers glowed in the remains of the fire. Belor still slept, his arm draped across her.

A thud outside caused Hadde's heart to skip a beat. Had something blown over? She shifted position and stared at the door, her ears straining against the night.

The door's latch rose in its slot.

"Belor, wake up," she hissed. Sitting, she grabbed her axe's handle. She heard more muffled noises outside as the door shifted against its braces.

"What is it?" he asked.

"Someone's outside! They tried to open the door."

Suddenly alert, he scrambled to his feet and drew his sword. Hadde belted her bowcase around her waist, picked up her bow, and stepped to the door. Belor joined her.

"What is it?" he whispered. "What's going on?"

She shook her head. "They can't be up to any good."

Belor reached for one of the posts Hadde had placed against the door.

"No, Belor, what if…"

Hadde's heart thudded as the latch lifted again. Belor grasped his sword in both hands as the door creaked. Hadde shoved her axe into her belt. Stepping back three paces, she nocked an arrow and aimed it at the door. The pressure on the door relaxed.

"Hadde, don your armor and saddle the horses. I'll guard the door."

"They'll wait by the door and ambush us as we leave."

"They won't expect us to charge out fully armed. Hurry with the horses."

Hadde saddled the horses and stowed their gear. She glanced up at Belor. "Anything?" she asked. He listened at the door and shook his head. "I doubt they just left. Hurry up."

She pulled her mail over her head, tied her belt and joined him. "Your turn." Before he could move the door burst from its hinges. Two men stumbled through the wreckage, a heavy beam held between them. More men crowded behind.

Before the attackers could recover their balance, Belor swung his sword, striking the first man in the face. The intruder screamed in pain and reeled backwards, blocking the doorway. Shouting a savage cry, Belor took a full swing and cut down the man he had wounded.

Hadde drew her arrow and shot the second attacker through the throat. He fell back gurgling and choking on the feathered shaft. She

42

loosed another arrow into the crowd pressing from behind. A man fell to his knees clutching the arrow in his chest.

No remorse, no fear, Hadde thought.

The three bodies, the ram, and the wreckage of the door blocked the entrance. Hadde loosed three more arrows in quick succession and the remaining attackers broke and ran. "Keep them back," Belor shouted. "I'll clear a path."

"Your armor!"

"No time."

Hadde drew another arrow and aimed it out the doorway as Belor pulled the bodies aside. An arrow from the darkness cracked against the doorframe. She saw the archer standing, moonlit, twenty strides away, partly sheltered by another cottage. She shot him in the shoulder and he fell out of view.

"Now, Hadde, mount up."

They ran from the doorway and leapt onto their horses. "Go left out the door," Hadde said. "Back to the fort."

"Now!" Belor shouted as Quickstep leapt out the door.

Too late, Hadde yelled, "Me first! Armor!"

Hadde dug her heels into Lightfoot's flanks and they raced after him. Windwalker trailed behind, her lead tied to Hadde's saddle. Arrows whipped close by as they emerged from the cottage. Hadde loosed an arrow as soon as she cleared the lintel, but didn't watch to see if she struck her target.

In front of her, Belor swung his sword in a vicious arc and struck down a spearman who attempted to bar their path. More arrows flew past, but Hadde didn't spare the effort to respond. She bent low in the saddle and raced for the safety of the night.

They had just cleared the village when Belor sagged in his saddle and fell. Pulling to a halt, Hadde sheathed her bow as she dismounted and ran to him. Belor sat on the ground, his hand holding Windwalker's reins and his sword lying on the ground next to him.

"Belor!"

He gasped and fell to his side. An arrow protruded from his abdomen.

Hadde looked toward the village. They were too close. Already, figures approached out of the darkness. "We have to get away from here. Can you ride?"

"I have to," he groaned.

"I'll take care of you, Belor. Just hold on!"

"I won't make it."

"You will!" She helped him onto his horse. He gritted his teeth in pain as he settled himself.

"We can do this! Ride!"

Belor could barely keep in his saddle. Hadde wanted to help him, but they dared not stop until they reached safety. She winced every time his horse stepped over a rough patch in the darkness and he hissed in pain.

They had gone a few dozen arrow flights when they stopped in a sheltered gully. Hadde quickly dismounted and helped Belor as he half fell from his saddle. She eased him to the ground as best she could.

"I have to take it out," she said. His face looked deathly pale even in the dim light of pre-dawn.

"No, just leave it," he gasped.

"We can't leave it in there. I have to treat your wound."

"I'm dead. You can do nothing for me. Let me go in peace." He grimaced and his head fell back.

"Don't say that. Don't give up hope. Let me do what I can."

"At least the Wasting won't take me." He moaned in agony.

"Old age will take you, Belor. Not this arrow. Not the Wasting." He lay still. Fear raced through her. She scrambled forward and felt his neck for a pulse. He groaned as she moved his head.

"For nothing," he whispered and closed his eyes.

"No! You're not going to die!"

He gasped and passed out. Hadde scoured their supplies and grabbed everything she thought she would need. Bending over him, she examined the arrow. It had pierced the right side of his abdomen. She caught a foul odor and recoiled. His intestines had been pierced. Blood soaked his breechcloth and leggings.

She fought back the grief that welled up in her. The wound was worse than she had thought. Hoping the arrow wasn't barbed, she grasped its fletching. "Hold still," she commanded, although she knew he was beyond hearing.

She took a deep breath to calm her own nerves and then pulled the arrow free. Belor cried out and convulsed once before lying still. At least it had come out smoothly. She tossed the arrow aside.

"Can you hear me?" she asked. He was still and silent. Hadde bound his wound as best she could. He had lost much blood, but there was nothing she could do about it. Hadde froze at a noise in the distance. She scrambled up the gully and peered toward the manor. Torches flickered as a line of men approached. Cursing, she slid back down.

The fort they had stayed in the night before was a half-day journey, but it was her only real hope of keeping Belor safe and sheltered. She quickly constructed a drag-litter by fastening two poles to either side of

Windwalker and tying a blanket between them. It wouldn't be an easy journey for him. But she had to get Belor to the fort. She had to save him. He was her friend. He was her love.

He would not die.

Chapter Six

Hadde turned in her saddle to check on Belor and found him sagging in a wretched heap at the bottom of the litter. She leapt from the saddle and ran to his side. Tying him in place hadn't worked and she feared moving him was doing him great harm. But what choice did she have? The Saladorans would have discovered them back in the gully. Even now the villagers could be in pursuit, although she hadn't seen a sign of them in hours.

Carefully, Hadde straightened Belor on the litter. The blanket she had covered him with had fallen askew, but when she reached out to fix it she found it soaked with blood. His bandages were a red ruin.

"Oh, Belor, you're so cold." She glanced in the direction of the tower and spotted it in the dim light of dawn. But seeing it did nothing to lift her spirits. Belor was dying. Getting to the tower was meaningless, she realized. There was nobody to save him. Nothing could save him. She sat beside Belor and, as gently as she could, lifted him and rested his head in her lap. His body was limp and heavy as she moved him.

"Shhh, all will be well, Belor." Tears welled in her eyes as she cradled him. He was almost gone. His breath was shallow and his face deathly pale. "I'm so sorry."

Unbidden images of evil Saladorans flashed through her mind. The man she had shot through the throat reeling backwards in pain and shock. Belor crumpled on the ground with an arrow in his side. "I should have left the cottage first," she said. "I was in armor."

He gave one last shuddering breath, and then lay still.

One of Hadde's tears fell on his cheek. She wiped it away only to leave a bloody smudge. "I should have known you would charge out the door. I should have stopped you. My mail would have turned the arrow."

She was the leader. She was responsible. They should have turned back and never tried for Sal-Oras. There probably wasn't even an elementar-king anyway. Mor-Oras was so much closer. Why had she let him convince her to go on? Belor would never see Landomere again. He wouldn't even feel the Great Forest's embrace in death.

Hadde led the horses off the broken path and into the woods,

46

searching for an appropriate place. She found it at the base of a young oak. She cleared the ground of debris and placed Belor under the tree's sheltering branches. His arms lay across his chest and he looked as if he had stopped to rest under the tree while on some pleasant journey. She paused a moment and then pulled his cloak over his body.

After removing her armor, Hadde gathered stones from a nearby creek bed. It took most of the afternoon to complete her work, but when she was done Belor was entombed under a sturdy cairn.

"Become one with the forest, Belor," Hadde said. "I'm sorry it isn't Landomere. But this tree is young and strong and has resisted the Wasting this long. Lend it your strength so that you may help it grow into a giant of its kind. May your spirit find happiness as it wanders amongst the trees."

Hadde dumped her gear on the floor of the fort's gate tower. She lit a fire and curled up in her blankets. It was still day, but she was exhausted. Wind and rain hammered against the tower's shuttered windows, waking her. For a moment she wondered where she was, and then the horror of the past day's events came to her. She grimaced at the memory and stared into the embers of her fire.

Somewhere to the west was Landomere. Hadde regretted the moment she had left her borders. She pulled the golden chain from beneath her shirt and looked at it in the firelight. Helna's Orb glimmered back at her. "Not much of a gift. More a curse."

She roused herself as the sound of rain faded and climbed the stairs to the top of the tower. Only a passing shower, she thought. She stood and watched the sun descend. The wan light did nothing to warm her. Tomorrow she would start her journey home.

Just as she turned to crawl through the trap door, a faint noise came to her on the breeze. The distant call of a horn. Her first thought was of Landomeri hunting horns, but that joy quickly faded. There would be no Lanomderi hunting party here. More likely the Saladorans had caught up to her. She leapt down the ladder into the tower, snatched up her bowcase, and returned.

A stronger horn blast pulled her eyes to the south. Her heart beat faster as she caught sight of a party of horsemen galloping up the ancient highway. They had just emerged from a patch of woods near where Hadde and Belor had first spotted the fort.

The slanting sunlight flashed off of steel as the strident horn called again. What would they do when they arrived? She felt a flash of fear. The tower door was locked, but the gate to the fort stood open. It had taken both Belor and her to close it the first time. She felt a flash of regret that she hadn't found a way to close it again.

Hadde studied the approaching party. There were more than just horsemen, she saw. A band of warriors on foot pursued the five riders. She tried to make sense of the scene. The riders seemed to be breaking free, when four men sprang out from ambush and hurled javelins at them. One of the riders toppled from his horse. A flame-red banner dipped as a mail-clad warrior lowered his lance and charged. A footman attempted to dodge, but the lance caught him and sent him reeling to the ground.

The remaining horsemen rode down the ambushers and charged for the fort, their pursuers hard on them. Hadde frowned. The footmen were too fast—almost keeping pace with the riders. But still the riders managed to gain a dozen strides on them. Not just riders, but knights, she realized. Saladoran knights. And she didn't need to see their eyes to realize who the footmen were. Their clothes and arms were identical to those of the strange warriors who had joined the Kiremi raiders.

It seemed the knights would break free when the lead pursuers cast a last volley of javelins. Two struck home and a horse stumbled and fell. The rider disappeared under his mount.

The fallen knight's companions wheeled their horses and raced to save their comrade. To Hadde's surprise, the thrown horseman sprang to his feet. One of the foot warriors struck at him with an axe, but the knight deflected it with his shield and cut the man down.

Hadde lost sight of the knight as his companions crashed into the crowd. Two of the knights leveled their lances and impaled their enemies. Another rode to the aid of the dismounted knight, pulling him onto the saddle. The rescued man and his savior broke free and rode for the fort, the other two knights guarding their escape.

Hadde pulled some tension into her bowstring. A slight crosswind blew from left to right. A stone post beside the road looked to be two hundred strides away. Her first arrow would land there. She adjusted her aim.

A javelin pierced one of the horse's flanks. The steed kept running, but fell behind the others. A knight riding a huge roan slowed to keep pace with the straggler. The roan's rider was the only knight still holding a lance; its red pennant fluttered in the wind.

Two of the silver-eyes closed on the last horseman as they passed Hadde's aiming post. She loosed an arrow but didn't watch its flight. As she shot her second arrow the first struck home. The lead silver-eye fell.

The slowest rider desperately swung his sword at an attacker. Another leaped forward and stabbed the horse. It reared up and fell, but the knight leapt clear. The roan knight charged, knocking aside two assailants.

Three more attackers ran at him, thwarting his effort at rescuing his comrade.

Hadde loosed another arrow. One of the silver-eyes staggered back, wounded. The dismounted knight hacked at his enemies but was hopelessly surrounded. Hadde loosed more arrows into the crowd of attackers, but it was to no avail. The beleaguered knight fell under the relentless attack.

The knight on the roan turned from his fallen comrade and spurred for the fort. Hadde reached to her bowcase for another arrow, but it was empty. Six unwounded attackers remained. She clutched her useless bow as the knight raced for the gate.

The big roan was fast. Hadde took a breath. The knight might make it. In the yard below, the men who had ridden double stood ready to shove the gate closed.

Javelins arced after the last knight. The roan swerved and they flew wide. Hooves hammered on the bridge as he charged to safety. Angry shouts rose from outside as the knights pushed the gate closed.

The knight pulled off his helm and dismounted as soon as he cleared the gate. He looked up at Hadde. "Archer, where is the lord of the manor? Why did no men ride out to us?" he shouted, his face flushed red with exertion. The other two knights barred the gate behind him.

"I don't know!" Hadde replied. "There was no one here when we arrived."

"What do you mean?"

A sudden hammering drew her to the wall. The six pursuers attacked the gate with their axes and swords. Hadde couldn't believe they were trying to hack through the heavy timbers. It was an impossible task.

"What's going on?" the knight demanded. "Why aren't you shooting at them? Where are the keep's defenders?"

"I'm alone," she yelled back, "and have no more arrows."

The knight gave her a hard look and glanced around the fort. He said something to one of the other knights, but Hadde couldn't hear him. The third knight tried to open the tower door.

"Come down here and open the door!" the roan knight shouted. He took one of the odd Saladoran bows and a quiver of arrows from a saddle case. Outside, the silver-eyes furiously attacked the gate.

Hadde ran down and opened the iron-bound door. The knight barely looked at her as he pushed into the room and headed for the stairs. Hadde caught a glimpse of the other two knights standing ready at the gate before she turned to follow him. As she passed Lightfoot she grabbed her saddle quiver from where it rested with her piled gear.

When she emerged onto the roof, the knight was pulling his

bowstring into place and sliding a short arrow into the groove carved on its wooden stock.

"Ambush us, will you? Cowardly bastards!" he swore. He lifted the bow to his shoulder and aimed it over the parapet. The string snapped forward and there was a cry of pain from below. "Bastards! Get you gone from Salador!"

He dodged backwards as a javelin skipped off of the parapet beside him. Hadde ran to the knight's side and nocked an arrow. She took aim and put an arrow into one of the attackers. It hit him in the collarbone and drove downward into his chest. He grunted and fell.

Beside her the knight had loaded his bow. His arrow cracked into the stone pavement. Hadde shot another attacker, wounding him.

The attack made no sense to Hadde. Two attackers continued to hammer at the gate. The others fruitlessly cast their axes at Hadde and the knight.

"Why aren't they running?" she asked as she drew another arrow.

"They're creatures of Dromost!" he said.

Hadde shot down two more attackers as the knight wounded another. The fight was over. Three of the bear-men lay wounded by the gate. Four others, further down the road, dragged themselves toward the woods.

"They're done, but for a few still wounded." the knight shouted over the wall. "Go out and see if anything can be done for our men!"

"I will, Sir Nidon!" came the reply.

The knight turned to face her. "Who are you?"

"I'm just a traveler here. My companion and I found this place abandoned."

"Your companion?" He was a large man, taller and broader than even Belor. His rugged face was crisscrossed with scars and a flat, crooked nose.

"I'm alone now. My companion was slain."

"You speak the High Tongue, but you're not Saladoran. What are you? Kiremi?" He looked her up and down with disapproval.

"I'm Landomeri."

A thud and a strangled cry from below drew her attention. Hadde looked over the wall to see one of the knights removing his sword from the neck of a fallen foe.

"Stay here," the knight said. "We'll return as soon as our companions have been seen to."

"I will come as well. I need to retrieve my arrows."

"As you will."

***

50

The three knights recovered the bodies of their fallen comrades and returned to the fort. Hadde stood aside as they took them to the center of the bailey and laid them to rest on the ground. The youngest knight led two horses toward the tower.

"Can I be of help?" Hadde asked him.

"No, it's my task," he replied as he walked by. One of the other knights, the one who had been thrown from his horse, turned at the sound of her voice.

"You! Woman!" he called out. "Get the archers and have them bring wood. We'll build a funeral pyre."

She was about to respond when the big knight named Nidon said, "There are no others, Earl Waltas. She's alone."

"What? Who was firing from the walls?"

"She was, Earl."

The earl looked at her and laughed. "What foolishness is this? She's a woman. Where are the others?"

"I was in the tower and saw for myself, Earl Waltas. I saw her wield the bow with expertise. There are no others."

Waltas strode purposefully toward Hadde. He was a young man with brown hair and brown eyes. His narrow features gave him a hawk-like appearance.

"Who are you? Where are you from?"

"My name is Hadde of Long Meadow. I'm Landomeri."

"How is it you speak the High Tongue?" He stood a few strides from her.

"I don't know what that is. I speak the language of my mother."

He looked her up and down with distaste. "You're no noblewoman."

"I… I make no claim to be one."

He laughed a curt laugh and looked back toward the other knight. "She speaks the High Tongue, but she's just a simple savage from the woods."

Hadde felt her face flush. "I don't know——"

"Shut up! You'll speak when spoken to. And when you speak you'll give due respect." Hadde's jaw dropped, but he continued before she could respond. "You carry arms, dress in uncouth manner, and don't know your place. Why are you in Salador? Are you a raider or a thief?"

"I'm neither! We were on a journey to see the king."

"You'll refer to me as 'my lord' or 'Earl Waltas.' And what business could the likes of you've with a king?"

"I'm an ambassador, Earl Waltas," she replied, bewildered at his assault.

"Foolishness!" he took a threatening step toward her. "Be off! Put

51

down that bow and cover yourself properly before I next see you."

Hadde took a few steps backward. She didn't know what to think. Pulling herself from the knight's glare, she turned and strode toward the tower door. Her mind whirled. What had she done? The ungrateful wretch! Hadn't she just saved him?

Only the fading light coming in the open door lighted the tower. The young knight was attending to the horses. He looked up in surprise as she entered the tower. For a moment she looked at him, not knowing what to say. Not wanting to be verbally assaulted by another Saladoran, she made her way to the stairs to the upper floor.

She had just reached the bottom step when he said, "We have lost much of our gear in the attack."

Hadde paused and looked in his direction. He wrung his hands. "Would you permit me the use of some of your stable gear?"

"I... of course," Hadde replied.

"We're also without food... for our horses," he added. He looked genuinely embarrassed at his need. "If you could spare some victuals, Sir Nidon would, I'm sure, reimburse you handsomely."

Hadde wasn't sure what was meant about reimbursement, but she understood the horses' needs. "I have little of my own," she replied, "but I'll share what I have. It's the Way of the Forest."

It was his turn to look confused, but he thanked her profusely. Hadde opened her packs and helped him take what he needed. As he returned to his horses, Hadde saw to her own mounts. For a time, they worked in silence.

Nidon appeared in the doorway. "Squire Melas, have you almost finished?" he asked.

"Yes, Sir Nidon," the young knight replied.

"Come and join us as soon as you're done. We must salvage more wood for the pyre. I don't wish to wait until morning."

"Sir Nidon," Melas said as Nidon turned to leave. "This woman was good enough to offer food for our horses. I wish to give her some payment."

"Go ahead. Now hurry and join us."

"I—I've lost my purse," the squire said and swallowed. "It was cut..."

Nidon frowned. "I've left my hauberk and sword outside for you to fetch. My purse is on my belt. You may take..." He paused and looked at Hadde. "How much do you want for two days food for our horses?"

She shook her head. "Nothing, Sir Nidon," she said, hoping she had pronounced his name correctly. "It is freely given."

"Don't be foolish." He turned to the squire and said, "Pay her a silver.

It's generous, but our need is great." He walked out the door before she could make any reply.

Hadde put more wood on the embers of her neglected fire. She set a cook pot on the fire to heat water for another meal of split peas and, after a moment's thought, added more water. As the water heated she moved her own blankets and gear to one side of the fireplace.

After pouring a large measure of peas into the pot, she mounted the ladder and climbed to the top of the tower. Night had fallen, but it wasn't yet completely dark. Stars filled the sky. A chill wind blew across the top of the tower. Hadde looked into the bailey and saw that the knights had completed their work. They had constructed a six foot tall wooden platform and placed their dead companions upon it. The structure was crudely built with wood stacked all around it.

She frowned and then nodded in understanding. The Kiremi honored their dead in the same way, leaving them on a raised platform so they could return to Helna without ever touching the soil. They thought the earth to be evil, tainted by Dromost, but the Landomeri knew differently. Dromost's followers may have lived in the dark places under the earth, but that didn't make the soil evil.

She shook her head at the knights. The fort might be abandoned, but anybody who came this way would certainly stop here. At least the Kiremi placed their dead in out-of-the-way places. All three knights held torches and, although she couldn't hear them, she realized they were holding some kind of ceremony for the dead. After a time they all walked closer to the pile and pushed their torches into the wood surrounding the platform.

Hadde stared at the scene in horror. She had to step away from the edge of the tower, repulsed at the thought of the bodies burning on the piled wood. It seemed a terrible affront to the Great Forest to burn wood to consume the dead. Not wanting to watch any more of the ritual, she returned to the tower room below.

"She will sleep with the horses," she heard Waltas say as the knights stomped up the stairs. Hadde clenched her jaw at the words. All three Saladorans walked into the tower room together. Nidon and Waltas carried their mail and sword belts, while Melas brought up the rear with a double armload of saddle packs. They glanced around the room and chose places to set down their gear.

"Squire Melas, go to the roof and stand guard," Earl Waltas ordered.

"Yes, my..."

"Earl Waltas," Nidon cut off the squire's reply. "If you would be so kind, but the squire is in my service."

The earl's face hardened. "Of course, Sir Nidon. My apologies. Would you have your squire stand guard?"

Nidon nodded at the squire, who laid the saddlebags on the floor before he climbed the ladder to the roof. He carried the bow Nidon had used earlier. Hadde hadn't seen another amongst their gear and assumed it was the only one.

As the squire departed, the two knights grabbed their baggage from the pile and settled themselves near the fire. All three Saladorans had been armed and armored in the same manner, but Hadde noticed they wore different sleeveless tunics over their clothes. Earl Waltas wore one of white, much spattered with blood, with two black hammers crossed upon it. Nidon's was red with a silver fringe and no symbol. The squire's was the same as Nidon's but displayed two crossed lightning bolts.

The knights proceeded to lay their weapons and harness out around them. Nidon drew his sword and set to work polishing it while Waltas cleaned his mail. Hadde watched for a moment and then moved to the fire to stir the porridge.

After a short time Nidon turned to her and asked, "How is it you're in Salador? You say you're an ambassador?" He used a smooth stone to get the nicks out of his sword's blade.

Hadde stirred the bubbling pot in front of her for a moment before replying. "I came as an ambassador of my people. To seek help from the king."

"Sir Nidon," Waltas corrected her. "You'll address him as Sir Nidon. And you'll address me as Earl Waltas."

"I'm sorry," she said. "In my land we don't use titles." She turned to Nidon. "We came here to see the king, Sir Nidon." She paused, hoping that they wouldn't laugh at what she was going to say next. "Is it true he's an elementar?"

Waltas snorted a derisive laugh. "You come seeking an elementar? You expect magic?"

Hadde hoped the darkness of the room hid her embarrassment. "I'm sorry. Our stories say that the kings of Salador were always elementars."

"And he is," Nidon said, casting a dark look at Waltas. "King Boradin is a great elementar, his brother less so," Nidon said. "And the king's son, Prince Handrin, shows great potential."

"Handrin?" Hadde asked. "Like Handrin the Great?"

"The prince is named for his ancestor," Nidon said. "They say he will be a great elementar."

Waltas snorted.

"Don't mock what you don't understand." Nidon shot Waltas a dark look.

"I understand perfectly well. There is no magic. There are only tricks that keep the ignorant in line."

"You'll learn the truth of it soon enough, Earl Waltas" Nidon said. He turned to Hadde. "Why do you seek the king?"

"I seek council. In the old stories Landomere and Salador were great allies, and we hope the king will be able to aid us in our time of need."

"You have two problems," Waltas said. "First of all, the king cannot help you. He cannot even help Salador. Secondly, you're a woman. Well, sort of." He laughed. "They won't let you in the front gate."

Hadde frowned. She didn't know how to respond.

"There is already an ambassador from Landomere in the king's court," Nidon said. "Orlos the Spiridus."

Hadde looked at him, not understanding for a moment. "Orlos? A spiridus from Landomere? One still lives?"

"You didn't know? He's the last of the spiridus. Over six hundred years old, I think. Everyone knows of him. He escaped the destruction of Belavil and has lived in Salador ever since. He's very old, though. I fear he won't live much longer."

"We didn't know he was there," Hadde said. She could hardly believe Nidon's words. A spiridus still lived? Her heart lurched in her chest at the thought. She had never imagined it possible. "I don't think even the elders know of him."

"So you see," Waltas said, "You can drag yourself back to the forest now. There's no need of you."

Hadde stared into the pot of bubbling porridge, her thoughts still on the spiridus. His presence in Sal-Oras had to mean something. Was there a connection between him and her golden chain?

"Serve us some of that soup," Waltas demanded.

Hadde looked at him in surprise, appalled at his lack of manners. She had intended to feed them, but gifts were meant to be given, not demanded.

"Hurry up," he said.

Hadde balled her fist. Even the youngest child knew not to demand food. She was about to tell him so when Nidon said, "You could say please, Earl Waltas." Nidon's tone was cold. He didn't look at the earl but continued working on his sword.

"What did you say, Sir Nidon?"

"Watch me, Earl Waltas," the knight said. He turned toward Hadde. "Hadde of Landomere, would you be kind enough to share your food

55

with us? Our recent battle left us without sufficient supplies."

"You go too far, Nidon," Waltas said.

Hadde took in the exchange but didn't understand what was going on. "I've made enough for all of us," Hadde said. She scooped a portion into a bowl and offered it to Nidon.

"Thank you," he replied, but didn't take it. "But as I'm a simple knight, and the earl outranks me, he should have the first bowl."

Hadde turned toward Waltas and offered the bowl to him. "Would you like some, Earl Waltas?"

"Bring it here and put it next to me," he said.

Hadde stood and walked behind Nidon to where Waltas sat at the opposite side of the fire. He glanced up at her as she set the bowl beside him. "Thank you," he said, but there was no kindness in it. The look he gave her sent a shiver up her spine.

She returned to the fire and spooned out two more bowls, one of which she gave to Nidon. He thanked her but didn't look at her as he did so. Hadde picked up the other bowl and carried it toward the ladder to the roof. She was almost there when Waltas called out, "Where are you going?"

"I was going to give the other knight his portion, Earl Waltas."

"He's a squire, not a knight. And no, you'll not. You cannot go up there with him alone."

"What? Why not?"

"It would be improper for him to be alone with a woman."

"Why?"

"You miserable savage, because it's uncivilized. Because it's inappropriate."

She kept a hold of her anger and replied, "If that's the case, you're welcome to join us." Turning her back on his scowl, she climbed the ladder.

"Peasant," Waltas muttered behind her.

The squire's eyes widened as Hadde emerged onto the roof. "I've brought you some food," she said, offering him the bowl.

"I... uh," he replied, glancing at the open trapdoor.

She offered the bowl again. Steam rose from it and dissipated into the darkness. The squire put down his bow and took the proffered food.

"Thank you lady... um."

"Call me Hadde. And you are Squire Melas?"

He nodded and said, "You have no title?"

"I'm called a huntress, but it's my calling, not a title."

"Ahh," he replied, but he looked confused. He spooned a mouthful of porridge.

"Have you seen any more of those creatures?"

He shook his head as he swallowed. "No, not a one."

It was very cold on the roof and Hadde hadn't thought to put on her cloak. "I'll come up to relieve you in a little while. You should not have to be up here so long."

"That isn't necessary. It's my task, and I'll do it until Sir Nidon sees fit to relieve me."

"I'll tell him of your plight," she said as she turned toward the trapdoor.

"No!" he yelped, sounding very young. "Don't do that."

"What?"

"Don't tell him I need help."

"You're cold, aren't you?"

"No, I'm fine. Don't try to help me. Don't tell Sir Nidon I need relief."

"I... well, if you say so." She started toward the door.

"Hadde, thank you for the porridge."

"You're welcome," she replied as she re-entered the tower. The Saladorans bewildered her—they were so different. The two knights had finished cleaning their equipment and were setting it aside as she stepped off the ladder. She walked to her side of the fireplace and set her bow and cloak to one side in preparation to return to the roof.

She was refilling her quiver when Waltas asked, "What are you doing?"

"I'm going to the roof so that Squire Melas may come down to rest and warm himself," she said. "Earl Waltas," she quickly added.

"No you'll not. Sir Nidon and I will relieve him at the appropriate times. You'll gather what you need and go downstairs to sleep."

"I'll do what?" she asked. "Why am I forbidden from taking a watch?"

"Because you're a woman and women cannot handle arms. It's inappropriate."

"I don't know who decided that, but it's nonsense. I've handled arms since childhood, and it's a good thing for you! Would you have made the gate if I couldn't handle a bow as I can, Earl Waltas?"

"You insolent bitch!" the earl spat back at her.

He looked as if he were about to rise when Nidon said, "I see no reason for anger, Earl Waltas, when what she says is true."

"What, Sir Nidon? Will you have commoners speak to us in such manner?"

"In the court of the king I've often met foreigners. Idorians, Estorians, and even a Nording chief. Their ways are all different from ours. They may be uncouth and strange, but our king tolerates them. We should follow his example."

Waltas turned his attention to the big knight. "You would side with this commoner, Nidon?"

"She did us a good deed with her archery. I'll not deny it. She deserves some courtesy."

"She's just a common girl. Foreign, no less. She deserves nothing! Is this what Sal-Oras nobility has come to? Are you an akinos that would…" He stopped mid-sentence and looked into the fire.

Hadde turned her eyes on Nidon and saw he was giving the earl a hard stare. "An akinos that would what, Earl?" Nidon asked. "You find my behavior to be…"

The earl left the question hanging and instead replied, "I suppose you would let her sleep in here? With us?"

It was Nidon's turn to look uncomfortable. "I… I don't want her in here with us, but it would be… it would be un-chivalrous of us to cast her into the stable."

"If she were a noble woman I would sleep in the stable. But she's not! She's a commoner. And foreign. Why do you protect her? What would people say of us if they learned we slept in the same room as this half-naked barbarian?"

Hadde balled her fists. She wouldn't be cast out of the tower without a fight. She looked at Nidon as he struggled to find a response. She didn't know why he was defending her.

The moment of silence dragged on.

"Well?" Waltas looked at Nidon with a smug grin.

"She's an ambassador," Nidon blurted out. "I wouldn't cast a foreign ambassador out. And as long as she keeps properly covered, it won't be a problem."

"She's already improperly covered. And you've no reason to name her ambassador. Where are her letters of cachet? Where is her token of office? The court will hear of your behavior, Nidon!"

Hadde glanced at Nidon, but he wasn't looking in her direction. She could see the tension on his face. She hadn't understood everything they were saying, but she could tell Nidon was losing the argument.

"What is a letter of catch-it? Or a token of office?" she asked.

Waltas threw his head back and laughed.

Nidon grimaced in defeat as he replied, "It's a letter from your sovereign announcing your mission to our king. The token is a badge, staff, or orb that's carried as a symbol of rank."

"Catch-it!" Waltas cried out and laughed again. "I don't think she has one of those. Do you, Sir Nidon?"

"But I have a token of rank," she said.

"What?" Waltas asked, a big grin on his face. "Let us see. Some twig from the forest?"

Hadde reached to her neck and pulled the chain from under her tunic. Both knights' eyes widened as it appeared. Waltas's mouth dropped open while Nidon smiled.

"May I see that, Hadde of Landomere?" he asked.

She removed the chain and held it out to Nidon. Only after handing it to him did she remember the warnings she had received. Not all Saladorans could be thieves, could they?

"A Spiridus Token. I've seen one before," he announced. He looked at Waltas. "One exactly like it. It's worn by Orlos the Spiridus, Ambassador of Landomere."

Nidon handed the Spiridus Token back to her. "Hadde of Landomere, you will see the king."

Chapter Seven

Waltas yanked open the trapdoor and stomped down the stairs. "Get up! It's nearly dawn."

Hadde roused herself and gathered her gear. With Belor's death she had abandoned her quest, but now she wondered if she had made the right decision. What should she make of Orlos? A spiridus still lived, and he wore a pendant exactly like hers. Was Belor right, and she was meant to travel to Sal-Oras? Perhaps Orlos had the answers she sought.

Following the knights' example, she donned her harness. Squire Melas assisted both knights with their aketons as she struggled with her own. Hadde picked up her mail corselet and began to pull it over her head when Waltas said, "What are you doing, woman?"

"I'm putting on my armor, Earl Waltas."

He shook his head. "The aketon is bad enough, but I'll not permit you to wear mail."

"Why not?"

"Because you're a woman and because it's the law of Salador. Only men of noble rank may wear mail."

"What if we're attacked by more of the silver-eyes?"

"They're called varcolac," Nidon said. He looked from Hadde to Waltas. "And I agree with Hadde. I think she should wear her corselet."

"You would let her flout our laws?"

"I think the situation calls for it, Earl Waltas. And as an ambassador I'm willing to give her some leeway."

"I've noticed, Sir Nidon. You're giving this barbarian woman quite a bit of leeway."

"I'll leave it for the king to decide if there is error in my judgment."

"What kind of a knight are you?" Waltas muttered.

The room went still.

"Are you challenging my fitness as a knight?" Nidon asked, his voice hard.

Waltas coughed and looked away. Nidon's gaze was unflinching as he stared at the other knight.

"I..." Waltas stammered. "We'll let the king decide." He paused and quickly added, "Decide what is appropriate for the woman."

Nidon turned his back on Waltas and finished donning his armor. Hadde pulled her corselet over her head and then cinched her belt tightly about her waist. She picked up Belor's sword and considered putting it on. He would have wanted me to wear it, she thought. He would have wanted me to continue his quest.

"You won't need that," Nidon said.

She looked up to find him staring at the sword. She was about to question him, but something in his eyes told her she shouldn't challenge him. And he was too important an ally to lose.

While the two knights finished their preparations, Hadde followed Melas downstairs. Once there she saddled Lightfoot while the squire took care of the Saladoran mounts. She had almost finished packing Windwalker and Quickstep when Melas said, "We have a problem."

"What's that?" Above them she could hear the two knights' footsteps as they stomped toward the stairwell.

"Earl Waltas's horse was slain. He has no mount."

Hadde shrugged. "He can ride Quickstep."

Melas' brows furrowed. "After what he has said to you? You would offer him a horse?"

"What does it gain me responding to his unkindness with my own?"

Melas opened his mouth to speak and then shut it. "I—," he started, but was interrupted by the arrival of the knights. Melas told them of Hadde's offer.

"Ride that?" Waltas snorted. "It's barely a horse."

Nidon smiled. "There doesn't seem to be much choice."

"I'll ride the squire's horse and he can ride the hobby."

"No," Nidon said, "Squire Melas isn't your vassal. He's a Squire of the House and is in the king's personal service."

Waltas flushed with anger but held his tongue. Pushing past Nidon, he walked to Quickstep. He sucked air through his teeth as he looked at the horse. "It's more a big dog than a horse. And this isn't a saddle. We'll replace it with my own."

"We have a saying in Landomere," Hadde said, as she pulled a strap tight. "Freely given, happily accepted."

Nidon laughed. "We say much the same. Most of us, at least."

Waltas ignored them and led the horse from the stable.

"Sir Nidon," Hadde said as they rode from the fort, "this is the road my companion and I were following. The manor we ride toward is where Belor and I were attacked."

"You were attacked on a manor? I assumed it was the varcolac."

"No, the villagers. They tried to rob us in the night, but we fought our way free. My friend was wounded and later died."

"No lord would allow this to happen on his manor," Waltas said. "More likely you were raiding it."

"There was no lord there, Earl Waltas. There were just men called yeomen. They said their lord had left them."

"We'll know the truth soon enough," Nidon said. "Let's waste no more time."

They rode off with Nidon and Waltas in the lead, Melas, Hadde, and Windwalker following behind. They made good time, even dismounting and marching for periods to save their horses. There was little conversation amongst the travelers. Every once in a while Nidon looked back as if checking on Hadde. She smiled and waved each time. He had nothing to fear; the pace was easy by her standards.

The manor was much as she had left it. Despite her warnings, the knights approached without caution. Hadde pulled her bow from its case and nocked an arrow. She ignored Waltas's glare. Nidon only shrugged. Unlike her previous arrival, there was no flight of villagers into the manor. The place seemed deserted but for the smoke rising from the chimney.

Nidon approached and called out a greeting, but there was no reply. He dismounted and strode to the gate, where he hammered upon the door with his mailed fist. Still no answer. With no means of entering, they gave up and retreated to the village to find a place to stay for the night.

"This is where we were attacked," Hadde said as they rode up to the battered cottage. Blood stained the shattered doorframe.

Nidon nodded appreciatively at the arrows embedded in the wall. "With the manor held against us, the signs of a fight, and the filthy state of this village, I'm inclined to believe Hadde's story."

"There is still some daylight left, Sir Nidon," Hadde said. "We could get some distance from here before we make camp."

"I see no need for that," Nidon said. "The sky is darkening and I have no desire to be rained upon."

"But what if the yeomen attack?"

"Bah!" Waltas snorted. "They wouldn't dare. If you're afraid, ride off and hide in the woods."

"We'll be safe," Nidon said as he dismounted. "We shall stay here."

"Don't you believe me when I tell you we were attacked? That these villagers are dangerous? I'm not making these stories up." She didn't try to hide the anger in her voice.

"We'll be safe," Nidon said, his tone final.

They made camp in a large cottage. Despite her discomfort, Hadde refused to take off her armor. She wouldn't be caught unprepared. The knights seemed less concerned about an attack but at least took the precaution of keeping watch.

Hadde settled down with her back against a wall and her bow across her lap, certain she wouldn't sleep at all that night. She remained alert for a while, starting at every noise, and fingering the fletching of a nocked arrow. Squire Melas stood the first watch.

She wished Belor were with her. He would have been filled with excitement that they had met Saladoran knights and were off on the next part of the journey. If only they had run into the knights a few days earlier Belor would still be alive.

Hadde dozed and woke up to find that Nidon had taken over for Melas. Her surprise that she had fallen asleep was short-lived. She fought her drooping eyelids for a while, but the effort was futile. She dreamed unsettled dreams of fire and violence and woke barely rested.

The following day, when there was still no sign those within the manor would open the gate, Nidon led the party northeast. Late in the evening they halted in a stand of trees next to a shallow brook.

"Two more nights under the stars," Nidon announced as they dismounted. "We're on the land of Earl Crane. Once we reach his manor our journey will become easier."

Hadde surveyed her surroundings. She had never feared sleeping in the open, but she found herself longing for the safety of four stout walls. Frowning at the thought of sharing a fire with the Saladorans, she led her horses to the far side of the clearing. The Saladorans paid her little attention as they established their own camp.

As she shrugged off her mail corselet, it came to Hadde that the next months could be very lonely. She was used to the solitude of the hunt, but it was a foreign feeling to be alone in the presence of others. She set up her lean-to and cared for her horses. From time to time she watched the Saladorans. Squire Melas established the camp while Nidon and Waltas saw to their arms, armor, and horses.

As she gathered wood, she noticed signs of game. Here and there small animals rooting for bugs had disturbed the mat of leaves. Was the Wasting not as strong in Salador? She still saw signs of it, but there was wildlife here. Was there some hope? She bent closer and grinned.
Turkey.

She glanced at the setting sun. Time was short. Dropping her armload of wood by the fire, she grabbed her bow and crept into the woods. Peering into the camp, she grinned at her successful escape from the Saladorans.

The wind blew from the north and she headed in that direction. As soon as she was out of sight she paused and took a deep breath. It was good to be a huntress again. Pulling an arrow from her belt, she listened to the wind and the babble of the little stream. Leaving the noise of the camp behind, she slipped deeper into the woods.

Hadde smiled. She was one with the forest and she let its spirit enshroud her. She knew she was no spiridus, but she felt like one as she glided invisibly between the trees. The trials of the journey were left behind. She felt like her true self again. She was a huntress and the woods were her home.

Hadde felt another presence in the forest nearby. She paused and slowly took a knee. Her heart beat a little faster as she cocked her head to one side. A tom turkey that hadn't yet bedded down for the night scratched a last meal from the forest floor. There were two other birds with him, but she barely spared the females a glance. The tom wasn't large, but it was big enough.

Hadde inched her bow into position. She wouldn't rush. Turkeys were the most elusive game she hunted and she knew them well. How many times had they escaped her at the last moment?

Not this time.

Willing herself to move slowly, Hadde drew her bow. She had a clean shot. She released. Squawking and thrashing erupted as she pulled another arrow from her belt. It wasn't needed. The tom was down and the others had vanished.

Hadde, cheered by her luck, took her catch and returned to camp. The two knights had a fire started and were seated next to it polishing their armor. Melas knelt over a pot sitting in the flames.

"Look what I've found!" she said as she held up her prize.

"Where have you…" Nidon started.

"Hah, we'll eat well tonight!" Melas cried out. He looked at Hadde with a childish grin.

A sour expression crossed Waltas's face. "I shouldn't have expected more," he said. "She's a poacher as well."

Hadde saw Nidon and Melas's happy expressions fade.

"What's poaching?" Hadde asked.

"Will you defend her again, Nidon?" Waltas said as he stood. "She's a common poacher and here she is with her ill gotten gains."

Hadde lowered the bird to her side. "What do you mean?"

"Poaching is hunting without permission on the lord's land," Nidon said with a sigh. "It's a crime in Salador."

"She must be punished," Waltas said gleefully. "We must take her to Earl Crane's court for trial."

"She doesn't know the law in Salador," said Nidon. "Now she does. Be reasonable, Earl Waltas, let us eat the bird and she will hunt no more. Is that correct, Hadde?"

"Be reasonable?" Waltas spat. "Now you want me to be reasonable?" He looked at Nidon with contempt. "You know the law. Claiming ignorance is no defense."

Hadde looked to Nidon for help, but he just stared at the ground stone-faced. Melas fixed his gaze on the bird in Hadde's hand.

"Give me that evidence," Waltas said as he took a step in Hadde's direction.

She took a step back. "I've never heard of such strange customs."

Nidon looked up and said, "Hadde, why did you kill the bird? *Who* did you kill it for?" He was staring intently into her eyes as he spoke. Waltas paused and looked at him. It was strange to have Nidon looking directly at her. The Saladorans had all avoided eye contact with her. "Why did you kill it? Who is it for?"

There was something to his intensity, but she didn't know what the meaning was. "I'm a huntress," she replied. "It's what I do. I hunt to provide food for my people. I bring gifts of food so my people can eat." She paused and held the turkey out again. "I brought this gift for you."

Nidon walked past Waltas and took the turkey from her. "And I accept your gift. And what is it you want in return?" he asked, still looking into her eyes.

"Nothing. It's the Way of the Forest."

Nidon nodded and smiled. He turned away from her and tossed the bird to Melas. "She's innocent," he stated and walked back to his place by the fire.

"What?" Waltas shouted. "That isn't for you to judge. It's for the lord of this land."

"You heard her, Earl Waltas. She didn't take the bird for her own gain. She gave it freely to me, a servant of the king, in pursuit of the king's business."

He looked away from the earl. "Melas, prepare the bird." Turning to Hadde he said, "I thank you for your gift."

"Your behavior has been outrageous, Sir Nidon," Waltas said. "This spiridus witch has you under her spell."

"She's no witch, just a woman," Nidon said as he sat down.

Just a woman. Even when they defended her, they insulted her. Hadde wanted nothing more than to be rid of these men. But could she leave? Go back to Landomere and...what? Have Lightfoot slaughtered for meat? Let the Wasting take her people?

Waltas shook with frustration. He opened his mouth to speak, and then with a grimace clamped it shut. Hadde sighed with resignation as she joined Melas. Together they plucked the bird. "A pot of boiling water would make this easier," she said.

"I don't mind. I'm just grateful for the meal."

"You are welcome to it."

"Hadde," he asked, "if a huntress gives away all of her food, how does she eat?"

"Each kill is brought back and the village takes what it needs. Whatever is left goes to the hunter."

His eyebrows rose. "But there would never be anything left."

"What do you mean?" she replied. "There's always something left."

"If you came back with a rabbit for fifty people, you're telling me there would be something left for you?"

"Yes."

He shook his head. "And you don't sell the rabbit? You just give it to them?"

"Yes."

"And they leave some for you?"

She smiled and chuckled. "Yes... well usually. Things have been harder recently. Some hunters have even been accused of eating their kills before returning to the village. It's wrong."

"Less talk, more food, Squire," Nidon called out.

"Yes, Sir Nidon."

For a time they stopped talking and put more effort into cleaning the bird. As Melas spitted it he said, "You know... it does make sense, I suppose."

"What?"

"That they leave some for the hunter. If they didn't, the hunter would starve and not hunt anymore. There would be no more food."

"Exactly. The Way of the Forest."

As the turkey cooked, Hadde retired to her lean-to where she cleaned and oiled her mail corselet. It was difficult to keep rust off on such a long journey. She was amazed at how bright and polished the armor and weapons of the Saladorans were. But then again they did little else.

She was so engrossed in her work that Melas surprised her when he walked up to her fire. He held a spit with a steaming turkey leg and thigh on it.

"A gift for the hunter," he said. "I'm sorry, but there was no plate to put it upon."

"That's no problem." She held up her wooden eating bowl and he slid the meat onto it. "I thank you for your gift."

He smiled. "It's the Way of the Forest."

"Will you join me, Squire?" she asked.

Melas glanced over his shoulder at the knights. "I cannot." The look on his face told her he wanted to.

Chapter Eight

Earl Crane's manor stood on a high promontory surrounded by a massive stone wall. Below the hill rested a walled town protected by a deep dry-moat. Hadde sucked in her breath as they passed through the gate leading into the town. Huge buildings arched overhead, threatening to smother her.

Within the keep she saw numerous signs of the Earl's wealth and power. Soldiers protected the gate, fine tapestries hung on the walls of the great hall, and servants scurried everywhere. Despite his wealth, Hadde saw that the Earl faced the same troubles as people elsewhere. The villages around the castle stood half abandoned, the people were haggard, and the livestock was thin and weak. His wealth only gave so much protection from the Wasting.

"The king can do nothing for you," Earl Crane said after greeting them in the castle's main hall. He looked and sounded as hard as the stone walls that protected his manor. He was as big as Nidon, and just as scarred, but he was thicker around the middle and gray stubble covered his chin. Hadde swallowed and nodded. She didn't want to believe what she was hearing. The king had to be able to help her. There were at least thirty Saladorans in the hall, all staring intently at her. Knights and their ladies, Hadde suspected.

"I must try, at least, Earl Crane," she said. "My people have no other hope."

"The king's own vassals see little enough help." Crane's glance cut for a moment to Sir Nidon and then back to Hadde. "A foreigner such as yourself has no reason for hope."

Hadde didn't know how to reply. She shifted awkwardly under the earl's glare.

"I shall fulfill my responsibilities as a host," Crane said. "Earl Waltas and Sir Nidon, you and your charges may stay as my guests for the night. My hospitality may not be as grand as you may be accustomed to in Sal-Oras. I hope you're not disappointed." He didn't hide the bitter tone in his voice.

"Thank you, Earl Crane," Nidon said.

"I cannot help but notice that you will make it back to Sal-Oras for the Festival of Spring," Crane said.

"That is correct, Earl Crane," Nidon replied. "Unless we meet with some unexpected delay. Will you attend the king?"

Crane laughed. "Attend the king? Would that I had time for such frivolities. My time is better spent here, with my people, not dancing, and feasting with the nobles of Sal-Oras. You'll thank the king for his hospitality on my behalf, won't you Nidon?"

"Of course. It would be my pleasure."

"In true fact," Waltas said, "we have already partaken of your hospitality, Earl Crane. The woman, a foreign commoner, poached a turkey from your lands."

Crane frowned at Hadde, but before he could speak Nidon said, "That isn't quite the case, Earl Crane. The bird was taken in order to feed my party. It wasn't poached, as I'm the king's man and it was taken for me."

"An excuse devised after the fact..." Waltas shot back, but the earl cut him off with a raised hand.

"I'm the king's loyal vassal," Crane said, "and won't begrudge his due, Earl Waltas." Crane looked pointedly at Nidon. "Just as I'm certain the king is doing everything in his power to fulfill his obligations to his vassals."

Hadde sighed in relief. She wanted no part of Saladoran justice. She smiled and glanced at Nidon, but he wasn't looking her way. Instead her gaze fell upon Waltas' evil glare.

They spent the night as the earl's guests. The three Saladorans were given quarters in the keep, while Hadde spent the night in a meager room next to the stables. She didn't mind. It was warm and dry and she wasn't in the presence of Earl Waltas.

Earl Crane had little to spare in the way of supplies, but he didn't deny Nidon or Waltas the aid they required. Hadde watched as Nidon gave Earl Crane a purse of silver for a few days worth of provisions. She smiled as Earl Waltas ranted at the immense price he paid for a warhorse, but the stable master wouldn't budge. It didn't surprise her to receive no thanks for the loan of Quickstep.

They rode northeast from the manor with Waltas and Nidon in the lead, followed by Melas. Hadde trailed behind. Barely a word was spoken as mile after mile passed behind them. She had the impression that Nidon wouldn't have said much under any circumstances.

Hadde found herself smiling at the prospect of the day. The chilly morning turned into a pleasantly mild winter afternoon. All rode without armor as Earl Crane had assured them of the security of his land. He had heard only rumors of the varcolac, and needed some convincing as to their existence. Nor had he cared about the fate of the lawless manor to the west. *"Not my land, not my problem,"* had been his only comment.

"Squire Melas," she finally said, "why do they ride side by side when they dislike each other so much?"

"Who? Them?" he asked, nodding at the two knights. "Neither could bear the thought of allowing the other in the lead. Sir Nidon is Champion of Salador, but by birth only a knight. Waltas is an earl, and the second most powerful noble in the South Teren. On the earl's land he would ride first. In the presence of the king, Sir Nidon would ride at the King's side. This is an unusual circumstance. Isn't it the same in Landomere?"

"I suppose, but not so strict. We elect our leaders before a hunt, or if there is a war. They would ride first. And I guess women never ride in front in Salador?"

"Well... no, not exactly. Of course a woman gains great status from her husband. And a noble woman ranks high above any low-born man. But women can't ride first, they are not as strong..." He looked away from Hadde. "Well, I mean, we have to protect..." His voice trailed off.

"So they're defenseless?" Hadde grinned at his discomfort. "And is there some woman in your life?"

"I, ah..." He glanced at the two knights riding ahead, and when they showed no sign of hearing, he leaned close to Hadde. Smiling he said, "There is someone. Our fathers are negotiating."

"Wonderful." Hadde paused. "What are they negotiating?"

"Jenae's dowry, of course."

"Her dowry?"

"Yes. It's what she will bring into our marriage. How much land, cattle, and vassals I'll gain by marrying her."

"Why does she have to bring anything?"

"To give me a reason to marry her."

"What? How can you say that?" she said, her voice so loud both Nidon and Waltas glanced over their shoulders at her. Quieter, she said, "What about love?"

He looked down at his hands. "Well, there is that as well."

"At least you Saladorans know what love is."

"We do. And I love her very much. She is the loveliest of all the Maidens in Waiting. She is the dawn to my day. She is...." And having opened up, the squire appeared unable to stop talking. Hadde didn't understand half of it but it made the miles pass easier. From time to time she told him of Landomere, but he seemed more baffled than she was.

Early in the afternoon, Nidon called a halt in a sunny, open glade with a grassy bank that led to a shallow stream. He had picked well, Hadde thought. And the Wasting *was* weaker here. Her spirits rose at the sight of green grass and the feel of the warm sun. It almost appeared winter had retreated.

"We'll rest here for a time," Nidon said, "and then push on to a barony down the road. We'll sleep indoors tonight."

After seeing to their horses, Nidon and Waltas sprawled out on the ground, well apart from one another. Nidon was soon asleep and snoring. Hadde built a fire and helped Melas prepare a meal.

Waltas watched them. Catching her eye, he said, "Hurry up, I'm hungry."

Hadde didn't reply but continued her preparations.

"This will take a little while," Melas said, staring into the stew pot.

"Then I'll wash up before we eat," Hadde said. "It seems forever since I last bathed, and it's a good day for it."

Melas blushed and turned away.

"What's wrong?" she asked.

Still facing away from her, he pretended to be in search of something in a small sack. "Don't ask me about such things," he said, his voice becoming a rough whisper towards the end.

She gave him a quizzical look and shrugged her shoulders. "Very well. I'm off to do the unmentionable."

"Well you probably shouldn't just go off, and, you know... alone."

"What, you want to come?"

"No!" he yelped. "Just, be... ah careful."

"Very well, Melas, I will." Hadde shook her head and, after grabbing a washrag and her change of clothes from her pack, walked to the water's edge and headed upstream. For a moment she thought of going back for her bow, but Earl Crane's lands seemed secure, and they'd seen no sign of danger. And she wouldn't have to go very far to put herself out of sight of the Saladorans.

The stream was only a few strides across with a bank that alternated between rocky and muddy. She found a spot where the stream turned and rocks dammed the water enough to make a decent pool. On the muddy bank a large flat stone provided a good place to sit. She wished it were deep enough to swim in. The air was cool and the water even colder, but the sun was high and would keep her warm enough.

If she were quick about her washing the men would never miss her. She smiled at the thought of being truly clean. Hadde stripped off her clothes and placed them on the rock. She let out a gasp as the freezing water flowed over her legs. Taking a breath, she plunged her face into the water.

71

"Too cold! Too cold!" she sputtered as she stood up. Grabbing her washcloth, she quickly scrubbed herself as she stood shivering in the stream. The sun wasn't as strong as she had hoped. She thought back to the big tub in her parent's cabin and wished she were there. And then she remembered it still needed mending.

Bracing herself, she plunged under the water a second time. She stepped out of the pool and onto the large rock. Crouching by the stream's edge, she twisted the water from her long hair. She considered washing her dirty clothes but knew she wouldn't have time.

"Brrr." She shivered one last time as she turned to pick up her clean clothes.

Earl Waltas stood behind her on the bank of the stream.

Hadde gave a start. "You surprised me."

"You've no shame," he said, staring. Hadde cringed at his gaze. For the first time in her life, in front of this Saladoran, she felt truly naked. "I came upstream so that I would be out of sight. I got the impression from Squire Melas that I should move out of sight to bathe."

He glanced toward the camp and then back at her. "You don't feel strange... naked in a man's presence?" He walked slowly down the bank toward her.

"Why would I?" She tried to sound confident, but she was afraid. She wouldn't give Waltas the pleasure of cowing her. She knelt and rinsed her towel and wrung the water out of it. The hilt of her hunting knife projected from her rolled clothing, but she resisted the urge to reach for it. He would just laugh at her cowardice.

He laughed a short laugh and then clasped his hands in front of him. "Yes, of course, why would you?" He glanced over his shoulder. "You've not seen Squire Melas, have you? I saw him leave the fire."

"No. Maybe he went for firewood. He knew I was going to bathe so I know he wouldn't have come this direction. He seemed, well... embarrassed."

"Silly boy," Waltas said.

"You appear to have gotten over it, however." She shuddered at the intensity of his stare.

He swallowed. "You're pretty, in a strange way. Exotic."

"I... thank you," she said, reaching for her tunic. "I guess it's time to eat."

As she spoke he stepped onto the rock. "Even those marks on your face. They make you... interesting." He unclasped his hands and clenched them at his sides. Hadde saw that he wore his dagger, but had left his sword back at camp. Still, she didn't want to take him on. She glanced past him to the stream bank and wondered how she could get past him.

As she lifted her tunic to pull it over her head, he lunged at her. Not caught by surprise, she flung it into his face and leaped into the pool. She slipped but regained her balance and ran for the bank.

Waltas charged after her.

"Stop!" she yelled as she ran, kicking up water with each stride. He tackled her from behind and sent her sprawling face down onto the muddy, rocky bank. Hadde scrambled forward but he grabbed her ankle and pulled her back. His crushing weight landed on top of her.

"Don't move!" he snarled in her ear. "Don't fight!"

"Stop! Please!" she said as she tried to get her hands under her. His forearm pressed against the back of her neck, pushing her face into the mud.

"You whore! I'm going to give you what you deserve."

Hadde couldn't move. The soft mud only gave way under her hands when she grasped for leverage. She felt his free hand fumbling at his trousers.

With all her strength, Hadde tried to kick free. "Help!" she cried out.

"Shut up!" Waltas hissed in her ear. "If you shout out again, I'll kill you. And don't think of telling him later. He won't believe you—no one will believe you. You're in Salador now."

She twisted and tried to throw the knight off. He struck her in the back of the head and pushed her face into the mud.

"Earl Waltas," a voice called out, "what...."

Hadde saw Melas at the edge of her vision.

"Get out of here, Squire. And keep your mouth shut. Be gone!" Melas stood frozen. Waltas thrust his fist at the squire. "Be gone." To Hadde's horror Melas took a step back, and then turned and ran.

She choked in anguish as he departed. "Back to work, eh, Hadde," Waltas said. The pressure on her back eased as he shoved his trousers down over his hips. With all her strength Hadde bucked up and lunged forward, throwing Waltas off balance. Before she could break free he grasped her calf and yanked her down.

Hadde screamed for help as his weight landed on top of her again. He hit her and her vision swirled. "Let's make this easy. You know you want this. The way you dress. The way you act. Prancing around half-naked."

He forced her legs apart.

She twisted sideways and then bucked hard in the opposite direction. "Damn it!" he gasped. "Just take it and it will be over. We'll both get what we want!" Gasping, Hadde twisted her body and tried to duck her head from another blow. She felt herself weakening and knew she couldn't take much more.

Suddenly Waltas's weight was pulled from atop her. Hadde found herself jerked sideways as Waltas fell into the stream. Nidon towered over Waltas. The king's champion smashed a huge fist into the earl's face, driving him under the water. The knight reached down, grasped Waltas's tunic collar, and pulled his head up.

Before Nidon could react, Hadde leapt past him and locked her hands around Waltas' throat. Her momentum tore Waltas from Nidon's grasp as she shoved his head back underwater. He struggled under her but couldn't find any purchase on the streambed.

Hadde screamed in rage as Nidon pulled her from Waltas. She kicked and twisted as she tried to free herself, but the knight was too powerful. "Stop," he said in her ear. His voice was calm, but strong. "Stop, Hadde, I'll take care of this. I'll take care of him."

He put her down on the rock by her clothes. Hadde grabbed the hilt of her knife, but Nidon's hand clamped down on her wrist. "Don't."

She stared at him, her anger making it impossible for her to speak. She was dimly aware of pounding footsteps as Melas ran up to them, sword in hand.

"You were in my charge and I failed you," Nidon said. "I've dishonored myself. This is my responsibility now. Let go of the knife."

Hadde looked past him as Waltas, choking and gasping got to his knees. Blood poured from his smashed nose. "You promise?" Hadde asked. "He'll be punished?"

"I promise." As he said the words, some of the rage went out of her and she let go of her knife.

"Dromost take you, Nidon!" Waltas sputtered. "Striking me when I wasn't ready."

"Give me your sword, Squire," Nidon commanded. Taking it, he strode toward Waltas.

The earl's eyes widened as the champion approached. He tried to get up, but the trousers around his knees tripped him. He fell backwards into the water. "You don't dare! Murder an earl for screwing a common whore?"

Nidon stood over him with the sword half raised. "She's under my protection, you bastard. I named her an ambassador."

"I wasn't going to kill her. She can still see the king."

"It is your good luck you have an audience with His Majesty."

Waltas brightened. "That's right," he said. "I must see the king."

"You promised, Sir Nidon," Hadde said. "You said he'd pay."

Nidon kept his eyes on the earl. "He will. But he'll face justice before the king. Pull up your trousers, Earl Waltas, and come with me. Squire,

74

stay with Hadde and make certain she remains unharmed."

As they departed Hadde reentered the stream and scrubbed the mud from her body. Melas stood facing the woods, his back to her. Hadde thought of Belor and wished he were still with her. None of this would have happened. But he was gone and she had no one to trust but herself. She wouldn't be caught at unawares again.

When she was done washing she stepped from the stream and sat down on the rock. "Why didn't you help me, Melas?"

"I... couldn't." He still faced away from her.

"Why? You saw I needed help."

"It isn't that easy." He remained with his back to her. His voice was quiet. "He's an earl. I'm only a squire."

"How does that matter?" she pulled her shirt over her head. Her tunic was soaked and she wrung it out.

"I'm sorry. It matters... a squire cannot.... I'm sorry; I didn't know what to do. I ran for Nidon."

She pulled on her breechcloth and leggings. "The next time you come upon such a situation, you do what Nidon did. You help!"

He flinched at her anger.

She picked up her belongings and strode past the squire. She heard him following close behind as she made her way to the camp.

"Where is he?" Hadde asked Nidon as she approached the fire.

"He's gone."

"Gone? You let him go?" Hadde shouted. "How could you?"

"I sent him to the king. Justice will be served."

"No it won't!" Her anger boiled over. "He'll ride home and never be seen from again."

"I made him swear on it. He will go to Sal-Oras. If he doesn't he will lose everything. It will mean a death warrant for him. It will mean disgrace and dishonor for his entire family. He will see justice before the king."

Chapter Nine

"The horses can't take much more of this, Sir Nidon. The rain is turning to ice," Hadde said.

"Not long now," he replied. "We'll be there well before nightfall. And Squire Melas will have prepared them for us."

She was glad that Melas had been sent ahead. At least Quickstep and Windwalker would be spared the soaking. Both Lightfoot and Nidon's mount, Thunder, were mud spattered and wretched looking.

Hadde pulled her heavy cloak closer about her as they passed though yet another village. Not a day passed that they didn't come across another village or town. Now that they were close to Sal-Oras, it was as if one village just blended into another. There were no wild lands any more, just one village's fields blending into another's.

But for all the people and all the towns, she still saw the Wasting all around them. Many of the cottages they passed were dark, and those that were inhabited all seemed to have fallen into disrepair. The cattle and sheep dotting the fields forlornly scrabbled at the few patches of weeds. The animals themselves were thin and many appeared sick.

"There, Hadde," Nidon said as they passed over a low ridge. She followed his outstretched arm and spied a river two arrow-flights distant, and further on through the gloom and freezing rain, the massive walls of Sal-Oras.

Pulling the hood of her cloak back, she said, "I never imagined anything so huge. Even in my dreams. I've seen the spiridus city of Belavil, but it's in ruins. This is...." She couldn't think what to say.

"Home," Nidon said, "and rest."

She caught movement to her left and was surprised to see a boat outracing them upstream. It seemed a hundred oars drove the boat forward. The river itself was over an arrow-flight wide, more water than Hadde had ever imagined.

"That boat," Hadde asked, "are there many like it?"

"A trading vessel from Idoria. Yes, there are many, but not so many as in years past."

As they rode closer Hadde saw that Sal-Oras sat on both banks of the river, although it seemed the larger half sat on the higher ground to the north. Two great towers sat in the river guarding the river entrance to the city. Just beyond them she saw a huge stone bridge linking the two banks.

Hadde glanced away from the city to find Nidon had ridden off without her. She tapped Lightfoot's flanks and quickly caught up to him. "An army could never take this city," she said as they approached the walls.

"It's been breached before," Nidon said over his shoulder. "Many times. In fact the entire South Bank has been taken. At one point in the War for the Orb, the entire city but for the Great Keep fell."

Huge blocks of stone, perfectly set, gray stone rose twenty strides above them. The ramparts seemed utterly unassailable. "How could anyone get past these walls?"

"Ladders, rolling towers, trebuchets, rams, mining... they have all been used." The road ran almost under the walls as they neared the gatehouse. A few footweary travelers walked the road ahead of them, heavy bundles on their backs. "Look there—and there. Hadde followed where Nidon pointed and saw the scars of ancient battles. In one place red bricks patched a five stride section of wall near its base. In another area the entire wall had been replaced with stones much smaller and rougher than the original.

"I was once in a battle," Hadde said. "When we lost the plains to the Kiremi. There were a thousand Landomeri riders, and as many archers on foot. I'd never seen so many people in one place. But this... how many soldiers did it take to storm these walls?"

"Thousands. But battles of that size haven't been fought in ages."

A dozen knights rode from the gate ahead. Each carried a lance with a red banner and bore the same device as Melas, crossed lightning bolts on a red field. The travelers on the road scattered as the knights approached.

"Our welcome," Nidon said.

The knights clattered to a halt. One rode closer. He removed his helm and said, "Who are you that ride armed before the gates of Sal-Oras?"

"I am Nidon, Champion of the Realm."

"Well met, Sir Nidon. I recognize you, and you may pass." He nudged his horse next to Nidon's. "It's good to see you, friend."

Nidon shook his hand. "And you as well, Gorwin. Shall we get out of the cold?"

"The sooner the better. The king awaits your return." The knight gave Hadde an appraising look. "So you are our Landomeri visitor. Squire Melas had much to say of you."

"I....," Hadde started, but Gorwin had already turned his mount away.

Nidon waved Hadde to follow as they rode through the massive gates. The tunnel beyond seemed a maw swallowing the two knights. Swallowing her fear, Hadde followed. Behind her rode the knights of Gorwin's escort, their horses' hoofbeats echoing off the walls and pounding against her. The tunnel seemed to close in on her. Would she ever pass through them again? She felt like a trapped animal.

A gust of wind-driven snow greeted them as they rode from the tunnel and onto a broad avenue. Tall stone houses rose on either side of the road. It was barely less oppressive than the tunnel. At least she could feel the snow on her face and see the cloudy sky above her.

Narrow alleys branched from the main road. Bundled pedestrians trudged along on either side of the street, paying no heed to the knights other than getting out of their path. In a few arrow-flights they passed many times the population of Long Meadow. But despite the numbers, the city had an air of emptiness, as if even this many people couldn't fill its vast spaces.

The citizens, most with ragged cloaks pulled close about them, shuffled along as close to the buildings as they could manage. The faces Hadde saw were pale and gaunt. A loud *crack* caused her to turn and stare at a small group walking past in a file. All wore white robes and walked with eyes downcast. As she watched they flailed short, stout ropes across their own backs. She flinched at the harsh sound. For a time she could only stare, finally saying, "Sir Nidon, who are they? Why are they whipping themselves?"

"Returnists." He barely gave the column a glance as the knights rode past.

"What are Returnists?"

"They believe in the imminent return of the Orb of Creation."

"Really?" She turned and watched the marchers with renewed interest. "But the Orb of Creation was lost long ago."

Nidon shrugged. "Tell them that."

"Why are they whipping themselves?" She had to turn away as she caught sight of the bloody stripes on their white garments.

"They punish themselves for their sins. They think moral purity will cause the Orb to return."

"Will it?"

"You're asking the wrong person."

Ahead Hadde saw a tower looming, standing guard over the bridge. Guards saluted as the party passed through the tower. They emerged onto the bridge only to be assailed by a vicious wind. No longer protected by the high buildings of the city, the full force of the storm drove them toward the edge of the bridge. Heavy snow whipped around them, so much she could barely see the water roiling below.

They passed through another tower and back into the city proper. A steeper hill led them toward a citadel cloaked in snow. Here was the Great Keep of Sal-Oras—the goal of her entire journey. Here she would find the Elementar King of Salador and salvation for her people.

The road emptied into a broad square surrounded by grand three-story houses. Across the square awaited the keep's massive gates. Hadde felt a moment's trepidation, but the knights didn't slow their pace as they rode under the portcullis and into a wide courtyard.

Walls even higher than those guarding the city surrounded the open space. Opposite the entrance stood the keep itself—several smaller gates set into it. Above the gates stood ranks of windows, and higher up, balconies.

The knights dismounted in unison leaving Hadde the only person still mounted. Squires and servants rushed up to take the knights' shields and lances while grooms saw to the horses. The escorting knights hurried up to Nidon and clapped him on the shoulder and asked for news.

Hadde bundled her cloak closer about her, the hood sheltering her face from the heavy snow. She patted Lightfoot's neck and thought of Belor—wishing he were with her.

"May I take your horses, sir?" a young voice asked.

Hadde glanced down to see a boy looking up at her. She didn't know what to say.

"May I take…" he started again and then stopped. "My apologies, madam. May I take your horse, my lady?"

She looked to Nidon for help, but he was talking with his companions. "Where are you taking her?"

"To the stables, lady."

"I'll take care of her," she replied as she dismounted.

The boy frowned.

"No, Hadde," Nidon said, rescuing her. "Let the groom take her. Lightfoot will be well cared for."

"What about my gear?"

"Everything will be sent to your chambers. Page!" he called out. A boy, younger than the groom, rushed to Nidon and bent to one knee in the thin layer of wet snow.

"This is Hadde of Landomere. See that she's taken to her chamber."

Hadde watched as the groom led Lightfoot away. Everything she needed to survive was on the horses.

"Lady, may I take you into the keep?" the page politely asked.

She ignored him and jogged after her horses. "Wait," she called out to the groom. "Stop!"

He turned and halted. "How may I help the lady?"

"I need a few things." She pulled her bowcase, arrow bag, and pack from Lightfoot's saddle.

"They will be sent to your chamber, lady," the groom objected.

"I'll take them," she said with an apologetic smile.

He dipped his head slightly, bowing and led the horses through a gate.

"I'm ready now," Hadde said to the page.

She knew they thought her behavior odd, but she couldn't help it. She was alone in a strange land and there were only a few things that gave her a sense of security. Her small pack, her bow, and arrows. She had survived many weeks alone in the forest of Landomere with only them. And she wouldn't let the Saladorans catch her unarmed.

"In what chamber are you staying, lady?"

"I… I've no idea."

He paused for a moment, looking around the courtyard. "I know whom to ask," he said as he led her through a heavy door and into the keep. Taking a lantern, he led her up a short flight of stairs, and into a windowless hallway.

Feeling lost and alone, Hadde followed the boy into the castle. The weight of the massive stone structure seemed to bear down upon her. She paused, brushing the snow from her shoulders, resisting the urge to run back outside. The boy, noticing she had fallen behind, turned and gaped at her Landomeri clothing. Hadde pulled her cloak closed.

"Please follow," he said, leading her higher into the keep. Hadde prided herself on her sense of direction, but soon became lost in the twists and turns of the keep. They entered a wide hall and the boy called out, "Mistress!" to a sour-faced woman in a fine blue dress. The woman waited for them to approach. "Mistress," he continued, "I'm to take this lady to her chamber, but don't know where to go."

"I am awaiting the arrival of a foreign lady." The woman said. Her narrow eyes looked Hadde up and down with open disapproval. She frowned at Hadde's baggage. "You're the Lady Hadde of Landomere? There must be some mistake."

"I'm Hadde."

"You speak Saladoran?"

"I speak my mother tongue. I know it as Landomeri."

"You speak with the accent of the court, but your attire…"

"It has been a long journey." Hadde said. She clutched her pack tighter. Even Saladoran women wouldn't treat her with any kindness.

"Of course," the woman sniffed, rolling her eyes. "My name is Lady Celena, and I keep the Maidens in Waiting in my charge. Follow me." She dismissed the boy with a wave of her hand and strode down the gloomy candle-lit hall. "I'm taking you to the Maiden Hall," Celena announced, over her shoulder. "Young ladies of noble birth are sent here to be educated in the ways of the court. They also attend to the needs of the greater ladies. Why you have been sent here, I have no idea."

They had not gone far when Celena stopped at an open door guarded by two armored men. Hadde peered down a long hallway. Doors lined both sides. "My chamber is the first on the right." Celena said. "I'll have a maiden show you to your room. She will attend you for the duration of your stay. There are always two squires on duty here. They are never to leave their post. They are also forbidden from entering the Maiden Hall," she added with a glare at the two men.

A door down the hall opened and a young woman strolled in their direction. "Jenae, please summon the Maiden Maret," Celena commanded. She turned to Hadde as the girl retreated. "The squires are also not to speak unless spoken to."

Hadde glanced at the two stone-faced squires. They ignored her and stared straight ahead. "I guess this means there is more than one Waltas in Salador."

"I don't understand. What do you mean?" Celena asked.

"It is nothing," Hadde replied.

Another door had opened and a second young woman hurried toward them, to Hadde she appeared sixteen or so. "Hadde of Landomere," Celena said, "this is Maret. She will show you to your chamber."

The young woman bent her knees and used her fingers to spread the sides of her dress. "At your service, Lady Hadde."

"I'm glad to meet you, Maret," Hadde replied.

"I've business to attend to," Celena said. "See to the lady's needs, Maret."

"I will, Madam."

As the older woman turned Hadde said, "Lady Celena, I've traveled here to see the king. How might I find him?"

"His Majesty is aware of your arrival. He will call for you when he's ready to see you."

"My task is very important."

"I'm certain that it is." She nodded to Hadde and departed.

"Please follow me, my lady," Maret said. She led Hadde down the Maiden Hall. They passed several chambers and were almost at the end of the hall when Maret turned and opened a door. She stood aside and motioned for Hadde to enter the room. As Hadde walked in, Maret followed, closing the door behind her.

The chamber, nearly as large as Hadde's cottage, contained a chest, a chair, and another piece of furniture with a curtain around it. The chair sat near a small fireplace with a barely flickering fire. A screen hid one corner of the room.

The far wall caught Hadde's attention. She put down her gear and walked to it. "What's this?"

"The window?"

"I know it's a window," Hadde said, perplexed. "But what is this?" She reached out and touched the cool, smooth substance. She could see through it to the courtyard far below. There she saw people moving, but they were all wavy. "It's like ice, but it can't be. It's too warm in this room."

"Do you mean the glass?"

"Glass?" Hadde tapped on it with her fingernail. "It's wonderful."

Maret pulled a lever and part of the window opened.

"Like a shutter," Hadde said. She looked outside. Despite the growing dark, she still saw people milling in the courtyard.

Snow swirled into the room and Maret pulled the window closed. "Many of the maidens' fathers don't have glass on their manors. My father does, but he's an important East Teren earl."

"This isn't your home?"

"No, my parents sent me here to learn to be a lady and to find a husband."

"How long have you been away from home?" Hadde asked as she warmed herself in front of the fireplace.

"Two years."

"I cannot imagine that." Hadde knelt by the hearth. A steaming kettle hung over the fire. "How old are you, Maret?"

"I'm fifteen, Lady." The girl was as tall as Hadde, with long dark brown hair and large brown eyes. Hadde thought Maret's eyes were very pretty. They were nothing like the grays, blues, and greens of her people.

"I'm twenty-one." Hadde said. "Fifteen seems so long ago. So much has happened." She took off her cloak and was about to lay it on the chair when she heard Maret gasp behind her. Hadde spun and saw Maret staring at her with wide eyes.

After a startled moment the girl looked away. "Lady! What are you wearing?"

Hadde sighed. "A tunic, breechcloth, and leggings. This is what we wear in my land."

"But I can see your legs! They're like men's clothes, but... worse."

"In my land, this is how all women dress. And, please, Maret, I've just spent over a week traveling with three Saladoran men who gave me nothing but misery. Could it be different between us?"

"Yes, Lady. I'm sorry. It's just... so strange."

Hadde shrugged. "In summer we wear even less. But what I would most like is to get out of these clothes and into something warm and dry."

"We have a hot bath prepared for you. We knew you were coming."

Hadde glanced around the room. "Where?"

"I'll show you. Please come with me, Lady." Maret started for the door, but stopped when she saw Hadde glance at her bow and pack. "You won't need those."

"I don't want to lose them. I—"

"We are just going a few doors down. Don't worry, there's no place safer than the Maiden Hall."

It was hard not to trust Maret. But how could she trust any Saladoran at all? She felt alone and trapped in the giant castle. Her hand grazed the antler handle of her hunting knife as she followed Maret out the door.

"Before I bathe I need to ask where one finds..." This was going to be difficult. She had no doubt she was about to offend the young girl again. "Where does one find..."

"Oh," Maret said knowingly and pointed to a door. "The bath is the next door down. I'll wait for you there, Lady."

"Thank you."

A low stone bench and a wooden seat with a hole cut in it sat in the small room. A basket filled with dried flowers and herbs couldn't mask the smell that told her she was in the correct place. Another basket held a generous supply of flaxen tow. A small window had been left cracked open. It made the room very cold, but Hadde had a feeling she was better off with it open.

"Where—" Hadde started as she entered the bathing room. Maret wasn't alone. An elderly woman in a drab brown dress knelt by a huge stone tub set into the wall. She pushed a log into a brightly burning fire in an oven under the tub and shut the door. The woman stood and pulled a folding screen partially in front of the tub before Maret waved her away.

"Thank you," Hadde said. The woman bowed and silently exited the room.

"This looks wonderful, Maret." The air was warm and moist with steam. Ice encrusted the room's single window.

"I had them make it extra hot, Lady. Your journey must have been difficult with the snow. What were you going to ask?"

"What?"

"When you came in. You started to ask something."

"Oh, yes. In the privy…where does it go?"

"Where does what go?"

"It," Hadde said. "You know."

"Urk." Maret swallowed. "I… well… I've no idea."

"But the shaft must fill up if it does not go somewhere."

Maret gasped, "A lady does not speak of such things."

Hadde laughed. She didn't want to think about being on the receiving end of that shaft. She looked at poor Maret, who had flushed red.

Glancing at the tub, Hadde said, "You don't know how long I've been waiting for this." She stripped off layers of clothing as fast as possible. Maret squealed and turned to face a corner of the room.

"Lady," she said, "the screen is there for your privacy."

"That's all right," Hadde replied. "I don't need any."

"We, um, don't expose our bodies to one another."

"Another difference between our lands." Wearing only the Spiridus Token and a smile of satisfaction, Hadde walked behind the screen, strode up a few steps and lowered herself into the hot water. It was wonderful. She sank until only her head were exposed. The tub was ridiculously large.

"Lady Hadde, you really… well, you really don't mind if someone sees you naked?"

"Why would I? We often bathe naked in the stream near our village. Or even if we're not bathing and it's really hot, we might wear only our breechcloths."

Maret laughed. "Lady Celena would be so scandalized. I would love to see her expression."

"So do it." Hadde swished the water in the tub and sighed. It was perfect.

"What would people say?"

"They would say there goes a pretty naked girl running down the hallway."

"Oh, no they wouldn't! They would call me mad. Or worse."

"But they would be wrong. So why would you care?" Hadde dunked her head. She came up sputtering. "This is beyond wonderful. Almost too hot, can you imagine? Do you get to do this often?"

"Once a week in summer. Less often now. Would the lady like me to call a nurse to help her bathe?"

"A nurse? No, I don't need any help. And, Maret, why do you call me 'lady'?"

"Because, you are a lady."

"But the Saladoran men I traveled with treated me terribly. They didn't call me lady."

"I don't know why, Lady. I was simply told you were a foreign lady from Landomere and that I was to see to your needs. You were assigned to the Maiden Hall, so you must be of noble birth."

Hadde thought better of pursuing the conversation further. She wondered what they would do to her if they discovered the truth.

"Lady, shall I have your clothes sent to be cleaned and mended?"

"That would be nice of you, but I'll do it if it's a bother," Hadde replied. "And Maret, would you simply call me Hadde?"

"Yes, Lady Hadde."

"No, just Hadde. It's the custom of my land. We don't use titles before our names."

"I shall do as you ask, Hadde."

She heard the girl shuffling behind the curtain as she gathered Hadde's clothing. A small tray next to the tub held a scrub brush, a comb, and a small decorated ceramic pot with a spout.

"What is in the pot?" Hadde asked.

"Scented oil. Pour a handful into the tub with you."

Hadde picked up the pot and put her nose to the spout. "It smells of flowers." She poured some into the water. "Do you know when I'll meet the king?"

"Lady Celena didn't mention it, but there will be a reception in two days. Perhaps then. I'm certain he will see you before the Festival of Spring."

"Two days? That long?" She could hardly bear the thought of being so close to the king only to be delayed for another two days.

"Yes, the king will receive petitioners in the morning and the festival will take place that evening. But if he does not see you then, you might wait two weeks or more."

"I had hoped to go home much sooner than that."

"It's for the Steward of the Court to decide when a petitioner sees the king. Shall I have some food brought up?"

"What? Thank you, yes."

"I'll summon a servant. I'll return soon."

Smiling, Hadde relaxed deeper into the water. Her little tub back home was nothing compared to this. A wave of homesickness swept over her as she thought about her parents and their little cottage in Long Meadow. "I'll be home soon."

A short time later the door opened. "Let me have those clothes," Maret said from behind the screen. "And take those to be cleaned and mended. And bring a lantern, it's getting dark."

"Yes, Maiden," a frail voice responded. The door opened and closed again.

Hadde was surprised at the authority with which Maret ordered people about. Even the tone of her voice changed. Always pleasant and light with Hadde, her voice hardened when she spoke to the workers. Their age seemed irrelevant; no respect was shown to them.

"Maret, who was that you were talking to?"

"Just a servant."

"What's her name?"

"Her name? I don't know. She's new. Oh, and there is food waiting for you...."

"Ahhh, I'll be right out. I'm starving."

"Wait!" Maret called. A linen towel appeared over the top of the screen.

Hadde stepped out of the tub and dried herself. "Would you pass my clothes?" she asked.

A white chemise and red dress showed up where the towel had been.

"What's this?" Hadde asked. "These aren't mine. My spare clothes are in my pack."

"I sent them to be cleaned as well. The red dress is one of mine. You and I are close to the same size."

Hadde wrapped the towel around herself and took the dress from the screen. "I've seen dresses during my journey here. They're very strange."

"You've never worn one?"

"No." Hadde pulled the white shirt over her head. "This shirt, I've never worn anything so nice. The linen is so fine."

"It isn't that special."

Hadde took the dress and held it up for inspection. "I suppose I won't be doing much hunting."

"Why would a lady do such?"

"To provide for her people."

"Those things are not for a lady to do. A lady manages her household and entertains her husband."

"Not in Landomere. How do you put this on?" Hadde fumbled with the dress. The only light came from a sputtering wall candle and the firebox heating the tub.

Hadde stepped out from behind the screen.

"Where is that—ack! You're naked, Lady!" Maret turned away.

"No, look. I'm wearing the shirt. It's very fine, thank you."

"Your legs, and well, it's much too revealing."

"You can only see my calves." She could see how embarrassed the girl was but couldn't understand why. She slid the dress over her head, but the waist was too narrow for her shoulders and she became stuck.

86

"Um… I need help."

"Oh!" Maret giggled despite her embarrassment. "You have to untie the drawstrings."

Hadde laughed at the absurdity of her predicament. She felt Maret's hands as she tugged and pulled. Eventually Hadde's head popped out the top of the dress.

Maret smiled at her. "I've never met anyone like you before."

"Now my hands are stuck."

Maret helped Hadde's hands through the cuffs. "These aren't like the sleeves on the dresses I saw at manors we passed through on the way here," Hadde said. "Those women wore sleeves that were so long they had to cut holes in them to get their hands out. These just cover your hand and have holes for your thumb and fingers."

"They were wearing dagged sleeves." Maret rolled her eyes. "Nobody has worn those for two or three years. Country nobles are always out of fashion. Here, let me help with your collar."

Maret reached for the buttons at Hadde's neck and said, "What's this? It's beautiful!"

Hadde put the necklace back under her collar.

"What? No!" Maret exclaimed. "It's a beautiful piece. You must show it off. Let me do it."

"I was worried about… well, I was fearful of thieves. I thought I should keep it hidden."

"Oh, that might be true in the lower quarters of the city, or in a town, but not within the Great Keep. You're perfectly safe here." Maret buttoned Hadde's collar. "There. Once we do your hair you'll look like a princess. You are very pretty."

"I… ah," Hadde started, surprised at the sudden complement. "Thank—"

A knock at the door interrupted her. The housekeeper stepped through and handed Maret a brass lantern. "Is there anything else I can bring you, Maiden?"

"There is food in Lady Hadde's chamber? And the fire has been stoked?"

"There is, Maiden."

"You may go."

"Wait, what is your name?" Hadde asked.

"They call me Gran."

"Thank you for taking such good care of us, Gran."

"You are welcome, Lady." A touch of a smile crossed her face, and bowing her head, she backed through the door.

Maret sighed. "Shall we eat now?"

"Yes, let's." Hadde smoothed the dress as she followed Maret out the door. "My parents would laugh until the sun came up if they saw me in this. How absurd."

Maret's back stiffened as she walked. "I'm sorry, but I had nothing finer to offer you."

"No, that's not what I meant. This is beautiful. The fabric and color are wonderful, much richer than anything we have in my village." The flowing skirt felt awkward around her legs. She stepped on the hem of the dress and nearly tripped when she turned around. "Thank you for loaning it to me. I'll return it as soon as I can."

"It fits you perfectly," Maret said as they entered Hadde's chamber. "Keep it until the tailors can make you some dresses."

"It fits? I feel like I can hardly breathe!" Hadde undid three buttons at her neck. "It fits so closely to my waist and ribs. Ooh, that looks delicious," Hadde said, spying a tray of food by the fire.

"There's beef stew, cheese, bread, and mulled wine. Let's sit and eat."

Hadde and Maret sat on padded stools next to the fire. An engraved wooden chest served as a table for their meal. "Thank you for the food, it looks wonderful."

"Go ahead, Hadde. Eat," Maret said as she stuck an iron poker into the fire.

The bread was crusty, light, and sweet; the cheese salty and strong; the stew rich and flavorful; the wine warm and spiced. Hadde had never tasted more delicious food in her life, even if the wine was a bit strong. For a time she didn't attempt to speak. Maret contented herself with a bit of bread and cheese. After a time she took the hot poker and used it to heat their wine.

"This meal is unbelievable," Hadde gushed. "I've never had anything so good." She took a long pull of wine. "I never knew anything like this existed."

"It's just a simple meal," Maret replied. "I apologize that it isn't enough. Shall I have a servant bring more?" Hadde stared at the nearly empty tray. A single slice of cheese and an end of bread were all that remained. "More? I cannot remember when I've ever eaten so much. I'm about to burst your dress." She sighed. "My poor family. My people. They aren't eating like this. They have nothing."

"The Wasting is strong on your manor?"

"In our village, yes. Worse than here, I think. I hope the king can help. I hope I can see him soon."

"You could be with us for some time. The king has very important affairs to attend to. I'll try to make your stay here comfortable."

"Well, don't worry about having that dress made for me. I don't intend on being here long. I want to go home as soon as I can."

"But you need some clothes… unless your baggage is still in route?"

"I have my own clothes." Hadde drank more wine. "You sent to have them cleaned."

"You can't wear those in court. They're not proper."

"Not proper?"

"I don't think the steward will let you enter the Great Hall in those clothes you were wearing. It would be as if you were naked."

Hadde finished off her goblet of wine. A flush of warmth spread through her veins. "I'll see him naked. It doesn't matter to me."

Maret's eyes widened.

Hadde smiled and yawned a tremendous yawn. "Would you like to hear about the time I went into battle naked?"

Maret's mouth worked open and closed, but no words came out. "I," she started, but was interrupted by loud knocking at the door. She frowned. "It's late for visitors."

Lady Celena barged into the room before the maiden had a chance to open the door. "A summons," Celena said, her hands clutched in front of her. "The king has called for Hadde of Landomere."

Chapter Ten

"Now?" Maret asked.

"Immediately," Celena replied. "Four Knights of the House wait to escort her."

Hadde stumbled as she stood, catching herself with a hand on the chimney. Her head spun with wine as her heart pounded a heavy drumbeat in her chest. "Everyone said it would be later."

"His Highness wishes to see you now. Hurry!"

Glancing at the pitch-dark window, Hadde wondered how late it was. She took a deep breath. "Very well. This is what I came for."

"She must have a cap and veil," Celena said to Maret. "And her feet are bare."

"I'll fetch a hat and shoes, my lady," Maret said as she rushed from the room.

"I'll tell the escort that you'll be with them shortly." Celena departed as suddenly as Maret.

Hadde found herself alone in the room, her hand still on the warm chimney. What would she say? How would the king react to her? She had thought so much of this moment, and now that it had finally arrived she had no idea what to do.

Maret reappeared bearing red slippers and a red flat-topped hat. "Sit and I'll prepare you."

As Maret combed Hadde's hair she asked, "What do I do? How do I speak to a king?"

"Always call him 'Your Majesty' or 'Your Highness'." Maret quickly fashioned Hadde's hair into two long braids that ran in front of her shoulders. "And never turn your back on him. The king isn't cruel. He won't mistreat you. But he's serious and deliberate. He doesn't tolerate fools." Maret placed the cap on Hadde's head, pushing the attached veil away from her face.

Hadde blanched. *"Doesn't tolerate fools?* I'm half-drunk and wearing this silly hat!"

"Oh no, it's not silly," Maret said. "You must keep it on in public."

"Yes, Your Highness."

90

"I shouldn't have given you so much wine. I didn't know it would have such an effect on you."

"I was so hungry and sleepy. And I thought he wasn't going to see me. You don't think the king will notice?" Hadde stood straight and brushed off her dress.

"Maybe we should tell the king you are sick from your journey."

"No! I'm not missing this chance. I came to see the king."

Maret shook her head. "Just think before you speak. Now, try these shoes." She forced the tight shoes onto Hadde's feet. "Perfect!"

"I can't wear these." Hadde hobbled across the room. "Where are my boots? Or my moccasins from my pack?"

"I put all of your things in the chest. But you cannot possibly wear your shoes with this dress. They don't match."

Hadde opened the chest, and after yanking off the red shoes, put on her moccasins. "These will have to do. And look, the dress covers my feet."

Celena appeared in the doorway, wringing her hands. "What's keeping you?"

"I'm ready," Hadde said.

The three women walked down the hall. Maret held Hadde's elbow, propelling her in a straight line. Hadde spotted the two squires on guard duty, and opposite them, the four fully armored knights standing at attention.

"I present Lady Hadde," Celena said to one of the knights.

Hadde swallowed at the sight of the knights. There was no sign of the Wasting on them. They were tall and broad and wore mail from head to toe, with gleaming helms on their heads and long red tabards covering their torsos. Their visors were up, but it didn't matter, all were stone-faced.

"Hadde of Landomere, I am Captain Palen. Please follow me," a knight said.

"Good luck to you, Hadde," Maret peeped as Palen motioned Hadde down the hall.

Hadde took a few strides and then halted so quickly one of the knights ran into her. *What am I doing?* she wondered. She needed Maret there to keep her from acting the fool. She turned past the knight, peering back at Maret. "Wait," she said, "can't Maret come as well?"

"She was not summoned," Palen said. "The king awaits your arrival."

"But—"

"She was not summoned." The knight's face showed no emotion, no hint of any sympathy.

"No! She has to come." Hadde pushed back against the panic that threatened to overwhelm her.

"Hadde," Maret said, her hand on Hadde's shoulder. "Please, don't argue. Just go with them and see the king."

Hadde ignored her. "Why can't she come?" she demanded. Somewhere in her mind, she realized her folly, but it wasn't enough to overcome her wine-enhanced outrage. "Why are you being so stubborn?"

"Are you refusing the king's summons?" Palen asked. He edged closer, towering over her.

"No, she isn't," Maret said. She turned to Hadde. "Please, Hadde, this is why you came. Don't spoil it. You don't need me."

Hadde's eyes locked with Maret's. The girl was right. This was the entire purpose of her mission. Belor had died so she could get here. She felt shame at her fear. She had killed Kiremi and varcolac and now she trembled at the thought of meeting the king? Was he more dangerous then they were? He wasn't going to kill her.

But maybe he was. If he couldn't help Long Meadow, it would mean the death of them all. Everyone she knew would perish to the Wasting. She drew a deep breath. She couldn't fail them. "I'll go," she said in a quiet voice. "Take me to the king."

Without a word, Palen turned and marched down the hall. Hadde followed with Maret's good wishes pursuing her. They wound their way through several dark corridors, the only sound the creak of the warriors' leather, the metallic rustle of their armor, and the stomp of their boots on the stone floor. Hadde felt woozy, but managed to keep pace with the knights. She felt the eyes of the knights behind her, and hoped she didn't look the fool she felt.

With the exception of their small party the keep seemed abandoned. Hadde hugged her arms around her body. Her mind still foggy with wine, she focused on placing one foot in front of the other. Over and over she rehearsed the words she would say to the king. And don't forget Maret's instructions, she thought. *Don't appear the fool.*

Hadde imagined a dark chamber filled with a pall of smoke and lit by a single candle. The king would be cloaked and hooded, his eyes glowing with magical fire. He would look into her soul and know that she was a fraud—that she was no ambassador.

They halted in front of an iron-bound door. "We have arrived," Palen said as he knocked twice at the door. He pulled it open without waiting for a response. "Please enter."

Taking a deep breath, Hadde strode through the portal. Tall glass windows let moonlight into the large chamber. Shelves lined the walls, each filled with hundreds of decorated boxes. Four lit candles atop a round table drew her eyes to the corner of the room. Four stuffed chairs surrounded the table, one filled with bundled blankets.

Hadde jumped as the door closed behind her. Her stomach roiled with fear as darkness closed in on her. She spun as a voice called out to her, "Greetings, Hadde. It has been a long time since I've seen one of my fellow Landomeri."

She wheeled toward the voice and was shocked to see an ancient man sitting on the blanket-covered chair. She had seen no one there before. The elaborate quilts covered him from head to toe—only his face and right arm lay exposed. He looked as if he had been seated for some time.

"I'm sorry," she said. "I didn't see you sitting there, Your Majesty."

The man's wizened visage broke into a smile and he laughed. It was a beautiful sound that brought her visions of sunny spring mornings in Landomere.

"I'm not the king, Hadde. My name is Orlos."

She gazed at him in awe. *The spiridus.*

"Come, sit with me." He motioned her to a chair opposite his own. "The king will soon arrive."

Heart pounding, she made her way to the chair. She stumbled as she sat. "I'm sorry," she said, cursing both the wine and the unfamiliar dress flapping at her legs.

He smiled. "Don't fret a moment."

"You don't look like a spiridus," she blurted out. The words hung there for a moment before she clamped her hand over her mouth. Her head sank as she removed her hand. "I'm acting such a fool."

"You've seen many spiridus?" Orlos asked, his tone light. Hadde shook her head, too embarrassed to speak. "I've looked this way for a long time," he continued. "A very long time. I think I've forgotten what I really am. I've not assumed spiridus form in more than a hundred years." He glanced out the window into the darkness before turning back to Hadde. "When you're spiridus it means you're one with the forest. That you can sense all of the life around you. It means freedom from want or need. It means never having to hurry."

"I didn't mean to pry. I'm at such a loss here."

"Ask me anything you wish. How often do you meet a spiridus?" He laughed, but the laugh quickly turned to a cough. The cough was deep and wracking. Hadde leaned forward, suddenly concerned for the ancient man.

"Should I summon help?" She started to rise, but Orlos waved her back down. She sat, helpless as his fit subsided.

"A couple of centuries hang heavy," Orlos said as he produced a handkerchief and wiped his mouth. "I'm sorry if I scared you."

"Is there someone who can help you? An herbalist or a healer?"

He shook his head. "There's nothing to be done. There is no cure for time. "

"Can you become... take spiridus form again? Maybe you could return to Landomere? You belong there. "

"Landomere doesn't want me. I'm exiled. I cannot return."

"Why?" She cursed herself for blurting out again.

Orlos closed his eyes and shook his head. "I would not speak of it."

"I'm sorry. I didn't mean—"

"It doesn't matter anymore. And even if I wished to return, I'm far too old. No, I would rather hear your story. I see that Landomere has presented you with a Token."

Hadde touched the chain around her neck. "I found it."

The door swung open and slammed against the wall. Hadde spun in her chair as a tall gaunt man strode into the room. He wore a tan tunic and dark brown trousers tucked into his high boots. A golden circlet kept unruly hair from his face. He appeared to be only a few years older than Hadde, but the years seemed to weigh heavily on his shoulders. Although he wore no armor, he was armed. He had a golden-flanged mace stuck through his belt and a shield slung on his back.

"You're late, Your Majesty, " Orlos said.

Your Majesty. Hadde sprang from her chair as the realization hit her. What had Maret told her to do?

"Your chair, " the king warned.

Hadde frowned in incomprehension as her chair crashed to the floor behind her. She spun toward it and started to lift it when she remembered Maret's warning. *Don't turn your back on the king.* She spun back toward him. "Your Majesty," she gasped.

Shaking his head, the king strode toward her. Hadde took an involuntary step back, wondering what she should do, when the king reached down and lifted her chair upright. "Please, be seated," he said.

Hadde shrank into the chair, humiliated, as the king took his seat. "I am Boradin, King of Salador. " He shoved his shield aside as he sat.

"I—" Hadde choked. He was not what she expected. He was young, and disheveled, and dressed in common clothes. "Why the shield?" she said. Her mouth dropped open as the king glared at her. *The wine!* She hadn't meant to speak aloud.

"It is my curse—it is my gift, I can never let it go. Give me—"

"But, why?"

The king's eyes narrowed at her interruption. "Who do you take—"

"Show her, Boradin," Orlos interrupted. He gave Hadde a reassuring smile. "You've scared the child to death."

"Very well." The king shifted the shield so that Hadde could see its face. Unlike those of the other knights she had seen, this shield was round. But like theirs it was painted red and bore two crossed lightning bolts upon it. Several black scars marred its face.

"It is Forsvar," Boradin said. "I must keep it with me all the time."

"Forsvar?" Hadde said. "His Gift? But…it's a legend."

"It is the first of the Three Gifts," Orlos said. "Not a legend."

"And not the last," Boradin said. "We will find the Orb and all will be made right again. But enough of this. Show me the Spiridus Token, Hadde of Landomere."

Trembling, Hadde drew the chain over her head and then, with fumbling fingers, dropped it on the table. As Boradin took the necklace, his gaze flicked over the candles and they flared, doubling in brightness.

Hadde gasped. "Was that magic?"

"Be silent," Boradin murmured.

Hadde's hat veil fell in her face. "Bother this," she muttered and pulled the hat off her head. Orlos chuckled as she dropped it on an empty chair next to her. Boradin spared her a single glance.

After silently inspecting the Token in the bright light of the candles, Boradin handed it to Orlos. "Tell me how it came into your possession," Boradin said. Neither man interrupted as she recounted her story. When she finished, Orlos said, "It is an authentic summoning. Landomere manifested herself in the form of the stag and led you to the Token."

"Where are you from, Hadde?" Boradin asked. "Western Landomere, by the look of your facial markings. Kiremi descended, no?"

"I'm from Long Meadow, Your Majesty. A small village in the southwest. But we're not Kiremi."

"There is spiridus in her as well," Orlos said.

"Really?" Hadde asked. "Part spiridus?"

Orlos smiled. "Let us say, from time to time the spiridus would… mingle with the humans living in the borders of Landomere. Her essence has touched you."

"Enough of her ancestry, Friend," Boradin said. He turned his gaze on Hadde. "Tell me, when you touched the Token, did a voice speak to you?" Hadde shook her head. "Did you feel anything?"

"No."

Boradin frowned at her. "Your guide was a stag? What were you thinking when you saw the stag in the forest?"

"I was thinking that if I should take it, it would help feed my people, Your Majesty."

"Did you feel a compulsion to come to Sal-Oras? Did a voice in your mind ever speak to you at a later time?"

"I came at the urging of my friend, Belor. I came because I was desperate. Belor thought maybe you could help us—that your elementar magic could fight the Wasting...." She glanced at the candles.

"It cannot."

The words hung for a moment as Hadde digested them. They were so final. "But... but you are an elementar, aren't you?"

"I am, but it doesn't matter one bit. Elemental magic has no bearing on the Wasting. I cannot call fire and burn it away. I cannot call the wind to blow it away. The Wasting is, simply, death. My magic is useless against it."

Hadde's head sank and she stared at her hands. All for nothing. Belor's death. Her family left behind. "I suppose I'll sell it."

"The Token? You thought of selling the Token?" Orlos asked, frowning.

"Is there something wrong? We thought to sell the token if all else failed. We would use the money to purchase supplies." She glanced from Orlos to the king and back.

"Someone gifted with a Token would never think of selling it," Orlos said. "Before the veden came and murdered the spiridus, the forest would often give us Tokens as a sign of some mission we were to accomplish. The Tokens took many forms. Some were specific to a certain task, such as a bow, a cord, or a knife. Yours, like mine, is a golden pendant."

He opened the blankets at his neck, revealing a necklace identical to hers. "But the Tokens always came with a voice," he said. "Landomere always spoke—." A coughing fit seized the spiridus, bending him almost double. Immediately, Boradin left his chair and knelt at Orlos's side. Hadde rose as well, but was lost as to what to do. She circled the table and stood beside Orlos, her hand on his back.

"I'll call a surgeon," Boradin said. "Hadde will stay with you."

Orlos shook his head trough the fit. "No," he gasped. "Nothing they can do."

"You can rest. We'll take you to your chamber."

"No. Must talk to Hadde." Orlos clutched her Token in his withered fist. "I must speak to it," he said as the coughing subsided. Tears trickled down his cheek. Hadde tentatively reached out and wiped one away with the back of her palm. His skin felt hot to her touch.

"You're warm," she said.

"It's nothing." He smiled up at her as he cupped her necklace's pendant in his hands. Closing his eyes, he sat in silence for a short time. Hadde stood beside him, her hand still resting on his back. The king retreated to his own chair, but his eyes never left the spiridus.

"It wants to speak, but its voice is too weak," Orlos said as he opened his eyes.

"What does it mean?" asked Hadde. "What should I do?"

"I cannot say for certain. When the spiridus were slain and Belavil destroyed, Landomere took a mortal wound. But it takes a long time for a forest to die. I don't even know if the Token was meant for you. It could have rested in that Spiridus Glade since the War for the Orb. It might be you didn't hear Landomere because the voice is too faint, or because you've too little spiridus blood."

"This isn't what I want to hear," Boradin said. "The Token must be a sign. It must have some meaning." He stood and paced along the heavily laden shelf behind him. "Orlos came to us when the Orb was lost, and now you arrive, bearing the same Token. Is it a sign that the Orb has returned? If it has, I must find it."

"How do you even know it still exists, Your Majesty? The old stories say it was destroyed."

"There are many legends about the fate of the Three Gifts." The king waved his hand at the shelves filling the room, as if the gesture would have some meaning to Hadde. "Not all say that the Orb was destroyed." He nodded toward Orlos. "We think that the varcolac are proof that it still exists. We think, at some point Akinos, or one of his descendants, must have gained some control over the Orb and used it to create the varcolac."

"How could they be created?" Hadde asked. "How could such a creature simply start to exist?"

"The Forever War ended when Helna the Creator banished herself and her two brothers." Orlos said. "Her brothers begged her to let them each leave a gift behind to aid their followers. Helna knew her brothers had left weapons of great power, and that her brothers' followers would continue the war until one side was victorious. Helna left the Orb in the care of the dragon, Agrep, commanding her to give it to the war's victor." He stopped and drew a deep breath. Hadde feared another fit.

"Easy, Friend, I'll tell it," Boradin said. He turned to Hadde. "Helna imbued the Orb with her own power. The power to create and give life. The Orb was to restore the land from the damage done by the Forever War and the wars that followed the gods' exile. When the War for the Orb ended, and Forsvar's followers had won, Agrep brought the Orb as promised. But the moment it was placed in King Handrin's hand, Akinos struck him down and stole it. Some of the Ancient Texts say it was destroyed."

"Sages have argued for five hundred years over that point," Orlos said as he returned Hadde's necklace to her. His hands shook as he placed it in her hand. "Most felt that without the Orb the land should have stayed the way it was at the end of the war. The Orb couldn't make it better, but the lack of the Orb should not have made it worse. That the Wasting exists counters that argument. Someone is denying the world the Orb's life-giving energies."

"Whoever has the Orb is using it," Boradin said. "They're creating varcolac and using the power of the Orb to destroy rather than to heal. As long as the Orb is misused, the Wasting will continue."

"What can you do, Your Majesty?" Hadde asked. "What can we do?"

"We can find the Orb."

"How?"

"By searching the library for clues."

"And what of my people?" Hadde asked. "Can you help them against the Wasting?"

"And what of your people?" Anger entered the king's voice. "Abandon all of my efforts here to help your little village? No, this is where the Wasting will be ended. In this room, in these books." He motioned to the shelves behind him. "The clues are in the Ancient Texts. In their prophecies. No, Hadde, I cannot help you. But perhaps you can help me."

"I don't know what I can do, Your Majesty. I'm only a huntress."

Boradin drummed his fingers on the table. "Can you read and write? Can you search the Ancient Texts?"

Hadde shook her head.

"Too much to ask."

Orlos' body jerked as he choked back another coughing fit. Boradin strode to his side. "Enough. Orlos must rest."

"No," Orlos said. "We must continue. We must find the Orb."

"Later, Friend. I need your help. We'll continue after you have rested." Boradin looked from Orlos to Hadde. "You'll stay in Salador while we research the meaning of your Token. If it leads to the Orb of Creation, we shall all be saved and your quest to save your people fulfilled. If it's unsuccessful, I shall take your Token in exchange for supplies for your village."

"I can't stay," Hadde said. "I have to return to Landomere. My people need me."

"You'll stay."

"For how long?" Hadde stared defiantly at the king. Nothing about this journey had gone as she had wished.

"You'll stay as long as it takes." He dismissed her with a wave of his hand. "Send the guards in as you leave."

"I won't stay. Long Meadow may not exist next spring. I have to leave now."

"Hadde," Orlos said, his voice weak, "stay with us a short time. Your

Token has some meaning. Give us time."

"Don't you understand? My parents are starving. They will die without me. They will die if I don't bring supplies." Her voice rose and her face flushed with anger. Just the mention of her parents brought a wave of homesickness over her. She wouldn't abandon them.

"Enough!" Boradin shouted. "Return to your chamber...or should I have you locked away? Well? The Maiden Hall or the dungeon...it's your choice."

Chapter Eleven

Hadde sat in front of the fire and put her face in her hands. She should have gone to Mor-Oras and sold the Token there. Belor wouldn't have died, and she would be well on her way home with provisions for Long Meadow. She pressed her palms against her eyes to fight off the tears that welled up at the thought of the tall Landomeri.

How she missed him. She wished he were with her. She missed his humor. She missed his enthusiasm. She missed his warmth. He would have been overjoyed at the success of their mission so far, she was certain. He probably would have imagined them on the verge of discovering the Orb of Creation.

Instead he was dead and she was alone. And in her eyes nothing had gone right.

A knock at the door disrupted her thoughts. She rubbed the tears from her eyes. "Hadde, I have good news for you," Maret announced as she entered. "I'm sorry. Are you not well?"

"I'm fine," Hadde lied. "Homesick. Please come in."

"The king has granted you an allowance. And he wishes for you to attend the reception of petitioners tomorrow morning. It's so exciting. You must have made a good impression last night."

Hadde shrugged. "If threatening me with the dungeon is a good thing, then yes, it went very well."

"What are you talking about? He is giving you a generous allowance. You can leave the Maiden Hall and let out private lodgings. Did you hear me, Hadde?"

"I heard you. What's an allowance?"

Maret sighed. "He's going to give you money every week. You'll be very comfortable."

"Comfortable—for a prisoner. You said I could get private lodgings with this money? Could I just stay here and save the money?"

"Of course, but I don't know why you would want to."

"I'll use the money to purchase food and clothing for my people. If the king lets me leave this winter I can still help Long Meadow. They won't survive much longer."

"I'm sure every——" A disturbance outside the door interrupted her. Hadde heard laughter and the patter of slippered feet running down the hall. "Ooh, what's happening?" Maret said. "Let me check."

A moment later Hadde heard a squeal from the hall followed by voices in excited conversation. Celena's voice angrily called out above the others. Maret rushed into the room, slammed the door, and smiling and breathless, leaned against it.

"What's happening?" Hadde asked.

"He's coming back." Maret scampered across the room and pulled open a window. A blast of cold air swept through the room. "I can't wait. I think I'll die."

"Who? Who's coming back?" Hadde joined Maret at the window.

"The prince."

"Isn't he a young boy? Sir Nidon mentioned Prince Handrin to me."

Maret rolled her eyes. "Not *Handrin!* Prince *Morin.*"

"I don't know of him. Why all the excitement?"

"Oh, Hadde, you don't know anything. Prince Morin is the bravest and most handsome man in Salador. In the world. And he's eligible. I'm going to marry him." She sighed.

"You've declared your love before your people?"

"If you're asking if we're engaged, we're not. Yet," the girl replied, staring out the window. "But I'm certain we will be. There's someone in my way." She paused. "I hope Felina of Kar-Oras dies."

Hadde looked askance at Maret. The viciousness of the words were not matched by cheery demeanor. "You don't really want her to die... surely?"

Maret continued staring out the window as she replied, "Well, not really. But she is hideous. It's not fair that her father is the Duke of the West Teren. It would be a political marriage, of course."

"Well, of course. We all know that."

Maret laughed. "You're making fun of me."

"Never." Hadde couldn't help herself, but laughed along with Maret.

A trumpet sounded, drawing their attention to the courtyard. "A fanfare," Maret said. "He's coming."

The Great Keep's gates opened and a lone rider entered the bailey. Hadde's stomach roiled at the sight. She drew in her breath as she recognized the rider. "What's wrong?" Maret asked as Hadde backed away from the window.

"That man, do you know who he is?"

Maret shook her head, her face crestfallen. "I've never seen him before." She stared out the window. "He looks a little worse for wear, but he must be important."

"Earl Waltas," Hadde said, making no effort to hide the contempt in her voice.

Maret shrugged. "My father is an East Teren earl. By his attire this Earl Waltas is South Teren. Do you know him?"

"I wish I didn't. I hoped he had returned to the South Teren. Close the window. I don't want to see him."

"Well, I wish it had been Prince Morin riding through the gate. I'll be very upset if I was misinformed."

Hadde returned to her chair. "Waltas," she muttered, "it only gets worse." Maret leapt to her feet as another fanfare sounded. "This time it's him. I know it." She said as she dashed to the window and yanked it open. "Look—the Black Company."

Hadde eased back to the window and watched as the prince's company thundered into the bailey. In perfect order the sixteen men wheeled into a double line facing the keep. Unlike the uniformed Knights of the House, each man in the Black Company seemed permitted his own colors. The only items they held in common were their black cloaks and the red pennants on their lances.

An ebony stallion, ridden by a tall, broad-shouldered knight, pranced to the front of the formation. Hadde watched as the black-clad rider expertly guided his horse with the barest touch of the reins.

"The prince," Maret whispered.

"Black Company." Morin's voice boomed off the bailey walls. "I give you my congratulations, and my thanks, for another victorious campaign. It has been a hard season, but one worthy of great praise. For those of you not wintering in Sal-Oras, I bid you a fond farewell until we reassemble next spring. The rest of you will have to suffer with seeing me through the dark winter. But do not fear, I'm sure we will liven up the time with the occasional drill." Several of the men grimaced and gave knowing glances as he spoke the last words.

"Perhaps one of you would take me in for the winter?" a knight said to a chorus of laughter.

Morin smiled and raised his hand for quiet. "I am proud to lead you." He paused. "I will not keep you from your rest and your families. Black Company... dismissed!" The command echoed off the keep's walls.

In unison the warriors dismounted from their horses. Squires and pages scurried from the keep to assist the knights. Before the young men reached the Black Company, another knight stepped out in front of the troop. Hadde recognized him as the man who had joked about leaving for the winter. He called out, "Three cheers for Captain Morin!"

"Hurrah!" The sound made the window glass shiver. "Hurrah!

Hurrah!"

Smiling, the prince bowed to his men.

"You're right, Maret," Hadde said. "He's very handsome. He looks nothing like the king."

"They're only half-brothers."

"And the king is so thin."

"They say he forgets to eat. He spends all of his time in his library reading the Ancient Texts—for all the good it does us." She lowered her voice to a whisper. "The prince—he's a real hero."

"And the other knight, the one who called for the cheer—who is he? He looks more like Prince Morin's brother than the king does."

"That's Sir Astor," Maret replied. "The prince's best friend. Astor lost his manor to the Wasting. Now all he has to his name are his arms and the prince's friendship." She gave a little shrug as if there was nothing more to be said of him.

Maret arrived in Hadde's room very early the following morning. "We must prepare you for the reception."

"There seems little point," Hadde said, talking as she munched bread she had toasted over her fire. She couldn't get over how plentiful food was in the Great Keep. "The king has made it clear he is unwilling to help me."

"Oh, you have to go. It will be your formal introduction into Saladoran society. It's very important; all of the most powerful nobles will attend. More than usual because of the Festival of Spring. And, besides, the king requires it. Let me fix your dress."

"It's mid-winter. Why do you call it the Festival of Spring?"

"Ahh, it is the Festival of Spring Coming. It celebrates the spring to be."

"And how many people will be there?" Hadde asked as Maret fussed over her.

"Oh, not many. A few hundred."

"Hundreds?" Dread washed over Hadde.

"Oh, that's nothing. The hall could fit over a thousand. Now, when you arrive the Steward of the Court will present you to the king. Don't forget to curtsy."

Hadde washed her last bite down with a gulp of tea. "What's a curtsy?"

Maret sighed and demonstrated. "It's the way a lady bows. What do you do in your land?"

"For a stranger we hold out both palms. With friends and family we clasp hands or embrace."

"Don't do that to the king." Maret laughed. "The Royal Guard will tackle you before you get close." She pushed a strand of Hadde's hair back into place. "I've been meaning to ask—what are the marks on your cheeks? The three stars?"

"Not stars. Rayed Orbs. They're my family marks. All Landomeri get family marks at their coming of age."

"Why?"

Hadde shrugged. "It's tradition. And they look pretty. You should see the Kiremi. They mark up their entire faces. It's hideous."

"They're pretty on you." Maret said as she brushed Hadde's hair. "You are very pretty. The men will be taken with your foreign looks."

"I... ah," Hadde stammered. "I...thank you." And then to change the topic she said, "My mother performed a ritual to Helna as the family marks were applied. She thinks the blessing has protected me."

"Oh... has it?"

"The gods are gone. They can't help us. But it makes my mother feel good."

"You—" A knock at the door interrupted them. With a last glance at Hadde, Maret opened it and spoke with someone in the hall. "Your guard has arrived early. It's time to go."

A tremor ran up Hadde's spine. "My guard? You're coming as well, aren't you, Maret?"

"I'm sorry, but I wasn't summoned. Maidens rarely serve in the Great Hall." Maret paused and then put her hand on Hadde's arm. "Here, I'll escort you there. They won't let me in, but I'll take you to the door."

"Thank you."

"Don't worry. The first time I was formally received I was very nervous as well. But there is nothing to fear. Believe me, after a while it becomes fun." Leaning close she whispered, "Just remember, they go to the privy just like you and me."

Hadde laughed as she stood. "Thank you, Maret. I'll try to remember that."

"Wait, you must put on your shoes." Maret picked up the red slippers.

"They don't fit. I'll wear my moccasins."

"You don't dare do that. It would be a disaster if you were caught wearing them."

With a groan, Hadde pulled on the tight shoes. "I'll do it this once."

"And your cap."

Hadde glanced around the room. "I...ah left it in the library."

"Oh, no. I don't have another that will match."

"So I won't wear one."

"No, you must. We'll do the best we can."

They started down the hall but stopped at Maret's door. The girl stepped inside and returned wearing her own cap and another for Hadde. "It's black, and doesn't go well with the dress."

"It doesn't matter," Hadde replied. "It's all the same to me. I'd rather wear my Landomeri clothes."

At the end of the hall stood four squires. Two guarded the door while two waited for Hadde and Maret.

"Hello, Hadde of Landomere," a squire said.

"Squire Melas!" Smiling, she stepped forward to hug him.

He recoiled, eyes wide with fear.

She halted mid-step. Saladorans don't hug, she reminded herself. "Squire, it's a pleasure to see you again."

"It's my pleasure as well, Hadde." He spoke formally, but she thought she spotted a hint of a smile on his face.

The squires led them through a maze of hallways. She soon lost all sense of direction. A group of ragged servants stood aside as Hadde's party passed. All were thin and pale. She was certain they were staring at her.

"I'm walking like I'm crippled, Maret," she whispered.

"You're doing fine."

They marched down a corridor larger than any Hadde had seen before.

"We're almost there," Maret said.

Hadde nodded and swallowed, her mouth suddenly dry. Two knights guarded the open entrance to the chamber. After saluting the knights, the squires departed. Maret took Hadde by the elbow and led her into the room.

Six men lounged in the chamber.

Hadde sucked in her breath at the sight of Earl Waltas. He glared at her as she entered the room. Purple bruises rimmed his eyes and his nose was crooked and swollen. She had not noticed his injuries when he had first arrived.

"What's wrong, Hadde?" Maret asked.

Hadde shook her head and turned away from the earl. Relief flooded through her at the sight of Sir Nidon speaking to one of the knights guarding the massive inner doors. The Champion appeared unconcerned with the presence of his battered enemy sitting just strides from him.

Nidon glanced at Hadde and nodded in recognition before returning to his discussion. She wondered at his calmness. But what did he have to fear? He was huge and strong, and she had seen his skill and bravery as he fought the varcolac. She couldn't imagine a greater warrior.

Two oddly-dressed men sat in chairs set along the right hand wall. Where Nidon and Waltas both wore fine, thigh-length tunics and trousers bloused into the tops of their high boots, these men wore long billowing robes of incredible richness. The closer man's robe was white, embroidered with hundreds of red and green flowers. The other wore black, decorated with golden scrollwork. Narrow-brimmed, peaked hats matched their robes. They paid Hadde little attention.

A short man in a red surcoat stepped up to Hadde and Maret as they entered the room. He looked at Hadde with disapproval. "You must be Hadde of Landomere," he said. "I'm Sir Fenre, Steward of the Court. I'll present you to the king. You'll follow the others and be presented last. Don't presume to speak to the king. You'll speak only when spoken to. Never turn your back on his highness."

Hadde nodded.

"Maiden Maret, you were not called," Fenre said.

"No, sir," she responded and curtsied. "I came only to accompany Lady Hadde."

"Lady Hadde?" Waltas snorted. "Ignorant girl, she's no lady. She's a commoner. A commoner of the lowest sort."

Maret turned toward the earl but kept her eyes lowered to the floor. "My apologies, my lord. I knew only that she had been sent to stay in the Maiden Hall and that I was to attend her."

Waltas laughed a harsh laugh. "Then you've been attending a commoner. What would your parents say?"

"I don't know, sir."

Waltas took a step toward them. "I see you've learned how to dress," he said to Hadde. "No longer the naked savage, are we?"

"Leave off, Earl Waltas," Nidon rumbled.

Waltas cast Nidon a hate-filled glance and stormed back to his chair.

"Maiden, take your charge and be seated over there," the steward said to Maret. He motioned to where the two robed men sat. Hadde and Maret put three empty chairs between themselves and the men.

Hadde turned to ask about them, but Maret looked away. "Maret?" The girl sat unmoving. "What's wrong, Maret?"

Maret wheeled and glared at Hadde with narrowed eyes. "Is it true? You're common?"

"I don't know, Maret."

"What do you mean, you don't know?" Tears welled in her eyes.

"In Landomere we have no commoners or nobles. We're all the same."

"But that lord, he said——"

"Rise for Prince Morin," the steward called out.

Hadde stood and faced the door. The tall prince stood at the chamber's entrance, a hint of a smile on his face. Unlike Waltas, his black clothing was immaculate. His gaze swept the room. For a moment Hadde's eyes locked with his. The Maidens didn't fawn over him without reason. He had chiseled features and dark, penetrating eyes. He strode into the room as if he owned it. As arrogant as Waltas, Hadde thought.

"Champion," Morin said, nodding to Nidon before turning to Waltas.

"Earl Waltas, it has been many years."

"Too long, Prince Morin," Waltas said, his face neutral.

"Not late, am I, Fenre?" Morin asked the steward.

"Of course not, my lord. The Landomeri just—" A fanfare of horns interrupted him. "It's time, gentlemen," the steward continued. "If you would…" He motioned to the inner doors. Morin took position at the head of the group. Nidon and Waltas stood behind him, followed by the two robed men, and Hadde in the rear. "Maiden Maret, you are dismissed," he said with a dismissive wave.

Hadde glanced at Maret as she departed, but the girl didn't look back as she hustled from the room. When all were in place, the steward stepped in front of the party and nodded to the guards. The knights pushed the doors open, revealing the Great Hall beyond.

Hadde stifled a gasp. Long Meadow would fit in the huge chamber. Giant pillars rose to a vaulted ceiling decorated with hundreds of pennants and streamers. High rectangular windows lining the walls illuminated the hall. A massive round window at the opposite end of the room lit a raised stone dais.

Hadde ignored her throbbing feet and concentrated on keeping her strides even as she approached the dais. Hundreds of people stood and watched as the group slowly progressed down the hall. She couldn't bear to look at them; instead she kept her eyes on the back of the black-robed man in front of her.

Reaching the far end of the Great Hall, the party stopped. The robed man in front of Hadde stepped aside, revealing the dais and the two royals. Boradin's face had a grim set to it. Hadde balked at the unfriendly gaze. Over his red tunic and trousers the king wore a matching red cloak trimmed with white fur. The clothing, while luxurious, sagged on his tall, gaunt frame. The shield, Forsvar, rested against his knees.

For a moment Boradin's gaze rested on Hadde, but he gave no sign of recognition. The queen reached over and touched his arm and he turned to her. Hadde watched as the two exchanged words.

The queen was the most elegant woman Hadde had ever seen. She felt like an awkward child in comparison. Two long auburn braids ran down the front of the queen's close fitting white dress. A white cape draped her shoulders. A silver circlet crowned her head.

The queen smiled and nodded as she spoke with the king, but to Hadde her cordiality seemed forced. Two knights in full armor stood to either side of the king and queen. Both stood at rigid attention with halberds held in front of them. At the base of the dais stood two more knights, each with a long handled torch. Hadde thought them odd in the well-lit room.

The steward's voice boomed out, "Your Royal Highnesses, Ladies and gentlemen, I present to you, Prince Morin."

Applause and a few loud cheers greeted the prince as he stepped to the base of the dais. As Hadde's eyes flitted back and forth she noticed that some in the crowd had failed to clap at all. She wondered at their lack of enthusiasm for the prince. Bending to one knee, Morin bowed his head.

"Prince Morin, welcome home," Boradin said.

"Thank you, brother." He rose to his feet.

"Another successful campaign against the savage Tyskmen?"

"It was, brother. Another season and their strength will be broken and the Namiri saved from their depredations." Scattered applause followed his words.

"And then what? From whom will you save us next?"

"I would be loath to announce my next target. We wouldn't wish to give them more time for their preparations, would we?"

"Of course not, Prince Morin. Your wisdom is equal to your strength." At a sign from the king, Morin bowed and strode to the right side of the dais where he joined another man. Hadde recognized him as Astor, the knight who led the cheer for Morin upon their arrival. He, like the prince, wore black and had a small white sword emblazoned upon his cloak. It struck her again that the two looked more like brothers than did Morin and the king.

"Your Royal Highnesses," Fenre called out. "I present to you, Sir Nidon, Champion of the Realm." Loud applause greeted Nidon as he strode to the base of the dais. There were no cheers, but the clapping was universal. Nidon took a knee.

"Sir Nidon," the king said, "I'm pleased you've returned safely. Your journey was long and difficult. I give you my thanks for accomplishing it so well."

"I exist to serve."

"Rise, Champion. Your faithful service is a tribute to the knighthood of Salador." Nidon took his place at the king's side. The knight who had been there saluted Nidon and marched from the dais.

"Your Royal Highnesses," the steward announced, "I present to you Earl Waltas of House Valen." Waltas stepped forward and took a knee. Stony silence greeted him.

"Earl Waltas, welcome to Sal-Oras," the king said.

"Thank you, Your Majesty."

"You're here representing Duke Kelos of Del-Oras?"

"Duke Kelos of the South Teren, Your Majesty," Waltas corrected.

Hushed gasps escaped the lips of many onlookers. The king leaned forward. "Yes, of course, of the South Teren." He paused a moment. "And the South Teren is a duchy of the Kingdom of Salador."

As Waltas started to stand the king put out his hand. "I didn't give you leave to rise."

Waltas paused, and then stood. A murmur rolled through the audience. "The South Teren does not fear you, King Boradin," Waltas said. "You might keep Sal-Oras in line with your illusions and magic tricks, but we do not fear you."

Boradin still held his hand outstretched. A frown crossed his face. "You doubt my magic?"

"I do."

Boradin clenched his fist and Waltas lurched forward, falling to his knees. Just as quickly he sprang to his feet. "A trick!" he shouted. Waltas snatched up a slate from the floor and tossed it at the base of the dais. "A loose slate and a trap lever. Just tricks!"

The king thrust his hand at Waltas and a blast of air struck the earl, staggering him back. The gust struck Hadde and she caught her breath at its strength. This was real magic.

"More trickery!" the earl shouted, but to Hadde he sounded less certain. "There is—there's a billows under your throne."

Hadde scanned the dais, but couldn't see any sign of a billows or a hole through which the wind could have blown.

"Bring me that torch," Boradin ordered. As soon as the knight handed the king the torch, he stood and hurled it at Waltas' feet.

Waltas laughed. "That's your magic? You toss—"

Boradin made a claw with his fist and aimed it at the torch. Waltas leaped back as a fireball erupted from the flames. The king twisted his hand and the fireball turned into a tornado of flame and surged toward the earl. With a cry of fear, Waltas leapt aside, stumbled, and fell to the floor.

Hadde and everyone assembled stepped back from the fiery display as a wave of heat washed over them.

Waltas scrambled away from the flames, but the tornado turned and pursued him. But with each passing instant it faded in strength. Unable to escape, Waltas curled into a ball as the last of the flames danced over him.

Hadde looked away at the last moment and her eyes fell on Morin. The prince wasn't looking at the fiery display; instead he stared at his brother. The king didn't notice his brother's gaze, but Nidon did. As Hadde watched, Nidon stepped closer to the throne, his right hand rested casually on his sword's pommel.

The king collapsed back into his throne. His breath came in ragged gasps, his face flushed bright red. "There's your magic, Earl Waltas," the king managed. "But it is not my place to kill you."

Waltas groaned and rolled to his knees. The fire had apparently done him no physical harm, but Hadde could see the fear on his face. She felt fear as well, even though the king's wrath hadn't been aimed at her. The stone on the floor, and the gust of wind could have been tricks, but the flame? There was no explaining that. The king was an elementar.

Boradin sat on his throne, one hand raised, a finger pointing at Waltas. "This spring you refused a royal call-to-arms. You challenge my rightful rule over the South Teren. You break my laws by attacking a foreign ambassador. You are not fit to be a knight of Salador. I declare your lands forfeit and your titles lost." Boradin wiped his sleeve across his sweaty face.

Waltas rose unsteadily to his feet. He clenched his shaking hands behind his back. He had to be terrified, Hadde thought. She wished she could take more pleasure in it, but it wouldn't be long before she stood in front of the king. Dread filled her.

"These charges are unjust," Waltas said. "You just hope to cow the other lords of the South Teren into submission with me as an example."

"I have spoken. You are dismissed."

"No." Waltas stood taller. "I demand a trial."

"Then you shall have it." Boradin smiled. "And since you demand one, it is my prerogative to choose its manner. You shall fight a trial by combat with Sir Nidon on the morning."

Waltas glanced at the champion and then around the hall as if looking for an escape. He took two steps back and then said, "You can't make me fight. It's the King's Peace until a week past the Festival of Spring."

Boradin paused a moment before replying. "So it is. You seem to know my laws well when it suits you. You will meet the Champion of Salador the day after the King's Peace. Now leave my sight. Or do you wish to be carried out?"

Waltas bowed and retreated from the chamber. Boradin waited until the doors closed behind the earl and then waved his hand for the steward to proceed.

"Your Royal Highnesses," Fenre announced, "I present to you the Dukes Emle and Giula of Arossa." The two robed men standing beside Hadde stepped in front of the dais. They didn't touch their knees to the ground, but instead bowed their heads.

"Duke Emle," the king nodded at the black robed man. He turned to one in white, "Duke Giula, welcome to Sal-Oras. Please excuse the churlish display by Earl Waltas."

"Please, Your Majesty," said Duke Giula, "it was a pleasure to see your display of elemental might." He reached inside one of his billowing, flower-decorated sleeves and produced a scroll, which he handed to Emle.

Hadde barely understood the duke's strong accent. His words all seemed to drone together. "High King Boradin of Salador," Emle said, "the nobles, burghers, guilds, and people of Arossa present this letter of thanks to his Royal Majesty the King of Salador, and to the people of the Kingdom of Salador, in appreciation for unselfish aid in our recent time of crisis."

"It was our pleasure," Boradin replied as the Sir Fenre received the scroll. "The restoration of peace in Idoria is of great importance to us all." The king turned to Giula. "You've done your country a great service. I regret your tenure as ambassador is at an end."

"Thank you, Your Majesty. But I'm certain you'll find Duke Emle my superior in all ways."

"I look forward to a long and fruitful relationship."

The two men bowed and stepped aside. Hadde found herself standing alone in front of the king. She tried to clear her throat, but couldn't.

"Your Royal Highnesses——," the steward started but the king's raised hand stopped him.

"Hadde of Landomere," the king said, "come closer."

Hadde's heart felt as if it were trying to leap from her chest as she walked to the dais. The crowd's murmurs came as an indistinct hum. She remembered Maret's admonition to curtsy, but Hadde doubted that she would do it right. Deciding that she must do something, she imitated the bent knee of the men who had gone before her. The murmurs from the crowd grew.

"Welcome to Sal-Oras, Hadde," Boradin said.

"Thank you... Your Majesty," she mumbled.

"Rise, Hadde."

As she attempted to stand, she suddenly pitched forward, whirling her arms for balance. Too late, she realized she had stepped on the skirt of her dress. She toppled clumsily to the ground and rolled to her knees. Laughter rolled across the audience.

Prince Morin was suddenly next to her, helping her to her feet. "Are you hurt?" he asked.

"I'm fine. I'm sorry," she said, blushing.

"No need to apologize," he said, and then he returned to his place beside Astor.

Despite the cold air in the Great Hall, beads of sweat gathered on Hadde's brow. Lowering her gaze, she saw a tear in the hem of her dress.

Boradin silenced the crowd with a raised hand. The king leaned forward in his chair and regarded her. "You are the ambassador of your people?"

Hadde swallowed hard and almost choked. "I am, Your Majesty."

"Your Majesty," a voice called out from the audience, "how can this—this woman—this bumbling ragamuffin—be an ambassador?" A chorus of voices agreed.

Boradin raised his hand for silence. "Different ways in different lands," he said. "Things weren't always as they are now. More of you should read the Ancient Texts." He returned his gaze to Hadde. "What brings you to Salador?"

"I...uh," Hadde stuttered. Why was he asking when he already knew her mission? "I... come on behalf of my people, Your Highness. The Wasting is taking a terrible toll on Landomere. I come in search of aid."

"Hadde of Landomere," the queen interrupted. "Why are you not married? Why are you not home caring for your children and your husband's household?"

The sudden change of subject bewildered Hadde. "Not married, Your Highness? I'm a huntress. As for children, well, the Wasting has left me barren. I've lain with a man, but—"

Someone shouted and pandemonium broke out. Women blanched and turned away. Others gasped and fanned their faces. Men yelled angrily at Hadde.

She looked around desperately for some escape. Had Waltas felt like this? The thought flashed through her mind.

A puff of wind struck her. *"You would think they never had sex."* The voice came from right behind her ear, but as if it had come from far off. Hadde spun, but saw no one.

A gentle breeze whirled around her and the world went strangely silent. People rushed to aid a stricken woman. Mouths opened and closed. Hadde couldn't hear a thing. Her face streamed with sweat and she wiped her brow.

"Hadde, it's I, Morin." The air suddenly cooled. *"They cannot hear us."*

Hadde faced the prince, her mouth agape.

112

"Watch." Smiling, he turned to the crowd. *"You're all a mass of ignorant fools,"* he called out.

She looked around, and while some stared at Morin, none showed any sign of having heard him.

"How?" Hadde asked.

"What do you think?" Boradin's voice cut in.

Hadde turned to the king. *"It's magic. Like you did to Waltas?"*

"In a way, very different," Boradin replied. *"My brother and I control the elements. If we don't wish the wind to carry our voices, it does not."* He turned to Morin. *"What are you thinking, Prince Morin? Why have you interrupted my assembly?"*

"The nobles put on quite a show of offense. The mood was turning on her, Brother. Saladorans are not used to foreign ways." He smiled at Hadde. *"It makes them furious when we do this. But then again half of them are worthless and the other half are jackasses."*

"Enough of this," Boradin said. He turned his attention on the audience.

"We must do more, Brother," Morin interrupted. *"She must be protected."*

Hadde stared at Morin in wonderment, her mind still reeling from the sudden chaos. Why was he doing this? His cocky self-assuredness had put her off at first. But now, here he was standing up for her, even against the king. Perhaps the prince was not another Waltas.

"Every moment we speak with her she gains status," Boradin said. *"They wonder why she's so important the king attends her so closely. It's enough."*

Morin shook his head. *"We must do more, Brother. If she's to stay in Sal-Oras, her official status must be clear to the people. She will be sorely tested as it is."*

"Very well." Boradin waved his hand in dismissal.

The breeze fell off and Hadde could hear again. There were no voices, just the sounds of people shuffling their feet, the rustle of fabric, and an occasional cough.

Boradin raised his left hand. "I declare that Hadde of Landomere is an ambassador from her land to myself. She is to be given all the rights, privileges, and immunities as such."

There were a few gasps from the crowd but nobody called out an objection.

"Furthermore, she's to be given the same respect one gives," the king cocked his head to one side as if thinking. "That one gives a baroness."

"Thank you, Your Majesty," Hadde said into the shocked silence.

The king took the queen's hand and rose to his feet. Around the room

113

people dropped to their knees, bowed, or curtsied. "I declare this audience at an end," Boradin said. A small entourage followed the king and queen as they departed through a side entrance. No one else moved.

The moment the door closed behind the king's party the room erupted. Several people rushed for the main door, but most remained where they were in animated discussion. Hadde had no idea what to do.

Morin appeared next to her, his friend Astor a step behind. Morin bowed low, and taking her hand, kissed it. "Congratulations, Ambassador."

Hadde swallowed. Dozens of people watched their exchange. "Prince Morin—"

"I've heard a bit of your journey to Sal-Oras. Extraordinary. Don't you think, Astor?"

"It was, Captain," Astor replied.

Hadde took a deep, calming breath. She had never met anyone like this prince. He commanded the attention of anyone near him, had more self-assurance than anyone she had ever seen, and seemingly knew no fear. And he had saved her.

"Your journey, Ambassador?"

"It was difficult," was all she managed.

"I was told you're quite an archer."

"In my own land I'm a huntress," Hadde said, recovering slightly. "I grew up with a bow in my hands."

A hushed crowd of onlookers encircled them. Morin appeared oblivious to them, his entire attention on Hadde.

"You even manage to wound a few of the varcolac?"

Hadde shook her head. "Wound? No, I slew at least four and injured more."

"Really?" The prince turned to his friend. "Did you hear that, Astor? I had an opportunity to speak with Earl Waltas when I arrived and he didn't mention that count." He turned back to Hadde. "You're certain that you are correct? Or maybe the earl is in error?"

Her flush turned to one of anger. "He—I think he miscounted in his haste to escape his pursuers."

Morin laughed. Many in the crowd joined him. "Is that so? I'll have to mention that to him." He glanced around the room as if looking for the South Teren noble. After a moment he looked back at Hadde. "It's said Landomeri archers are the best to be found. I wonder if that's true. It's a shame none of your male countrymen came with you."

"One did, Prince Morin, but he was slain by Saladoran brigands."

"Oh? I'm sorry. I didn't know." For the first time his self-assurance seemed to falter.

"And, Prince Morin," Hadde said, "I'm as fine an archer as any man."

"Really?" His smile returned. "We must have a contest. Are you occupied tomorrow afternoon?"

"I don't know." Hadde glanced at the crowd, wondering what she had gotten herself into.

"Ahh, it will be fun. Something to help pass a winter's day."

"I…"

"Come now, don't let me down."

She met his gaze. For a moment she said nothing. She was a Landomeri huntress, maybe she could show this prince a thing or two. "I promise I won't."

Chapter Twelve

"Come in," Hadde called to the knock at her door.

"Hadde, I——" Maret started. "You're wearing your old clothes."

"I had Celena return them to me. At first she refused, but I said I would go naked rather than wear Saladoran attire."

"You said that? What did she do?"

"She began to argue, so I started to undress in front of her." Maret stared wide-eyed. "She didn't take it well," Hadde continued. "But I felt like a fool in Saladoran clothing. I couldn't bear the way people treated me."

Maret bowed her head. "That's why I'm here. I want to apologize for my behavior yesterday. When that vile earl said that you were common, well, I thought that you had been tricking me all along. But then I saw how the king and Prince Morin treated you, and I knew that I had nothing to be ashamed of."

"I don't understand. You were there? I saw you leave."

"I... I came back to see... to see the audience." She paused a moment before adding, "I saw that you must be very important."

"And if I wasn't important you would like me less?" Hadde turned from Maret and threw another split log on the fire. A shower of sparks flew up the chimney. She never wanted for wood, and never had to cut or fetch it herself. It was good to be a Saladoran noble.

"No, not that." Maret paused. "I just couldn't associate with you any more. It wouldn't be proper."

"I just don't understand what makes you think you're any better than anyone else."

"But we're *nobles.*" She said the last word as if it explained everything.

Hadde sat, staring into the fire and contemplating her response. These Saladorans were so *different.* Would she ever understand them?

Several *thunks* outside the window pulled her from her thoughts. Through the wavy glass she saw activity in the courtyard. She opened the window and smiled. Four men practiced with their odd Saladoran bows as a dozen more watched. "Come and see this, Maret."

They knelt by the window and watched as the men loaded and loosed arrows at targets fifty strides away. After a few shots a group of boys scurried up to the targets and recovered the missiles.

"What are those bows called?" Hadde asked.

"Their crossbows?"

"Is that what they are? Crossbows?" Hadde watched a bit longer and said, "They aren't very good, are they? I mean... they're competent, but...."

Maret giggled. "They aren't the best in Salador, but I think they are pretty good. Look, that one hit the middle. Oops, that one missed." A stray bolt flew across the courtyard and smacked into the stone wall beyond. "The Footmen of the House are better. Some of the Guild Companies are among the best, they say."

"Then why aren't they taking part in the contest tomorrow?"

"The squires are noble. It makes it more entertaining for the members of the court. And the squires are good enough to beat..." Maret's voice faded into awkward silence.

"They are good enough... good enough to beat me, you mean."

"I... ah...."

Hadde laughed returned her attention to the squires. "You truly think they're good?"

"Well, yes, don't you? Especially the squire on the far right. Many people are putting money on him."

"Putting money on him?"

"Gambling. They're wagering money that he will win. Do you place bets in Landomere?"

"Of course we do. We just don't use money." Hadde paused. "Are many people placing bets?"

Maret nodded. "Gambling is very popular."

"Is anyone...putting money on me?"

"I...I don't know."

"Be honest, Maret."

"Um, not that I know of."

"Are you betting on me?"

"Don't be silly. You're a woman."

Hadde's grip on the windowsill tightened as she resisted the urge to rail at Maret. The girl's ignorance was infuriating. But it wasn't just her—it was all Saladorans. They needed to be taught a lesson.

"Did you say something?" Maret asked.

"No, nothing." Hadde forced a smile. "That red dress you loaned me. May I give you something for it?"

Maret perked up. "You want to buy it from me?"

"I guess… I've never bought anything before."

"Of course I'll sell it to you." Maret smiled. "I'm so happy you changed your mind and will wear a dress again. You look so pretty in it."

"I'll wear it once more, at least."

Hadde woke early the following morning, dressed, and ate a light breakfast brought by servants. Being served and treated with deference felt so strange. She hated it. Why would anyone bow before another? Why would someone expect it of others?

She polished her bow and checked the fletching of her arrows until the hour of the contest arrived. Maret tried to visit, but Hadde wanted to be alone.

"They're waiting for you outside, Ambassador," the stable boy said as Hadde arrived. "They sent someone to fetch you."

"Thank you for saddling my horse." Hadde said as she patted Lightfoot's neck.

"Gran came this morning and told us you wanted your pony. You're certain you don't want it rigged sidesaddle?"

"No, that isn't necessary." She finished strapping her bowcase to the saddle.

"But you're wearing a dress."

"I know."

He gaped as she sprang into the saddle. Hadde had cut the dress' skirt in half and sewn the parts into two billowy trouser legs. When she stood or walked with slow, even steps the folds of the fabric hid what she had done. However, when she mounted her horse, she could separate her legs and put a foot in the stirrups on either side.

"What's your name?" Hadde asked.

"Puddle, Lady."

"Thank you for taking care of Lightfoot. I think I'm ready now."

She straightened the folds of the dress, Puddle opened the door to the courtyard. Tapping her heels to Lightfoot's flanks, Hadde emerged into bright autumn sunlight.

The crowd closest to the door took first notice. A few snickers were followed by gales of laughter. Acting as if she hadn't heard them, Hadde leaned forward and patted Lightfoot's neck.

"Let them laugh." Looking up, she smiled at the hundreds of spectators in the courtyard. More poked their heads out from the keep's windows or watched from the parapets above.

Five firing lanes crossed the courtyard, the center lane empty. A crossbowman and a page stood in the others. Prince Morin stood in front of the contestants. He gave Hadde a curt bow and motioned her to the open lane.

Hadde rode Lightfoot to her position on the firing line. It lined up with the closed main gate of the keep. Morin approached her wearing a frown. "Ambassador Hadde, why are you mounted?"

She looked around as if suddenly noticing there were no other horses. "This isn't a mounted contest?"

Morin laughed, as did all of those who heard her. "No, of course not. Let me help you from your horse."

"But why are the targets so close if we're not shooting mounted?" She pressed her right leg to Lightfoot's flank and Morin stepped back as the horse turned in place. "Silly horse. Stand still." She kept up the pressure and Lightfoot continued to turn. Hadde rotated her head to keep her eyes on the prince. The crowd roared with laughter. Lightfoot stopped and Hadde dramatically wiped her brow.

"Are you ready to begin?" Morin asked.

Hadde nodded and fought not to laugh at his discomfiture.

"Are you going to dismount?"

Hadde shook her head.

"Very well." He stepped in front of the firing line. "Each of you will fire ten arrows into the target. The red center is worth three points, the white two, and the blue one. At the end of ten arrows the man with the highest score will be counted the winner of the contest. A tie will be broken with first death."

"First death? That sounds dangerous," Hadde said. A ripple of laughter rolled across the crowd.

Morin rolled his eyes. "First death, Ambassador Hadde, means that each competitor fires one arrow at a time and the first to score an uncontested three wins." He faced all of the competitors. "We'll start from the right of the line. Let the contest begin!"

Hadde pulled her bow from its case and watched as the first squire scored one point. His page handed him another bolt as the second man earned two points. Hadde pretended to fumble for an arrow as Lightfoot rotated to the right.

The second crossbowman moved to grab Lightfoot's bridle. He was a stride away when she drew her bow and sent an arrow into the target.

Her baffled competitor stopped and stared at the target. Three points. Startled gasps emanated from the onlookers. The laughter stopped.

Lightfoot continued rotating.

Hadde drew and loosed another arrow as the target came into view. Three points. Someone clapped, but for the most part the crowd stood silent. A third shot scored two more points.

"Ambassador Hadde, one at a time please," Morin called out.

Lightfoot stopped and Hadde sat facing the crowd. "My apologies, Prince Morin, I couldn't seem to stop."

He grimaced. "Shall we continue?"

Hadde nodded and turned Lightfoot toward the targets.

She passed on the next two rounds. The two squires on her right had scored five and four points respectively. Hadde had eight. The two men to her left had two and three points each.

As Hadde nocked her fourth arrow, Lightfoot broke into a trot and wheeled to her right. Hadde rode a figure eight around two of her competitors. As she circled each one she loosed an arrow into her target. Five more points with two arrows. Her competitors looked sullen but there was more laughter and applause from the crowd.

"Prince Morin," she called out. "My frail, womanly arm is tired. Would you mind skipping me for a few rounds?"

"Very well."

She allowed her competitors to skip her on their next four turns. All eyes watched expectantly as she pulled five arrows from her bowcase and dismounted. Morin gave her an odd look as she placed all five arrows in her left hand—the same hand in which she held her bow. She gave him a quick smile and then loosed the arrows one after another as fast as she could, pulling another arrow from her fingers the instant the previous one left her bow. She wasn't concerned with her aim, she knew they would be close enough.

The four arrows hit the target in the span of six heartbeats. She lowered the bow—the final arrow still held under her little finger.

Grinning, Hadde looked back at Morin and was surprised to see him still staring at her. He glanced at the target. "Impressive. You're up by one." He paused before ordering the three lowest scorers to fire their last bolts. The prince didn't pay their efforts any attention. Nor did the crowd. The initial applause following her rapid fire demonstration had quickly faded. Now all she heard were angry murmurs.

"Last round," Morin said.

"You fir...." The words died on her lips as Hadde faced the last competitor. Venom filled his stare. She balked at his anger. What had she done to deserve it? The thought vanished as soon as she had it.

What had she done? She had humiliated him. Hadde's eyes flicked away from him and across the crowd. Some were smiling, clearly entertained by the show. But the others....

Frowning at her lapse, Morin waved to the squire. "Go ahead."

With a final glare at Hadde, he lifted his crossbow, and with only a momentary pause, pulled the trigger. The bolt flew into the target, striking the line dividing the bulls-eye and the two point circle. He lowered his bow, relief plain on his face.

"Three points to win," Morin said to Hadde.

"Thank you, Prince Morin. Numbers simply baffle me." She nocked her arrow and took aim. A simple shot dismounted and at this range. As she let the air out of her lungs and prepared to release she heard Morin say, "Wait, you're—"

She ignored him and let fly. The arrow struck the target with a crack. The crowd roared. Hadde let a smile cross her face as she regarded her handiwork. Her arrow protruded from the red circle of her competitor's target, a half-finger from his bolt.

Chaos ruled the crowd. Some cheered, many argued, while others shouted angrily at Morin that her points were invalid. The prince raised his hand and the mass quieted. "Hadde of Landomere, you appear to have scored three points, but on the wrong target. Those points don't count. Perhaps you're unfamiliar with the rules? Would you like another opportunity?"

"No fair!" someone shouted from the crowd.

"Ten arrows only!" called another.

Morin raised his hand again.

"The rules are the rules, Prince Morin," Hadde said before he could speak. "It was foolish of me not to pay more attention to what I was doing. The squire is obviously my better."

"You were amazing, Hadde," Maret gushed. She stared out Hadde's window into the courtyard. Workers were already removing the stands. "I've never... never... it was magnificent!"

Hadde smiled as she placed her bowcase on her bed. "It was fun."

"May I see it?" Maret asked, motioning toward the bow.

"Of course." Hadde slid the bow from its protective sheath and handed it to the maiden. "It's named Hawkeye."

"What a perfect name. It seems so... exotic... so dangerous."

Hadde laughed. "Here, this is how you hold it." She showed Maret how to properly take up the bow. "I draw it with my thumb. But you might want to use four fingers."

Maret grimaced as she attempted to draw the bow. The string hardly moved. "It's impossible," she said. "How do you do it?"

"I grew up with a bow in my hand—all Landomeri do. But I started with a simple bow. Hawkeye is a composite of wood, sinew, and horn." She motioned to where Belor's bow leaned, unstrung against the wall.

"That bow has an even heavier draw than this one."

Maret stared at Hadde, incomprehension plain on her face. "I don't know what you're talking about. All I know is that I could never do it."

Hadde took Hawkeye back and placed it on her bed. "You could. It would just take time. I'm going to change clothes," she warned.

As Hadde unbuttoned her dress Maret turned her gaze outside. "You almost won, Hadde. Many people were rooting for you even if they didn't want to show it. It was so exciting." She paused a moment. "You know, I'll bet you would have won if you hadn't ridden your horse."

"Hmmm," Hadde said as she stepped out of the dress and pulled on her tunic and leggings.

"Well, you could have."

"I did win, Maret."

"But..."

A knock sounded at the door. "One moment." Hadde called out. She finished tying her leggings and opened the door. A maiden stepped into the room. "Ambassador Hadde, Prince Morin has sent you a note."

"A note?"

"Yes, here it is." The maiden walked into the room and handed Hadde a folded piece of paper.

"Read it, Hadde," Maret exclaimed.

"I can't."

"Why not?"

"I don't know how to read."

Both girls stared at her. Hadde shrugged. "We have no books in Landomere."

"Oh, I'm sorry," Maret said.

"No need to feel sorry. Would you read it for me, Maret?"

"Of course. Look, it has his seal on it."

Maret carefully removed the wax. "He wants to meet you. He wants to discuss archery He says to bring your bow and arrows."

"When?" Hadde asked. She felt a flutter in her stomach. Had the afternoon's display gained her another enemy?

Chapter Thirteen

"Hadde of Landomere, a most impressive show," Morin said, holding up the ten arrows she had loosed in the contest. He glanced past her, and with a wave of his hand and a word of thanks sent off her escort.

"Where are we, my lord?" Hadde asked. The squire had led her to an unfamiliar part of the Great Keep.

"Please come in," he pushed open a heavy door. "This is the Weapons Gymnasium."

As she stepped through the door, she gasped. The chamber was almost as large as the Great Hall. She stared, awestruck, at the vast collection of weapons and armor lining the walls. Practice dummies of leather stuffed with straw were scattered throughout the room. Some were mounted on wooden horses, while others hung from the ceiling by ropes.

She jumped as the door banged closed behind her. As the prince turned from it, she realized they were alone. An image of Waltas's leering face appeared in her mind. Would this Saladoran turn out as evil? She resisted the urge to run for the door, swearing to herself that no man would take her at unawares.

Resting her hand on her knife's hilt, she said, "You could equip an entire army from this one room, my lord." She hoped he hadn't caught the quaver in her voice.

He smiled a broad smile. "Not much of an army. The weapons are for practice. They're either blunted for mock combat or weighted to build strength. And enough with the 'my lords.' I find it tiresome."

She nodded. "Do you spend much time here..."

"Call me Morin. And yes, all knights do. I think I spent most of my childhood here. But I didn't ask you here to talk about me. I want to talk about you. You cost me a considerable amount of money. You nearly ruined my friend Astor."

Hadde swallowed. Money might mean little to her, but she knew how much Saladorans loved it. "I'm sorry," she said.

He laughed a good-natured laugh. "Not only me and Astor, but Sir Nidon, and Squire Melas as well."

"You bet on me in the contest? I didn't know. I would have…."

He arched his eyebrows. "You would have what?"

"I was told that no one put money on me. I just wanted to prove a point."

"Oh, that you did." He chuckled. "In fact I was actually expecting competence from you. I've spent much time in foreign lands. Enough to know that women are not utterly inept in all masculine tasks. Nidon and Melas also had much to say about you. You made quite an impression on them." The prince's smile seemed to hint at a secret that he alone knew.

"I was raised an archer."

"I saw that." He put his hand on his chin. "Tell me, are there many people from your land who can do such things?"

"From western Landomere there are. We live on the edge of the Kiremi plains. I used to be a better rider, but I spend most of my time in the forest now. Several years ago we fought a battle against the Kiremi in hopes of maintaining our access to the plains and the aurochs that live there. We drew the battle, but our losses were too great. We couldn't afford to keep fighting and so moved deeper into the forest."

Morin nodded. "The Kiremi are your enemies?"

"Only recently. We used to exist with them peacefully. The Wasting ended that. They didn't want to share the aurochs with us."

"The Kiremi fight mounted, with bows, as you do?"

"Yes, but they also carry small shields and spears. Some of them have armor as well. I don't think their archery is as good, though."

He paused in thought. "Here, have a seat." He led her to a bench along the wall. Hadde sat, but the prince remained standing, pacing in front of her. "How long are you in Sal-Oras?"

"I don't know. I want to return home, but the king wants me to stay." She thought of her parents and imagined what they were doing. How hard were things in Long Meadow? She should be with them.

"You must be very important." Morin paused.

"He said that he had to read books and study prophecies."

"That damned library. He spends his life in there while the Wasting takes the world. Forsvar is a decoration he wears around his neck. So he won't let you go until he finds the answers he's looking for? You may be with us quite a while—he'll never find what he's looking for."

"Never?" She wondered how long she would be stuck in Sal-Oras. She couldn't bear living at ease while her people wasted away.

"The Orb isn't in that library. It's out there somewhere." He waved his hand in a sweeping gesture.

"But I must go home. If the king cannot cure the Wasting I have to take supplies home." Hadde stood. She felt ill at ease sitting with the prince pacing back and forth in front of her.

"Don't worry. I'll do what I can for you," he said. "I'll not let my brother make a prisoner of you."

"Thank you, Prince Morin."

"But there is one thing that I would like to ask of you," he said. A moment of apprehension caused Hadde to pause. What would this man ask of her? "I'll do what I can," she forced herself to say.

"May I take a look at your bow? Would you mind?"

"Of course not." Hadde stood and drew her bow from its case at her side and handed it to him.

Morin ran his fingers along the arc of the bow. "It's beautiful."

"Hawkeye. My father made it for me."

"It's perfect."

Hadde watched as he ineptly drew the bow. She struggled to keep the smirk from her face. "You think this is funny?" His smile put her at ease. "This is what I want...I would like for you to instruct me in archery."

Hadde couldn't hide her surprise. "I thought archery was beneath Saladorans."

"It may be, but I'm not like other Saladorans."

Hadde whistled a happy tune as she made her way toward the Maiden Hall. Turning a corner, she saw a man walking ahead of her. He paid her no notice as she fell in behind him. Still remembering her meeting with Morin, she followed the man for a score of strides before something about him made her slow her pace. She frowned. What was it about him?

The white tabard. Earl Waltas.

Choking back a cry, she threw herself into the shelter of a doorway. The earl didn't turn, but continued down the hall. Hadde breathed easier when he disappeared around a corner. But what was he doing so close to the Maiden Hall? He wouldn't dare seek her out, would he? Not after what Nidon had done to him. Not after she had been given the king's protection.

Her hand went to Hawkeye. Touching the bow dispelled some of her fears. The thought of putting an arrow into him flittered through her head, but she knew she couldn't. The rage she felt the days after her attack had chilled. She would put her trust in Nidon's sword.

And who would they suspect if Waltas turned up dead of an arrow wound? She almost smiled. It wouldn't make much of a mystery.

She stepped out from her hiding place. But instead of following in Waltas's steps, she turned and took a longer route. She wouldn't take the risk he would ambush her as she turned a corner. Hadde strode down two halls and up the stairs that led to the Maiden Hall. The tension eased from her shoulders as she passed the two armored squires standing guard.

Noticing Maret's door stood ajar, Hadde knocked and said, "Maret, are you in?"

"Come in." Two maidens sat in the room with Maret. Fabric lay piled around all three. Their eyes widened as they noticed Hadde's bow at her side.

"Hadde, this is Jenae," Maret said, nodding at a tall brown-haired girl. "And this is Tira. Their fathers are West-Teren barons."

Hadde had seen both before, but had never been introduced. It had been Tira who had brought Morin's letter to her. "It's nice to meet you. I'm Hadde." And then, tired of their arrogance, she added, "My father's a hunter."

"A what? Really?" Tira asked.

"A hunter," Hadde said, smiling at the pretty, auburn-haired girl.

"But what's his title?"

"They have no titles in Landomere," Maret said, her tone expressing her satisfaction at her knowledge. "Ambassador Hadde resides here on the king's command."

"Well, we all know that," Tira said.

"The contest was amazing, Ambassador Hadde," Jenae said. "How did you shoot like that?"

"Riding and archery have always been a part of my life. And please, call me Hadde."

"Everyone is talking about it," Maret said. "You're famous."

"And you had a private audience with Prince Morin." Tira giggled. "He's magnificent."

"What did he say?" Maret asked. "You were with him such a long time."

Hadde shrugged and then patted her bow. "He wants me to teach him archery."

"He what?" The girls couldn't hide their surprise.

Hadde shrugged. "He thought horse archery might have military significance. At least that's what he said when he walked me back to the Maiden Hall."

Jenae gasped. "He escorted you?"

Hadde glanced at the open-mouthed girls. "Not the entire way. But, yes, after his lesson."

The girls exchanged looks.

"Did I do something wrong?"

"No," Jenae replied. "It's just that, well, he showed you unusual favor."

"He was just being polite." Hadde shifted her weight from foot to foot under the girl's scrutiny. She certainly didn't want more enemies. "What are you working on?" She asked to break the silence.

"Our gowns for the Festival of Spring," Maret said. "It's coming up soon."

"Do you already have your gown?" Tira asked as she appraised Hadde's hunting attire.

"No," Hadde laughed. "I'm finished with Saladoran clothing. In any case, I wasn't invited."

"Oh, everyone is invited. It isn't a private party."

"The prince didn't mention the feast to you, did he?" Maret asked.

"No. Only archery." Relief spread across the girls' faces. Hadde laughed to herself. They had nothing to worry about except their party. "Your dresses are beautiful. Have fun at the ball." She turned to leave and then paused. "I'm going to go for a ride tomorrow. Would any of you like to come?"

"Go for a ride?" Maret asked.

"Yes. I would like to get out of the keep and see some of the city."

"Hadde, real ladies don't ride for pleasure." She made no effort to hide her disapproval.

"Ah, but I'm not a real lady," Hadde replied as she departed.

Hadde woke early the following morning and made her way to the stables. Stable hands were already tending to the Great Keep's horses. Puddle ran up to her as she made her way to Lightfoot. He was terribly thin, with straw from his night's sleep still in his hair.

"Is the lady going to ride?" he asked as he brushed off.

"I am. I wish to see a little of the city."

"I'll see to your horse," he said. He spoke with the accent of the commoners, but Hadde found she had no difficulty understanding them now.

"I think I'll take all three, Quickstep and Windwalker as well as Lightfoot."

"All three saddled?"

"No, just Lightfoot, unless... would you like to come with me? You could be my guide."

"Lady? Me?"

"Yes, you. And here, take this as well," she replied as she handed him a hunk of bread and a quarter of cheese folded in a cloth. She had another for herself.

"I—I thank you, Lady!"

"It's no problem. Thank you for taking care of my horses. Now let's go for a ride."

"I have to get permission," he said as he dashed off. Hadde went to Lightfoot and stroked her muzzle. She was there only a moment when Puddle returned with a man Hadde's age. "I'm the Stable Journeyman, Ambassador," he said. "Puddle says you wish to ride with him."

"I do."

"That doesn't seem proper. He's just an apprentice."

"I want him to come. It will be fun."

"I should check with the Stable Master."

"No," Hadde said as he turned to leave. She had had enough of Saladorans and their silly rules. "We're just going for a short ride."

"As you wish. But I'll let the Master know." He shot Puddle a dark look before giving her a curt bow and begging her leave to depart.

After saddling the horses, Hadde and Puddle mounted and rode into the courtyard. Dawn had just broken and only a few people were up and about. Hadde drew a deep breath of cold winter air and pulled her heavy cloak closer about her. When she noticed Puddle's ragged cloak, she insisted he return to the stable for something warmer. He returned with a horse blanket wrapped around his thin shoulders.

"You've nothing warmer?" Hadde asked. The nobles certainly didn't lack for food or winter attire.

"No, Ambassador. But I'll be fine. I don't notice the cold much." As they made their way to the gate a Knight of the House stepped in front of them. Two guardsmen stood nearby.

"Ambassador Hadde," the knight called out as she approached. "I'm Captain Palen. May I be of service?"

"I remember you," Hadde said. "You took me to the king on the day I arrived."

"I'm surprised you remember me," he said with no hint of humor. "You were in quite a state."

Hadde laughed. "Yes... I didn't expect to see the king that evening. But today I want to go for a ride. I'd like to see the city."

"But you must have an escort, Ambassador."

Hadde rubbed her face in frustration. "But I do." She turned to the stable boy. "Puddle, right?"

He smiled. "Yes, lady."

"There you are, Sir Palen. Puddle is my escort."

"That's not acceptable. You must be properly escorted."

"Properly escorted?"

"By a gentleman."

"Very well, Captain Palen." Hadde sighed. "You may come as well."

He looked startled. "Me? I cannot, I'm Captain of the Gate this morning." He paused. "Do you have the king's permission to leave the Great Keep?"

"I wasn't aware I needed it. Am I a captive?"

"I——"

"Captain, it's very cold out in this open courtyard and I would like to start my ride."

"One moment," he said, and turned to one of the guards. "Fetch my horse. And inform Sir Gorwin that he commands the gate until I return."

"You could ride Quickstep," Hadde offered as Palen turned back to her.

"I..." He glanced at the little horse. "Thank you, but I'll ride my own." He mounted as soon as the guard brought the horse up. They started out the gate, Hadde and the captain in the lead, Puddle and Quickstep a few strides behind.

"Where are we going?" Palen asked.

"I don't know." She scanned the broad square lined with three story mansions of white plaster and dark timbers. "I wanted to exercise my horses and thought I would see the city while doing so. I thought an early ride would be best as fewer people would be out." She directed Lightfoot down one of the three streets leading from the square.

"Begging the ambassador's pardon, but I was just about to be relieved of duty. I was going to break my fast and get some real rest."

Hadde held her temper in check. She hadn't asked for his company. "I'm sorry, Captain," she said. "I didn't know. You can go back now. I'll be fine."

"But you must be escorted."

"Captain Palen, you're free to do as you wish. I demand nothing of you." She examined one of the houses lining the street. A servant had just opened the shutters, revealing large glass-paned windows. Behind the windows hung heavy blue curtains decorated with gold thread. She glanced around and noticed that all of the homes surrounding the square were just as rich.

"What's wrong if I ride with Puddle? Isn't it safe?"

"It's safe, especially at this time of day and in this quarter of the city. But it wouldn't be proper. You're an ambassador and a woman."

Hadde turned down a side street. She shook her head at the sheer size of the city. The entire population of Long Meadow could fit into a row of four or five houses. "Why do women need protection?"

Palen stared at her. "Are you mocking me? You expect me to believe you don't know the answer?"

"But I don't."

He snorted. "Bah, they need protection because they're fair and weak and must be protected from harm."

Hadde stopped trying to hide her anger. "I'm neither weak nor foolish, Captain. I don't need protection. Did you know that I've been in a battle, that I've killed men and even varcolac?"

It took a few moments for him to reply. "I don't know the circumstances under which you accomplished those feats. But I do know that women are weak. It's the way they were created."

They entered a new part of the city. The streets narrowed and the buildings weren't as grand. Stores lined the street, each with a sign over the door depicting its wares. "How can you say women were created weak?"

"Just look at the gods," Palen replied. "Helna may have created the world, but what happened when her brothers arrived? They changed her creation as they wished, and what did she do to stop them? Nothing! She was powerless. Forsvar and Dromost were strong and she was weak."

"Her brothers fought and caused destruction. Wasn't it Helna who created a perfect world before they arrived?"

"Of course they fought. They fought to protect their charges. Just as men do today. Women produce new life while men fight to protect them."

As the sun rose above the rooftops, more people joined them on the streets. Hadde and her companions entered an alleyway of cobblers. The foot traffic moved aside as the riders approached, but otherwise they were ignored.

"Captain Palen, was it not Helna who banished the gods from earth? Didn't she compel Forsvar and Dromost to leave with her?"

"They saw what the war was doing to their followers. All three gods left on their own accord."

"That's not the way I learned it." Hadde spotted the river through a gap in the buildings. Turning right, they rode downhill toward the water. Buildings with cracked and crumbling facades lined the street. Piles of refuse lay in front of many of them. It reminded her of the manor where she and Belor had been attacked. She shook off the memory. Poor Belor, she thought. How much she missed him.

She sighed as she stared down the street. So much poverty so close to so much wealth. Why did they stand for it? They rode several hundred more strides when Hadde halted. A wretchedly clothed woman, bent nearly double and with her arms clutched across her body, shuffled past.

"Let's not tarry here," Palen said.

"Wait a moment." Hadde reached into her saddle bag and pulled out her bread and cheese. She dismounted and jogged up to the old woman.

The woman's eyes widened in fear and she shied back as Hadde approached.

"Please, take these," Hadde said, offering the food. The woman snatched the food from Hadde's hands and tucked it under her shawl. "Thank you, Lady," she said, glancing warily up and down the street.

"I wish I had more for you."

"More than I've had in days." The old woman shuffled off.

As Hadde remounted, Palen said, "What did you do that for? It will do no good."

"No good? She's starving."

"And you changed that?"

"For now."

"Maybe not." Palen nodded in the direction of the old lady. Three gaunt youths kept pace with her as she shuffled her way up the street. One shot Hadde an angry glare. The glance was cold and pitiless.

"They're up to no good," Hadde said, motioning toward the boys.

"And what would you have me do?"

"Protect her."

"You'd have me escort every old hag in the city?"

"If you won't help her, I will."

As she turned Lightfoot toward the trio, Palen reached out and grabbed her arm. "No, I'll do it," he said.

Hadde wrenched her arm free and charged the boys. They scattered with a shout. Two scurried down an alley. The third dashed across the street and into an abandoned building. The woman huddled against the wall in fear.

"A lot of good that will do," Palen said as Hadde rejoined him. "Come, let's return to the keep."

"We'll take her with us," Hadde said. She turned to look for the woman, but she had disappeared. The activity had caught the attention of nearby pedestrians. They stared at the riders, and more often than not the looks were unfriendly. "Why are they so angry?" Hadde asked.

"They forget their place. They think it unfair that they're common."

"It isn't?"

"Hardly. They don't realize how hard it is to be noble. They don't understand the pressure or the responsibility."

She shook her head and turned to Puddle. "Do you agree with the captain?"

The stable boy looked at her in surprise. "What ma'am?" His face reddened. "I'm sorry, but I wasn't listnin'."

Hadde sighed. "Puddle, do you think it's right that the nobles live in fine houses and eat good food while the poor are cold and hungry?"

The boy glanced at the knight and then at Hadde. "What do you mean?"

"Do you think it's fair the nobles live so much better than everyone else?"

"But they're nobles."

Hadde frowned at the ragged boy. He obviously didn't understand. "Puddle, would you rather live like a noble?"

"But I'm a stable boy."

"But would you not rather be a noble? A squire or a knight?"

"Ambassador, Hadde," Palen interrupted, "he knows his place. It's the way things are supposed to be."

Hadde sighed and looked away in frustration. Down the street a mass of people walked in their direction. At the front of the group marched a dozen men cloaked in white, most with hoods pulled over their heads. They appeared somehow familiar to her. After a moment it came to her. "Returnists."

The crowd included men, women, and children. All wore something white, even if it was as small as a white scrap of cloth tied around an arm. The mass slowly made its way toward the riders. The leaders chanted as they walked, but Hadde couldn't make out the words.

"We should get out of the way." Hadde said. The three horses took up much of the street.

"Only if we wish. If we choose to stay they will have to find another street."

"But there are only three of us."

"And they're commoners. I'll not make way for them unless it pleases me."

Hadde took in the size of the approaching crowd and felt a tinge of fear. "There are so many of them. I think we should move aside."

"Are you afraid?" Palen scoffed. "There is nothing to fear from them. They're just returning from their morning rituals down by the river." Turning to the crowd he shouted, "Hello Returnists, have another Gathering did we?"

The white-cloaked men in the front ranks stopped and the crowd halted behind them.

"The day is near, my lord!" the foremost of them called. "Join us so that the scales will be tipped in favor of righteousness."

Cries of "The Orb returns!" came from the crowd.

"Join you?" Palen asked. "Put on a white cloak and walk the streets?"

"Cast off the mantle of your rank. Cast off privilege. Desire is the root of evil! 'Depart from worldly desire and the Orb will come.' So said the Messenger."

"The Orb returns!" the crowd shouted.

"Join you?" Palen laughed. "Become a shoeless beggar and the Orb of Creation shall return?" He laughed again and turned his horse from the crowd. He opened his mouth to say something to Hadde when a voice called out, "Down with him! Down with the nobles!"

Palen's sword swept from its sheath as his horse wheeled into the crowd. "Who said that?"

"The nobles are Dromost's servants!" yelled another.

"You!" Palen pointed his sword at the man. "How dare you curse your superior?"

The Returnist spat at Palen.

"No! No!" the white-clad leader bellowed. "Be at peace! Anger brings anger!" His words were too late. Palen's sword flashed as he brought the flat of his blade down across the back of the Returnist. An angry roar went up from the crowd.

Someone leaped up and grabbed Palen's arm. Others pulled at his horse's bridle.

"No! Stop!" Hadde shouted and urged Lightfoot into the crowd. She reeled in pain as a chunk of ice hit her in the chest. Snowballs, ice, and rocks soon pelted both her and Lightfoot.

Hadde looked on helplessly as the rioters pulled the surprised Palen from his saddle. The Returnist leader grabbed Lightfoot's bridle and forced her back from the crowd. "Ride off!" he cried. "Flee!"

The crowd surged toward Hadde and Puddle. The leader turned and tried to hold them back, yelling over his shoulder, "Ride! Ride from here!"

"Go, Puddle! Run away!" Hadde shouted. As he rode off Hadde put her heels to Lightfoot's flanks and drove the little horse into the crowd. Men grabbed at her, but she kicked them away. She searched for Palen in the masses. His horse bucked and ran through the crowd.

A bloody staff rose and fell ahead of her. The crowd fell back from the ferocious blows, revealing Palen on the ground. His helm had been pulled from his head and blood matted his hair. "Die, noble, die!" The man screamed over and over as he rained blows upon the knight's corpse. Hadde turned away from the awful sight.

She tried to turn Lightfoot, but a Returnist had grabbed her bridle. Hadde drew her hunting knife and, leaning forward, slashed at the man. He fell back with a cry, clutching at a long gash in his arm. Lightfoot reared up and kicked another Returnist.

Shouting, Hadde slashed at those nearest her. They fell back, and she charged through the gap. Lightfoot raced up the street, the mob close behind her. Puddle was just ahead. A large cart blocked the way before him. Desperately, she searched for an escape and spotted an alley to their left. "This way!"

The few people in the alley leaped aside as they galloped past and onto a broader boulevard beyond. Hadde pulled Lightfoot in as Puddle stopped next to her. Red clad Knights of the House rode uphill toward them.

Pointing in the other direction, she said to Puddle, "Ride for the keep. Tell the captain of the guard what happened." The boy didn't need any more urging as he raced off on Windwalker, Quickstep in tow.

Hadde rode to the oncoming knights, blocking their path. They halted as she approached.

"What are you doing?" their leader demanded as she stopped in front of them.

"Sir Palen has been attacked. One street over." Hadde waved her arm in the direction of the attack.

"What are you talking about? Attacked? By whom?"

"A mob of Returnists. They pulled him from his horse."

"Captain, up there," a knight said. The Returnist mob poured from the alley Hadde had just left. They didn't pause, but immediately started in the direction of Hadde and the knights.

"Draw swords!" the captain ordered.

In unison a dozen swords sang from their scabbards.

The sight of the drawn blades caused the front ranks of the mob to pause. From behind them stones and rubbish flew at the knights. Hadde dodged a rock hurled at her head.

"Move to the rear," the captain ordered her. As soon as she was past, he ordered, "Escort, four abreast! Forward! As the dozen knights rode by, Hadde realized they weren't alone. Duke Giula of Arossa sat nervously on his horse, craning his head to see what was happening. Four knights remained with him.

"Ambassador, what's going on?" he asked. A tremendous shout prevented any response. Hadde watched as the knights plowed into the mass. Blades plunged and rose, blood-stained. It looked as if the knights would put the crowd to rout until more Returnists emerged from a second alleyway. Hadde, Giula, and his escorts were cut off.

For a moment the Returnists seemed not to know what to make of the situation. Then someone cried out, "The Orb returns! Slay the nobles!" Hadde watched, dumbfounded, as the unarmed horde attacked the knights.

Giula's escort charged, abandoning the two of them. "We must escape!" Hadde yelled.

Giula just stared at the carnage ahead.

"Duke! We must go!"

Knights hacked down at the masses around them. But as each Returnist fell, another took his place. A knight was pulled from his saddle. Hadde grabbed Giula's arm. The knights would soon be overwhelmed. "Now! We must ride now!"

He stared at her and nodded. Before he could move, a stone struck him in the side of the head. His eyes flew wide in pain and surprise. Hadde pulled him across Lightfoot's saddle before he could fall to the street.

Hadde kicked her heels and Lightfoot sprang away from the onrushing crowd. The little horse struggled under the weight of two riders, but managed to evade the closest pursuers. They rode downhill. Below them lay the river. No escape there. Hadde knew she had to make her way uphill to the safety of the Great Keep.

The sounds of battle diminished behind her as she rode. She entered a wide avenue, but panicked when it turned downhill. She saw the docks ahead of her. She turned right and rode on for a time, and then halted. She was lost. Giula lay still across Lightfoot's saddle.

Dilapidated buildings filled this section of the city. Many had collapsed. The few people she saw looked at her with suspicion. She listened for the sound of fighting but heard nothing. "Calm yourself." She took a deep breath. If she kept riding it was likely she would run into the mob again. She looked for the three bridges that spanned the river, but couldn't see any from the narrow street.

A shout from behind startled her. Without looking, she put her heels to Lightfoot's flanks.

Her hands clenched to keep them from shaking, Hadde slowly advanced to where King Boradin sat staring at her from his throne. She glanced at the others in the Great Hall. Orlos the Spiridus, looking pale and wrapped in heavy blankets, sat on a chair to the king's right. The queen lounged on her throne to the king's left. To her left stood Morin. A dozen nobles gathered at the base of the dais.

"Ambassador, I wish to thank you for saving Duke Giula of Arossa. It would have done great harm had he fallen."

"I wish I could have saved more, Your Majesty."

"Tell me what happened."

Hadde recounted the story of the ride, the street fight, and of finding her way back to the Great Keep. The king nodded as she spoke, his expression tight. The others watched her in silence.

"The Returnist leader tried to stop the crowd, but failed?" Orlos asked in a frail voice when she finished. He seemed much weaker than when she had last seen him.

"Yes."

"Such behavior isn't like them," Boradin said. "They have always been peaceful." He drummed his fingers on Forsvar's gold rim. "Ambassador, you're forbidden from leaving the Great Keep. I don't wish to lose you or your Spiridus Token. Sir Palen shouldn't have allowed you to leave."

"So I'm a prisoner now?" Hadde asked without thinking.

"Sir Palen is dead because you wanted to go for a ride," the king snapped. "It is for your own safety."

Palen is dead because your land is sick. Hadde held the words in check. The king waved her off and she retreated to the edge of the crowd.

From behind, Hadde heard booted feet striding the length of the Great Hall. She turned and saw Nidon. The champion wore full armor, his helm under his left arm, and his broadsword at his side. Blood spattered his clothing. Upon reaching the dais, he knelt.

"Rise, Champion. What is your report?" Boradin said.

"Your Majesty, the riot has been dispersed. I've sent the First Company of the House to assist the Guild Companies in restoring order. I have two prisoners with me."

"What were our losses?"

"Five Knights of the House, Your Majesty."

The king's right hand gripped his shield. "Bring in the prisoners."

Four knights marched through the door. Between them they dragged two men in blood-soaked white robes. Ten paces in front of the king, the warriors forced the prisoners to their knees.

"How were they taken?" Boradin demanded.

"Your Majesty," Nidon said, "as you ordered, I rode with four mounted lances to investigate reports of varcolac in the vicinity of Tenomas. As we rode over the Bridge of Heroes we became aware of commotion in the city below. We saw household knights fighting in the streets and rode to their aid. Unfortunately, by the time we arrived, four had been unhorsed and murdered by the mob.

"We charged into the crowd. Many were slain before they realized we were upon them. These two we took as prisoners as the others fled. Shortly after we charged, footmen of the Guild Companies arrived."

Hadde glanced from Nidon to the king. How could they be so matter-of-fact about a massacre? It seemed to mean nothing to them that scores had died.

"Thank you, Sir Nidon." The king turned his attention to the prisoners. Both had been roughly handled—their faces were purple and bruised and blood ran down the front of their tunics. The younger of the two shook uncontrollably, but the older appeared defiant. "What are your names?" Boradin asked.

"Your Majesty, my name—" the scared one started.

"Shut up!" his companion snarled. A knight struck the Returnist in the back of the head, sending him sprawling to the floor.

"No need for that, Sir Eslon," Boradin said. "Pull him up." The knight grabbed the bound prisoner and forced him back to his knees.

The king turned to the man who had started to speak and said, "Now, tell me, what is your name?"

"Don't tell…"

Boradin raised his hand and the older prisoner's body suddenly twitched. Hadde frowned as a wave of heat passed over her. The man gasped, unable to draw a breath. His eyes bulged as his flesh reddened. Blisters appeared on his skin and Hadde nearly gagged at the odor of burnt flesh. The audience of nobles stood silently and watched as he fell thrashing to his side. Even Morin looked on without emotion.

"Stop it! You're killing him," Hadde said.

"Silence," the queen hissed. "He deserves no less."

"My lungs!" The returnist howled in pain as he clutched at his chest.

Nidon's sword flashed from its scabbard and before Hadde could blink, the champion ran the returnist through. He gasped once and fell to the floor.

Boradin stared at Nidon for a moment, but Hadde couldn't read the king's expression. Was it anger? Nidon appeared not to notice as he wiped his sword clean on the returnists robe.

"Your friend is unwise," Boradin said to the remaining prisoner. The king's breath came heavy and sweat stood out on his brow. I've no patience for his behavior. Now, tell me your name."

Hadde looked from the prisoner to Boradin. He had just killed a man for refusing to talk. And the death meant nothing to him. What kind of man was this king?

"Speak!" Boradin commanded. Nidon grabbed the prisoner by his hair and forced him to look at the king. Even though the Returnist faced the king, his eyes were locked on his dead companion.

"Do you think you can pay attention now?" Boradin asked.

The prisoner quivered. A dark stain spread across his crotch and down his leg. "Y—Your Majesty, my name is D—Dulen. I'm a journeyman carpenter."

"Journeyman Dulen, you are a Returnist?"

"I am," he said, looking at the king's feet.

"Journeyman Dulen, why did the Returnists lay hands on my knights and the ambassador from Arossa?"

"It—it wasn't my idea, Your Majesty. I just went along to watch."

"Of course you did," Boradin replied, his voice more gentle. "But why was it done? I've not moved against the Returnists. Before today you've been peaceful and loyal subjects. And we share the same ultimate goal. I, too, wish for the Orb's return. Why have you turned on me?"

"Forgive me, Your Majesty." Dulen started to cry.

"Now there, there's no reason for that. Tell us, why did you attack?"

Dulen looked desperately at the people gathered around him. "We had a Gathering this morning, Your Majesty. Our leaders spoke to us and told us that the Messenger wasn't pleased."

"Who is this Messenger?"

"He's a divine creature sent by the Orb of Creation to instruct us. He speaks to our leaders and gives them the blessed message of the Holy Orb."

Hadde touched her pendant. What if the Returnists were right? What if the Orb were about to be restored to the world? She wished Landomere had spoken to her and told her what her part in all this was.

"Who is the Messenger? What is his name?" Boradin asked.

Dulen shook his head. "I'm sorry, Your Majesty. I'm not one of the worthy. I've never seen the Messenger."

"Dulen, was it the Messenger who asked you to attack my knights?"

"No, Your Majesty. Our leader said the Messenger told him the Orb wouldn't return until we had purified ourselves. He said our society is corrupt and that we must heal it in order to for the Orb to return."

"Corrupt? How?"

The man swallowed and looked around. "The nobility is corrupt and the Orb is withholding its grace from us because of them."

"And so the Messenger urged you to attack nobles?"

"No, Your Highness. But during the Gathering some of the faithful had become impassioned." He sobbed. "We're so hungry, Your Highness. Half of winter and we're so hungry. We saw those nobles and the Arossan and the crowd became enraged. Please, we're hungry and the nobles eat so well. And it's their fault the Orb won't return. Their impurity brought the Wasting upon us.

"That knight… when he rode into the crowd and struck one of us with his sword, it was too much to bear. Someone yelled out to kill him. That's when the fighting started."

King Boradin steepled his fingertips and nodded. "I've heard enough." He turned to Eslon. "Lock him up." The knights dragged both the prisoner and the corpse from the chamber.

"Your Majesty, if I may?" A richly dressed man stepped to the front

138

of the crowd.

Hadde gaped at the man. Despite his size, she hadn't seen him in the crowd. He was immensely fat. His meals would feed a dozen Landomeri, she thought.

Boradin nodded in his direction. "Guild Speaker Felden, what can you add?"

"Your Majesty, the Guild Masters have become concerned with the rising membership of the Returnists. Many of the apprentices and journeymen of the Upper City Guilds are now joining the cult. It has become a plague in the Lower City. There are renewed rumors of a Returnist boycott. In the past it was no great concern, but their numbers have been growing."

Orlos started to speak, but his words collapsed into a fit of coughing. The king went to him, waving a guard closer. "This is too much for him. Take him to his chamber." Boradin turned to a nearby noble. "Call for the surgeons."

The guard easily lifted Orlos, and carried him from the room. Hadde could still hear the ancient spiridus coughing as they disappeared down the hall. "May I go with him?" she asked. She didn't know what she could do, but she felt she had to be with him.

"No," Boradin said. "You'll stay here. Orlos must rest."

"I want to help him," she started from the room when a gust of wind suddenly struck her chest, knocking her back and taking the breath from her. Eyes wide with fear she looked to the king.

"You will attend me," Boradin said as he lowered his hand. "Or must I order Sir Nidon to hold you here?"

"I will stay, Your Majesty," she said, catching her breath. She returned to her place, but the nearby nobles shuffled a few strides from her. Awkwardly alone, she glanced up to see Morin looking at her. He gave her a reassuring smile and a slight wave of his hand that told her to stay calm.

"What do they wish to accomplish with a boycott, Guild Speaker?" asked the queen.

"Many Masters have forbidden their apprentices and journeymen from becoming Returnists, Your Highness. The Returnists would like to see these restrictions removed in order to gain more recruits in the guilds. They also wish us to reduce prices for commoners while raising prices for the nobles."

"This is absurd," Queen Ilana cried out. "Kill them! Just kill them and the problem will be done with."

The vicious snarl took Hadde by surprise. There was no doubt that the queen meant every word. Hadde understood having anger toward one's enemies—there was no love lost between the Landomeri and the Kiremi. But this was different. It was anger towards one's own. It was passionate hatred.

"Your Highness," Felden responded, "It isn't that easy. The Returnists have become popular. An attack could spark a revolt that could ruin many guilds and cost a fortune in gold."

"Guildsmen! Gold is all you care about," Ilana said. "We should take these Returnist leaders and put their heads on pikes throughout the city. That will teach them their place. That will teach them to obey." The queen stood, her face red with anger.

Hadde wondered at the deep well of anger that filled the queen. She was as bitter as any person Hadde had ever met. It stunned her that anyone could speak so casually about having people killed just to make a point.

"I must retire to my chambers," Ilana said. She glanced at the Guild Speaker and then at her husband. "I'm suddenly feeling quite ill." The assembled nobles bowed as she started for the door.

"Sir Nidon, please escort the queen," Boradin commanded. The knight nodded and followed Ilana as she departed.

Morin cleared his throat. "The Wasting, the scourge of the varcolac, the rise of the Returnists and the Messenger, the arrival of Hadde and her Spiridus Token, these are all signs." His gaze wandered over the audience. "Not only does the Orb of Creation exist, but the power of its wielder is rising. We do not have much time left."

"Obvious, but true none the less," Boradin replied. "Everything is meaningless except for the return of the Orb to its rightful hands. If I can find the Orb, all damage can be undone. Famine, revolt, plague, none of it matters. They will all end."

"And what will you do if the Orb does not return?" Morin asked. "What if it doesn't show up at the front gate and present itself to you?"

Boradin glared at his brother. "I'm not simply awaiting its return, as you well know."

"You do nothing but read the Ancients in hopes they will deliver it to you," Morin scoffed.

"And how do you help? You run off to adventure in the Three Duchies and kill Tysk barbarians, or hold archery tournaments. In the long term, you do nothing for us."

"And what have you accomplished? At least when I fight, Salador is preserved, the Wasting is held off, and hope is kept alive."

"This is why I give you permission to go off on your adventures. It preserves me from distraction." Boradin dismissed his brother with a wave of his hand.

"I never asked for your permission."

"You grow too bold, Brother."

"Will you roast me as well?"

"Maybe I should have. A long time ago."

Hadde shrank back from the angry exchange between the two brothers. She didn't know who was in the right, and felt horribly out of place amongst the powerful nobles. A thought struck her; was Morin an elementar as well? Who would be victorious in a contest between the two brothers?

Morin must have seen her move, and looked in her direction. His face was flushed with anger, but she thought she could see merriment in his eyes.

"Do you have the fire, brother?" Morin asked. "Do you?"

Chapter Fourteen

"Are you ready to learn to wield a sword?" Morin asked.

"I can't imagine having much use for one," Hadde replied. She unstrung Hawkeye and laid it by the gymnasium entrance. Each day for three days she had spent her mornings teaching Morin archery. He was an enthusiastic student and, unlike other Saladoran men, truly respected her. There were no derogatory comments about womanly weakness or innate inferiority. Instead there was praise of her strength and skill.

The afternoons and evenings with Maret and the other maidens were slow torture. Hadde didn't know how much more gossip and sewing she could take. It wasn't the sewing that bothered her—she did it often enough at home. So while the maidens worked on dresses Hadde sewed clothes for her parents. The Saladoran wool and linen were as fine as Hadde had ever worked with. By spring she could have clothes for all Long Meadow. *By spring.* The thought depressed her. Would the king even let her leave then?

More and more the Great Keep felt like a prison. And always there were thoughts of home nagging at her. She could escape, she thought. It wasn't as if she was under close guard. But what good would it do to return home empty-handed? And there was Morin. He had promised her aid.

"Let a sword lesson be some repayment for your archery lessons." He pulled arrows from his target and placed them in a large basket.

"That isn't necessary. In any case, you've already aided me. You saved me the day I appeared before the king in the Great Hall. What I really want...."

"What is it? My kingdom is at your feet," he said as he gave her a silly bow.

"You've already done a lot for me, and I hate to ask for more. But I would really like to see Orlos. I send notes to the king every day asking for permission, but there is never a response."

"Orlos isn't well," Morin said. "My brother fears doing anything that will tire him."

"I have to see him. He's the last spiridus."

142

"I'll see what I can do. But for now, let me give you a sword lesson."

"But I have my bow. And my knife if I need it." She patted her hip where her knife usually rested.

Morin laughed. "Forget something?"

Hadde reddened. "I always have it with me at home. I've grown lazy living in this keep."

"Your dagger is too short to take on a long blade. And your bow won't always be of use. What if it's pouring rain? What if a fierce wind is blowing? What if you're out of arrows? You can't always choose the circumstances of your battle." He picked out two wooden training swords.

"I've only been in one major battle," Hadde said. "No one got close enough to swing a sword. It was entirely decided by archery." She touched her head. "Although a varcolac once did do his best to brain me."

"Well, I've been in dozens of battles and swords were swung in every one of them." He gave a sword to her and crouched in a fighting stance. "This is how you hold the sword at the ready. Keep the point facing your enemy's throat. Now, you do it."

Hadde quickly lost track of time as Morin led her through the sword lesson. After teaching her several basic cuts and parries, he demonstrated practice patterns and exercises. "Good! Very good, Hadde. Enough?"

"No." She smiled. "I'm enjoying this." In fact she would gladly spend the entire day with him. Not only was he handsome and intelligent, but also, like Hadde, he didn't settle for half measures. He wanted to be the best in all he attempted. He had a passion about everything he did. And, she admitted, it made her happy that his passion for both teaching and learning centered on her.

"Very well," he said. "One last activity. Face me and we'll do the same patterns, but this time sword against sword."

"Am I ready for that?"

"Here." He led her to the wall and pulled down a padded aketon. "Just in case."

She took off her heavy hunting tunic and pulled on the aketon. As she finished, Morin placed a skullcap on her head.

"There, the shortest, prettiest knight I've ever seen." He paused. "What's wrong? Did I say something wrong? Your face—"

"No, I'm sorry. Your words reminded me of something a friend of mine once said." She thought back to when Belor had teased her about being a short, skinny, Saladoran knight in her uncle Segreg's smithy. "Beware, Sir Hadde," she said as she forced a smile.

Morin laughed with her. It was a pure laugh. One that hid nothing.

One that told her he enjoyed her company as much as she did his. The thought caused a twinge of guilt to twist in her.

"Let's begin," Morin said. "Take your training ready stance."

"Are you going to put on a helm?"

"You won't hit me. Pattern one—begin."

They went through the exercises slowly at first, gaining speed with each evolution. It wasn't long before Hadde was soaked with sweat. She didn't care. The challenge and the thrill were worth the discomfort.

Morin stopped. "Why are you grinning like that?"

"I'm enjoying this. You're very good, Prince Morin. You haven't made a mistake yet."

"And you're as good a student as you're a teacher, Ambassador Hadde of Landomere." He gave her a curt bow. "Have you had enough? Here, I'll take your sword and helm."

"Thank you." She handed him the gear. "Who's the finest swordsman in Salador?"

"With a sword, only Nidon is my better. As is my brother with magic."

"So… you're an elementar as well?"

"Not really. Not like my brother. I'm better with one of these." He raised the blade in a salute.

"I've seen Sir Nidon fight. He's a great warrior." Hadde shrugged off her aketon as Morin returned their blades to the rack. The air was cold after the heat of exercise.

"Nidon is big, but—"

Hadde glanced up and saw Morin staring at her. She looked down and saw that her fine linen shirt had completely soaked through with sweat and her breasts were clearly visible through the fabric.

He turned away. "Excuse me. I didn't mean to look."

"No, I'm sorry for embarrassing you." She snatched her woolen tunic from where it lay on the floor. "We Landomeri are not self-conscious, and I forget myself sometimes." She pulled her tunic over her head. "You can look now."

"I apologize again. It wasn't chivalrous of me to stare that way."

"Please, Morin, there is no reason to apologize. I'm not offended."

"Why are you grinning?"

"Mighty Prince Morin." Her smile broadened. "Challenged only by his brother's magic, Nidon's sword, and Hadde's breasts." She couldn't help laughing. "I think if I ever go into battle with a Saladoran I shall go naked."

She grinned at his wide-eyed reaction. "The chivalrous ones won't dare to look at me and the others will be too distracted to hit me. I would be perfectly safe."

"I wouldn't advise it."

"Oh, I've done it——" She clamped her mouth shut, but the words had already escaped.

He stared at her with one eyebrow raised. "Oh, you've done what?"

Hadde caught herself whistling a happy tune as she made her way back to the Maiden Hall. She laughed at herself. What was Morin doing to her? An image of Belor passed through her mind. The two men were much alike. Both were confident men of action. Both thought they could make the world a better place. Or, at least, Belor had believed those things. The smile fell from her face at the thought.

As usual, a guard had arrived to summon Morin for some meeting or another. At least he had assured her there would be another archery lesson the following day. As Hadde started up a spiral stairway, a female servant carrying a lamp appeared around a bend and yelped, "You scared the life out of me."

"I'm sorry. I wasn't paying attention," Hadde said.

"You just popped up out of the dark. How could you see?"

"It isn't that dark," Hadde replied. "It's never so dark you can't see."

The servant gave Hadde a wide berth as she slipped past her down the stairs. "In this hall it is."

Hadde shrugged. Some of the interior halls were dark, especially those in the lower levels of the keep. But it was never *that* dark. Maybe the Saladorans were dark-blind. She chuckled at the idea.

Hadde continued up the stairs. She was one level below the Maiden Hall when she saw lantern light approaching from ahead. An open door exited the stairwell to her left.

"Coming up!" Hadde warned.

Waltas slammed into her. His left hand gripped her right wrist and pressed it against the wall. His right forearm crushed her neck. With her free hand she pushed against his arm, trying to stop him from choking her. She tried to cry out, but only a gasp escaped her.

He held his face close to hers. "You're coming with me." He jerked his head toward the door behind him.

There was no Nidon to rescue her this time. Hadde jammed her thumb into Waltas' eye. As he fell back she wrenched her arm free and leapt down the stairs. Her legs flew over the steps, but not fast enough on the tight spiral. The sound of Waltas's pursuit echoed after her.

Suddenly, she found herself at the bottom of the stair. She had missed the door that led to the Weapons Gymnasium. A straight hallway stretched in front of her. She was lost.

"Halt!" Waltas yelled from above. "You can't hide there in the dark." She heard some movement and then all went quiet.

Breathing deeply, she looked up the stairs for any sign of the earl. She didn't dare go up. The hall behind her was dank and narrow. A foul stench wafted through it. Ice crawled down her spine.

Dim light appeared from above. He was creeping down the stairs. Hadde scrambled down the hall, looking for some escape. She cursed herself a fool for not bringing her knife. And Morin had her bow. *What an idiot I've become!* She had been thinking too much of Morin and now she might pay for it with her life. Hadde passed several empty chambers, praying to Helna for a way out.

She glanced over her shoulder as she arrived at an intersection. The bright glow of a lantern neared the base of the stairs. She ducked into a side hallway as Waltas appeared. He held a lantern in one hand and a dagger in the other.

Hadde didn't wait. She padded down the corridor. It was dank and dark and reeked. No one had been there in ages. Like the last hall, there were empty rooms to either side. It came to a dead end.

She slipped into a room before Waltas reached the intersection. The room stank of excrement. Hadde glanced around for some way out, but saw nothing but rubbish and a low stone bench. A rat scurried across it and through a hole. A privy.

Hadde glanced out the door. Waltas stood in the intersection. For a moment she thought he might choose another hall. Her hopes fell as he headed in her direction. She scanned the room for anything she might use as a club or a staff. Nothing.

Hadde crept to the privy. A rotten wooden lid covered it. She looked through the hole and saw a short drop to a pile of rubble. It hadn't been used in years. A tunnel led off to one side.

Quiet footsteps approached. With one last glance over her shoulder, Hadde pulled the wooden cover from the privy. Not waiting to see if Waltas heard, she lowered herself over the side and dropped into the hole.

Pebbles clattered beside her as she landed on the fallen masonry. A narrow gap in the wall led to a stone walkway running next to a ditch filled with a sluggish stream. She gagged at the awful odor and looked above her. She had no choice.

Breathing through her mouth, Hadde slid through the opening and onto the path. Turning right, she crept carefully along the narrow sewer walkway. A darting movement in the darkness ahead caused her to leap back and give a startled shout. She crouched, ready to flee, as a large rat jumped into the stream and swam to the other side.

Hadde sighed and looked behind her for any sign of Waltas. None yet, but he must have heard her. She continued along the path, rats scurrying everywhere. After a few dozen strides, the ditch beside her emptied into an even larger stream. The stream flowed to the right and Hadde crept in that direction.

The tight confines of the tunnel pressed in around her. Ahead, the path ahead had collapsed, partially filling the stream and creating a small dam. The path continued on the far side of the gap. A long jump, and not one to miss.

Rocks clattered behind her. She turned, and to her dismay, she saw the glow of lamplight reflecting off the walls.

Hadde glanced at the stream of muck she had to leap. If she missed, Waltas would surely be on her before she could climb out. She heard the sound of his rapid approach. She didn't dare risk it.

Grabbing a piece of rubble in either fist, she turned to face her pursuer. Hadde's hurled rock caught Waltas flush in the face as he turned the corner. He reeled against the wall, lost his balance, and fell into the ditch. Darkness engulfed the sewer as his lantern followed him.

Retching, he emerged from the filth only to be struck by the second of Hadde's rocks. Crying out in pain and anger, he heaved himself onto the path where he knelt, coughing and gagging.

If only she had her knife she might take him on. Hadde picked up two more rocks. She heaved one at Waltas, striking him in the shoulder.

Choking out a gasp of pain, he blindly scrambled on all fours toward the corner. Following, Hadde kept up a furious barrage of stones. She clenched her jaws as she threw each missile, wishing that she could do more harm, cause him more pain. He scrambled away from her, finally climbing through the privy hole.

She halted just below him. She heard him, still choking and coughing, on the other side of the narrow gap. She couldn't follow him through. *Wait here until he leaves or continue through the sewers?* She crouched and listened. He was waiting. But how long?

"You're dead, you bitch!" Waltas roared into the tunnel. "I'm going to tear your head off!"

She stepped back as his shout echoed off the tunnel walls. "Why don't you come back down? This is where your kind lives," she shouted in reply. His curses followed her as she crept back down the sewer path. The rat still sat on the dam, cleaning itself.

Striding a few paces back, she took a deep breath and sprinted forward. Planting her foot, she leapt the stream, her head narrowly missing the low ceiling. Her feet hit the path, but her momentum carried her into the wall. Rebounding, she flailed her arms for balance. Her heels slipped over the edge and loose gravel gave way under her feet. Madly contorting her body, she regained her balance.

She moved on. Twice the sewer branch she followed connected with larger streams. And twice again she was forced to leap a gap or retrace her steps to find an alternate route. It wouldn't have been as bad if she had grown accustomed to the cloying stench. But instead, her stomach roiled and her eyes burned with the fumes.

Rubbing her hands across her goose-pimpled forearms, she stared at the stone ceiling above her. She imagined the weight of the tons of stone above her. What if she couldn't get out?

She continued down the path a short distance when a light appeared in front of her. *Lamplight.* Her heart thumped in her chest. Could Waltas somehow have gotten in front of her?

Hadde hid in a small side tunnel and watched the light approach. It wasn't Waltas, but a gray-haired man pushing a wheelbarrow filled with tools. He was strides away when Hadde called out, "Hello! Can you help me?"

"What? What's that?" the man cried out, nearly dropping his load into the ditch. The lantern, attached to the front of the cart, swayed wildly.

"I'm sorry, I didn't mean to scare you. I'm lost."

"Who's there?" He pulled a shovel out of his wheelbarrow and held it defensively. He spoke with the heavy accent of a commoner. "Who's out there?"

Hadde stepped into the lamplight. "I'm lost. I need help finding my way out of here."

He stepped a few paces backwards as she approached the outer edges of the light. "Where did you come from?"

"I was chased here by a man who wanted to harm me."

"How—how did you find your way? It's pitch dark in here and you've no light." He looked closely at her.

Hadde didn't understand what he was getting to. Did all Saladorans have bad vision? Was that why they were so poor at archery?

"It's darker than Dromost's soul in here. How come you didn't fall in?"

"What do you mean?" Hadde asked.

"What are you? Some kind of spiri..." He took another look at her. Hadde held her hands wide to show that she was no threat. "I'm no spiridus. Just a visitor from Landomere. I'm lost and I need a way out."

He eyed her suspiciously. "You were being chased?"

"There is a man in the keep who wants to hurt me. I'm afraid he could be waiting for me."

"Where did you find your way into the sewers?"

As best she could, Hadde described the route she had followed. He nodded in understanding. "I could take you out of the sewers and you could make your way back through the city. Or I know of another way into the keep from the sewers."

"I would rather not go through the town," Hadde replied, thinking of the Returnists.

"I'll show you out, but we've got to go to my hut first. I got to get more candles." Hadde glanced into the wheelbarrow as he removed the lamp pole. He cackled. "Give you the grand tour, I will."

"What is it you do down here?" Hadde asked.

"I'm the shit farmer."

Her brows arced. "A what?"

"In the old days the keep's shitters used to drain themselves. Used to run down the sewers all the way to the river and nobody had to do a thing. Some of 'em still work but many is clogged. I come in and shovel out the shit traps."

"That's an awful job. Why do you do it?"

He cackled. "You wouldn't believe what I find." He reached into a wooden pail hanging from one of the cart handles. "Just found this today." He held up a metallic object.

"What is it?"

"Come and take a look."

Hadde shook her head.

"Well, I'll tell you then. It's a silver brooch. There I was, shoveling away, and plop, this here brooch lands right next to me." He cackled again. "A good day to be a shit farmer. You know, the shit farmer before me, he found a whole sack of silver. He was cleaning...."

Hadde turned at a sound behind her. The tunnel was clear, but she was certain that she had heard something. A rat? "I'm sorry," she whispered, interrupting the shit farmer's tale. "The man I spoke of, he could still be here."

"Don't you worry. I'll get you out."

Hadde warily made her way back to the Maiden Hall. She didn't think it likely Waltas would be roaming the corridors of the Great Keep, but she wasn't about to let herself be caught again. Despite her filthy, disheveled appearance, she kept to the more populated areas of the keep. She ignored the stares of those she passed by, alert only to any sign of Waltas. She only felt some security when she spotted the two squires on duty at the entrance to the Maiden Hall.

She stopped in front of one of the squires. "I've been attacked by Earl Waltas. I wish to speak to Sir Nidon."

His eyes widened as he glanced her up and down. "Yes, Ambassador, would you like an escort to take you to him?"

"No," she snapped. "I want him to come to me. I'm covered in filth." She stormed past the squires. "They promised me!"

But it was her fault, she thought. She had become too comfortable in this strange world. She had let her guard down. It wasn't Landomere, where she knew the sounds of the forest and when something was wrong. This was Salador, where knives waited around corners in cold stone corridors.

She passed two maidens talking by an open door. One of them said something to her, but Hadde paid them no heed. Passing her own room, she yanked open the door to the bathing room. Gran gasped at Hadde's sudden appearance.

"Hadde," the servant said, "a maiden is using—"

"She'll have to wait." Hadde pulled her tunic off as she strode past the privacy screen. A maiden screeched with surprise and pulled her unbuttoned dress back together. Hadde barely slowed as she stripped off her leggings and moccasins and stomped up the stairs and splashed into the hot tub. She didn't spare a glance as the maiden fled the room. The world went silent as she submerged under the water.

Hadde stayed under as long as she could, cocooned in heat and isolation. She rose, sputtering to find Gran glaring at her, wagging her finger in Hadde's direction. "You shouldn't have done that," Gran scolded. "Sent the poor girl off crying."

"I've been attacked," Hadde shot back.

Gran paused for just a moment. "Was it that little one who attacked you?"

"No, it was—"

"Then you've no right to treat her that way."

Hadde stared into the old woman's eyes for a moment before sinking back. "They think they can do anything. They think everything belongs to them."

"It's the men you're talking about, aye? Well, some of 'em do. I spent years dodging the worst of them. Suppose I'm lucky now, too old for that sport."

"I won't let him catch me again," Hadde said, quieter. The hot water had sapped some of her anger. "I'll kill him."

Gran put her hands on her hips. "You can't do that. You can't go killing nobles. I heard that Sir Nidon's to have at him. That earl's as good as dead unless he gets real lucky. But you kill a noble and your life

150

is forfeit. They'll hang you."

"They said they'd keep him away from me."

"You tell Sir Nidon what happened. He's one of the good ones. At least as good as they come. Now, get washed up and apologize to poor Maiden Tira. I'll fetch some clothes for you."

"Thank you Gran. I'm sorry."

"Don't be sorry to me. An angry nekkid girl is no worry to me."

Gran brought Hadde a towel and her red dress rather than let the naked, wet Landomeri walk down the hall to her room. Gran also brought word that both Nidon and Morin had arrived at the Maiden Hall.

Hadde quickly dressed and then dried and brushed her hair. Maret entered the bathing room just as Hadde finished. "I just heard," Maret said. "Are you hurt?"

"No, just angry."

"Prince Morin and Sir Nidon are here. Sir Astor as well. You mustn't keep them waiting."

"I know," Hadde said, letting some of her impatience show.

"Would you mind if I escorted you to them?"

Hadde shrugged. "I think they are just at the end of the hall. But let's go." She ignored the many maidens who loitered in the hall or by their doors. However, she heard the words *Prince Morin* uttered more than once. Lady Celena passed Hadde and Maret in the opposite direction scolding the girls back into their rooms.

The two squire guards stood at rigid attention in front of Morin and Nidon. Morin, arms crossed, paced back and forth. Nidon stood rigid, hands clasped behind him. Astor rested with his back against the wall. Morin looked Hadde up and down as she approached.

"Are you hurt?" Concern crossed his face.

"No. I escaped. But just barely."

"I've failed you again," Nidon said. "I didn't see... I can't imagine what he was thinking."

"Tell us what happened, Hadde—wait," Morin started. "Maiden Maret, thank you for bringing Ambassador Hadde to us. You may retire."

Maret curtsied. "Perhaps I could stay and comfort the Ambassador."

"She will be fine, thank you."

"As you wish, My Prince."

Morin's face grew grim as the maiden departed. "Hadde?"

"After I left you Waltas attacked me on the stairwell. I broke free, but took a wrong turn and ended up in a cellar. He pursued me and forced me to flee into the sewer. I lost him there."

Morin turned to Nidon. "Have him detained."

Nidon nodded, but his brow furrowed. "Ambassador Hadde, did

151

anyone see him?"

"I don't know. I passed a servant on the stairwell, and maybe she saw him. The shit farmer helped me find my way back into the keep, but never saw Waltas. What would it matter?"

"I need just cause to detain him," Nidon said. "He's an earl. I cannot just clap him in irons."

"But I just told you—he attacked me."

"It's not enough."

"What? Prince Morin, you can order it, can't you? Or your brother? He's the king!"

"Meaning no insult to Ambassador Hadde," Nidon said, "but she is common. A common accusation isn't enough."

"My brother declared her an ambassador and a baroness...."

"Not enough, I think," Nidon said. "Those are just honorary, she's not really a baroness. I'll take it to the Council of Judges."

"And my brother's relations with the council are a frayed rope," Morin said.

"What is all this?" Hadde demanded. "I don't understand. Can't a king do as he wishes?"

Astor laughed. "No," he said, speaking for the first time. "Especially not a weak king."

Nidon shot Astor a stern look. "The strength or weakness of the crown is not of importance. It's the law that matters. Hadde, can you imagine the chaos that would reign if commoners could bring up false charges against nobles? Who would have the experience to rule?"

"Oh, well we couldn't have that, could we?" She turned from Nidon to Morin. "Can't you do something, Morin?"

"I'll tell you what we can do," Astor said, as he moved away from the wall. "We could make Earl Waltas disappear."

"What are you saying?" Nidon demanded.

"I'm saying there are ways of dealing with this problem."

"We are Knights of Salador," Nidon said. "I'll hear no more of this, Sir Astor."

"These are difficult times," Astor said. "A good end justifies—"

Morin put up his hand. "Nidon, have eyes placed on Earl Waltas," he said. "And see if the judges will swear out a warrant." He fixed Hadde with his eyes. "I will speak with Waltas. He will bother you no more."

Chapter Fifteen

Hadde stood outside Orlos' chamber, her two knight-escorts taking position with the guards already standing at the spiridus' door. Despite her enthusiasm to speak with the spiridus, part of her mind still roiled on the day's turbulent events. She missed the simplicity of Landomere. She missed her family and Belor.

A rap on the door, and a muffled "enter" interrupted her thoughts. A guard opened the door and she stepped into the simply furnished room. The only luxuries were an oversized fireplace and a large stuffed chair. Books and papers lay piled on the table, chairs, and floor. The door closed behind her.

"I was told..." Hadde's gaze swept the room, but she didn't see anyone. There were no other doors. A wardrobe stood to her right.

She yelped as Orlos appeared next to her. "You scared me. You appeared from nowhere."

"Now that doesn't make any sense," he said with a grin as he shuffled past, a heavy blanket draped across his narrow shoulders. "How can someone be nowhere? Come in, sit down."

"Thank you for inviting me," Hadde said, her heart still thumping in her chest. She looked to her left, to where the fireplace stood. How had she not seen him? "I've asked many times to see you, but received no response."

"Sit, Hadde." He lowered himself into his stuffed chair, and waved her to a padded stool next to him. "I have been ill, as I am certain you have noticed. I'm afraid that I am not long for this world. The weight of centuries hangs heavily on me." He rubbed his temple with a bone-thin hand.

His hand trembled as he placed it back on his lap. "Isn't there anything that can be done for you?" Hadde asked as she sat.

"There is no cure for age—or at least for my kind of age." He gave a rueful smile and a slight shrug. "But I didn't ask you here to tell you of my woes. It is you I want to hear about. Things are difficult for you here," he said.

"It is strange here. Everything is strange." She smoothed her red dress across her lap. "You know of Earl Waltas?"

"I do. And you must be careful of him. Don't trust too much in Saladoran law to protect you. Politics and power always trump law."

"Prince Morin and Sir Nidon have said they will help me. And Nidon is to fight Waltas soon."

Orlos stared into the glowing embers of the fire. "Earl Waltas is entangled in the web of politics. That is why Nidon brought him here. They won't fight if Nidon accepts his apology."

"If Waltas apologizes to Nidon? I'm the one he should apologize to."

Orlos smiled, and reaching out, patted her on the arm. His hand was withered with age and trembled. "Sir Nidon won't accept the apology unless you accept the apology."

"Never, I'd——"

"At what price would you accept an apology? Five mules loaded with grain and salt? Ten?" Orlos took a deep breath and stifled a cough.

Hadde looked down at her hands. Was that what it would come to? The aid she needed for her people if she accepted an apology. She would do it, of course. To Dromost with Earl Waltas. But how much would she ask for? She glanced back at the spiridus. "Prince Morin said he would try to help."

"Hmmm…Prince Morin. You are enjoying your time with him?"

Hadde shifted in her seat. She hoped he couldn't see her blush in the dim light. "He was kind to me in the Great Hall. And he reminds me of someone I loved. He is filled with passion and thinks he can make the world a better place."

"You are teaching him archery."

"Yes. He's learning, but he'll never be Landomeri. He speaks a lot of military tactics and strategy."

"And gets to pass his winter mornings with a pretty Landomeri girl."

Hadde bit her lip as she struggled for a response.

"I think you will soon have bigger things to think of." He cleared his throat. "The archer's offspring shall slay the sun," Orlos intoned.

"Excuse me?"

"The archer's offspring shall slay the sun. It's a fragment, Hadde. Part of an ancient prophecy." He gave a short, rasping cough before continuing. "Or it might be hunter's offspring. The translation is not certain."

"You've discovered something?" Hadde leaned closer to the wizened spiridus. "You've learned the meaning of my Token?" She touched the pendant as she spoke.

"Perhaps. It's impossible to be certain. I discovered it while reading the Blind Prophecies. Much of it has been destroyed or reads as gibberish. But this one fragment stuck out."

"What does it mean?"

"That is why I called you here. What do you think it means?" He stared at her with piercing gray eyes.

Hadde shook her head. "It means nothing to me."

"Do you have any children?"

"No."

Orlos drummed his fingers against the chair's arm. "Do you know what *the sun* could mean?"

"Helna is the sun goddess and the life bringer. But an archer can't slay a goddess."

"But her symbol is the Orb of Creation."

"I still don't know what it could mean," Hadde said.

"Another name—an ancient name—for the King of Salador is the Sun King."

"An archer's child will slay the king?"

"Or destroy the Orb."

"You think I'm the archer?" A chill crept up her arms.

"You bear the Spiridus Token—Helna's Orb."

"But I've no child."

"Not yet."

"The Wasting has left me barren. Like many others, I can't bear children."

"So I heard." He paused a moment and then said, "Perhaps you are the offspring that shall slay the sun. You father is an archer, correct? And a hunter? A Saladoran wouldn't think a woman a threat, but I know better." He chuckled, but it turned into a fit. Hadde held his hand as the coughing wracked his body.

"Can I get you something?" she asked as the fit subsided. He waved her to a mug sitting by the fire. Orlos drank and then sat for a moment contemplating the fire. "After your archery display, they won't make the mistake of assuming you are a harmless woman," he said.

Hadde wrapped her arms around her body. The room was cold and yet the huge fireplace held only a small fire. "Let me stoke the fire," she said.

"No, leave it for a moment." He waved her back. "I've not shown this prophecy to the king. I'm concerned how he might react."

"But—" A knock at the door interrupted her.

"I was afraid this might happen. I must cut our discussion short."

"No... I have to learn more. I need to speak with you." Hadde glanced at the door, wishing the visitor would leave. "I've waited so long to speak with you."

155

"I know, Hadde, but I am meeting Prince Handrin. I promise to see you again, and soon. Stay for a time with us." He turned to the door and called, "Enter."

The door opened and round-faced boy of seven or eight stepped into the room. He stared at Hadde. She smiled back. Handrin wore rich clothes of red embroidered with silver and was as chubby as any child Hadde had ever seen. Certainly no Landomeri child ate as well as he did. A knight stepped into the room behind him and gave Hadde an appraising look.

"Thank you, sir knight," Orlos said. "He'll be safe with us." The knight nodded and backed out.

"Prince Handrin," Orlos said from his chair, "I present to you Ambassador Hadde of Landomere."

She stood, "I'm glad to meet you... Your Majesty?" She hadn't intended for it to come out as a question.

"Call him Prince Handrin," Orlos said.

"Are you a spiridus?" the prince asked. He wore a red outfit that exactly copied those of the Knights of the House.

"No, Prince Handrin."

"Not entirely correct," Orlos said. "There's a fair amount of spiridus in you."

Hadde turned to him, surprised at his comment. "What do you mean?"

"I see it in you," he said. "The spiridus and the Landomeri used to be on very... ah... friendly terms," he said with a glance at Handrin.

"You aren't wearing those strange clothes," Handrin interrupted. "And what's that on your face?"

"She usually dresses in Landomeri attire, Handrin," Orlos said. "But not this evening. And many Landomeri have face-marks. Now, be a young gentleman and greet Ambassador Hadde properly."

The Prince faced Hadde and, bowing at the waist, said, "It is my pleasure to meet you, Ambassador Hadde of Landomere."

"Very good." Orlos looked at Hadde. "Stay a little longer. You will enjoy this. Handrin, I grow chilly. Will you tend the fire?"

"Yes, Master Orlos." The child stepped closer to the fire.

"What are you doing?" Orlos asked, his tone sharper than before. He pulled his blankets closer around him.

"I'm tending the fire, Master Orlos."

Orlos sighed and then choked back a cough. "Perhaps I was not specific enough. Would you tend the fire, young elementar?"

Handrin grinned. "My apologies, teacher."

Hadde watched as the boy narrowed his eyes and leaned closer to the fire.

"Remember," Orlos said. "The four elements are all tied together. All linked by magic. You are an elementar, and your will controls that magic. Think about what you wish to accomplish. The greater the task, the greater the energy that will be taken from you. Now, how will you tend the fire?"

"I'll use my will and urge the element of fire to consume the log."

"Hmmmm... I suppose you could do it that way."

Handrin took a deep breath but Orlos' dramatic sigh interrupted him. Hadde wanted to laugh at the old spiridus. The prince let out his breath.

"I can make it burn," Handrin said.

"I am certain you can," Orlos replied, but he looked unconvinced. Hadde watched as the prince clenched his fists and stared into the fire. Hadde felt the hair on the back of her neck prickle.

"Are you trying to kill us?" Orlos asked.

"But what do—what do you want me to do? I'm trying to make the log burn brighter!"

"What element are you using?"

"Fire."

"Is it the only element?" Orlos settled deeper into his blankets. "Is it the only element that makes things burn?" Hadde could see the child puzzling over the question. The prince rocked from side to side as he thought. "You're not going to squeeze water from the stones of the fireplace?" Orlos asked.

The boy grinned, pursed his lips, and gently blew at the fire. Hadde saw the flames react to a sudden onrush of wind. The flames fanned higher. It was as if a large bellows blew into the hot coals.

"Why did you use the element of air?" Orlos asked. Hadde watched as the prince relaxed. The wind stopped but the fire crackled brightly.

"Master Orlos, I used air because it's the easiest to master. It also uses the least strength."

"Why else?"

The boy paused a moment and then said, "It's the complement of fire."

"Well done." The spiridus pulled his blankets up to his chin. "But it is still chilly. Throw another log on the fire, young prince."

"Master Orlos?" Handrin asked as he gathered wood. "Is it possible that my magic could get weaker?"

"What do you mean, Handrin? It is like any exercise. As you practice and study the skills you will get stronger. If you exhaust yourself your magic becomes weaker. With old age and illness it will become weaker. You won't reach the prime of your power for many years."

"But when I practice lately, it is harder and harder to do. The flames are weaker, the wind is weaker——"

"Are you ill?"

"No, Master Orlos."

"I will speak to your father. He knows the elements better than any. Don't worry yourself."

But to Hadde it seemed Orlos was worried. "Are there only three elementars?" she asked.

"Just the three: father, brother, and son. The magic is passed through the bloodline, but not always for certain. Less frequently since the Orb of Creation was lost."

"And elemental magic cannot end the Wasting?"

Orlos shook his head. "No form of magic can end it. There used to be other forms of magic besides elemental——blood, song, spirit, but they are long gone. Only the Orb of Creation can save us. And it is out there."

"My father will find it." Handrin said. "He is a great king."

"Yes, yes he is," Orlos said.

But Hadde wondered if he meant it.

"You might want to consider leaving Salador," Orlos had said before she departed.

"But the king hasn't given me permission."

"Hadde, if he discovers the Blind Prophesy and deems it a threat, you will wish you had."

"You were with Prince Morin again. Before Earl Waltas attacked you." Maret said.

"What?" Hadde shook herself back to the present. She and Maret sat in Hadde's room, it was late evening and exhaustion from the long day's events settled over her. Half a loaf of bread and a slab of butter lay on a tray beside her. She didn't want it. Guilt washed over her. Weeks ago not wanting food was unimaginable. She was certain no one in Long Meadow would pass up food.

"You were with Prince Morin today," Maret said.

"Yes, he's becoming proficient with a bow."

Maret buttered her toast, but pressed so hard the bread ripped. "I don't know why he would want to learn the bow. It's a peasant weapon."

Hadde glanced at Maret and then back into the fire. She didn't want to talk archery. "That's what most Saladorans think. But he sees some potential in it."

"Do you like him?" Maret dropped her toast onto the tray.

"Like him? He's been very kind to me. Next to you, he has treated me better than any Saladoran."

Maret stared into the fire. "People are starting to talk."

"About what?"

"Don't act as if you don't know."

"Maret, speak plainly to me. We're friends. You can tell me."

The young girl glared at Hadde. "They're talking about you and Prince Morin. They say you've used a spiridus spell on him to make him love you."

Hadde laughed. "That's absurd. Who is saying these things?"

"People."

"Maret, the prince does not love me. He wants to learn to wield a bow." She paused. Maybe it wasn't exactly the truth. There was some spark between them. Morin hadn't done anything overt, but she had felt the growing attraction. "What would you have me do? Sit in my room? There is little else of interest in this place."

"Well, that isn't what I've heard. I've heard—"

"You're hearing it from me. The prince and I are not in love." She laughed, hoping that it sounded more convincing than her words. "After all, what Saladoran man would be interested in a barbarian from the forest?"

"Well... I guess you're right. But you should be careful."

More warnings.

Chapter Sixteen

"Let me show you something new, Hadde." Morin placed Hawkeye next to the Weapons Gymnasium door. "I told you that you needed to study the broadsword in case you lost your bow. But what if you lost your sword as well?"

"You're going to tell me running away isn't an option." She smiled at Morin. Two days more with him had convinced her that she was, in fact, deeply attracted to the prince. He was much like Belor in his enthusiasm and conviction that the Wasting would end and that they could make the world a better place. But there was something more to Morin, a sense of underlying power—even danger, which she had never felt with Belor.

"No, running away isn't an option."

"I would use my knife, I suppose."

"And how will that go? You with your little blade against my sword."

"Not well." She smiled. "That's why I wanted to run."

"This is where harness fighting comes in. Harness fighting is simply wrestling in armor. It's used when you've lost your weapon or you wish to subdue an enemy without killing him."

Morin took a training sword, shield, and dagger from the wall. He handed the dagger to Hadde while he stood in front of her with the broadsword.

"You see how unfair it is?"

She nodded.

"Now if you wait for me to attack, you're finished. You have to attack me. But that isn't easy. I can fend you off with my shield and you've this big butcher's blade to worry about. If you could get me to the ground, it would be much easier. My sword would be useless and I would be vulnerable to stabs to the eyes, under my coif, or under my armpits. Put your dagger down."

He placed his sword and shield on the floor next to her dagger and stood in front of her. "Could you win a wrestling match with me, Hadde?"

"It would be hard."

He laughed. "I should have expected that answer. You're not one to concede defeat. Now, why would it be so hard?"

"Because you're so much bigger and stronger than I am. And you're an experienced fighter."

"Isn't it hopeless for you?"

"No, because if I kicked you in the crotch you would curl up on the floor and cry like a child."

Morin's mouth dropped open as he took a step back. Hadde smiled. "I, um," he stammered, "I thought you were going to say you were faster than me, or you were strong for your size."

"I once tried to stab a varcolac raider in the privates. But I missed and stuck him in the thigh." She couldn't help herself and laughed at the shocked look on Morin's face.

"I guess you know more than I thought about harness fighting."

"It wasn't something I planned, but it worked."

"Perhaps I can formalize some of your raw talent and teach you some new skills. Here, a quick demonstration." Morin picked up the sword and handed it to Hadde. "You're going to take a swing at me. Slowly, so you can see what I'm doing."

Hadde took a step back. "Ready?" At his nod she slowly swung the sword overhand and down toward his head. Morin blocked her at her wrist. Very quickly he brought his leg forward and locked it behind hers. He paused with their two bodies pressed close against one another. "This is called a hip throw." Morin's face was just inches from hers.

"It's very romantic."

"I...um." He flushed.

She smiled and asked, "Is this how it ends?"

Suddenly, she found herself lifted from the floor, swung over his hip, and planted gently on her back. He looked down at her. "That's how it ends."

He helped her to her feet.

"Do it again," Hadde said. "This time I'll try to stop you."

"Very well. And we'll go a little faster."

Without warning, Hadde shouted and swung the sword. In a whirl of motion she found herself planted on the floor. This time it ended with Morin straddling her, his knees on either side of her body and his left hand pinning her sword arm to the floor.

"I—that was fast," she said, breathless.

He grinned down at her and waved his right hand in front of her face. "This is my dagger hand. If you were a Tyskman..." He drew his finger gently across her throat.

Hadde licked her lips. "But I'm not a Tyskman. I'm Lando—"

He leaned down and kissed her. She greeted him enthusiastically.

Much too soon, he broke off the kiss. "You're much nicer to Landomeri than you are to Tyskmen," she said.

"Landomeri are much more beautiful." He bent forward to kiss her again, but she put her free left hand on his chest and pushed him back. "My turn," she said.

Morin frowned. "Your turn?"

"My turn to throw you." She pushed harder.

"I suppose." He looked crestfallen.

They stood, and taking the sword, Morin advanced on her. Hadde blocked the sword, locked his leg, and tried to throw him. He didn't budge. She strained harder but he barely moved.

"What's wrong?" She frowned as she looked up at his face. "I think you're too big."

He smiled. "It's all in the hips. You've to get yours lower, and put your right arm below my ribs. There, now——"

Morin rose over her hip and toppled to the floor, Hadde falling on top of him. She scrambled to pin his arms to the floor.

"I didn't hurt you, did I?" she asked.

"No, I'm fine. Now you have me right where you want me. If you keep your weight on me, I can't move. Lock your arms."

Hadde leaned forward and put more weight on her arms. "Now your fate is in my hands."

"And how do Landomeri treat their prisoners?" he asked.

Still pinning him to the floor, she leaned forward and kissed him. Eventually, she broke the kiss. "What do you think?"

"It wouldn't work," he said.

"Wouldn't work?" she frowned.

Straining with the effort, Morin lifted his arms from the floor. Hadde shifted her weight forward and pushed with all her strength. After a few moments he gave up.

"You're strong," he gasped. She leaned forward and they kissed again. She waited much longer before stopping this time. "Are you going to let me move, Hadde of Landomere?" he said.

She shook her head. "I like you where you are. If I let you up, you might try to escape."

"I promise I won't."

"I'm not giving you the chance. Oh, and I want five wagons of food for my people."

"Only five? Not ten?"

"And I want to know something...."

He smiled. "Go on."

"I want to know what you see in me."

"This is a tough interrogation."

"Tell the truth, Prince Morin. You're in my power." He pressed against her, but she forced his hands back down.

"So I am," he said. "I'll tell you the truth. When I first saw you in the great hall I saw a beautiful foreigner just asking to be conquered."

"Is that right?"

"It is. But now... now I see much more. I see a woman of passion. I see someone who, like me, feels a duty to make the world a better place."

"And...."

"And I've had enough of this interrogation."

"Too bad. I like what I'm hearing."

He gave her a crooked smile. "You're very certain I can't escape on my own."

"No, you can't."

He relaxed under her, pursed his lips and blew air at her.

She grinned. "What was—"

A blast of wind suddenly struck her and her long hair whipped around her face. She recoiled in surprise. Morin lunged upward and she suddenly found herself sitting on his lap, her legs around his thighs and his right arm around her waist. The wind stopped.

"Magic?" she exclaimed, gasping for breath. "You cheated!"

"In battle you do what you have to."

"Hmmph! Magic is really useful."

"It has saved me from time to time," he said as he pulled her close. He kissed her more passionately than he had before.

"Can you do more than mess up hair?"

Someone pounded on the door. "Prince Morin," a voice called.

"Off," Morin said. "Grab your sword." Hadde untangled herself from him and, after snatching up her weapon, rolled to her feet. Morin stood before her in a ready stance. "We can't be seen like that," he said to her in a hushed voice. Louder he called, "Come in!"

Astor stood in the doorway. "Captain, His Highness wishes to speak with you. He's in a foul temper."

"Let him know I'll be with him shortly. Oh, and what of our South Teren friend?"

Astor shrugged. "Keeping to himself. No accidents yet," he said. He caught Hadde's eye and gave her a slight smile.

She felt her face redden. He knows what we were up to, she thought.

Astor gave Morin a quick salute and retreated from the room.

"Off to knock some sense into my brother," Morin said. "Perhaps we might continue the lesson at a later time?"

She smiled. "I think we will."

Hadde repaired the fletching on her arrows as Maret, Tira, and Jenae continued their furious sewing efforts. The Festival of Spring was only a day away and the maidens were in a panic that they wouldn't finish their gowns. Their efforts, however, did not make a dent on the pace of their gossip. Hadde mostly ignored their chatter, but it seemed to be the same conversation over and over. Perhaps she could change its course?

"You know," Hadde said, "I hear all this talk of Prince Morin and this or that knight or squire, but none of you talk of marrying Prince Handrin."

"What?" Tira squawked. "But he's... he's just a boy."

"There will be no choice in the matter," Jenae said. "The choice will be made for him."

"I met him." Hadde said. "I watched Orlos give him a magic lesson."

"Prince Morin can do magic," Tira announced.

"I know."

"You've seen him do magic?"

"I—ah—he showed me some at our last archery lesson." Hadde tried not to blush at the memory of the romantic interlude. Hoping to change the subject, she turned to Jenae. "Do you think you'll have your dress done by tomorrow night?"

"I'll not sleep a minute. It will get done."

"She wants to impress Squire Melas," Tira giggled.

"Really? So you were the Maiden he mentioned," Hadde said.

The girls all turned to face her. "What? He mentioned me?" Jenae asked.

"Yes, during our journey to Sal-Oras. He said something about his father negotiating with a young lady's father."

"So it's true!" Tira said.

"I knew it," Maret said. "He will propose at the ball."

Hadde made her way to the window as the girls chattered about this new turn of events. Wavy figures moved in the courtyard below. Many wore the royal red of the House. But two standing beside a horse wore black.

Cracking open the window she peered out. As she had hoped, one of the two men was Morin. The other was Astor. She thought for a moment of telling the girls of Morin's presence, knowing how much it would please them.

Her gaze flicked towards the maidens and back to Morin. They would just crowd her from the window. She let them gossip on. Below, Morin clapped his friend on the shoulder and then they shook hands.

"Hadde, did he say anything else?" Tira asked.

"No, nothing. But, to me, he seemed very much in love." She paused as the maidens burst into a fresh round of giggles. She watched as Astor mounted and rode out the gate. Morin turned and strode for the Great Keep. His gaze flicked over the keep's facade, and for a moment she thought he spotted her looking down at him. But his stride didn't slacken and he soon disappeared from view.

"A package for Ambassador Hadde of Landomere," Gran called from the doorway. Maret waved the elderly servant into the room. She handed Hadde a linen bundle tied with red ribbon. Under the ribbon lay a sealed note.

"Shall I read the note for you?" Maret asked.

"Maret, don't be rude," Jenae said.

"I'll do it," Maret said. "Hadde can't read."

"Maret! Shhhh!" Tira said.

Hadde laughed at the girls. "I don't mind, Jenae. I know I cannot read." Hadde took the note from under the ribbon and handed it to Maret.

Maret frowned as she looked at the letter. "The royal seal, again. It must be from Prince Morin." She cleared her throat as she opened the letter. "'Dear Hadde,' it says." She paused and pursed her lips. "'I'm sending this gift in thanks for my archery lessons. I know it isn't your fashion, but it would please me if you would accept it. My thanks again, Morin.'"

"He signed it, Morin?" Tira asked. She snatched the note from Maret's hands and read it. Then she put it to her nose and breathed deeply. "Oh, if he would only marry me."

"Please, Tira," Jenae said, "He's not going to marry you. Maret, maybe, but not you."

"I've as much a chance as she does."

Jenae rolled her eyes.

"Don't fool yourself," Maret snapped. "I'd put you twelfth in line."

"Twelfth!" Tira shrieked. "How dare you!"

"You know how powerful my father—"

"Stop it." Jenae interrupted. "Don't fight. Neither of you are going to marry him." Both girls glared at Jenae, but held their tongues.

"Open it, Hadde," Maret demanded.

Hadde glanced at their unsmiling faces before resting the package on her lap. She hesitated before opening it. What would she find? And how would the girls react to it? She could only imagine their reaction if they knew the truth about her and Morin.

She untied the ribbon and unfolded the linen cloth. The girls gasped

165

as she revealed a luxurious black dress. The rich wool cloth was finer than any other Hadde had ever seen.

"Look at that gold embroidery." Jenae was clearly awed.

"Look, there is a belt and a circlet and slippers and a fine chemise," Tira added.

Hadde ran her hand over the belt of gold links shaped like ivy. The circlet's swirling pattern matched the embroidery of the dress.

"It's as fine as anything I've ever seen the queen wear," Tira said.

"He's not going to marry you," Maret announced, staring at Hadde.

"Of course not," Jenae said. "But look at that dress. You must try it on, Hadde."

Hadde examined the dress doubtfully.

"You must."

Hadde took the package to her room. Why would Morin have given her a dress? The last time she had worn a dress it was to mock Saladoran men. He had to mean something by it. Did he want her to try to fit into Saladoran society? Why? She felt a momentary flutter in her stomach. Did he mean for her to stay? It couldn't be. It was impossible. She had to return to Landomere. No matter how she felt about Morin.

She ran her hand over the dress. It wouldn't hurt to try it on.

The dress fit well, but without lacing it up she couldn't be certain. Unlike Maret's red dress, the sleeves went only to her wrists. The frilled white cuffs of the shirt stuck out beyond them. She supposed it was intended. The girls would correct her if not. The high collar of the dress didn't close either. She pulled the Spiridus Token from under the shirt and laid it outside the collar.

Hadde linked the belt around her waist and, smoothing her hair, put the circlet over her brow. The slippers were impossibly small. She put on her moccasins and walked back to Maret's room.

Hadde smiled at the awestruck looks on the girls' faces. Jenae jumped up and tightened the laces that ran up the back of the dress. "Too tight," Hadde said, but Jenae would hear nothing of it.

"It's wonderful," Jenae said as she stepped in front of Hadde.

"What is wrong with the neck?" Tira asked.

Jenae looked at the high collar of the dress. "It looks like the dressmaker forgot to put buttons on the collar. That's odd on such a fine dress." She tried to pull the edges of the collar closed. "Hmmm, it won't close."

"I don't think it's supposed to," Hadde said.

"It has to. You cannot go around revealing your neck like that."

"I do all the time," Hadde replied. "None of my tunics have high collars."

"Well, they're Landomeri clothes. That's different. This is a Saladoran dress. What will men think? I can see your neck all the way to your collarbone. I mean, if they can see your collarbone, what comes next?"

"I like the sleeves," Jenae said. She lifted Hadde's arm and looked at the cuff. "I think I'll do this with my dress."

"You should wear your collar like this, too," Hadde said.

Jenae laughed. "That would be so scandalous. You can get away with it, Hadde, but I never could."

"Lady Celena will never let you cut your cuffs that short, Jenae," Tira said.

"It's beautiful," Maret said. "Are you going to wear it, Hadde?"

"I don't know." She glanced at the girls. They stared at her expectantly, but she also sensed their jealousy. She sighed. There would be no harm in her wearing a dress once. "I guess so."

"You have to," Jenae said, sounding relieved. "It's too beautiful not to wear. Just look at the gold alone!"

"I thought you didn't like dresses," Maret said.

"I don't, really," Hadde replied. "But it was a gift."

"When I asked you before, you said you wouldn't wear one."

"Maret," Jenae said, "whatever she said before doesn't matter. This is a gift from Prince Morin. She has to wear it."

"You don't see it?" Maret snapped. "You don't see what she's trying to do? She will steal him away!"

Hadde took a step back from Maret's anger. Jenae and Tira stared in silence.

"I'm not stealing him," Hadde said. *But I could if I wanted to.* She left the words unspoken, but her heart raced at the thought. It would be so easy to crush the silly little girl's spirits. Maret might think they were rivals, but it wasn't a contest.

"Prove it. Stay here. Don't go to the festival."

Hadde's cheeks flushed red with anger. She had enough of Saladorans telling her what to do. Even Maret. "I'll go where I will, and no one will stop me."

Chapter Seventeen

"I think I need a rest," Hadde said. "My head is spinning just trying to keep up with these dances."

"Let's refresh ourselves with some wine," Morin replied. He took her by the elbow and led her from the dance floor. Bright streamers and pennants filled the Great Hall, making the atmosphere festive and light. It was a huge change from the ominous tone of her previous visits. The nobles, too, were clad in their finest. Gold, silver, and jewels sparkled everywhere. It was as if the Wasting didn't exist.

"I'm sorry for stepping on your foot," Hadde said.

"You dance as if you've been doing it your entire life."

"You lie, but it's kind of you to say so." Hadde took the cup of cooled white wine he offered. The cold drink was a welcome relief. The crowded press filling the Great Hall, combined with the dancing, had her flushed.

She sipped her wine and surveyed the room. Leaning close to Morin, she whispered, "Everyone is looking at us."

He smiled and glanced around. "Not us, you. You've turned quite a few heads this evening."

"It's the dress. Thank you for sending it. I never thought I would put one on again."

"The dress is magnificent. But on any other woman it wouldn't be as fine."

"You've a way with words, Prince Morin."

"I mean every one of them. Here, let's move away from this crowd."

"The feast was wonderful," Hadde said as they walked from the refreshments table.

"Only twice a year do we eat like that."

"It makes me feel guilty," Hadde said. "I can't help thinking what it's like in Long Meadow. My parents are probably eating horsemeat and split peas." She paused. "I should be home with them. I wish your brother would let me leave."

"I'll take care of——" Morin stared across the room. "What is he doing back already?"

Hadde followed his gaze.

Astor, strode across the hall toward them. His fine black clothes were travel-stained, making him appear out of place amongst the elegant nobles. A huge grin spread across his face as he approached.

Morin left Hadde's side and embraced his friend in a back-pounding hug. "Astor! Back already? You're smiling too much for something to have gone amiss."

The two men had attracted the attention of many standing nearby. Astor glanced at the crowd. "Bad weather forced me back." And then, more quietly, he said, "Good news."

"Yes?"

"We should talk. Now."

Morin looked at Hadde. "Would you mind if I took a moment with Astor?"

"Not at all," Hadde replied.

"I—um," Astor said, looking Hadde up and down. "What happened to you?"

"A model of eloquence, my friend here." Morin laughed.

"I—just, you look beautiful, Ambassador Hadde."

"Thank you, Sir Astor." She glanced at the revelers surrounding them. Most had returned to their own conversations, or at least had pretended to. "Don't worry about me, Prince Morin. I can fend for myself."

"Thank you, Hadde."

As the two men departed, she turned and headed for the refreshment table. She helped herself to another cup of wine and stood by one of the huge pillars holding up the vaulted ceiling. Across the hall she spied Maret among a group of maidens tracking Morin's progress. They looked like a pack of wolf pups pondering how they would take down a stag. They didn't even know the hunt was over. Hadde smiled at the thought. It gave her more than a small amount of pleasure she could claim Morin as her own. Now the fine ladies of Salador were envious of *her*.

Just the act of appearing at Morin's side had changed Hadde's status in Sal-Oras. Noble men and ladies who had never given her a kind glance were eager to speak with her tonight. It was the dress, she was certain. Everyone knew Morin had given it to her. Did they think they could gain his friendship through their kindness to her?

She sighed. Better to not think about it. It wasn't her future. Her future was Landomere and the struggle against the Wasting.

"Would you do me the favor of this dance?" a voice asked from behind her.

Hadde gasped and took a step back. "No!"

169

Waltas leered at her. "Come now, I'm not going to accost you in the Great Hall, am I?"

Hadde searched the hall for Morin.

"Don't worry, he came to see me. We have an understanding."

"An understanding? What understanding?" She glared at the earl. He just grinned in reply, as if he had no fears in the world. Not at all like a man with a trial by combat looming ahead of him.

Waltas glanced at the nearby partygoers. "I'll just say... we can all be friends now."

She turned and had only taken a step when he said, "Don't turn your back on me."

She wheeled on him. "Champion Nidon is supposed to kill you at some point, isn't he?"

His eyes widened briefly at the mention of Nidon's name. But then he smiled and shook his head. "All that's left is for me to beg forgiveness and all will be well."

Orlos had been right. "And what of my forgiveness?" It felt like the ancient spiridus was speaking through her.

"You don't matter. Only Nidon."

"Is that so? I'll have to remind him that his honor has been stained and his name is less than it used to be." She turned her back on the earl.

"You'll pay, you bitch," he hissed as she walked away. "You common whore!" The few people close enough to overhear his last words glanced sourly in his direction.

Hadde ignored him and kept walking. Morin was still engrossed in his conversation with Astor. As Hadde scanned the room for any sign of Nidon, a Lady in Waiting stepped in front of her.

"Ambassador Hadde, Her Royal Highness, the Queen, wishes to see to you," the woman said.

"Me? You're certain?"

"I'll take you to her." Her guide turned and sauntered to the base of the dais, never looking back to see if Hadde followed or not. The queen sat upon her throne, deep in discussion with an elderly woman seated on a short padded stool.

"Wait here," the escort commanded, before abandoning Hadde to join six other Ladies in Waiting gossiping in a huddle.

Hadde stood alone waiting for some sign of what she should do. She couldn't imagine any reason for the summons. Queen Ilana was a cold woman, but she didn't have any reason to harbor a grudge against Hadde.

At least none she knew of.

The queen seemed not to have noticed that Hadde had arrived. In vain, Hadde scanned the hall for Morin. Instead, she spotted Nidon in conversation with a young noblewoman. The knight shifted from foot to foot. He looked awkward and afraid in front of the tiny woman. Not far from him, King Boradin stood in the middle of a large group of noblemen at the outer edge of the dance floor. He looked bizarre with the shield, Forsvar, on his back.

"The queen will see you now."

Hadde jumped at the unexpected voice.

"Thank you," Hadde replied. The Ladies in Waiting stopped talking as Hadde approached the queen. Ilana wore a dress of cream and white decorated with hundreds of lustrous white beads. Already beautiful, she was dazzling in the rich gown.

Hadde bowed. "Your Majesty."

"Please be seated, Hadde of Landomere."

Hadde sat, careful to keep her moccasins concealed beneath her hem.

"You're dressed like a queen," Ilana said, looking Hadde up and down.

"Thank you, Your Majesty. The dress was a gift."

"Yes, of course it was. When I said that you're dressed like a queen, I meant it quite literally. You're wearing my mother-in-law's dress." The queen laughed—a joyless sound. "Don't worry, she has been dead for some time now." Ilana bent forward and traced her finger along the open collar. "I see it has been tailored to fit your daring sense of style."

"It was that way when it was given to me."

"Was it now?" Ilana sat back in her throne. "He thinks of everything," she said as she looked over the dance floor.

Hadde followed the queen's gaze, but couldn't make out the object of her attention. The Ladies in Waiting stood at the bottom of the dais, pretending not to pay any mind to Hadde and Ilana. Beyond the ladies, dancers swirled across the floor. Hadde caught a glimpse of Morin dancing with Maret. The maiden's face beamed with joy. "Ah, you see him now. Did you know that he was supposed to marry me?" the queen asked.

Hadde shook her head, wondering where this was heading. She had no doubt that Ilana would take the conversation to a bitter end.

"Everyone expected Boradin to marry an Idorian princess," Ilana continued. "I was the second choice and should have married Morin. And then that silly Idorian wench had to fall ill and die. I married Boradin. Morin was quite crushed."

Hadde looked at the queen, not knowing what to say.

"I would have taken him as a lover." Ilana sighed. "But my husband is incredibly jealous. He watches me like a hawk. Why do you think he lets Morin run off on his adventures? To keep him away from me. Well, that and to keep Morin from rebelling again. Did you know about that? That Prince Morin is a traitor?"

"I don't want to hear this," Hadde said. The man the queen described wasn't Morin.

"But you will. I'm the queen." Ilana paused and gave Hadde an icy smile. "Did you ever wonder why my husband keeps Forsvar with him at all times? The last time he let it out of his sight—years ago—Morin attacked him. Boradin barely fended his brother off.

"But, I don't tell you these things because I want to. You poor, innocent common girl. I tell you these things to save you. You're so naïve, so trusting. I tell you these things to save you from heartbreak. What you want, you cannot have."

"I just want to help my people." Hadde caught Morin's eye as he whirled across the dance floor, Maret by his side. He gave Hadde a wink as the dance carried him away.

"He will do anything to become king," Ilana whispered. "And if he succeeds, he will take me as his wife and adopt Handrin as his heir. You, Hadde, are just a momentary distraction from grander schemes."

Hadde wanted nothing more than to escape Ilana's venomous tongue. None of it was true. Morin couldn't be the man the queen described. But somewhere deep inside, a worm of doubt gnawed at her.

Boradin arrived, marching up the steps to the thrones, leaving a band of noblemen at the base. He swung the shield off his back as he approached. Hadde started to stand, but Boradin motioned for her to remain seated.

"A study in contrasts," he said, admiring Hadde and Ilana as he sat down. "White and black but both beautiful. What was it the Ancient philosopher Endanar said? White and black, day and night, life and death, you cannot have one without the other."

"Yes, I'm certain I read that somewhere," Ilana said, looking away from him.

"Hadde, I know that you're anxious to return home," Boradin said, "but you'll be happy to hear I've made some progress on your Token. I found a scrap of a prophecy by Ergos the Blind. It starts, 'the archer's offspring shall,' but the rest of the text is corrupted. But I'm certain that Orlos or I will find the full text soon."

Hadde's heart skipped a beat, and a trickle of sweat crept down her back. She nodded, attempting to appear calm, not daring any reply.

"The archer's offspring... you've no children, correct?" Boradin asked.

"I'm barren," she blurted out. "I cannot have children."

"Not for lack of trying," Ilana said, flicking a mote of dust from her dress. "As we all know."

Boradin ignored his wife. "At least the prophecy gives us a place from which to start."

"It's time, Your Majesty," Fenre the steward called from the base of the dais.

The king nodded and waved him off. "Enjoy the rest of your evening, Ambassador Hadde. Bah, I always dread these events, but once I get to them... I do have some fun."

Standing, Hadde bowed and backed down the dais. Relief at escaping the royals flooded through her, but it was tinged with fear. Fear that Boradin would soon discover the rest of the prophecy. And fear that the things Ilana said might be true.

As Hadde reached the floor Boradin stood and, taking the queen's hand, raised her to her feet. The music stopped. A herald blew a fanfare. All turned to face the pair as they descended the dais. They halted on the lowest step.

"I wish to attend to one matter before I call out the Winter Swan," Boradin said to the crowd. All stared at him expectantly. "Squire Melas, Maiden Jenae, come forth."

The two young people slowly made their way through the crowd. Melas walked proudly, a broad smile across his face. Jenae blushed under the attention of the gathered nobles. Melas bowed, and Jenae curtsied before the king and queen.

"Squire Melas," Boradin said. "I received good news today. An answer to an inquiry I made of Maiden Jenae's father some time ago. Would you like to know how he responded?"

"I would, Your Majesty."

Boradin smiled. "The answer was 'yes.'"

For a moment nothing happened. Hadde scanned the audience. All beamed at the scene before them. Hadde could hardly believe what she was seeing. Here were two young people who wished to declare themselves to one another. Not only were their fathers involved, but now the king.

"Well, then, young squire. What are you waiting for?" Boradin asked.

"I, ah, yes, Your Majesty." Melas turned to Jenae and knelt before her. "Jenae, long have I loved you from afar. And now, at long last, I've permission to do as I've long desired. Jenae, will you do me the pleasure of becoming my wife?"

"I will, Melas. I love you so," she replied.

A cheer rose. Hadde smiled and joined in the applause. The Saladorans were so odd. They even needed the king's permission to declare their love. They couldn't even kiss right, she thought as the two lovers exchanged a quick peck on the cheek.

"And now it's time for the Squires and Maidens to retire," Boradin said as the applause faded. "All of them," he added, staring at the two lovers in front of him. "Although, perhaps, the Squire Melas might be permitted to escort the Maiden Jenae to her hall."

The squires and maidens bowed to the assembled lords and made their way from the hall. "And now the climax to our feast." Boradin raised his hands above his head. "Behold the Winter Swan."

The huge doors at the opposite end of the Great Hall swung open. Six liveried squires marched into the chamber carrying a large cloth-covered table. On the table stood a beautiful ice sculpture of a swan. The crowd silently parted as the squires brought the sculpture to the center of the room. After gently lowering the table to the floor, the squires bowed to the king.

"Ladies and gentlemen, it is midnight," Boradin called out from atop the dais. His voice carried easily across the room. "Fall is ended and winter is upon us. But in our hearts we know a new spring is on the way. Let us rejoice this night, and let the warmth of our merriment melt the Winter Swan. Strike up the Dance of Spring."

Applause greeted his words. But to Hadde the king's words had seemed flat and joyless. As if Boradin didn't truly believe that a new spring would come. He took the queen's hand and led her to the statue.

"I see you had a private audience with the queen," Morin whispered.

Hadde whirled to see Morin smiling at her.

"And the king as well," he added. "Did they have anything interesting to say?"

She opened her mouth, but didn't know what to say. The queen's words burned within her and she wanted Morin to dispel them. But she couldn't bring herself to speak. She glanced at the royal pair. "Morin, do you believe in prophecy?" she finally asked.

He frowned. "It's hard to say. There is so much of it, and so much is false, it's nearly impossible to use. But in the right hands, and interpreted properly, it can be very powerful." He took her elbow and led her away from the dais.

"Orlos warned me of a prophecy that he has discovered. 'The archer's offspring shall slay the sun.'"

Morin stopped and gave her a sharp look. "He warned you?"

"He said that the king could interpret it as a threat."

Rubbing his face with his hand, Morin glanced at his younger brother. "Does he know of it?"

"He has only discovered the first part."

For a short time Morin stood and stared off. Shaking his head, he took

174

Hadde's hand in his and smiled at her. "I hardly think my brother would move against you. I mean no offense, Hadde, but what threat are you? Come, we'll join them. It's the Dance of Spring."

"I don't know this dance."

"It's simple."

As the music began, everyone in the hall faced the Winter Swan and walked slowly to the right. The crowd soon organized itself into a half dozen rings surrounding the table. Despite the morose tolling of the music, the people in the crowd appeared unaffected and wore smiles on their faces.

The music unexpectedly stopped and Hadde bumped into Morin. All around her the dancers released their neighbors' hands and gave a single clap. Hadde, not expecting it, was late in clapping. Others were late as well, shielding her from embarrassment.

The circles started in the opposite direction as the music began again. This time the rhythm was faster and the tune more upbeat. There were steps that went along with the dance, but Hadde couldn't make out what they were. She skipped along with the momentum of the group.

When the crowd stopped and clapped a second time, Hadde got the idea. Off they went in the opposite direction. Faster and faster the dance repeated until the guests were almost jogging around the Winter Swan.

At some point the neighboring rings started dancing in opposite directions. Hadde laughed as she tried to keep up with what was going on.

With a final fanfare, the music stopped, and all stood staring at the sculpture. Many breathed hard after the exertion. Hadde joined in as everyone in the crowd took a deep breath and blew toward the sculpture. Cheers and clapping followed. Hadde glanced around, bewildered at the sudden end to the dance.

Servants moved into the crowd offering ceramic goblets of wine. Morin took two and offered one to Hadde.

"That was fun," she said. "Why did everyone blow at the swan?"

"It's an old tradition. If the Winter Swan melts before dawn it means a short winter and an early spring. The Dance of Spring starts out slowly to represent winter and then increases in energy as spring arrives. Once everyone is heated by the dance they blow on the Winter Swan to help it melt faster." He took Hadde's elbow and led her toward the swan.

"I've never seen anything like it," Hadde said. "The streams in Landomere rarely ice over. If they do it's just for a day or two."

"This ice comes from the Treteren River, north of the King's Crossing. It used to come from Namir, but cold winters bring ice much farther south these days."

"It's a beautiful sculpture. It's a shame to think of it melting away."

"Nothing lasts forever. It's part of the tradition. Even winter, though it seems it may last forever, will someday end. There is always hope."

"Does it work? If the sculpture melts will winter end early?" She felt a little foolish for asking.

He shook his head. "It doesn't matter what the sculpture does. Winter gets longer every year. The Wasting is stronger than tradition."

"Why do people do it, then?"

"Old traditions die hard. And, I think, people want to have hope. The Winter Swan gives them hope." The musicians started into another tune, and Morin led Hadde to the dance floor. The intricate dance involved groups of four couples. She tried to follow along as best she could, without looking too clumsy. Morin and the other men were kind enough not to make her feel out of place.

At the end of the dance the king and queen departed the Great Hall. A quarter of the guests followed them. "I thought our revelry was supposed to melt the Winter Swan," Hadde said as she watched them leave.

"My brother has little time for fun. He thinks it deprives him of time he could better spend on more important matters. At least he gives us leave to carry on. Otherwise the festivities would end with his departure."

"Why did the queen leave?"

"It would be inappropriate for her to be present without her husband. She has to leave with him. The others were here to curry the king's favor. They have no reason to stay. Speaking of currying favor, did she have anything to say to you?"

"She… she said very unpleasant things."

"As I would expect. She grows uglier by the day. She's like a beautiful tree rotting at its core."

"She said you once attacked your brother. That you want to be king."

"She did?" He snorted in derision. "She exaggerates. He and I had an argument. A scuffle, that's all. I felt I should have been made king, but our father chose otherwise. He thought magical talent more important than leadership. Boradin won and I'm the prince. And that's that."

"How could Boradin have ever defeated you?"

"The shield. Forsvar is also known as 'The Defender.' It protects its wielder against magical harm. Even those allies standing nearby, they say." He shrugged.

"She also said you loved her." Hadde stared at Morin for any sign he might give at the words.

Morin looked surprised, but after a moment shook his head. "Once I might have. But she's not that person anymore. My heart lies with another, now."

The look Morin gave her dismissed any question as to whom he loved. She stared into his eyes. There was no doubting him. Morin was the brave, honest man she was falling for. And the queen was a vile woman who wished only to spread dissent. Heart pounding, she leaned close to kiss him, but he stopped her with a barely perceptible shake of his head.

"Not here," he said.

"But—"

"There are others. They cannot see us. I'm sorry, but it's the way it has to be."

She furtively glanced at the people around them. None seemed to be paying the two of them any mind. She wanted so much to hold him close. She hated the Saladorans and their silly rules about love. "I want to be with you."

"Soon, I promise."

Chapter Eighteen

Hadde ran the polishing cloth over Belor's bow one last time and then gently leaned it against the wall next to his bowcase. A score of white-fletched arrows rose from the case—the feathers perfectly smooth. The bow had been Belor's most prized possession, just as Hawkeye was hers. Both unstrung bows rested beside each other, Belor's noticeably larger.

It wouldn't be too big for Morin, she thought. But could she part with it? Morin had given her the dress, and more than that she had fallen for him. It was too fast, she thought. It was all too fast. She stared at Belor's bow. Not yet. She couldn't part with it.

Hadde turned to a knock at her door. "Come in," she said.

The door opened to reveal Maret. The girl's eyes were downcast. "Hello, Hadde," she said.

"Hello, Maret." Hadde kept her tone neutral.

"I came to visit earlier."

"I was down at the stable visiting my horses," Hadde said, as she absently tossed a stick into the fire. "I think Lightfoot wants to do more than just ride around the yard."

Maret nodded and stood silent for a few moments. "I've come to apologize," she finlly said. "I was awful to you before."

Hadde stood. "Come in, Maret. And there's no need to apologize." She smiled at the girl. After last night, it was hard to summon up any anger.

"I should have known better. After all, it's ridiculous to think a prince would marry a... well, you know."

Hadde's face flushed. So much for a real apology. "Yes, I know."

Maret strode into the room and seated herself on the hearth. A smile brightened her face. "The ball was wonderful. Everything was perfect. Did you see us?"

"Yes, I saw all the maidens there." Hadde busied herself buttering a piece of bread. She had woken up late, but had not had much interest in food for the first few hours after she rose.

"No, not them. Prince Morin danced with me. He came up to me and asked me to dance."

"Oh, I saw you. You were very happy."

"It's a shame he didn't show you much attention. Well, besides the dress. It was nice of him to let you wear it."

"What do you mean?"

"Well, he did dance with you a little early on, but he favored me far more. I only wish they allowed the maidens to stay for the Dance of Spring. I'm sure he would have danced with me again. I was the only maiden he danced with, you know. It just isn't fair that we have to leave before midnight."

"Well, I'm glad you had a good time," Hadde said. She wondered how crushed Maret would be to find out the truth. It would be so easy to put the girl in her place. But she couldn't. Morin was intent on keeping his love for Hadde secret.

Maret sprang to her feet. "That's all, really. I just wanted to let you know that I was sorry for speaking unkindly to you. I should have known better."

"I'm glad we cleared everything up," Hadde replied.

"I must be going," Maret said as she headed for the door. A piece of paper fluttered to the floor behind her.

"Wait," Hadde called. She put down her bread and picked up the paper as Maret turned.

"Let me have that!" Maret demanded, her face suddenly white.

Hadde glanced at the meaningless scribble and held it out to Maret. Hadde forced a smile and said, "That must be important. Is it from someone special?"

"Yes—no! No, it isn't." Maret tucked the note in her sleeve and backed from the room. "I have to go."

Hadde lay down in bed and pulled the thick comforter up around her neck. She stared into the brightly burning fire. The day had been a disappointment. A queasy morning, brought on by far too much drink, followed by Maret's bizarre appearance. And then her hopes for seeing Morin dashed.

Maret had delivered the letter just after lunch. "So sorry, Hadde," Maret had said, her voice anything but sorrowful, "but Prince Morin has cancelled his lesson with you."

Sleet rattled against the dark window. She imagined her cottage in Long Meadow. Her parents would be curled on their sleeping mat near the fire. She hoped that they were well. She glanced at the tapestry-hung stone walls and longed for the wooden timbers of home. Sleep came slowly.

She awoke to pounding on her door.

"Wake up! Hadde, wake up!" a girl's voice shouted. The door flew open.

"What is it?" Hadde sat up, her mind still foggy with dreams. "Is it the Kiremi?"

She reached for her bow and then shook her head. *Kiremi?* She blinked her eyes. She was in Salador. There were no Kiremi.

Jenae ran to Hadde's bed. "She's been attacked!" Sobbing, the maiden put down her lantern and threw her arms around Hadde's neck. "She's going to die."

Hadde's heart lurched in her chest. "What are you talking about?" She took the girl by the shoulders and pushed her back so she could see her face.

"Maret! Someone attacked Maret!"

Still sleep-addled, Hadde couldn't grasp what she had said. "What?" She shook her head. "She what?"

"Maret's in the surgeon's parlor." Jenae collapsed into Hadde's bed, sobbing uncontrollably.

Hadde pulled on her hose and moccasins, yanked on her tunic, and ran from the room. Crying girls filled the hall. Lady Celena fruitlessly attempted to settle them.

Brushing past, Hadde ran to the end of the hall. Torches lit the intersection and instead of just two guards, there were a half dozen in full harness. "Let me through," Hadde yelled as she approached. "Move aside."

Someone grabbed her by arm. A knight. "Ambassador Hadde, you can't leave. The murderer is still on the loose."

"She's not dead! She can't be. Let me go. I have to see her." She wrenched herself free. Tears pouring from her eyes, she shoved her way through the crowd. It didn't matter how the girl had behaved before. She was still Hadde's friend. And someone had hurt her. She wanted to run, but didn't know the way. Suddenly Morin was there.

"Someone attacked Maret," she said. "I have to see her."

"I know. I was just with her." He took Hadde by the hand and led her down the hall. Armed escorts fell in behind them. "She's alive, but barely."

"Make way. Make way for Prince Morin," someone called from in front of them. A path opened. Turning, they entered a bright, lavishly decorated room. Fresh tears sprung to Hadde's eyes as she spotted Maret lying on a couch. Blood-soaked bandages covered her face and arms. A man and two women stood over her, working to staunch the bleeding, but it looked hopeless.

Hadde walked to the couch. The man was stitching a terrible cut that ran down Maret's face from her temple to her jaw. Where her skin wasn't covered in blood, it was deathly pale. "How did it happen?" Hadde asked. Someone stepped up to her and wrapped a blanket around her shoulders. Hadde didn't take her eyes from Maret.

"We don't know yet," Morin said from just behind her. "She left the Maiden Hall last evening and never returned. It was midnight before Lady Celena discovered Maret was missing. A team of squires searched for her, and one of them discovered her and her assailant in an abandoned apartment. The villain knocked the squire to the floor and ran off. The squire chose to aid Maret rather than pursue her attacker."

"Who would do this? She never hurt anyone."

The surgeon stood up. "I've done all I can do. She's alive, but I fear she won't be for long."

Hadde bent low over her friend. "Maret? Can you hear me?" She wanted to touch the girl, but it seemed every part of her was bandaged. "Who would do this? She has no enemies."

"Make way for the king!"

"Stand back, Morin," Boradin commanded as he strode up to the bed. His wore Forsvar on his arm as if prepared for a fight. Morin backed away as his brother commanded.

"Your Majesty?" Hadde asked. "Can you do something with your magic?"

He shook his head as he examined Maret's wounds. "It doesn't work that way."

"What do you mean? Look at her. She's dying!"

"I wish I could help, Hadde, but I'm a master of elemental magic."

"What good is magic if it cannot help her?"

"Send for Orlos," Morin said from across the room. "He is our greatest healer."

Boradin shook his head. "Orlos isn't well. He cannot help."

"The South Teren has turned against you, and now you'll risk the East? You'll tell Earl Seremar you let his only daughter die?"

Boradin paused a moment, regarding his brother with a cold stare. "Lord Fenre, wake Master Orlos and bring him here. Be gentle with him."

Someone maneuvered Hadde into a chair. A mug of mulled wine was thrust into her hands, but she couldn't drink it. In the background she heard the surgeon shooing people from the room.

Nidon's friend, Sir Gorwin, entered the room. He held a bloody parchment in his hand. "I found a letter. From the killer."

"She's not dead!" Hadde snapped.

The knight blanched "I mean it was found——"

"Give it to me." Boradin ordered. He unfolded the letter and read it. "Where did you find it?"

"Your Highness, I found it in the room where the maiden was attacked."

The king scanned the letter and looked around the room. "It's an invitation to a... a lover's meeting," the king said. "There's no name. No address."

"A lover's meeting?" Hadde asked.

"You know something of this?" the king demanded.

"I saw that note. Maret dropped it this morning."

"Did she say who sent it?"

"No. She wanted to keep it secret." Hadde glanced around the room, her eyes momentarily meeting Morin's. "She has no lover though. I would know it."

"I was on duty then, my lord," a squire said. "A page brought a letter very early this morning, but it was for Ambassador Hadde. I gave it to Maiden Jenae to take down the hall to Ambassador Hadde."

"How did it get into Maiden Maret's hands?"

"I was at the stable with Lightfoot in the morning," Hadde said, "Jenae must have taken it to Maret."

Boradin examined the letter again. "It's unsigned. She thought it was for her. But who would she expect such an invitation from?" He stared around the room as if expecting a response.

Hadde glanced at Morin again. Had he sent her a letter only to have it intercepted by Maret? Maret would have eagerly accepted an invitation for a secret meeting from him. But even if Maret had shown up instead of Hadde, it was impossible to think he would have done such a thing to her.

"It is unfortunate that the girl thought the letter was for her," Morin said. "But this attack was planned against Hadde. The letter was intended for her."

"Waltas," Hadde said, suddenly certain of herself. "Earl Waltas did it."

"Find him," Boradin ordered. "Bring him to me."

"I warned him," Morin said. "I told him to stay away from you, Hadde."

"She's alive," Hadde announced to the mob of girls who surrounded her as she entered the Maiden Hall. "They've summoned Orlos." The words were greeted by a fresh outpouring of emotion. Hadde couldn't

182

bear to tell them the true extent of Maret's injuries.

She made her way through the crowd to Maret's room. Someone had pulled the blankets back, but Maret's deception was still obvious. Piled clothing under the blankets had fooled Celena when she had taken roll. The stupid hag hadn't made much of an effort to check on her wards.

Rage welled within Hadde. But only a small part of it at Celena. She thought of Waltas. The bastard would suffer. Hadde ran to her room and threw open her storage chest. In moments she had her bowcase, cloak, and pack. Only twenty arrows, but they would be enough. She pulled on her boots and ran out the door.

She didn't need to be told that Waltas had departed the keep. She knew it. He had attempted to take his revenge on her, had failed and nearly been caught. Hadde ignored the girls calling out their questions as she jogged down the hall. Her tears had stopped and her torment had been replaced by grim determination.

She pushed past the knights who tried to stop her at the end of the hall and ran the entire way to the stables. There, she discovered stable boys already preparing horses for the pursuit.

Hadde ran to Lightfoot and dropped her gear next to the stall. "Sorry for getting you up, but there's something we must do." Puddle scampered up to her. "What is going on, Lady Hadde?"

"I need to leave quickly, Puddle. Maiden Maret has been attacked. Help me saddle Lightfoot and Windwalker."

Soon, Hadde was mounted and riding for the stable exit. The throng of stable hands, squires, and knights preparing their mounts frustrated her efforts at making a rapid departure. Nidon stepped in front of her as she finally reached the door. He grabbed Lightfoot's bridle. "What are you doing?"

"The same as you, I think, Sir Nidon."

"You can't go after him. It's too dangerous."

"It's too dangerous for that bastard. Not for me. Last night he hunted me. Today, I hunt him."

"No, leave him to me. He came to me and attempted to apologize. I rejected it and told him he had to face me in combat, so instead he sought his revenge and fled. I couldn't accept his apology after what he had done to you. And now this…"

Hadde ignored the look of anguish that crossed Nidon's face. "Leave him to you?" she asked. "You Saladorans let this happen. I will end it. Let go of my bridle."

For a moment Nidon held her horse fast, holding Hadde's gaze in his own. Finally, he released Lightfoot. "Aim true."

Hadde urged Lightfoot through the open stable entrance. The Great

Keep's courtyard was dark but for a few torch-lit entrances and the brightly illuminated gatehouse. Snowflakes brushed her cheeks as she rode toward the gates. "Who goes there?" a Knight asked as she approached.

"Hadde of Landomere. Open the gate."

"The gates are sealed."

"Why?" Hadde glared at the forbidding gates in front of her.

"By the king's order."

"Did you let Earl Waltas through?"

"Yes, but the gates were not sealed then."

"You let a murderer through."

"There was no reason to stop him."

She held back the rage that threatened to overwhelm her. It would do no good to scream at the fool. "If that murdering bastard escapes because you delayed me at this gate I shall make certain you take full blame for it. Open the gate."

"I cannot, Ambassador. You're forbidden from departing."

"Open it!" Morin's voice boomed. She turned and saw him striding toward her. The guard recoiled at the prince's onslaught.

"But the king——"

"I'm Prince Morin, Lord Protector of Salador. If you defy me I'll have your head."

"Yes, my lord. Open the gate!"

Morin turned to Hadde and grasped her hand. "I just spoke with Nidon. I know you won't wait for us, so I'll not ask it of you. But we will be close behind. Don't risk too much."

"Thank you for letting me go." He truly wasn't like other Saladorans. Not only was he letting her go, but he assumed that she could handle herself alone. Morin released her hand and she put her heels to Lightfoot. They raced through the city streets, the houses a blur in the darkness. Hadde ignored the snow that stung her face. There was no hint of the coming morning.

At the city gates a soldier hailed her. "What's going on? The alarm bells rang, but we've had no other word."

"I'm Ambassador Hadde of Landomere. There has been a murder attempt in the Great Keep. A maiden lies on her deathbed. Has anyone passed this gate tonight? The villain is attempting to escape."

"No one has passed this gate."

"Are you sure?"

"I'm certain of it."

Hadde looked around in desperation. She had assumed Waltas was heading for the South Teren. "Is there another gate?"

"There are two others on the East Bank. The East Pass Gate and the Ost-Oras Gate. Both in that direction." He pointed. She rode hard for the next gate. There, the Gate Captain told her Earl Waltas had passed through.

Hadde dismounted as they opened the sally port for her. "Does this road lead to Del-Oras?"

"It ends at the East Pass, a hundred miles from Del-Oras."

What was Waltas up to? Had he decided not to return to his homeland? Was he taking a different route? She cursed the snow as it fell more heavily. His trail would soon be covered. "Where does the East Pass lead?"

The captain shrugged. "The land of Belen, but nobody has used the East Pass in hundreds of years. It's closed."

"Thank you, Captain. Send word to Prince Morin that Waltas passed this gate."

"I will, Ambassador." The sally port slammed shut behind her. Light from the gate illuminated partially obscured hoof prints. The trail followed the highway to the southeast. She switched leads and mounted Windwalker.

As long as she didn't lose his trail, she could catch Waltas. Saladoran warhorses were large and strong but they were not suited for fast-paced rides over long distances. She rode hard, almost missing the indentations in the snow marking where Waltas had ridden his horse off of the road.

She glanced back toward Sal-Oras. Darkness and the falling snow obscured the walls from view. Even the torches lighting the gates were invisible. She guided Windwalker down the embankment. The horse slid but kept his balance.

At first Hadde thought Waltas had made a mistake in leaving the road. The broken country around Sal-Oras would only slow him down. But soon she saw the purpose in it. Waltas had ridden into a pine forest where the snow had not penetrated. She found herself forced to dismount on several occasions as she searched for disturbances in the fallen pine needles carpeting the ground.

She could tell from his horse's hoof prints that he was pressing his horse hard. But his haste had also made his trail easier to follow. He had knocked clumps of snow from some branches, and in a few places he had snapped small limbs.

"He's in too much of a hurry," Hadde said aloud as she patted Windwalker's neck. Or he had not thought Hadde would be the one pursuing him—the one person in Sal-Oras who had no problem seeing well in the dark. And the one person who had been a forest huntress for almost a decade.

She still didn't understand the Saladorans' night blindness, but right now it was to her advantage. Waltas had gained ground on her, of that she was certain. But he had also failed to lose her. She knew her two little Landomeri horses would make up the lost time.

The sky lightened as she came upon the Del-Oras Highway. She stared southeast, into the South Teren. Waltas' trail ran straight and clear. He was heading home. She set off after him.

As dawn brightened the sky the snow slacked off. There was little sound besides the breathing of her horses and the thudding of their hooves on the road.

The arrow-flights rapidly passed as the cloud-hazed sun slowly crawled into the sky. Hadde reined in Windwalker as she came upon a disturbed patch of snow. She dismounted and searched the ground— quickly finding a broken wagon wheel partially obscured by the snow. Waltas' horse had fallen, she realized. She jogged along Waltas' trail as it continued South. A grin crossed her face. His horse was lame. He would never escape. She mounted Lightfoot and set off in pursuit.

In only a few hundred strides she caught sight of him. Waltas led his limping horse through a shallow valley. Beyond him she spied a small village nestled in a tree line. Perhaps if he made the village he could find remounts, or even allies to help him fend her off. Who knew what story he would tell them? All they would know was that he was a Saladoran nobleman in need of help. A few crossbowmen could make her task impossible.

But he wouldn't make the village. She would make certain of that. Her heart thudded in her chest. She was a huntress, and he was doomed. He would pay dearly for what he had done to Maret.

She untied Windwalker's lead line and let it fall. Pushing Lightfoot to a canter, she rose in her stirrups, her legs evening out the ride. Waltas cocked his head and turned. Hadde was close enough she could see the look of horror that crossed his face at the sight of her. Just as fast, he dropped his horse's reins and ran.

Hadde calculated the distances and smiled grimly. He had no hope of escape. A part of her enjoyed watching his futile efforts. She wanted the bastard to taste some of the fear Maret must have felt.

Waltas was still a hundred strides from the nearest hut when Hadde pulled abreast of him. He yanked his sword from its sheath, but she rode well clear of him. Narrowing her eyes, she drew her bowstring and let fly. Waltas tumbled to the ground in an explosion of snow.

Hadde nocked another arrow as Lightfoot skidded to a stop. Waltas struggled to his feet, her arrow protruding from his thigh. He still held his sword. Blood streamed down his face from a gash in his scalp.

Grimacing, he glanced at her and then at the village. She didn't give him time to think. Her second arrow hit him just above the left knee. Screaming, he toppled to the ground. Hadde pulled another arrow from the bowcase.

"Stop. No more," he moaned as he clutched at the shaft in his thigh. His blood stood out starkly against the white snow. Hadde drew the bowstring to her ear. Before he could react she loosed the arrow. He screamed as the arrow struck him in the shin. She guided Lightfoot closer.

"No. Please, no more."

She nocked another arrow.

"They will hang you," he said. "You can't kill a noble."

Pausing, Hadde glanced toward Sal-Oras. Would they? She turned back to him and shrugged. She was beyond caring.

"They will string you up by the neck," he continued, his voice stronger. "Run now and you might escape."

She would run, but not yet. Soon enough. She would ride to Landomere and be done with these Saladorans. What did she have to stay for? She thought of Morin. Would he punish her for killing Waltas? Would he turn against her?

She shook her head. The Saladorans hated Waltas as much as she did. They wanted revenge for what he had done to Maret. And she wouldn't give Waltas a chance to talk himself out of trouble. Waltas deserved this. The Way of the Forest didn't protect murderers. He had forfeited his right to live.

"You tried to kill Maret. How could you?" She stopped Lightfoot five strides from Waltas.

"I didn't mean to," he grunted. "I didn't know it was her."

Hadde half drew her bow and aimed it at Waltas's face. He closed his eyes and lifted both arms for protection. "She was innocent," Hadde said as she shot him in the arm.

Crying out, he clutched at the newest arrow. "It was supposed to be you," he gasped. "Everyone heard about Morin's letters. Why did you send the girl?"

"I didn't send her, you bastard. She read my letter and thought it was for her. She loves Morin and wanted to see him."

She half-drew another arrow. He flinched back and she shot him in the other arm. "No more—" An arrow impaled his palm as he tried to defend himself. "Argh! Whore!" he yelled. He rolled in agony. Red slush plastered his body. "If you're going to kill me, be done with it!"

She ignored his pain, pushing it out of her mind. He was vile. He deserved every moment. "What was that? Five? Six?" Hadde looked down at her bowcase. "We've just begun."

"Bitch." He groaned through clenched teeth. "You whore." An arrow hit him in the shoulder and he fell onto his back. Hadde pictured Maret on the surgeon's couch and nocked another arrow.

Chapter Nineteen

Hadde stared at the still form of Waltas. Blood spattered the snow for strides around him. Her rage was gone, leaving only emptiness. She stared southeast toward home. It would be so easy. The Saladorans would never catch her. She would be free of them forever. But how long was forever? How long until everyone in Long Meadow died?

She turned at the sound of approaching horsemen. Two black cloaked men on big warhorses—and they had Windwalker. How would they react to the sight of Waltas laying dead in the snow? Her hand moved to her bowcase. Fight, flee, or return to Sal-Oras?

The horses pounded closer, their hooves thudding in the fresh snow.

Morin. It was Morin and his friend Astor. Relief washed over her. Her decision delayed for a short time at least.

"You're safe?" Morin reined in next to her.

She nodded. "Maret? How is she?"

"Not well, but she lives." He looked past her. "You caught him."

"It's done. But, I don't know what to do. I want to see Maret. But what will happen because of this?" She nodded in Waltas' direction.

Morin shook his head. "There's no going back to Sal-Oras. Not for a while at least."

"Because I killed Waltas? He said that they would hang me."

"No. My brother wouldn't kill you for that alone. But it might give him the excuse he's looking for." Morin glanced at Astor and then back to Hadde. "You have a decision to make, Hadde. You can ride for home, alone, or you can ride with us to the East Teren."

"I don't understand. What excuse? Why does he want to kill me? And why the East Teren? If I can't go to Sal-Oras I want to go home." Hadde slid her bow into its case and took up Lightfoot's reins.

"Maret is alive and safe, but Orlos died in the effort to save her."

"What? No! That can't be. He's the last of the spiridus. Now Landomere is truly dead." A tremendous sense of loss filled Hadde. She hadn't even known Orlos existed just a short time ago, and now she felt his death as strongly as she would had anyone in Long Meadow died. The fact he lived had given her some hope for the Great Forest.

"My brother blames you for Orlos' death," Morin said, his face grim. "He said it never would have happened if not for you."

"If not for me? What of Waltas? He nearly killed Maret. He's responsible for Orlos' death."

"We know that." Morin's glance included Astor. "There's more. Boradin found the second half of the prophecy yesterday. It couldn't be worse timing. He thinks Orlos, the prophecy, and you are all related. He will arrest you if you return to Sal-Oras."

Hadde stared down at her hands toying with the reins. "Everything I have done has been for nothing. Everything I touch comes to harm," she said.

"I promised to help you, and I will. You have the Spiridus Token. If you want I'll give you more gold as well. You and Astor can ride for Mor-Oras and buy all the supplies you want for your people."

Hadde raised her head. "Astor and I? What about you?"

"What—" Astor started, his face showing surprise.

Morin raised his hand to cut them off. "It's not what I want. I want both of you to come with me to the East Teren. Hadde, Astor has found a way for us to save everyone. He's found the Orb of Creation."

She stared in disbelief. "How do you know?"

"I'll explain as we go. We cannot stay here—I don't want my brother's men to discover us. Please, have faith in me."

Have faith? What had faith in Saladorans gotten her? Hadde looked toward home. She pictured her parents' faces. How much she wanted to see them. But what had she accomplished? She would return a failure. But if Morin was right... if he possessed the Orb....

"Your part in all of this isn't finished," Morin continued. "It wasn't chance that gave you the Spiridus Token. You must see this out."

"Just the three of us?" Hadde asked. "If we're to retrieve the Orb, shouldn't we take a larger party? And what of your brother?"

"We don't need more people," Astor replied. "Please, we must go. Captain, she doesn't have to come."

Morin ignored his friend and stared at Hadde. "We have little time. I want you to come with me. Not because of any prophecy, or your Token, but because I want you there with me when I take the Orb."

Hadde met Morin's gaze. He was her last hope to save Long Meadow—whether it was through the Orb or a gift of gold and supplies. But it was more than that... it was more than just what he offered Long Meadow. "I'll come," she said.

"Good. I'm glad." He smiled at her and then glanced toward Sal-Oras. "We can't wait. Let's ride."

"A shame to leave good arrows," Astor said as they rode past Waltas' corpse. "There must be two dozen in him."

"Fifteen," Hadde replied. "One for each year of Maret's life."

He looked at her, dumbfounded.

"What should we do with him?" Astor asked Morin.

"Leave him," Morin replied. "He's an akinos. By his deeds he gave up the right to a noble treatment. Let Dromost take his soul. Hadde, do you want your arrows?"

She shook her head. "I'd leave them in as a warning to anyone who hurts a friend of Landomere, but I only have five remaining to me."

As Hadde dismounted Astor called out, "You won't need them! Let's be on our way."

"Who knows what we might run into?" Hadde said.

"I do know," Astor replied. "You won't need them." He looked to Morin for support.

"Come, Hadde, we must ride," Morin said. She gave Waltas' corpse one last glance and then mounted Lightfoot. She felt no emotion toward the South Teren noble. Pulling the arrows from his corpse would have meant nothing to her. She only felt regret at leaving the good arrows behind. Who knew what might happen as they rode for the Orb?

Morin led them south along the highway until they reached the village Waltas had been running for. It turned out to be long abandoned. As they rode through it Morin used his magic to light several of the buildings on fire. "It will obscure our path and sow confusion amongst our pursuers," he explained.

They rode south the entire day, only leaving the highway to avoid a town blocking their path. Hadde and Morin rode around the town while Astor entered to purchase supplies. He met them on the opposite side where they halted for brief meal out of sight of the road. The day had become warm enough to melt the night's wet snow.

"How much further south will we travel?" Hadde asked.

"We'll turn east now," Morin replied. "I think we have confused the trail enough."

"And how long until we recover the Orb?"

"Six days," Astor said, "unless the weather turns against us."

"How can you be so certain?"

"You've heard of the Messengers, I'm sure," Astor said, meeting her gaze. A smile crossed his face. "I captured one. From him I learned that Akinos holds the Orb near Ost-Oras."

"Akinos?" Hadde asked. "Who is he? Who would be known by that name?"

"Not just some person," Morin said. "It is *the* Akinos. The Slayer."

"It is him," Astor said, his head bobbing with enthusiasm. "The Orb has sustained Akinos' life, but now he's ancient and dying. Morin can take the Orb from him."

"I don't believe it," Hadde said. It went far beyond seeing magic to believing that Akinos the Slayer still lived and wielded the Orb of Creation. And that Astor had somehow learned of his location. "If what you say is true, why do the Messengers or the varcolac not take the Orb for themselves?"

"They're creatures of the Orb. They cannot harm its wielder no matter how weak he may be," Astor said.

"But how do you know it isn't a trap?"

"You would have to meet one of these Messengers to understand," Astor said. "I'm certain he told the truth. In fact, the Messengers want Morin to have the Orb. They want a leader they can believe in. A rightful king. A true descendant of Handrin the Great."

Hadde stood and crossed her arms. Frowning, she said, "Maybe they're just good liars."

Morin laughed. "Hadde, you don't know Astor as I do. There is no one I trust more." He clapped his friend on the shoulder. And then, more serious, he said, "We have to try. There's too much at stake not to."

For five days they rode northeast, the first two cutting across hill country, the following three on the Ost-Oras highway. They passed many manors, some occupied, some abandoned. At none did Morin reveal his true identity. Both he and Astor had removed the Black Company badges from their cloaks. Only their fine swords hinted at their status.

Late on the fifth day they arrived at the walled town of Egoras. Hadde and Astor followed Morin as he led them to a small inn. The few people on the streets eyed the strangers warily.

"This place has seen better days," Astor said, looking at the stone building in front of them.

Hadde followed his gaze. On one corner, a web of cracks stretched ominously upward from the foundation. The entire section appeared ready to fall. Ancient paint peeled from the closed shutters and the roof thatch was long overdue for replacement.

But bright light streamed from behind the shutters, and the smell of cooking food made Hadde's stomach rumble. "I'll risk it for a night of comfort," she said. Morin laughed. "Me too. And no one will know me here."

As they rode up to the front door, a young man and a boy ran out to see to their horses. Astor tossed each a copper. An elderly woman approached as they entered the inn's main room. She glanced at the men's swords and fine cloaks. A hint of surprise crossed her face as she took Hadde in.

"Would your lordships require chambers?" the woman asked as she wiped her dirty hands on a dirtier apron.

"Three. Your best," Astor said.

"We've only two. Many has come in from the country due to the varcolac."

"You've had trouble with them?" Morin asked.

"Worse and worse each day it seems."

"Two rooms, then," Astor said. "And hot water for washing up."

"Freg, set fires for our guests," she said to a serving woman.

Hadde surveyed the room as Astor paid. Two long tables rested before a roaring fire. Eight men sat in two groups, food and flagons before them. The patrons stared at the three travelers, all conversation having ended upon their entrance. None of their expressions were welcoming.

Each of the men wore a white armband, Hadde noticed. Returnists. All of them.

"We'll take our meals upstairs," Morin said.

"You wouldn't rather eat here?" Their host waved expansively toward the fire. "It's not often that we receive visitors. We'd love to hear news of goings-on."

"Upstairs."

"As you wish." She led them up a creaking staircase and down a hall. Two rooms, one much larger than the other, were opened to them. The thin Freg, the hem of her oft-mended dress reduced to a tatter, finished lighting the fire and scurried from the room.

The three travelers were soon settled in front of a roaring fire, eating a meal of thin stew and coarse bread. "Nothing like poor food, poor wine, and poor accommodations," Morin said, toasting them with his cup. "Only the best for my companions."

"At least we're not at the corner about to collapse," Astor said. "Maybe our side will still be standing in the morning."

"It isn't so bad," Hadde said.

Morin snorted. "I suppose. Compared to sleeping under a bush. What do you say, Astor?"

"Oh, much better," he replied. He suddenly stood and strode to the window and stared out. Hadde wondered what he was possibly looking at, the panes were so dirty as to be impossible to see through. "We're close," he almost whispered the words.

Hadde glanced at Morin and then at Astor. "You are certain of this, Astor? You really believe Morin will take the Orb?"

He turned from the window, beaming. "I know it!" He returned to the table, snatched up his wine, and downed it in a gulp. "Let's start early tomorrow. We are only a day—maybe two from our goal." Taking his cloak, he headed for the door. "I'll wake you in the morning."

"Good night," Morin said as Astor departed.

Hadde glanced from the door to Morin, who was intently pouring more wine. Nobody had spoken of sleeping arrangements, and now she found herself alone with Morin in the larger of the two rooms. It was their first time alone outside the confines of the Great Keep. The first time without the threat of prying Saladoran eyes and wagging Saladoran tongues.

Morin took a long pull of wine. "This is really awful stuff."

Hadde drank from her own cup. "Then why are you drinking so much?"

"Because I'm happy."

"You do look happy." She got up and stepped in front of the fire. The heat washed against her, driving off the memory of their cold journey.

"It *is* close, Hadde. I feel it."

"The Orb? How do you know? Magic?"

He stared into his cup. "No, not like that. I'm just certain of it. And when I get it, everything will change. The Wasting will end and all will be made whole again."

Hadde turned from the fire and smiled at him.

He grinned in return. "You don't believe me."

"Oh, I believe you. I believe you would accomplish anything you set your mind to." She paused a moment and her smile faded. "What of Maret? Will you heal her? I wish I could have seen her before we left."

"The Orb of Creation can heal all harm, or so say the Ancient Texts. But no matter the cost, I'll heal what Waltas did to her."

"Good. I care for her very much. Even if she can be a silly girl." She turned back to the fire and pulled off her heavy overtunic. Extending her palms toward the fire, she said, "Sometimes I think I've made the wrong choice. Maybe I never should have come on this journey. But now... maybe something truly great is going to happen."

"You never should have come on this journey to Ost-Oras? To win the Orb? Or you never should have departed Landomere at all?"

"I never should have left home. I abandoned my family and lost Belor. And look what has come of Maret." She touched the token at her neck. "I should have sold it and returned home."

"You should have no regrets. We do the best we can with what we have. You had to save your people. You had to do something more than sit and let the Wasting take you. You and I, Hadde, are much alike.

We're people of action."

She turned and let the heat warm her back. Morin sat leaning against the table, staring at her. His face rested against his right hand. He smiled. "Tell me the rest of the story."

"Which story?"

"The one you almost told me in the gymnasium. The one that has to do with fighting naked."

She brushed a lock of hair from her face. "You would like that?"

He nodded.

"One day, years ago, I was swimming with my friend in a stream near our village when the Kiremi attacked. There was no time to dress and I ran back to my house naked. With no safe place to go, I took my bow and climbed onto the roof.

"I stood there, naked, loosing arrow after arrow at the raiders. I can't imagine I was much to look at, just a skinny girl, but it seemed to work. Only a single arrow grazed my ribs." She touched the place where the scar rested. "They called me Hadde the Naked after that. My father always teases me."

"Clothed in armor of your natural beauty, you're nearly invulnerable." Morin dramatically spoke the words as he gestured with his cup. "Your radiance would have blinded me to such a degree that my arrows couldn't have come close to touching your flawless body."

Hadde laughed. "You've a honey tongue." She turned toward him, and he met her gaze. Wood crackled in the fire behind her.

"I seem to remember," he said, "that same day. We had just finished training with swords. You took off your tunic and sweat had turned your linen chemise transparent. There I was, staring at your breasts——"

"And you red-faced with embarrassment."

"I didn't know you so well then. And that isn't the point I'm trying to make. Do you remember what you told me then? You told me if you ever went into battle with Saladorans you would go naked because it would be such a distraction. I remember thinking you were incredibly bold, very unusual, and very beautiful."

"And what made you think of that right now?"

"Because I see you standing there, and all I can think is that I wish your tunic were transparent."

Hadde laughed, and then slowly undid the laces at her tunic's neck. Morin's eyes widened.

"And would it work?" she asked. "How distracted would you be?"

He swallowed. "Very."

Turning from him, she drew her tunic over her head and dropped it on the hearth. Keeping her arms across her chest, she turned slightly and smiled. "You know," she said, "I wonder what would have happened if the guard hadn't come along that day."

"I'll show you," he said as his chair clattered to the floor.

Chapter Twenty

The following morning Hadde and Morin made their way downstairs to the inn's great room. Astor waited for them at a table set with bowls of stew and bread. Hadde ignored the hint of a grin she thought she saw on his face. Let him smirk all he wants, she though. He had slept alone last night.

There were no other guests. The innkeeper hustled from the kitchen to the hearth, preparing for the day. She gave Hadde and Morin an off-hand wave as she went about her tasks.

"A fog rolled in last night. Thick as soup," Astor said as they approached the table.

"It's bad?" Morin asked. "I'm not in much mood to wait for it to burn off."

"No, we shouldn't wait," Astor replied. "We need to move on."

Hadde glanced at the table. "You've eaten, Astor?"

"And saddled the horses. I guess I wasn't as tired as the two of you this morning."

"But you wish you were," Morin said as he sat down.

Astor laughed and cuffed Morin on the shoulder. "I'll go and see to the last of our gear, so there's no delay."

"We'll be with you soon," Morin said. He smiled at Hadde as he sat. "This will be a great day."

"Your good mood continues," she replied. His smile was infectious.

"How couldn't it, after last night." He reached across the table and squeezed her hand.

"I think I prefer staying at this inn with you to the comforts of Sal-Oras," Hadde said.

"Once I take the Orb we can have both. Now, let's eat and be on our way."

Hadde took a bite of the stew. She hardly tasted it as she pondered Morin's response. He wanted her to stay with him in Sal-Oras? She had never thought that far into the future. She was a Landomeri huntress, and no matter how comfortable the Great Keep might be, she couldn't imagine living her life there.

"Things will be different soon," Morin continued. "Imagine a world without the Wasting. Imagine Salador under a real ruler. My brother has been such a failure. But that will all end soon."

"What will happen to your brother? And his son?"

"They will be princes of Salador. My brother is no fool. He will realize who the true king of Salador is when he sees me with the Orb."

They quickly finished the meal and hurried for the door. "Don't go out in that mess, your lordship," the innkeeper said. "You won't see the varcolac until they're right on you."

"Thank you for your warning—and for your hospitality, but we must be off."

Outside, a young stablehand stood beside Astor, watching over their horses. Astor tossed him a coin as they mounted. Hadde patted Windwalker's neck and mounted Lightfoot. In a few moments they reached the town gate and the highway.

Astor hadn't lied about the fog. Hadde doubted she could see more than thirty strides ahead of her. But Morin seemed utterly unconcerned with the poor visibility. He led them off at a rapid pace.

After a hundred strides Astor muttered, "I can't see my damned hand."

"Morin, can you magic off this fog?" Hadde asked. "You're an elementar."

"No, we'll have to ride through it." His head swiveled from side to side, alert for danger, but his pace did not diminish.

"Just blow it away." She waved her hand as if wielding the wind.

He chuckled. "Call in a foggy wind to blow off the fog? Or burn it off with fire? The effort would exhaust me within two hundred strides. No, sometimes it's best not to fight nature." They rode on, the fog swallowing both voices and hoof beats.

Hadde regarded the two men. Morin seemed unperturbed by the fog while Astor would give a sudden start as a tree or boulder appeared out of the mist. With each passing arrow flight, Astor grew more nervous. Hadde glanced at the sky. A milky sun stood well over the horizon. The fog wouldn't last.

Astor half-drew his sword at the sight of a bush emerging from the mist.

"What's wrong, Astor?" she asked.

"What? Nervous of varcolac, I suppose," he replied, his voice too loud. "They could be lurking anywhere."

"Morin doesn't seem worried."

"Well, he's an elementar." He forced a laugh. "He'll just fly away if things get too hot."

"If only it were that easy," Morin replied. "If only."

They rode on. The sun burned away at the fog. Wooded slopes rose to either side of them. It was a good sign, Hadde thought. Morin had told her that Ost-Oras was built on a low mountain range.

A birdcall trilled. Hadde knew immediately no bird had made that sound. She drew her bow from its case and nocked an arrow. Only five arrows, why had she listened to Astor? She glanced toward the sound and saw ghostly forms flitting through the woods. "Morin! There are men to our left—in the woods," Hadde said.

His sword sang from its sheath. "Ride!" He spurred his stallion forward. Hadde leaned low and put her heels to Lightfoot. Windwalker galloped obediently behind. Someone shouted in front of her. Men scattered as Morin and Astor plowed into them.

Morin's sword flashed and a man fell. His horse reared up, hooves lashing out to strike another. Astor cut down a third. "They're fleeing," she called out. A dozen men leaped through the trees as they ran. She relaxed the tension in her bow.

Several bodies lay in the road, all clad in rough fur clothing and wearing their hair in dozens of long braids. "Tyskmen," Morin said. "They should not be here. No Tyskman has ever come this far south."

"Bandits?" Astor asked. "Look! Here is what they were after."

Another body rested on the road just ahead, a Saladoran. His horse lay nearby.

Morin dismounted and knelt by the body, and then peered down the road. "A herald. He was riding for Sal-Oras. I wonder what news he carried."

"Morin, they're coming back," Hadde said. Dozens of forms slipped through the woods in their direction. Two appeared much larger than the others. Impossibly large. She dismissed it as some trick of the light. "More than before."

"We'll ride for it," Morin said, remounting.

"Which way?" Hadde glanced back in the direction of Egoras and safety.

"Onward," Astor said. "The Messenger awaits us."

Morin nodded his agreement. "Let's go."

The three riders set off with the howling Tyskmen running in pursuit. Dozens of warriors emerged from the woods. At the back of the pack lumbered the two huge figures. It hadn't been the light, Hadde thought.

The warriors quickly fell behind, only to be enshrouded in the remaining mist. Hadde took a deep breath. At least they weren't varcolac. She remembered their chasing down Nidon and his companions when she had first arrived in Salador.

Once well clear Morin slowed the pace. "That was no group of bandits. It was a warband," he said.

"I don't understand it," Astor said. He still held his bloody sword in his hand. Hadde thought his face looked pained, or maybe fearful. But he hadn't shown any fear during the fight. He had cut down one Tyskmen and chased others from the road.

"Duke Avran will have to raise a force to clear the highway." Morin said. "I can't believe my brother has let Salador fall into such a sorry state. Astor, your Messenger friend is close? Could the Tyskmen have found him?"

Astor just stared into the distance.

"Astor!" Morin snapped. "Where is the Messenger?"

"Ahead... today... we will meet him today."

"And he's safe from these Tysk raiders?"

"Yes, he's safe. They won't harm him." Astor didn't look at Morin as he spoke, but stared down the road behind them.

"How do you know?" Hadde asked.

"He's too powerful. The Tysk cannot harm him."

"Then how did you capture him?"

"I surprised him!" Astor shouted, his face red with anger. "And I'm no Tyskman—I'm a knight of Salador. Now let's go!" He rode off without waiting for them.

"What's wrong with him?" Hadde asked Morin as Astor rode clear.

"The Wasting has taken everything from him—his family and his manor. All he has left is his empty title. He thinks himself a failure. Finding the Orb and restoring it to me will be a great accomplishment. He will have done something greater than any other knight of Salador. No one will be able to look down on him again."

Several hundred arrow-flights later, the fog had burned off and the sun shone brightly. "We've left them well behind," Astor said. "Without horses there is little chance they'll try to follow."

"How do you know they have no horses?" Hadde asked.

"I know the Tysk," he said sharply. "They don't ride."

"Very well." She held up her hands to fend off his anger.

"This is where the Messenger will meet us." Astor said. "Let's leave the road and take shelter. I know a place."

"You're certain he will show?" Morin asked, craning his neck to look up the road. "How long will we have to wait for him?"

"He will ride to this place late each afternoon and then ride back toward Ost-Oras. He should be here soon," Astor said with a glance to the afternoon sun. He wiped his forearm across his brow and then rubbed his palms on his trousers. "Come, follow me."

Hadde wondered at the sweat running down his temple. It was a sunny day, but it was still just past midwinter and a cold breeze blew down the shallow valley. She and Morin followed Astor as he led them off the road and into a gully. The surrounding trees were bare of leaves, and many showed signs of Wasting-sickness. They were no healthier than the trees of Landomere. It was a stark reminder of the Wasting's strength.

The rocky gully was clear of trees. An old firepit had been built up against a large boulder. It made sense, the gully made an excellent sheltered camp. Except for one thing. "Astor, we can't see much from down here. What if the Tysk come upon us?"

"I'll stand watch," he said as he dismounted. He started back up the slope toward the road. "Take care of the horses and have something to eat. There is food in Windwalker's saddle bags," he called as he disappeared.

"Morin, there's something wrong with him," Hadde said.

"Just nervous," he replied. "I have to admit, I am too." He clapped his hands together and rubbed them back and forth. "The Orb changes everything."

"I don't know," Hadde said. "I don't feel it." She took their provisions to the rock near the firepit. The rock formed a natural table, if a little sloped. "I've seen your magic, and your brother's. I've also seen the varcolac. I suppose the Orb should not seem so impossible to me."

Hadde drew her knife and cut thick slices from a dry sausage. She offered a piece to Morin, but he waved it away. "Not now," he said. She shrugged and took a bite. As she chewed she glanced up the slope for a sign of Astor. She'd cut some for him, although she doubted he would have an appetite.

She saw some motion, and then Astor appeared at the top of the slope. And he had someone with him. Hadde's eyes widened in surprise and she quickly swallowed her mouthful. "Look!" she said, pointing with her knife.

Morin quickly rose from where he crouched next to her. Hadde wiped her blade, sheathed it, and stood with him.

The white-cloaked figure stood tall and broad-shouldered. A deep hood concealed his face. Astor beamed as he led the stranger into the gully. "Who are you?" Morin asked as the figure approached. Morin's hand rested on his sword hilt.

"Well met, Prince Morin," the stranger said. He had a strong, deep voice. "I am Brother Resnam, Messenger of the Order of Eternal Knights. I am here to lead you to the Orb of Creation."

Morin looked to Astor and then at Resnam. "The Orb is near?" Morin asked.

"Not far. It awaits you."

Hadde stared at the stranger. His robes concealed all. She peered beneath his cowl, but it shrouded his face too much for her to see anything. The robes were as white as any she had ever seen. She noticed Helna's Orb stitched in gold on the right breast.

"You are the Orb's true master," the man continued. "You are the rightful heir. You will restore Salador to glory."

Morin stared at the hooded man in silence.

"We should listen to him," Astor urged. "Here's the chance you've——"

Morin cut him off with a raised hand. "And how can I trust you, Brother Resnam? You who won't even show your face."

"Very well," Resnam said. Hadde gasped as he removed his hands from his sleeves. Both were the color of liquid silver and shone brightly even under the shadow of the trees. Slowly, he lifted his hands and drew back his hood. His face, his hair, his eyes—every feature gleamed in flowing argent.

"What manner of creature are you?" Morin asked. Hadde couldn't believe how stoically he reacted to the sight of the man's skin. She had recoiled two steps without even realizing it.

"I'm a man, like yourself. But I'm also an Eternal Knight." Spreading his hands in front of him he said, "I've touched the Orb of Creation and been blessed by it. It has granted me eternal life and health. It's the fountain of all life. There is no need for doubt, Prince Morin. Permit me to lay my hands upon you, and you'll feel the power and the glory of the Holy Orb."

Smiling, he stepped toward Morin.

In an instant Morin's sword flashed from its sheath and pointed at Resnam's neck.

"Morin, no!" Astor stepped forward and grasped Morin's hand. "Let him touch you. I've felt the touch of a Messenger. There is nothing to fear. Their blessing is like touching the source of life itself. You can feel the goodness in it."

"You said nothing of this to me," Morin said, his voice cold. "You didn't tell me that *this* was what a Messenger would be." Hadde slowly stepped aside, moving herself closer to Lightfoot and her bow.

"I am unarmed, my prince," Resnam said. "My only wish is to show you the glory of the Holy Orb. Let me lay my hands upon you and then take you to the Orb of Creation."

"No," Morin said. "You'll instead come with me to Ost-Oras. There—"

"Morin, you can trust him," Astor said. He faced Resnam. "Will you touch me, and demonstrate your trustworthiness to Prince Morin?"

"Come forward, Sir Astor, and feel the blessing of the Orb."

"Don't do it, Astor," Morin warned.

The men paid her no attention as Hadde pulled Hawkeye and her arrows from their case. *Five arrows!*

"I've felt their touch," Astor said. "It's *good*. To touch them is to touch Helna. It is to touch the hand of the goddess."

Astor knelt before the Eternal Knight. Hadde watched, awed, as the eternal placed his hands upon Astor's head. Golden-silver light poured from Resnam's hands and suffused Astor's head. For a moment, Astor's head gleamed as silver as the Eternal Knight's.

"Be blessed, Sir Astor," Resnam said.

Astor sagged for a moment as the eternal lifted his hands.

"It's goodness," Astor said. He turned to Morin, a rapturous expression on his face. "Let him touch you."

Morin sheathed his sword. "If anyone but you asked me to do this, I would refuse."

"You can trust me, Morin." Astor stepped aside as the eternal approached the prince.

"No. Don't," Hadde said. She glanced from Astor to Morin. "It doesn't feel right. I don't trust them." She gripped the arrows in her bow hand, ready to nock and loose in one swift motion.

Morin paused. "If I can't trust Astor, I can trust no one at all."

"This... it just isn't right." Hadde said. She didn't know how she felt what she felt. She glanced around, a sudden feeling of oppression overcoming her.

"I would give my life for Morin!" Astor shouted. His hands shook as he spoke. "He's my prince, my captain, and my friend. I'd do anything for him."

"Hadde," Morin said, "Astor is my brother-in-arms. We've faced death together. I trust him."

"But I don't," she said. "He—"

"Stop," Morin cut her off. "I'm a magus elementar. I can handle myself. And if this is the path to the Orb of Creation, I must follow it. Believe in me."

Hadde took a deep breath and glanced from Morin to Resnam. Was it really happening? Was Morin going to get the Orb? It was too simple. No more suffering. No more pain. After all these years the Wasting would finally end.

The eternal stood in front of Morin and then dropped to his knees. "Let me take your hand, my prince." Morin sheathed his sword and then pulled off his glove and offered his hand to Resnam.

"My lord," the Eternal Knight said as he took Morin's hand in both of his own. For a moment nothing happened. And then Resnam said, "Open yourself to me, my prince. You shield yourself from the Orb of Creation."

"No. Unhand me."

Morin pulled his hand back, but the eternal clasped Morin's wrist. "Please, my lord," Resnam begged. "It's easier this way. There is no harm."

"Unhand me!"

Hadde cried out as the Resnam lunged forward and tackled Morin to the ground. Showers of sparks and fire erupted from Morin's hands as he fought off the eternal.

Resnam's robes burst into flame, but still he pinned the prince beneath him.

"Get him off!" Morin shouted.

Hadde drew her bow and shot Resnam in the chest. She was only strides away, and the arrow penetrated deep into his body.

He grunted in pain but didn't let go.

"Stop!" Astor shouted, his voice frantic.

Hadde shot another arrow into Resnam, but still he held Morin fast.

The Eternal Knight's robes burned away, revealing silver skin beneath. But where Morin's magical fire was strongest, the skin went iron black, as had two large patches where Hadde's arrows stuck.

"Stop, Hadde!" Astor charged at her.

She ignored him and shot again. The arrow struck within a handbreadth of the others, and finally Morin cast the eternal aside.

Morin leaped to his feet, his sword suddenly in his hand.

"Don't!" Astor turned from Hadde and grasped Morin's sword arm.

"What are you doing? Leave off!" Morin shouted. The two men struggled for his sword.

Resnam staggered to his feet. Hadde stared as he pulled one of her arrows from his body. It was impossible. Silver blood dripped from the shaft. The drops turned black as they fell. The eternal cast the arrow to the ground.

From the forest came shouts and footsteps crashing toward them. Hadde wanted to turn, but Resnam was advancing on Morin. As the eternal lurched forward, he pulled another arrow from his chest.

Astor reeled as Morin punched him in the face. Leaping past his stunned friend, Morin struck the eternal a savage stroke to the neck. A raised arm partially deflected the blow, but the sword sank deep into the eternal's throat. Brilliant silver blood gushed from Resnam's neck as his body toppled heavily to the ground.

Astor fell across Resnam's body. "What have you done?" he sobbed.

"Run, Hadde!" Morin shouted. Startled, she looked up to see a dozen eternals, dressed in white and gold, charging toward them.

"The horses!" Morin turned to face the attack. He raised his arms and a wall of fire descended on the eternals. Four fell, their robes engulfed in flames. But most charged through the inferno.

Hadde turned to Lightfoot only to have an eternal lunge for her. She desperately dodged him and was knocked to the ground. Hadde rolled to her feet, but the eternal was past—heading for Morin. The eternals had nearly surrounded him. All wore cloaks and armor scorched by flame. But none except Resnam, had been slain.

"Morin! Behind you!"

He turned and a jet of fire struck the eternal. He fell back, clothes afire, but still standing.

As the eternal reeled back from Morin's fire, his companions advanced. The prince turned his fire on them. But the flames were weaker and the eternals pushed forward. Morin staggered, although he hadn't been struck by any blow.

An eternal leaped and tackled Morin from behind. A swirling maelstrom of dirt and leaves rose around the melee, and he disappeared from view.

"Morin!" she shouted.

The war-cries of a score of varcolac overwhelmed her cry. Silver-eyed warriors poured over the slope and into the camp. Hadde loosed an arrow, felling the first. Her last arrow struck another in the leg.

With no time to even mount, Hadde scrambled to the firepit and put her back against the boulder. Dropping Hawkeye, she drew her knife, knowing that it was hopeless.

The wind roared. Hadde turned as Morin leaped from the cloud of debris, buffeted by gusts of wind. He landed outside the ring of eternals, staggered to his feet, and stumbled toward her. He fell at her feet just before the first varcolac arrived.

Hadde lifted a stone from the fire-ring and heaved it at the varcolac. It caught him flush in the forehead. He stood in front of her, stunned, just two strides away. The varcolac behind him roared in anger.

Morin staggered to his feet as three varcolac cast javelins. The missiles veered off, caught by a gust of magical wind. All cracked into the boulder behind Hadde.

Morin fell to one knee. His breath came in ragged gasps. The white-clad eternals he had just escaped surged in their direction, blocked from closing by the varcolac.

Hadde snatched a javelin from the ground. As she rose, two varcolac leapt at Morin. He slashed at them with his sword and they fell back. Hadde raised the javelin.

Morin feebly waved his sword at the varcolac. A short jet of fire flickered and went out. It was hopeless. There would be no escape.

"Back! Leave off the prince!" an eternal shouted, but two varcolac had already thrown themselves atop Morin. He toppled backward, his sword clattering to the ground.

Hadde lunged at a varcolac just as another hurled his javelin at her. She watched as its gleaming head spiraled at her. For an instant she felt helpless, more helpless than she had ever felt in her life. Arrows had been shot at her before, an axe swung at her, but always there had been some hope of evading them. Not now.

The javelin struck her in the chest with terrible force. Harder than any blow she had ever taken. Her breastbone shattered as the speartip plunged into her and slammed her against the boulder. Her hands clutched the smooth javelin shaft as she slumped forward. So smooth. Polished.

Blood covered her hands. *Her blood.* She toppled to her side. Pain. So much pain.

She tried to draw a breath, but choked and gagged on the hot blood filling her mouth. Her lungs burned as if filled with flaming embers.

The varcolac held Morin fast in front of her.

He stared at her. His mouth opened and closed, but she heard nothing.

She tried to say his name, but couldn't draw a breath, tried to reach out to him, but couldn't move her arm.

She wished she could touch him one last time. Then she died.

Chapter Twenty-one

Hadde stared through the open cottage door at the two corpses huddled together in front of the cold hearth. They had starved to death in each other's arms. The Wasting had taken them.

She was too late.

"Mother?" she whispered into the dark room. "Father?"

"Return unto us, Hadde," a man's voice called out to her.

She ignored him. She would die here, with her parents. She didn't deserve to live.

"Depart that fell place," the voice ordered her.

She ran down a dark stone corridor. Maret's anguished screams urged her on. But no matter how fast she tried to run, some invisible barrier held her back.

Hadde saw the dagger as it was drawn across Maret's face. She saw the terror in the girl's eyes. "Save me, Hadde!" the maiden screamed.

"Where are you?" Hadde shouted. The corridor went on forever, thousands of doors lining both walls.

The dagger plunged into Maret's chest.

Hadde fell to her knees. It was all her fault.

"She lives yet. Return unto us, fair Hadde."

The stones of Belor's cairn lurched as if something under them moved. Hadde tried to step back, but her feet were rooted to the ground.

A skeletal hand burst from the mound. Flesh and muscle hung in tattered ropes from the bones.

"No!" She tried to close her eyes, but couldn't.

Belor erupted from the mound. His worm-eaten corpse shambled up to Hadde. The stench of death overwhelmed her.

"You did this to me," he hissed as he wrapped his hands around her neck.

She fell into a black abyss as fear overwhelmed her. Downward she plummeted, screaming her anguish. She had failed them all.

"Do not relinquish faith. Hold fast."

She flailed her arms as she fell. There would be no return. Dromost would take her and reward her failure with an eternity of pain.

A hand grasped her wrist as light cut the darkness. Rays of gold and argent played upon her. She searched for the source but saw only its brightness.

"Live."

Warmth engulfed her as the golden glow suffused her body. She wanted it to last forever.

She opened her eyes. Above her a roof of multicolored fabrics shimmered in the sunlight, mesmerizing her. A tent—a monstrous tent. So large even a Landomeri oak could easily fit within it. A spider web of ropes held the gay roof aloft.

She lowered her eyes to the tapestry walls surrounding her. The partitions were three strides tall—frameworks of wood covered with wonderfully embroidered pastoral scenes of people at work in lush green fields.

Light shimmered over her as the canopy wafted in the breeze. Laughter came to her from some nearby part of the tent—girl's laughter. It reminded her of Maret and Jenae giggling over Morin. The sound was so full of life.

Life.

Hadde touched herself where the spear had impaled her. Her hand came to rest on a soft quilt. She lowered the quilt and stared at her naked chest. There was no wound. She sat up and stared closer, moving her Spiridus Token in case it hid any sign of injury.

Nothing. *I am alive... but how?* She remembered the chaotic fight, the eternals, and the varcolac. But how had she come to be here? She was clean, uninjured, and resting in a soft bed of white sheets. It made no sense.

The scent of roasted fowl wafted through the room. Her stomach rumbled. In the room rested a small table with two stools beside it and a camp chest. Next to the chest rested Hawkeye and her bowcase. She frowned. They had left her armed. They had even refilled her case with arrows. But why? She had killed varcolac and an eternal. Who held her?

She got out of bed and crouched by the chest, glancing over her shoulder at the curtain door. She ran her hand over her bow. It was undamaged. Opening the chest, she found a white dress, a linen chemise, and tall, soft boots inside. Her pack and hunting knife were there as well. Her cloak was there, but her other clothes were missing.

Hadde pulled the tunic and dress over her head. The fabric was as fine as any Maret had shared with her but much more plain. She stared at her knife as she slipped on the boots. She reached for it and then, glancing over her shoulder, pulled her hand back. She shook off the fear that someone was watching her. They wouldn't have left the knife if they didn't intend her to have it. She belted it around her waist.

"Pardon. May I enter?" A girl's voice asked from beyond the tapestry-covered entry.

Startled by the voice, Hadde's hand went to her knife. But what danger was there here? Whoever held her had left her armed. "Come in," Hadde replied. She rose and faced the door.

A fair-haired, light-skinned girl entered the room, carrying a tray of food. She wore a plain white dress and felt boots like Hadde's. Pastries and a cup of steaming liquid sat on the tray. "I am called Nadas. I serve to you. You are hungry?" the girl asked. She spoke in a heavily accented singsong voice.

Hadde glanced at the food. She was hungry, but shook her head, no. "Where am I? Where is Prince Morin?"

"You are with Akinos—in his tent." The girl smiled and placed the food on the table. "Eat now. More with prince, later."

"Akinos? It's true? He is alive after all this time?"

"Yes-yes. He lives a long life. The Orb brings him long life."

Impossible, Hadde thought. The Orb had been stolen five hundred years ago. But then there were many things she had seen that just a few weeks ago she would have thought impossible. "May I leave? Go out and see Prince Morin?"

"No. He is very occupied." The girl smiled as if hoping to soften the refusal.

"What about my horse? Can I see Lightfoot?"

"Horse? I do not know. I will ask. You eat." She smiled again as turned for the entrance.

"Wait," Hadde said, "Can you stay and talk? I want to know more. I want to know what is happening."

"I am sorry, but I go. Another visitor comes to see you soon."

"Who?"

"Commander Seremar comes. I must go. Eat. He comes soon." The girl gave Hadde another smile and departed.

Hadde watched her go, more curious than ever. She wished she had asked about her wound. How any of it was possible. Unable to resist her hunger, Hadde ate one of the pastries. It was light and sweet, filled with some berry filling. The mug of tea was hot, if a little bitter. She paused and chuckled as she stared at a half-eaten morsel. *Akinos the Betrayer serves sweet tarts and herb tea to his prisoners.*

"Hadde of Landomere, may I come in?" a man's voice asked from beyond the curtained entrance.

Hadde gulped some tea to wash down the tart filling her mouth. "Who are you?" she asked as she brushed flakes from her mouth.

"Brother Seremar."

Brother. Dread swept over her. An Eternal Knight. She put down the pastry. Could she flee? The walls were only hanging tapestries. She could slash the ties that connected them at the corners and be gone in a moment.

"Hadde?" he called again.

She pushed back against her fear. Even if she escaped the room, where would she go? "Come in," she said. The curtain rose and the eternal entered. Save for his bare head, he wore a full suit of armor. Unlike the other eternals he wasn't accoutered in white and gold. He wore a yellow tabard decorated with a black dragon rampant. The knight had a sword at his waist and carried his helm in the crook of his right arm.

He bowed his head in greeting. It was disconcerting meeting his silver gaze. The liquid silver of his skin flowed and swirled as she stared at him. It made his face almost impossible to read.

"You don't look... I mean dress... like the other eternals," Hadde said, pulling her gaze from his face.

"Not only am I a Brother of the Eternal Order, but I am an East Teren earl as well. I command Akinos' Saladoran knights. He permits me to wear my family coat-of-arms." Laughing, he removed a gauntlet and held his silver hand in front of his face. He worked his fingers as he turned his hand over. "There are some, even those who have known me long, who have trouble distinguishing between me and the other brethren. My colors set me apart so that they might better recognize me. They let the knights of the East Teren know that I am still one of them."

"I see," Hadde said. Something about the earl's tabard looked familiar, as if she had seen it before. But there were so many knights in Sal-Oras, she couldn't be certain of it.

"You are well?" Seremar asked.

"I am. Although confused by what has happened to me. I don't even know how I am still alive. I was dead—I felt the javelin strike me."

"I understand, and maybe I can bring you some answers. As for your healing, that will wait for another to answer." He paused. "I was told you wish to see your horses."

"I do. And Prince Morin as well."

"He will come to you later. But I can take you to your steed." He motioned toward the entrance. "I have some time. And wish to speak to you in any case."

She grabbed her cloak and followed him out of the room and down a short corridor bordered by rooms created by fabric partitions. Brightly clothed guards in scale armor saluted them as they departed the massive tent.

Sunlight momentarily blinded Hadde. Shading her eyes, she stared up at a fortress jutting from a steep hill. A sea of tents rested between Akinos' pavilion and the walls. "Is that Ost-Oras?" Hadde asked.

"It is," he said. "A great city." The fortress stood on a hill north of a shallow stream. Walls, greater than those of Sal-Oras, ringed the city. A huge keep protected the western end of the city, where the hill was the least steep and the approaches easier.

"Why do you wish to speak with me?" Hadde asked as Seremar led her toward the city gates. Near the gates she spied a corral. She searched for Lightfoot and Windwalker amongst the many warhorses gathered there. "Because I know that you were in Sal-Oras and might have word of my daughter."

"Your daughter? How would I know of her?"

"You might. She's a Maiden in Waiting in Sal-Oras. Her name is Maret."

Hadde gasped. "Your daughter? But you're—"

"Eternal. I only recently accepted Akinos' touch. Maret does not yet know of my transformation." He smiled. "She will join me soon enough. Tell me of her. Is she well?"

Hadde opened her mouth to reply and stopped. What should she say to him? What would Maret say if she knew what had become of her father?

"I see by your expression that all isn't well. Tell me."

"She was attacked."

"Attacked?" He grabbed her arm.

She tried to pull away, but his grip was vice-like. "She's alive, but she's badly hurt."

"Who did this?" he demanded.

"Earl Waltas. From—"

"I know of him. Is he still in Sal-Oras?"

"It happened only days ago. Please let go, you're hurting my arm."

The eternal's vice-like grip tightened. "She's badly injured? In danger of dying?"

Hadde grimaced in pain. "Orlos the Spiridus was summoned to help heal her. Morin told me that Maret was still alive."

He released her. "Orlos' presence gives me some comfort. What happened to Waltas?"

"He's dead," Hadde said. She rubbed her arm where he had gripped it. The man's hold on her had been impossibly strong.

211

"Who killed him? Champion Nidon?"

"I did it." Hadde glared at the eternal. "Maret is very dear to me. After Waltas attacked her he fled. I couldn't let him escape."

For a time Seremar stood silently. Hadde thought she saw a tear on his gleaming face, but it was difficult to tell against his silver skin. "How severe were her injuries?" Seremar asked.

"Prince Morin had hope for her." Hadde wouldn't say more. How would Seremar react if he knew the full nature of her wounds?

The eternal wiped a hand across his face and stood taller. "As long as she survives until the Orb arrives in Sal-Oras, all harm will be cured then. Come, let us find your horse." They walked silently to the corral. Hadde smiled as she spotted her two horses. She whistled; Lightfoot snorted and trotted to her. Windwalker followed loyally.

Hadde jumped the fence and hugged her horse. "She's well. I was worried about her."

"Akinos' Rigarians don't know horses, but there are enough Saladorans in the host to watch over our few mounts."

"Rigaria?" Hadde asked as she petted her horse's neck. "That's the place of legend where the veden lived."

"The veden are long gone. Humans live there now."

"And varcolac."

"And all are good," he said, his tone softer. "All serve Akinos."

"I…" Hadde paused and scanned the encampment below Ost-Oras' walls. "You are saying the varcolac are good? And look at this army. I don't like it. I don't see the good in it."

"You will meet Akinos and then you will understand. It's hard to overcome a lifetime of false teaching. But Akinos isn't evil."

"But how can I believe you? You're one of his Eternal Knights."

"I may be eternal, but I still have free will. And you don't have to trust me. I'll show you Akinos' goodness. Come with me."

Hadde patted Lightfoot goodbye and followed Seremar to Ost-Oras' great gate. They walked past a slow-moving train of wagons entering the city. The guards bowed to Seremar as he passed.

"The city fell quickly," Seremar said as they passed a second defensive wall. "The Returnists within opened the gates to us. But, unfortunately, others resisted."

Hadde froze. "A giant!" The man crossing their path was nine feet tall and massively built. He carried a huge wooden beam on his shoulder. And then she remembered the giants moving through the fog when the Tyskmen had ambushed them on the road east of the town of Egoras. "There are giants in Akinos' army?"

"Do not fear them. The capcaun, the urias, and the varcolac are all children of Akinos." He nodded toward the giant. "The capcaun, and their children, the urias, are giant in stature. But they are all Children of the Orb and serve a just cause."

"What just cause?"

"The cause of salvation."

They exited a second gate-tunnel into a large square. Everywhere Hadde looked she saw activity. Directly across from her, crowds of Saladorans watched as giants and Rigarians swarmed over a partially destroyed building. The sounds of their hammers and saws echoed across the square as they rebuilt the structure.

To her left she spied long lines of Saladorans waiting in front of six large wagons. As they reached the front of the line, measures of grain were poured into sacks and given to them. Steam rose from a dozen cauldrons next to the wagons. Rigarians ladled bowls of food to those waiting for their rations.

"The people were starving," Seremar said. "Akinos made his army's stores available to them. There isn't much to spare, but he saw the people's need."

"What is happening over there?" Hadde asked. To her right a shorter line of people waited in front of a large white tent. A man walked hunched over, covered by tattered blankets and cloaks. Others leaned upon crutches or another's arm for support.

"Follow me."

As they approached, Hadde watched white-robed men and women wander up the line sorting the city's residents into two groups. Surgeons and their apprentices attended to the larger group. The smaller group awaited entry to the tent.

"They're healers?" Hadde asked.

"Rigarian surgeons are unmatched in their skill. But they're limited to mortal means." Seremar led her into the white tent. "Eternals, however, are limited only by the Orb of Creation."

Two Eternal Knights attended those permitted entry into the tent. Both wore robes of white and gold. Their bared silver arms and heads shone brilliantly in the shelter of the tent.

A boy, thin and pale, and coughing violently, was led before one of the eternals. The child weakly resisted the elderly man pulling him forward.

"I'm scared," the boy whimpered before another fit doubled him over.

The eternal strode forward and placed his hands upon the child's head. Silver veins shot through the boy's skin, and almost instantly the coughing ended, and the boy stood upright.

He paused a moment, staring up at the eternal, and then lunged forward and embraced the knight.

The second eternal healed a man whose arm was covered with a bloody bandage. He exclaimed in surprise as he unwrapped the coverings to find his arm healed.

"I am your servant," the man said, kneeling before the Eternal Knight.

"Give your thanks to Akinos. It's he who will save us all."

"Is this what happened to me?" Hadde asked.

"This and more." Seremar took Hadde's elbow and guided her from the tent. His touch was cold—metallic.

She looked at the line of sick and injured waiting to get into the tent. "Why are some turned away? Can't the eternals... can't you heal everyone?" she asked.

"Akinos does as much as he can. But his power isn't limitless. Each healing takes a bit of Akinos' life... it ages him and he is old already. We heal only the most needy. For the time being, the others will have to make do with human care. But their wait won't be long. Soon all will be healed. "

Seremar led her back to Akinos' tent. She said nothing as they walked, lost deep in thought. Nothing she had seen was as she had expected. In fact, it appeared the opposite. Akinos, a creature of legendary evil was healing the sick and rebuilding ruined buildings.

But the behavior of his varcolac nagged at her. Their brutality was at odds with all else she had seen. "Why use war and terror as your means to spread peace?" Hadde asked. "Why use an army to demonstrate goodness?"

"All will be explained. I have to leave you now," Seremar said as they neared Hadde's room. "And... thank you for dealing with Sir Waltas. I'm glad that it was a woman who killed him."

"It doesn't matter who did it. He had to pay for what he did to Maret."

"As you will," he said. "I have matters I must attend to. I will see you again." He gave her a short bow and departed.

The curtain to Hadde's chamber opened behind her. Nadas appeared and motioned Hadde in. "I go to fetch your dinner," the young attendant said. "Akinos comes soon."

"What do you mean? Akinos is coming here?"

"He does," she beamed at Hadde. "He grants you great... courtesy."

214

Chapter Twenty-two

"He comes," Nadas said.

Hadde stood from her barely-touched meal and backed from the chamber's entrance. Her heart pounded a heavy beat in her chest.

"No, do not be afraid." The attendant rushed to her side and held her hand. "It is good. He comes."

The curtain parted and two blond giants strode in. Both were half again as tall, and more massively built, than any man Hadde had ever seen. They wore white tunics with golden-rayed Orbs displayed upon them. The first giant carried a stout wooden chair that he placed upon the floor. The second carried a frail man. Gently, the giant eased the elderly man into the chair. With graceful bows they backed from the room.

Nadas gave Hadde's hand a squeeze. "I go as well," she said.

Hadde clasped her hands in front of her to stop their shaking. Akinos was ancient. More so than even Orlos. Gaunt, almost skeletal, no part of his skin was untouched by deep crevasses of age. He wore robes of the purest white trimmed in gold. Hadde wondered that she didn't fear him, this legendary evil. But there was a kindliness to his large, brown eyes that set her mind at ease. His eyes were untouched by age, bright and clear and happy.

"Be seated," Akinos said as he motioned to the bed beside her. She obeyed without thought.

"How is it—" Hadde started and caught her breath. In his right hand he held a crystal sphere. It fit easily in the palm of his hand. At its center burned a gold and silver flame that pulsed like a heartbeat.

The Orb of Creation.

Hadde took a deep breath. "I was dead. Did you save me with… it?"

"Death held thine spirit in her dark shroud. Thou dreamest the nightmares of regret before the final darkness. Thou wert as close as one might come to that final end and still return."

Hadde had no difficulty following his speech. Although strange, it was easier to comprehend than that of the commoners. He didn't sound foreign, just *different.*

"But a spear struck me," she said.

215

"Thou wert fortunate a full score Brothers of the Eternal Order surrounded thee. Through their hands flowed the healing grace of the Orb of Creation. They held thine death at bay until thou wert borne here."

"But why? Why did they save me?"

"Thou wouldst prefer death?" He chuckled.

"But I'm just... I'm nobody special."

He laughed again. "King Boradin does not agree. Nor does Orlos. And what does thou wearest around thine neck but a Spiridus Token? The Great Spirit of Landomere loves thee. Who is Akinos to let thee perish?"

"How do you know all this?"

"Akinos knows." He nodded and raised his brows. "Akinos knows."

Hadde looked into his eyes. They seemed like deep wells—wells of knowledge. Again, he smiled and nodded, as if he knew her thoughts. "And Morin?" Hadde asked. "How is he?"

"Safe and unharmed. Thou shalt see him forthwith."

She stared at the Orb for a moment, and then at the old man's face. His accent wasn't strange, nor foreign. It was *old.* "How are you... how can you be Akinos?" she whispered.

He smiled. "Akinos sits before thee."

"But you can't be. You don't look—"

He laughed. It was a young sound that gave no hint of his age. "Thou wert imagining a monster? A flame-scaled giant with a mighty ram's head? Dagger-like steel talons? Perhaps dragon wings as well? Akinos is none of those things, as thou canst well see."

Hadde tore her gaze from the Orb and looked into Akinos' eyes. It wasn't possible. This couldn't be Akinos. But how could she deny the Orb?

"Five hundred years of lies have turned Akinos into a horrible beast," he continued. "Five hundred years of stories and legends reviling his deeds have turned him into the Slayer, the Betrayer, the Lord of Death." He leaned closer in his chair. "But there is another story. One thou hast not been told.

"Akinos' dear brother was Handrin the Great. Savior of the Light, wielder of the Godshield Forsvar, victor of the War for the Orb, and a most horrible tyrant."

"But Handrin was good," she said. "All the stories say so."

"Thusly his descendants, or shall we name them worshippers, want one to believe. They wrote the legends that have been passed down over the centuries. Dost thou think the House of Handrin wants the truth to be known?" Akinos shook his head. "If Akinos had not slain him, Handrin

216

would have taken the Orb and used it to make himself, not the keeper of life, as Helna intended, but the absolute master of all life. He would have used the Orb of Creation to enslave the world for his own vile pleasures."

"He was a great man," Hadde objected. "He slew the veden."

"Ahh, yes, the veden. The evil slayers of the innocent spiridus—the beautiful, fey creatures of Landomere who lived in harmony with the Great Forest." Akinos laughed again, but this time the sound was humorless. "Thou hast learned how the evil veden slaughtered them, but those stories are all purest falsehoods."

"They were not evil," he continued. "They were only the veden. And their only wrongdoing was being on the losing side of a war. The veden were a graceful, magical people. Does it make them evil that they preferred night over day? The stars and the moon over the sun? Thusly their god created them. They worked no evil in their hearts."

He pointed a finger at her. "Thou thinkest they destroyed the spiridus, dost thou not? The spiridus joined the War for the Orb late—thine own legends tell thee so. But the legends lie when they tell thee the Army of Light was near destruction and the veden were on the verge of conquering all under their evil onslaught. Wishest thou to know the truth, Hadde?"

"I know the truth," she said. "They were evil. The veden came to Landomere and killed all of the spiridus. They destroyed Belavil. I've seen the ruins." In her mind she pictures the beautiful ruins as they must have once appeared—terraces overflowing with gardens of flowers, homes carved from the mountain itself and adorned with flowing scrollwork vines. The veden had left the city a shattered ruin. She had been told so her entire life.

"In truth, the veden dangled on the brink of destruction. They barely held strong their last refuge, in Antok. But so strong was Antok that Handrin and the other human elementars could not break its ramparts asunder.

"The spiridus were convinced to join the war when Handrin promised to craft them another forest in Rigaria, the veden homeland. It was Orlos who made this vile deal and sealed the fate of both the veden and the spiridus. And so the invisible spiridus crept into Antok and massacred the entire population of veden women and children. Every last one was slain."

"That isn't true! Orlos—"

"Akinos was there!" The Orb's pulse quickened and its light momentarily blinded Hadde. She recoiled from Akinos' anger. "It happened! Only after this heinous crime did the veden swear revenge on Landomere. Only then did the veden take flight, knowing all was lost and their race doomed. They went to Landomere and lay waste to it. The spiridus earned their just reward."

Akinos fell back in his chair, his breath labored.

Hadde could only stare and shake her head. None of it was true. How could it be? Everything he said went against everything she had ever learned. Her parents, the village elders, everyone knew the story of the destruction of Belavil by the Demon Lords. Akinos denied it all, and there he sat in front of her, Helna's golden orb in his hand. "I'm part spiridus. All Landomeri are," she whispered. "The Spiridus never would have..."

"And thou wert told silly fables of midnight trysts and frolicking in the woods only to come back pregnant, always hoping to be kidnapped again. Dost thou wish to know the truth? It is named rape. But that does not make for nearly so charming a tale."

She glanced from Akinos' face to the Orb. Her head swam with images from her people's stories. Were they all lies? She didn't want to believe it, but her doubt couldn't get past the Orb of Creation. It brought her back from death. She *felt* its goodness.

"And what about you? What about the evil you've wrought? What about the varcolac?" she asked.

"Some suffering must be endured if the world is to be redeemed." He leaned forward in his chair. "It took centuries to master the Orb. It would have been easier had Akinos been an elementar. But sadly, he lacked his brother's blessing. For a time Akinos fled from place to place, pursued by Handrin's henchmen. He finally found refuge deep under Antok in Rigaria. There, with the help of lore locked in veden tomes, he made his first advances. It took time to accomplish his goals, so at first he used the Orb only to sustain his own life. To extend it and nourish it. That accomplished, he sought answers."

"To what?" Hadde asked. "What would he—you—accomplish?"

"Akinos sought to create a perfect world. A paradise without want. For in want rests all evil. But just as he found the answer, the Wasting struck. Akinos needed more time, but the Wasting forced his hand. Although he was not yet ready, he had to emerge from hiding. But how would he be received? Could he just ride forth from Rigaria and announce himself? Come everyone, Akinos the Good has come to save you! Would anyone believe him? Would anyone trust him?"

"Maybe they would have. Maybe you could have proven yourself to them." She didn't believe her own words as she said them. There was no word more vile than Akinos' own name. There was no stronger word for evil—for treachery.

"Akinos prove himself redeemed? The monster who slew Handrin the

Great? Thou thinkest the House of Handrin would rejoice at the arrival of their ancient relative? Akinos had to use other means. He dared not risk a long struggle and possible defeat. Were he defeated, the Wasting would swallow us all. He devised a plan. One that would cause pain, he knew, but only for a short time.

"It was imperative that Akinos accomplish two tasks. Weaken Salador and divide Boradin and Morin. United they could defeat him."

"Why did you cause so much pain?" Hadde asked. "The varcolac have terrorized so many. They attacked my village! My people! Did you send them out? Did you create them?"

"Do not blame the varcolac. They are not evil. They issued forth to demonstrate unto the people of Salador that their king could not protect them. And so Akinos sent forth the varcolac to do what necessity dictated. If some went to Landomere, Akinos apologizes. They ranged too far."

Hadde frowned. There was no excuse for what the varcolac did.

"Akinos caused some pain in order to accomplish his goal," he continued. "But is he unique in this, Hadde? Prince Morin is good, is he not?"

"Yes, he wants to save his people. He wants to end the Wasting."

"And his answer to fighting the Wasting is slaughtering the Tysk? Knowest thou how he treats them? He and his men slay their warriors by the hundreds. The women and children he steals as slaves for sale in Estoria—those that they deem valuable. The weak, the old, the very young, they kill."

Hadde clenched her fists. "You're lying. Morin would never do such things. The Tysk are savage raiders."

"How dost thou know this? Because he tells you so? Ending the Wasting is not his true motivation. He fights the Tysk to gain the Teborans and Namiri as allies. For what purpose? To overthrow his brother. That is his only goal, Hadde. That is what consumes him."

Hadde looked away. She wanted to deny him, but she had heard the same words before. *Did you know that Prince Morin is a traitor?* Queen Ilana's words echoed in Hadde's mind. *He will do anything to become king. And if he succeeds he will take me as his wife and adopt Handrin as his heir. You, Hadde, are just a momentary distraction from grander schemes.*

Akinos' voice brought her back. "Why do people do evil things to one another? Because of desire. They covet what others have. Riches, power, and the pleasures of the flesh… and when they cannot have what they covet, they take it. Is this not so, Hadde?"

She shook her head. She wanted to refuse him, but she knew that his words were true. "I've seen what you are talking about. Especially in Salador. But people don't behave that way in Landomere. We treat each other with kindness and generosity."

"Has it saved you?"

"It has saved us from murder and jealousy and theft. We don't have those things."

"But has it saved you from the Wasting?" Akinos asked.

"No, but we cannot control the Wasting. It's a force of nature."

"Thou art wrong. The Wasting reflects human evil. It is nature's response to our wickedness. How do we end the Wasting? We end our own evil. How do we end our own evil? We eliminate want. We eliminate human desire."

"That cannot be done. Everyone wants something, at least a little."

"The eternals do not want for anything. They do not fear the Wasting. The Orb of Creation provides all they need in life. They feel no hunger, no pain, no sickness, no fatigue, and no jealousy. They feel none of those things because the Orb protects and nourishes them. They do not even fear time itself. The Eternal Knights are immortal."

"I've seen them hurt. Morin slew one."

"They can be slain." He grimaced. "What a terrible loss it is. But as soon as our goal is accomplished there will be no more fighting. We will all be eternal."

"What do you mean? You wish to make us all eternal? We'll all be like the silver men?"

"That is the paradise Akinos seeks."

Hadde recoiled at the thought. "But I never... I don't want—"

The Orb flashed in his hand as he held it toward her. "Touch it, Hadde."

She shook her head.

"It will do you no harm. It saved you."

Hadde knew his words were true. The Orb had saved her. Without taking her eyes from the flashing crystal, and almost without thought, she reached out and gently placed her fingertips on the sphere. In an instant its magic overwhelmed her. She gasped as the Orb's magic thrilled through her torso and into her limbs; the pleasure of it was beyond any she had ever felt. Beyond any she had ever imagined. A warm golden glow enveloped her and left her unable to think or move.

After a while, she had no idea how long, Akinos' voice emanated from the golden light surrounding her. *Where is the evil, Hadde?*

"There isn't any."

"Wouldst thou deny the world the grace of the Orb? Wouldst thou delay the moment at which all could feel the healing touch?"

220

"No."

"Then help Akinos, Hadde. Help him heal the world."

The wonderful cocoon surrounding her receded. Hadde cried out for it to return.

"Akinos is sorry, Hadde," Akinos replied. *"If he could, he would make thee eternal. Thou couldst feel the touch of the Orb at every moment. But he cannot. Not yet. He has not the strength."*

The golden glow receded and Hadde found herself still touching the Orb, but it was cold and the magic was gone. She slowly withdrew her hand.

"Therein lies the problem," he said, his voice weary. "Akinos lacks the strength. He cannot accomplish his goal because he is too weak. It takes much of the Orb's strength simply to keep him alive."

"Why not make yourself eternal?"

"Akinos tried, but it nearly killed him. To become eternal one must be strong of body and of spirit. Akinos is too old. He needs an heir. One to whom he can pass on both the Orb and his knowledge."

"Who? Morin?"

"No. Akinos desires Morin as an ally, but not as an heir. Nor his brother. They are too set in their ways. Akinos wishes young Handrin to be his heir. He has the innate talent. He is young enough. He will complete Akinos' vision."

"Why do you call him an heir? Can't the Orb sustain you forever?"

He closed his eyes. "And so Akinos prepares himself for the ultimate sacrifice. The moment the Orb leaves his hand, Akinos dies. But his death shall free the Orb's power to save us all. He must sacrifice himself to save you." Akinos sagged in his chair. "Akinos grows weary. His children, his eternals, the healing, all draw his strength. But I... Akinos does not begrudge it. They accomplish much as our victory nears.

"Morin will come to you soon. Tell him what thou hast seen. Tell him what thou hast experienced. And soon, this evening perhaps, Akinos will see you both before him."

Akinos closed his eyes, and for a moment Hadde thought he had fallen asleep. Then, without warning, the two capcaun returned and gently carried him from the room.

For a time Hadde sat and wondered at what Akinos had told her. Could she believe him? She stared at her hands. Whom could she believe? Akinos, Boradin, Morin—all had their own stories. They all thought themselves good.

Maybe Akinos wasn't the villain she had always thought him to be. She felt the lingering warmth of the Orb of Creation. Certainly nothing about its touch was evil.

It wasn't long before six eternals escorted Morin into Hadde's chamber. He rushed to her and pulled her close as the eternals withdrew. Suddenly, the background sounds of the tent disappeared and silence enveloped them. It seemed to her a gentle breeze swirled around the room. She glanced around, confused, and then remembered that Morin had done the same thing when she first arrived in Sal-Oras.

"I couldn't believe it when they said you weren't dead," Morin said.

"*You* couldn't believe it?" Hadde laughed, glad to be with him. "What about me? I remember everything."

He hugged her close. "Well, they've shown they don't want us dead. At least not yet."

"They don't want us dead at all. Akinos wants you as an ally," she said, her arms wrapped tightly around him.

Morin pulled back a little. "How do you know?"

"I spoke with him—it was just a short time ago."

He grabbed her shoulders and stared her in the eyes. "You spoke with Akinos?"

She nodded. "He healed me, Morin. I *was* dead. Not close to it, but dead, and he brought me back."

"What did he say?" He paused and stared into her eyes. "Why are you frowning?"

"I didn't like what he said. He told me things about you." She paused and then said, "Is it true you take slaves?"

He looked past her.

"And that you plan to overthrow your brother?"

"Let's sit, Hadde." He took her arm and led her to the edge of the bed. "How long was Akinos with you?"

"We talked for a long time. What about the slaves?" Hadde watched Morin intently. She didn't want to imagine him as a slaver.

A dark look crossed his face. "They're Tysk. Savage, brutal people. Each spring they lay waste to Namir. So, yes, when we defeat them we take the women as slaves and sell them to the Estorians. We don't keep slaves in Salador, as you know."

"You don't need them. You have peasants." She didn't try to hide the anger in her voice.

"We do what we have to do, Hadde. We need the money to fight the Tysk. There is nothing good about that race."

"You need the money to overthrow your brother. Isn't that what you are up to?"

"No, my goal is to end the Wasting. But to do that I need to replace my brother. I should be the king. My brother is a fool."

"That's why you didn't tell your brother you knew where the Orb was. You wanted to take it so you would be more powerful than he is. So you could be the king."

"I wanted to take it because it belongs to me. I'm the true heir to the throne. The true descendant of Handrin the great."

Her eyes narrowed. "Yes, I think you are."

"What do you mean?"

"Akinos told me of Handrin the Great, and of the veden and how they were slaughtered by the spiridus."

"Whatever he said was a set of lies. Akinos is a murderer and a thief. He has deceived you. Has he turned you into one of his followers? Are you, like Astor, a Returnist?"

"The Orb has returned."

"Am I an evil person, Hadde?"

"No." For a moment the word caught in her throat. She wondered at her own hesitation.

"I fight the Tysk, who are murderous savages. Yes, I sell their women, but the only alternative is killing them. I make no profit from it. The money funds my efforts to fight the Wasting and continue my war against their evil kind."

"He said you do kill some of them—the elderly."

"More lies. And I'll not harm my brother; I only wish to supplant him. Because he's ineffective. Because he has done nothing to save us from the Wasting. Because he has led Salador to discord and division. The South Teren is nearly in revolt and the Returnists threaten Sal-Oras itself. If I ruled, it would free him to use his magic for greater good."

Hadde wanted to believe him. She wanted to believe that he was the hero he claimed to be. She closed her eyes. A jumble of conflicting voices assaulted her. Whom could she trust? She saw Morin's face in her mind.

His strong hand cupped her face. She opened her eyes and looked into his. "I love you, Hadde. I've nothing to gain in lying to you."

Hadde reached up and put her hand over his as it rested on her cheek. He did love her. She was certain of it. "I want it to be you, Morin. I want it to be you who saves us."

"Akinos seeks dominion. He will say and do anything to get it. He uses Helna's Gift to create those silver monsters to do his bidding."

"He wants more than that," Hadde replied. "He wants to transform us all into eternals."

"What?" Morin frowned and withdrew his hand from her face.

"He wants everyone in the world to become eternal, but he doesn't have the power to do it. He wants Prince Handrin to do it for him."

"Akinos is mad." Morin settled back in his chair. "How can he think such a thing possible?"

"He thinks he has used the Orb to the extent he can. He thinks only a true elementar can wield it to its fullest potential. The Orb's power is amazing, Morin. I touched it."

Morin leaned close. "You did? Tell me."

"It was indescribable. Perfect."

"What happened when you touched it?"

"Golden light surrounded me. I was frozen by the pleasure of it."

"Why didn't you take it from him?"

"What? Take it? I never thought to. And I couldn't have if I wanted to."

"You are kind and generous and trusting, and I love you for your innocence. But, you had the Orb of Creation in your hand. You are too trusting. Akinos is using you."

"You weren't there," she said. "I wish I could explain it better. And maybe you're right and I'm too trusting, but there wasn't anything evil in the touch of the Orb."

"I wonder," Morin said. "I wonder if he will let me touch it and see for myself."

Chapter Twenty-three

That evening a dozen Eternal Knights escorted Hadde and Morin from their room into the tent's huge central chamber. Sunlight played across the roof's multi-hued panels and lit the room below with a soft light. Four tall tent-poles supported the structure, forming the corners of a square reception hall. Brightly patterned rugs filled the area on the ground between the poles. At the edge of the closest rug sat two high-backed wooden chairs.

The eternals filed silently past, forming a semi-circle behind Hadde and Morin. She glanced at him, but he stared impassively at the far side of the chamber. His customary grin was missing.

"Morin—"

"Look."

Curtains were drawn aside, and four giant capcaun strode into the room carrying a chaise on their shoulders. There sat Akinos on a lacquered wooden throne, the Orb of Creation clutched in his hand. Brilliant golden light shone from it.

Morin drew in his breath.

The capcaun, clad in armor of golden scales, marched onto the rugs and easily lowered Akinos' chair to the floor. From behind them appeared a dozen Eternal Knights, all in purest white bearing the symbol of the golden Orb upon their tabards. The knights spread out, completing the circle of eternals. The four giants drew great golden-headed maces from their belts and faced outward from Akinos' chair.

"Akinos bids welcome to Morin, Prince of Salador," Akinos said. "And to you too, Hadde of Landomere. Please be seated." He motioned to the two chairs. "Is there anything you need?"

"Nothing, thank you," Hadde replied. Morin shook his head.

"Hadde, it pleases Akinos to see thee once again. Prince Morin, Akinos is glad to have finally made thine acquaintance."

"The circumstances are not exactly as I would have chosen," Morin replied, his voice light despite the circumstances. Despite his efforts, Hadde heard the tension in it.

"Understandable. But it is Akinos' hope to change thine opinion of him. He wishes to prove to thee that he is not the evil creature thou hast been taught."

"I think your task is nearly complete, Akinos," Morin said. "Hadde spoke to me at great length today. She was quite convincing. She told me of your meeting and I have great faith in her judgment."

Hadde's heart thudded in her chest. What was Morin thinking? She knew he was lying to Akinos, but what did he hope to gain? How could he think he might possibly gain the Orb with so many of Akinos' minions so close?

"That is most pleasing," Akinos said, smiling at her. "We have the same goals, all of us. We wish to end the pain and suffering of this world. We wish an end to the Wasting."

"Hadde told me you wish to save us by making us all eternal." Morin waved his hand at the knights surrounding them. "And I can see the logic in that."

"A perfect world, a world without desire, without want, is within our reach." Akinos leaned forward in his chair. "But Akinos cannot do it without thee, Prince Morin. Thou shalt lead us to redemption."

"I can't say I completely embrace all that you've done," Morin said. "What of the varcolac, and these giants? What is their purpose?"

Akinos sighed. "For centuries Akinos labored to perfect the human race. The capcaun, or giants as you call them, were the first of his efforts. How easy he thought it was when he finished. They are men and women, like you and Hadde, but in all ways superior. Greater in size, and strength, intelligence, and emotion. How proud Akinos was."

Hadde stared at one of the capcaun as Akinos spoke. The giant stood, unmoving, his arms across his body, the gleaming mace at the ready. His face, partially obscured by his helm, was unreadable.

"But Akinos had failed. The children of the capcaun are the urias. They are large and strong, but their physical form is flawed and their minds are brutish. They are obedient and hard-working, but they are not... well, they are not the capcaun. The capcaun with Akinos now are the last, and youngest, of those he transformed. When they are gone there will be no more of their kind. And, sadly, the children of the urias are urias, but weaker yet. Akinos loves them dearly, as do the capcaun, but they are not perfect."

"Nobody can be perfect," Hadde said. "It's part of being human."

"Thou art wrong." He waved a finger at her as if scolding a child. "Akinos came a step closer when he created the varcolac. With the varcolac he did not focus on size, but on... intensity. Akinos wanted to create humans who were, like the capcaun, stronger and more durable than other mortals. He also wanted to give them minds that were more focused... more able to concentrate."

Akinos grimaced and took a deep breath before continuing. "But they are flawed as well," he said. "The varcolac are ruled by their passions. They are berserk with emotion. Ah, Akinos was so close! The varcolac are wonderful, blessed children, but when their passions get hold of them there is little that can control them. But ultimately Akinos succeeded. The human race has found perfection in the eternals. They are the salvation of us all."

"And to accomplish your mission, the transformation of the world, you need the strength of true elementars," Morin said.

Akinos smiled. "Akinos needs a successor, one with the innate strength of magic that he lacks. And, he fears, in order to achieve what he dreams of, he must die. When Akinos hands the Orb to his successor, five hundred years will fall upon him all at once."

"And you wish for Crown Prince Handrin to be your successor?"

"He has the strength. And he is young enough that he has not been overly corrupted."

"And for me and my brother?"

"Thou shalt support Handrin in his endeavors to create an eternal world. A perfect world."

Morin nodded as if convinced. Hadde glanced at the circle of eternals and the four massive capcaun. Morin couldn't fight them all. She wished she knew what he had in mind.

"One last question," Morin said. "How can I trust you? How can I be certain you aren't simply seeking dominion over the world?"

"Thou wouldst like proof?"

"I would."

"Then Akinos shall give it unto thee. He will permit thee to peer into his soul. Akinos will prove himself to thee, just as he proved himself to Hadde of Landomere. He will let thee touch the Orb of Creation."

Hadde glanced at Morin to see his reaction to Akinos' offer, but she couldn't read his expression. His lips formed a tight line and there was tension in his eyes. He shifted his weight as if to stand, but Akinos halted him with an upraised hand.

"Akinos places one condition on thee, Prince Morin. If thou lookest into the Orb and see it is what Akinos hath promised, thou shalt swear fealty unto him."

Morin paused only a moment before standing. "If I see what you've promised, and what Hadde has described, I'll do as you ask."

Hadde clutched the arms of her chair. She couldn't imagine that Morin would submit so easily. She knew he wouldn't. Morin was going to do what had never crossed her mind. He would steal the Orb.

"Then come, Prince Morin. Behold the Orb of Creation."

Morin took a deep breath. He walked forward, his back rigid and his hands fisted at his sides. Hadde wished she could be in Morin's place so that she could touch the Orb again. She swallowed as Morin's hand reached for the glowing sphere.

The air crackled.

An explosion of brilliant light threw her from her chair to the floor. The force knocked the wind out of her, but the rugs cushioned her from harm. Wind whipped through the tent and the air hummed with power. Eternal Knights raced past her with naked blades.

"Stop!" Akinos shouted. The power of his voice caused the tent to shudder. The eternals froze a few strides from Morin, their weapons poised to strike.

Morin and Akinos stared at one other, seemingly frozen in place. Morin's hand quivered a hand's-breadth from the Orb. An argent tongue of flame connected his hand to it. A golden nimbus surrounded the two men.

"Withdraw," Akinos said, his voice full of strength, "or Akinos will destroy you."

Hadde stared at Morin. He wasn't truly frozen. His body twisted as his muscles strained against invisible bonds.

"Stop, Morin," Akinos intoned. "You do not have the strength to steal the Orb. Akinos does not want to kill you."

Morin's face grimaced in agony as his hand inched toward the Orb. Hadde pulled her legs under her and was about to spring to his aid when an eternal grasped her arm. "You cannot help him," the knight said.

She grabbed at the eternal's silver hand and the strength suddenly seeped from her body. His fingers might as well have been made of stone. "He's in pain," she said, gasping.

"The pain does not last."

The wind stopped and the light dimmed. Hadde turned back to the throne. The silver flame connecting Morin and the Orb had disappeared, but the glowing aura still surrounded him. The tension went out of his body.

"If thou summonest thine magic Akinos will destroy thee. Dost thou understand?"

"I do," Morin replied. He fell to his knees and partially supported his weight with one hand on the floor. The aura disappeared.

"Akinos pities thee, Morin. He pities thine lack of trust. Thine lack of faith. Now stand—reach out and touch the Orb."

Morin warily got to his feet. He reached toward the Orb of Creation and froze the moment his fingertips touched its surface.

"Dost thou feel Helna's grace, Morin?" Akinos asked. "Dost thou feel the hand of the Creator?"

"I…"

"Thou dost not, because thou art resisting it."

"You ask too much." There was anguish in Morin's voice. "I cannot surrender myself to you."

"Morin, thou hast nothing to fear." Akinos' voice softened. "Hadde of Landomere, thou hast felt the Orb, hast thou not?"

"I have," she responded from where she knelt. The eternal still held her arm.

"Didst thou resist it?"

"No, I didn't think to."

"Didst any harm come unto thee?"

"No." She thought desperately for some way to aid Morin. He was in need and she was helpless. Why did Akinos want Morin to accept the Orb? Why not just touch him with it? She glanced at one of the silver-skinned eternals and it came to her. Seremar had said it. He had accepted Akinos' touch. Becoming eternal had to be voluntary.

"Hadde, does Morin have aught to fear?"

She drew a breath to shout a warning when the eternal holding her touched her cheek. Golden warmth engulfed her. The pleasure of Helna's grace paralyzed her. The eternal was with her, in her mind. But this time it wasn't Akinos' benevolent aura.

"Tell Morin he has nothing to fear," the eternal said.

"No!" Hadde pushed against the presence in her mind. *"Get out!"* For a moment she felt the eternal recoil.

"You're strong," he said, surprise in his voice.

Hadde flinched in pain as the eternal clawed back into her mind. *"Now do it! Tell him he has nothing to fear."*

She gathered herself to resist, but this time the eternal was prepared. The power of his presence smashed through her mental guards and she succumbed.

"There is…nothing…to fear," she said. She tried to choke off the words, but it was impossible. The eternal forced them out of her. "The Orb…it is good. I wish…I wish I could…touch it again."

Akinos laughed a jolly, happy laugh. "Thou shalt, Hadde. In good time." He leaned closer to Morin. "Do not resist the Orb. Akinos can feel your magic. Akinos wishes you no harm. Hadde felt the goodness of the Orb and it did no harm unto her. Thou fearest becoming powerless? Thou fearest lack of control? Let go of it! Let go of fear, Morin!"

"It isn't that easy," Morin replied. The words seemed to cause him pain.

Hadde struggled against the weight crushing down upon her mind.

She wanted to break free but the eternal held her too tightly.

"Morin, if Akinos wanted you dead, you would be. He could strike you down at this very moment. Free thine self from the fear that cripples thee. Open thine self. Trust Akinos as you trust in Hadde."

Morin nodded. "Hadde, is it true?" He stared into the Orb. "Can I trust Akinos?"

She threw herself against the shadow that controlled her mind, fighting to drive the eternal out. For a moment he seemed to give way, and then his will crushed hers.

The eternals turned their silver eyes upon her, as did Akinos. "It is good," she heard her voice say. "Everything about it…is good. Its touch filled me…its touch filled me with warmth. With healing warmth and with love."

"Do not resist it, Morin," Akinos said quietly. "Let it engulf you. Let it become you." Morin's shoulders lowered as the tension left his body. The Orb pulsed faster. Hadde felt waves of heat wash over her.

"Morin, dost thou feel the strength of the Orb of Creation? Dost thou feel how it sustains thee?" Akinos asked.

"I do."

"Dost thou feel the goodness of Helna's Grace?"

"Yes." Morin's skin began to glow as silver rays split the golden aura surrounding him.

"Dost thou always want the strength and the sustenance of the Orb with thee?"

"I… I do." His voice sounded distant.

Hadde reeled as the eternal released her mind. Gasping, she looked up to see silver veins spread through Morin's skin. "What are you doing to him?" she shouted at Akinos.

Neither Akinos nor Morin responded. Hadde tried to pull away from the Eternal Knight holding her, but he wouldn't let go. She struck at his wrist, but it was hopeless.

When she looked back at Morin she cried out in fear. The skin on his face and hands cracked and split. As human flesh disappeared, liquid silver replaced it.

"Morin!" she screamed.

"He cannot hear you," the eternal said.

"Morin, dost thou swear fealty unto the Orb of Creation?" Akinos intoned. "Dost thou swear to protect it and to serve it?"

"I do," Morin replied.

"Dost thou swear it now and through eternity?"

"No, Morin, don't!" Hadde yelled, but it was too late.

"I do," Morin replied. As soon as the words left his mouth he cried out in agony and fell. Golden fire engulfed his body and the silver veins covering his skin disappeared as he turned completely black.

Hadde screamed in rage and lunged toward him, but she was held fast by the eternal behind her. Morin lay still on the floor. The golden fire vanished as Akinos collapsed into his chair. The gathered eternals looked expectantly at Morin's still form. Hadde slumped against the legs of the knight behind her.

Morin's skin slowly lightened, the black fading to gray. Then silver streaked the gray. Hadde wanted to turn away but couldn't pull her gaze from his transformation. "What have you done?" she cried out. Hadde pulled forward and the eternal holding her let go. She ran to Morin and cradled his head in her arms. "Morin, can you hear me?"

He opened his eyes and Hadde recoiled in horror. They were silver. No iris, pupil, or whites. Unblinking eyes gazed up at her.

"I'm here. Don't be afraid," he said. The voice was weak, but it was Morin's.

She looked up at Akinos. "What have you done to him?"

"Akinos has given him the greatest gift imaginable. He is eternal. Tell her, Morin. How dost thou feel?"

"I feel life. Power."

Hadde stared down at him. She still cradled his head in her arms. Silver veins broadened and formed patches on his skin. It wouldn't be long.

"Thou art the last of Akinos' children, Morin. He lacks the strength to create more. Our salvation will come at the hands of another. Dost thou understand Akinos' mission? Dost thou understand what he wishes to accomplish?"

"I do." Morin's voice grew stronger. His flesh gleamed, untainted by any blemish. The light of the Orb reflected in rainbow hues that swirled across his silver skin.

He sat up and held his hands in front of his face, flexing his fingers. "I see it now. You'll save us all."

Morin smiled at Hadde and then suddenly sprang up, lifting her to her feet as easily as he would have lifted a child. "It's true. Akinos is our salvation."

She stared into his unreadable eyes. Was it really Morin? His features were unchanged, but there was no expression. No emotion.

He touched her face with his hand and she felt an instant thrill of pleasure. Power surged through her. Morin's flesh and the Orb were one and the same.

You did this to me, his voice said in her mind. *You helped him turn me into a monster. He will destroy us all.*

Chapter Twenty-four

Hadde sat on a sun-warmed rock in the middle of a stream. Water gurgled as it flowed around her. She let her gaze wander over the lush grass and patches of fragrant Everbloom that made their way down the bank to the edge of the water. Great trees, filled with life and covered in green leaves, bordered the stream as far as she could see.

Landomere lived again.

"Hadde?"

She turned, expecting to see Belor emerge from the water beside her. But that wasn't right. He was dead.

"Hadde?"

She knew that voice. Where had she heard it before? "Morin, is that you?" she asked, her heart beating a little faster. Had he come to visit her in Landomere? "Where are you?"

He appeared beside her on the rock, garbed in his usual black, but with the silver skin of an eternal.

"Is this what you dream of?" he asked as his eyes took in their surroundings.

"Dream?" She glanced around. "I'm dreaming?"

"It's the power of the Orb. I'm in your room. I'm touching you in your sleep."

"I can't wake up. I want to wake up."

"It's better this way. No one can hear us. We don't have much time, so you must listen carefully."

"Morin, I'm so sorry. I didn't mean to help Akinos. I didn't mean—"

"What's done is done and cannot be taken back."

"I couldn't help it."

"I know. Your mortal mind is too weak to resist the power of the Orb." He paused and stared at her for a moment. "I need something of you—a task to be done. But I don't know if I can trust you."

"You can trust me, Morin. I was under the control of that eternal. I tried to fight—"

"You're the only one who can save us. I've no choice but to trust you."

232

"You aren't listening to me!" Hadde couldn't keep the anger from her voice. "I couldn't warn you."

He stared past her into the dream forest. "You loved me once."

"And I still do."

"Then in the name of our love do this. Return to Sal-Oras and see my brother. Warn him."

"Of what?"

"Akinos is the Wasting, Hadde. The eternals are the Wasting."

Hadde shook her head. "I don't understand. How can they be the Wasting?"

"Akinos is no Magus Elementar. He has no magic himself. He has power only because of the Orb, but has no sense of it. He can use the Orb, but he does not *feel* it."

"What do you mean?"

He paused a moment. "It's the difference between knowing how to wield a bow and knowing how to make one. Most people can figure out how to shoot an arrow, but only a few truly understand the crafting of the bow and the forces at work when one is drawn."

"Your magic is like this?"

"Yes. It's part of me. I feel it as it passes through me. I feel the power, but I also know the energy it takes. When Akinos uses the Orb of Creation to maintain his own life, he must steal life from others in order to do so. But he does not understand what he's doing. He does not feel the energy he's draining from others. Akinos should be five hundred years dead. He draws life force from all around him just to sustain himself."

"And that's why there is a Wasting? Because Akinos is keeping himself alive?"

Morin stared into the forest. "If it was only him we would hardly notice. But he created the eternals. We eternals are all dead, and there are over a hundred of us. The Orb—"

"What do you mean? You're dead?"

"Dead in that the Orb sustains us and gives us life. We no longer eat or even breathe. Magic courses through our veins, not blood. The Orb gives us strength and health and regenerates us if we come to harm. But it is the very act of creating and sustaining eternals that creates the Wasting. "

"Morin, will you ever live again? Will you ever be flesh and blood?"

He shook his head. "Only if Akinos is slain and the Orb of Creation is taken from him. That's why I'm here, Hadde. I need your help.

"Did you tell him about the eternals and the Wasting?"

"I told him tonight. I told him everything I just told you. He wouldn't believe me. He flew into a rage and accused me of wanting to take the Orb. He called me blind and ignorant."

"He seemed... well... rational to me."

"Hadde, he's mad. The eternals are the realization of a dream five hundred years in the making. He's convinced, to the very depths of his soul, that the eternals are the world's salvation. Accuse him of causing the Wasting and you'll see his anger."

Hadde watched the water as it swirled around her boulder. "Now that you're eternal, could you take it from him?"

Morin laughed. "The Orb sustains me and he controls the Orb. He can slay me with a thought. Worse yet, he could weaken me. Make me as helpless as an infant crawling on the floor.

"Only my brother can save us. He's a strong elementar. And he bears Forsvar. He must defeat Akinos and take the Orb from him. That's why I need you to tell my brother everything that has happened since you left Sal-Oras. Tell him that the longer Akinos remains unchallenged the more powerful he will become."

"Even if Boradin is warned is he powerful enough? Akinos has an army, and he has the eternals, varcolac, and capcaun."

"The might of Salador is not to be taken lightly. But time is Akinos' ally. Tomorrow he marches for King's Crossing, not far from Sal-Oras. An army of Namiri and Teborans will join him there. If those armies join, it will be nearly impossible to stop him. The world will perish under the weight of the eternals."

"Maybe your brother is already on the way."

"My brother doesn't even know of the threat. Ost-Oras is five days fallen and Boradin is unaware that Salador has been invaded."

"How is that possible?"

"The varcolac and Tyskmen have done their job well. Their raids have cut off all communications." He laughed a bitter laugh. "This is a secret invasion. We didn't even know Rigaria was inhabited. And now an army has marched out of it." He touched her arm. "That's why your task is so important. You must warn Boradin."

"And you, Morin? What will happen to you?"

He looked into Hadde's dream forest. "When Akinos dies I'll live again. But my brother won't forgive me this time, I fear. I knew the location of the Orb and tried to take it for myself. And the Namiri and Teborans are my allies; he will blame me for their joining Akinos' cause. I'll have to flee Boradin's wrath." He turned his gaze on her and smiled. "Perhaps I'll exile in Landomere."

"I would like that," Hadde said. She forced a smile, barely able to meet his argent visage. His grin reassured her, but she couldn't read the truth in his silver eyes. She wished they would give her some sign. She wanted his eyes to tell her all he said was true.

"We have no time to waste," he said. "It's very late and the army will soon awaken. I'll get you out of the camp. But all else depends on you. Ride cross-country until you reach Egoras—the town we stayed in the night before we encountered the Tyskmen. From there, take the ancient highway to Sal-Oras. Be wary of patrols of Tyskmen and varcolac."

"How will I escape the camp? What about guards?"

"I'll take care of them."

Hadde frowned. "You'll kill them?"

"No. I have… new gifts." He paused and held his silver hand out in front of him. "My touch can give life, but it can also take it away. I can restore stamina or cause fatigue. I'll exhaust the pickets with my touch. They will think only that they fell asleep while on guard. We cannot delay any longer."

She grabbed his sleeve. "Come with me, Morin."

"If I disappear, Akinos will slay me. I must remain with him and play my part." He paused. "Hadde, remember the prophecy Orlos told you?"

"The archer's offspring shall slay the sun?"

"I know what it means. Akinos is the sun and you are the archer. Your offspring is the message that you bear for my brother. Landomere must have sensed this when she gave you a Spiridus Token bearing the sign of the Orb. Landomere must have known that it would come to this."

Hadde touched her Token. "I was sent as a messenger?"

"I'm certain of it. We must go now. I'm going to awaken you."

Hadde woke in her dark room in Akinos' tent. Morin bent over her, his black cloak pulled over him. He withdrew his hand from her brow. She reached out and took his hand. "I want to go back into that dream. I want to see the living Landomere again." She paused. Morin's hand felt cold and smooth. "Why do I not feel anything in your touch?"

"I control the magic that flows into and out of me. I can touch you and you would feel nothing at all." He put both of his hands around hers. "Or I can let you tap Helna's Grace." For a fleeting moment warmth and life coursed through Hadde. And then it stopped and Morin pulled her to her feet. "And just as easily I can sap the energy from your veins. Come now."

The tent was eerily quiet, and she realized he was using his magic to shroud them in silence. She pulled on her boots and grabbed her bow and case. She still wore the white Rigarian dress.

Morin wrapped a heavy cloak around her shoulders before creeping to the tapestry door to peer out. He waved Hadde after him as he passed through.

As they entered the hallway, Hadde was surprised to see Nadas snoring blissfully by the entrance. Hadde wondered if it was Morin's magic, or if the girl truly slept so deeply. They came to a curtained exit to the tent. Torchlight flickered just beyond. Morin motioned Hadde to halt. "Be ready," he whispered.

With a wave of his hand the light extinguished in a gust of wind. He reached through the curtain and a guard slumped into the tent. Hadde saw another guard, his back to them, staring at the smoldering torch beside him. Morin grabbed the second guard's neck with one hand and touched his face with the other. The guard fell to the ground. Morin ignored him and scanned the darkness beyond.

As Morin looked away, Hadde quickly knelt and put her hand to the guard's throat. His pulse beat strongly. She stood before Morin could turn back. Smiling, she followed his gaze outside the tent and into the camp beyond. She could trust him. He hadn't killed them even when he had the chance.

A village of tents surrounded Akinos' great pavilion. Three nearby torches cast circles of light. Two guards stood near them. A torch fell to the ground as Morin flicked his hand in its direction. He glanced right and a gust knocked another torch against a tent. Guards sprang toward it.

Morin tugged Hadde forward. Crouching, they dashed from shadow to shadow. Twice more, Morin used his magic to darken their path. A hundred strides from Akinos' tent, the camp was night-shrouded and silent. "Stand now, and walk as if nothing is wrong," Morin ordered.

Hadde followed him as he strode confidently forward. Ahead lay the ancient highway to Ost-Oras. A horse stood picketed near it. A smile came to her lips. Even in the dark she recognized Lightfoot.

"In here." Morin led her into a small tent near her horse. They knelt in the shadow of its entrance. "I'll be back soon. I must clear the way for you. When I return, take your horse to the stream as if you're watering him."

"Where is Windwalker?"

"I couldn't get to him."

"But—"

"I tried, Hadde. But it would have aroused too much suspicion. Lightfoot will have to do."

"I could steal him."

"There's no time, and I'll not risk it. Our survival depends on this journey. You must escape. We won't have time to speak again, so leave as soon as I return. Act as if nothing is unusual. Water your horse, cross the stream, and ride for the gap between the hills. From there ride west to

236

Egoras and then to Sal-Oras. Keep well south of the highway."

"What if something goes wrong? What if something happens to you and you don't return? How will I escape the camp?"

"Nothing will happen to me. But if it does, you'll hear it. I'll use my magic to cut a path to freedom for you. Then you must ride as hard as you can. I must go. Take this." He slipped a golden ring onto her finger. "Show it to my brother. Tell him everything."

"I miss your touch, Morin. Your hands are so cold now."

He smiled and took her hand between his. Warmth flowed into them.

She grinned at him, but before she could speak, he was gone. The warmth fled with him, and it crossed her mind that it hadn't been Morin's heat that touched her, but the Orb's. Hadde watched until he cleared the embankment and the road and then settled in to wait. Looking to the eastern sky, she saw a ruddy glow.

Morin startled her with his return. "It's clear?" she asked.

"Clear." He helped her to her feet and thrust her bow and case into her hands. "Good luck, Hadde. I love you." He touched her face and strode away.

"I love you, too," she said to his back, but she didn't think he heard. She drew a deep breath. Would he still be an eternal when she saw him again? If she ever saw him. His last words brought her some comfort. His transformation hadn't taken away his ability to love.

Steeling herself to the task ahead, she crept out from the tent. She wouldn't fail. She wouldn't betray Morin's trust in her. And when all was done, the Wasting ended and Morin restored, they would...

She shook the thought from her mind. Later.

Hadde untied Lightfoot from her picket and, taking a deep breath, led the horse across the road. She glanced left and right as she started down the bank. A few people moved in the pre-dawn light, but none paid her any attention. If their night vision were as poor as that of the Saladorans she had met, she would be no more than a shadow to them.

She paused at the stream's edge and then mounted. Peering up the hill before her, she looked for any sign of the guards Morin had subdued. A small campfire burned to her right, but other than that she saw nothing.

She and Lightfoot splashed across the stream and trotted up the opposite slope. Hadde tensed, ready to push her horse to a gallop at the first cry of alarm.

Chapter Twenty-five

The open gates of Sal-Oras beckoned Hadde. A fever chill passed over her as she urged Lightfoot forward. For five days she had dodged Tyskmen and varcolac as she had made her way cross country. Morin had ensured she was well-provisioned, but fatigue and bad weather had taken their toll on both her and Lightfoot.

It didn't matter. She had made it, and Boradin would get his message. Hadde stroked Lightfoot's neck. She had ridden the horse mercilessly. "I'm sorry. We're done now. We can both rest."

"Pull back that hood and let me see your eyes," a gate guard ordered.

"What? My eyes?" Hadde asked. She shook her head to clear her fog-shrouded mind.

"Do it! Or are you varcolac?" He tightened his grip on his spear.

"I'm no varcolac."

His eyes opened wide as she pulled her hood back. "I'm Hadde of Landomere," she continued. "Ambassador to the King. Please take me to him." It was an effort just to say the words. Her head nodded with fatigue.

"The Landomeri! The one we were warned about!" he shouted as he seized Lightfoot's bridle. Hadde jerked upright and tried to yank Lightfoot free, but the guard held the horse fast.

"Take her, idiot! Don't let her flee!" he shouted. Before the words could register, strong hands seized Hadde and pulled her from the saddle. She cried out as her head struck the paved road. Two men pinned her to the ground.

"I must see the king," she shouted. Her voice seemed distant.

"You'll see him soon enough." Two guards hauled her to her feet. She tried to twist away, but they held her firmly between them. A wave of dizziness passed over her. Fever and fatigue had robbed her of all her strength. "My horse," was all she could manage.

A knight stepped in front of her and pulled her hunting knife from its sheath. "See to the horse," he commanded. "And take the prisoner to the king."

Two Knights of the House dragged Hadde down the Great Hall toward Boradin's throne. She barely managed to lift her head. The hall was nearly empty. Six nobles stood at the base of the king's dais. She recognized Sir Fenre, the Steward, amongst them.

"Why are you——" Hadde started.

"Silence," a knight ordered.

They dropped her to her knees before the king. Hadde sagged onto her hands, too tired to raise herself. "Why are you doing this to me? What have I done?" she asked.

"Where is Morin?" Boradin demanded.

Hadde caught her breath. "Morin is in Ost-Oras, Your Majesty. Please, why are you treating me this way?"

"Because you conspire with him. Now tell me why he's there."

"Akinos is there. With the Orb of Creation," she said. The gathered nobles murmured at her words. "Morin sent me back to warn you," she continued. "He sent this." She held out her hand with Morin's ring upon it.

"Bring it to me."

A knight forced the ring from Hadde's finger and took it to the king.

"What is his warning?" Boradin asked.

"Akinos is the Wasting. He's using the Orb of Creation to sustain his own life and to create beings called Eternal Knights." She paused and caught her breath. "One of them was the Messenger the Returnist prisoner spoke of. But the eternals require so much life-force from the Orb that none is left for the rest of us. Morin says that you must defeat Akinos or he will continue making eternals until all life is destroyed." Hadde sagged to the floor as pain, confusion, and sickness overwhelmed her. The knight pulled her up so that she sat facing the king.

"And my brother? What is he doing?"

"Akinos made him eternal. He's a slave to Akinos now. Morin helped me escape so that I would bring you this message. Akinos' army is marching for King's Crossing. If he gets there and joins his allies, all is lost. We shall all perish."

"Morin is one of these creatures now? Why did Akinos do that to him?"

"I tried to stop him. I…" She trailed off. How could she explain that terrible moment? Would they believe her when she told them of the eternal who had used her to convince Morin to become eternal? "Morin is powerless against Akinos now. None of the eternals can harm the wielder of the Orb."

"My brother didn't fight?"

"The Orb is too strong. But he said that you were strong enough to fight Akinos. You and Forsvar."

"And these allies you spoke of?"

"The Namiri and the Tebar."

"Teborans," Boradin corrected. He turned to Sir Fenre. "Send for Champion Nidon. Tell him I wish for the Knights of the House to prepare to ride. Call for my couriers as well. We must marshal the army. As many as possible in just a few days."

"All this on her word, Your Majesty?" the steward asked, casting a doubtful glance toward her.

"On *my* word! Do it!" Relief flooded Hadde as Fenre ran from the chamber. "Thank you, Your Majesty," she said.

"I don't do this for you. Akinos lives. The Orb has returned. It isn't just your word that pushes me to action. My eyes see far. My ears hear much."

"Prince Morin said that this was my purpose," Hadde said, touching her Spiridus Token. "That Landomere wanted me to bring you this message."

"Perhaps," Boradin said. "But the Blind Prophet's writings say differently. I'll take no risks. Not with Akinos, nor Morin, nor with you." The king turned to one of her guards. "Lock her up."

"Tower or dungeon, Your Majesty?"

"What? Why——" Hadde started, but the guard cuffed her into silence. Blinding pain flashed through her skull as waves of darkness threatened.

The king stared at her. "Tower. And send a surgeon."

Hadde pulled from the knight's grasp. "Why imprison me?"

"The archer's offspring shall slay the sun," he replied. "You're a danger to me and my son."

"No! Morin said that Akinos was the sun and my message was the offspring that would bring his doom."

"Morin says much, but understands little." He waved his hand. "Take her away."

The surgeon looked down at Hadde as she lay exhausted on the straw pallet. "A bit banged up, but you'll live. At least the king doesn't want you dead. If he did, he'd have locked you in the dungeon instead."

"Tell the king he must send an army…" she managed before darkness overcame her. From time to time she awoke, alone in her cell. Her bedding smelled of old straw and the blanket was coarse, but at least there was a pitcher of water beside her. But she never woke for long, and each time she fell asleep she dreamt fever-fueled dreams of fire and violence.

Keys jangling in the lock woke her. She blinked against the bright light as the door opened. "Leave us," a familiar voice commanded. Hadde struggled to put a name to the voice as she raised herself onto her elbows. She blinked her bleary eyes clear as the girl sat down on the bed next to her. "Maret?" she said, her mind still addled with fatigue. "What happened to your face?"

The girl recoiled and shielded her face with her hands. Even the veil she wore could not completely hide the bandages and long scars. Hadde saw that even Maret's hands were bandaged. "But, Hadde... you know what happened."

Hadde rubbed away the fatigue that tried to pull her back to sleep. She glanced around the room and frowned at the unfamiliar sights. And then, in a sudden rush, it all came back to her. She reached to Maret and pulled the girl's hands from her face. "Maret, I'm so sorry."

"No, Hadde, I'm the one to blame. It was my stupidity. My jealousy. I was a fool."

"No! It wasn't your fault. It was Waltas." Hadde pulled Maret closer and weakly embraced her. An image of Maret on the surgeon's table came to her mind, and she couldn't stop the tears that followed. Maret hugged her close and for a time they both cried at the memory.

"How are you up and healed so soon?" Hadde asked.

"Orlos did it. He healed me. But he died in the effort." Maret pulled back and stared Hadde in the eyes. "Is it true what they said about Waltas?"

Hadde frowned. "What do you mean?"

"They said he looked like a porcupine." Maret's eyes narrowed as she spoke.

Hadde saw Waltas sprawled in the blood-spattered snow. She quickly pushed the image from her mind. "He did," was all she managed to say.

"I hope it hurt."

"More than you could..." Hadde tailed off. Maret could imagine that kind of pain. "It hurt a lot."

"Good." Maret turned away and picked up a tray from the floor. "I've brought you some food. And that brazier for warmth." She placed the tray on Hadde's lap and walked to the door, the floor threshes rustling as she walked. The only pieces of furniture were the bed and the brazier, Hadde noticed. A tall narrow window let in light.

"Guard!" Maret called through the door's grate. "Bring five fresh blankets, a linen shift, and a bucket of clean water." She turned away from the door before the response came.

The girl's tone surprised Hadde. "You sound different."

Maret returned to her seat beside Hadde. "Have some food. I brought some chicken broth." As Hadde obeyed, Maret said, "It was the king's responsibility to safeguard me, and he failed. Everyone knows it. I'm a living stain on his honor. He will give me whatever I ask."

"But even so, how is it you're ordering guards around?"

"You're not in the dungeon, Hadde. You're just being confined until the king decides to set you free."

"What's the difference?"

"The difference is I can make your stay comfortable. At least until King Boradin finds a way to be rid of me."

"Be rid of you?"

"Send me home. I can't stay here any longer. He will negotiate some agreement with my father, compensating him for the damages to me. I'm no good to my father anymore. Who would marry me now?" She put down the bowl and looked out the window. "I'll be a lonely spinster hidden away in my father's keep."

"Your father—" Seremar's silver visage appeared in Hadde's mind. How could she tell Maret of what had become of him? Her mission leaped back into her thoughts. "I must see the king! I have to convince him to go to King's Crossing to fight Akinos."

"He already left. This morning."

"But I just spoke with him."

"Two days ago, Hadde. You've been asleep. Don't you remember any of the conversations we have had?" Maret gave a little laugh. "I suppose it was all fever-talk. Your journey took a terrible toll on you." She paused.

"We spoke?" Hadde stared down at her plate, bewildered. "I don't remember anything. Just some bad dreams."

"We spoke," Maret said, "but that doesn't mean I understood much. Please tell me what is happening. There are rumors of Morin and Akinos and the Orb of Creation."

Hadde recounted her story to the maiden, leaving out only the details of her relationship with Morin and the meeting she had with Maret's father. "Don't give up," she concluded. "King Boradin will return with the Orb and heal you."

"You think so?" Maret traced a scar across her palm. "I've been so miserable since it happened. Only Orlos' words have kept me from... kept me going."

"Orlos spoke to you?"

"When he healed me. I was in darkness and I was terribly afraid. I kept thinking Earl Waltas would come back and attack me again. Then I saw a point of light in front of me. It was Orlos. When he came close the darkness disappeared and we were alone in a great forest. Orlos was young. He told me I would be safe, and I believed him.

"He showed me Landomere. It was so wonderful—I didn't want to leave. He put his Spiridus Token around my neck and I fell asleep. When I woke Orlos was dead and I had this." Maret pulled Orlos' Token from under her collar.

"He saved me, Hadde. But I feel guilty. He was the last of the spiridus, and he's gone because of me."

"Maret, he was dying. I saw him. I spoke with him and he was very ill. Even the spiridus cannot live forever, and he knew he was going to die soon. You gave his death significance," Hadde said, absently fingering her own Token. "Saving you allowed him to leave us with one last gift. You."

Maret took a deep breath. "Orlos told me something else as well." After a long pause she said, "I'm pregnant."

Hadde gaped. "How could you know so soon?"

"He knew. When he told me, I wanted to die. I couldn't bear the thought of giving birth to Waltas's child. But then Orlos told me something very strange. He told me it wasn't the earl's child anymore. Orlos said, because his spirit was in me, the child had become his. Is that possible? Could he do that?"

"I... I don't know. The spiridus are very magical. They and the dragons were the firstborn among Helna's creations." Hadde paused. She didn't know the answer, but she could see the hope in Maret's eyes. She had been through enough pain. "If Orlos said it, it must be true. The child is his."

Hadde woke with a start and stared blearily around her chamber. She heard a shout in the distance. An acrid stench hung heavy in the room. Despite her weakness, she jumped from the bed and ran to the window. A haze of smoke drifted over the bailey. But from outside the keep or within?

Steel clashed on steel. More faint shouts came from below. She pressed her face against the window's narrow opening. To her right she saw the front face of the Great Keep. To her left stood the gate towers. Footsteps pounded past her door. "What is happening?" she called out. She went to the door and shouted for the guard, but there was no response.

She returned to the window. A dozen soldiers ran across the bailey. Before they reached the gate, its huge doors swung wide. Roaring a victory cry, a white-cloaked, torch-wielding mob swarmed into the courtyard.

Returnists.

Hadde gasped at the sight of three silver-skinned eternals leading the attack. Their argent skin seemed ablaze as it reflected the torchlight. The mob swarmed the soldiers in the courtyard. Three ran for the keep as the others were cut down.

"Shut the doors!" Hadde shouted. Her cry was lost in the fury of the crowd. Led by the eternals, the Returnists stormed the Great Keep. From within the keep she heard the muffled sounds of combat. Hadde picked up the stoutest stick from the few that lay on her little woodpile. It was a pitiful weapon, but better than none. She took it to the door and hid herself against the wall.

Looking at the stick clutched in her hands, she wondered what she was doing. Was she going to beat the first person that came through the door? Sighing, she sagged until she sat on the floor. She was a prisoner. Helpless. All she could do was listen to the sounds of the struggle.

The battle was short-lived; silence soon overtook the keep. The odor of smoke slowly faded. By dawn only a few Returnists walked in the bailey below. A score of dead soldiers lay heaped next to the gates. There was no sign of the eternals.

She considered calling out to the Returnists and asking them to let her out of her cell, but thought better of it. How much did they know? Would they know that she had warned Boradin against Akinos? It was too much to risk. She could wait.

Settling herself at her window, she watched as the Returnists brought arms and supplies into the Great Keep. The dead soldiers were removed as stores were piled in the bailey. It was obvious the Returnists planned on remaining for a long time, and that they thought someone would try to force them out.

A day passed. Then another. Hadde's food ran out and her water nearly so. No one came for her, and she resisted calling out for help. She had seen enough to know that the Returnists expected an attack.

All through the night Hadde listened to the sounds of the Returnists making their preparations. It was dawn when the first warning shouts rang out. She watched as Returnists manned the gate towers. They rained crossbow bolts and stones upon unseen attackers beyond the keep's walls.

More Returnists spilled from the keep and formed a shield wall facing the gates. Only half wore armor, and many held their weapons awkwardly, but all stared at the gates with equal intensity. They cheered as one of the eternals joined them.

The eternal stood facing the Returnists with his back to the gate. "The

244

Orb returns!" he called out. "It marches to us as I speak. But an enemy would see it taken from you. We must be strong. We must hold out until our salvation arrives. Praise the Orb!"

"The Orb returns! Praise..." The chant faltered as many in the crowd pointed toward the gate. A few still cried out with enthusiasm, but most shuffled in the ranks.

Hadde followed their gazes. Flames engulfed the gates, burning them as if doused in oil. Hadde had never seen a fire so intense. The gate's defenders desperately hurled missiles at the unseen enemy beyond the wall.

"They're coming!" A shout echoed from the tower. Just as the eternal turned to face the fire, there was a terrible crack, and the gates exploded. Flaming shards of wood sprayed the defending ranks of Returnists. The blast threw many to the ground.

Boradin and the Knights of the House charged through the smoking ruins. The king held Forsvar in front of him. The Godshield blazed with blue-white fire and the Returnists recoiled from its piercing light.

The eternal, thrown to the ground by the explosion, leaped to his feet. "Stand!" he shouted. The massed Returnists wavered. A few ran for the keep, but most rallied around him. Boradin strode into the bailey, his golden mace held aloft. He thrust it forward and flames engulfed the eternal.

The knight screamed at the fiery onslaught and charged the king.

Boradin collapsed to one knee and his fiery assault died. Nidon leapt in front of him to take the eternal's charge, but the charge never arrived. Ten strides from the king the eternal stumbled and collapsed to the ground. His silver skin turned black as he crawled a few strides and then lay still.

The Knights of the House shouted, "Salador!" as they raced forward. The Returnists broke and fled for the keep, but their comrades had barred the doors behind them. The knights hacked down the fleeing masses as the Returnists crushed one another in their efforts to escape. Their lack of arms and training hastened the slaughter.

Hadde turned away from the massacre and curled upon the floor. Cries of agony poured through the window. She pressed her hands against her ears, but couldn't stop the sound.

A piercing scream, higher than the others, caused Hadde to look toward the window. Another followed soon after. Someone bellowed orders. Nidon? The noise of slaughter stopped. Hadde raised herself and peered out.

Returnists, their white clothes covered in blood, lay piled in heaps against the Great Keep. Dozens still lived, huddled against the walls, their arms raised to shield themselves. But they need not have made the effort. The Knights of the House had given ground before the walls. In the open space between the knights and the Returnists, two girls in dresses lay sprawled on the gravel.

Hadde gasped. Two maidens.

"More will follow if you don't leave the bailey!" a voice shouted from above. Hadde looked to a crowded balcony high on the keep's face.

There, amongst a crowd of Returnists, stood an eternal. Above his head he held a maiden. Returnists held more maidens to either side of him. Hadde recognized them all. She saw Jenae, and then she spotted the queen.

"No," Hadde murmured. How could any man be so wicked? So twisted? She didn't want to believe it possible. But he already had.

"Villain!" Boradin shouted. He stood in the bailey glaring up at the eternal. "Put her down!"

"As you wish." The eternal cast the girl from the balcony. Hadde couldn't turn away. The girl screamed as she plunged headfirst for the ground. A moan of dismay rose from the knights as she fell.

Boradin raised both arms and a gale rose up and swirled around the falling maiden. Nidon sprang forward and caught her, but she struck him with such force that both were thrown to the ground. A second knight ran forward, his shield raised high to protect the champion and the maiden. Hadde cheered as she recognized Melas.

More cheers joined hers. "Magus Elementar!" the knights cried. "Boradin! Nidon!"

Nidon stood, lifting the girl easily in his arms. She clung to him as he carried her to safety. Melas guarded their retreat. But something had happened to Boradin. He knelt on the ground on all fours and vomited into the gravel.

Nidon passed the maiden off to another knight and rushed to the king's side. Other knights joined him. The eternal laughed. "Save this one then!" All eyes rose to the balcony. The eternal held another maiden before him, a dagger at her throat.

Hadde recognized her. "Jenae," she whispered. At the same moment Melas shouted her name from the courtyard. He ran to stand below the balcony.

"Stop this outrage, Brother Gredoc!" Another eternal shouted as he shoved his way onto the balcony. He gazed down into the courtyard and saw the dead maidens and then stared at the eternal holding Jenae. "You cannot do this!"

"They must be taught a lesson," Gredoc replied. The two eternals started arguing, but Hadde couldn't make out the words. The second eternal lunged forward as Gredoc drew his dagger across Jenae's throat. Blood jetted from the deep slash as the eternals struggled over her. Jenae was flung over the balcony in a shower of blood.

"No!" a howl of rage and anguish rose from the knights. Gredoc seized another hostage. Queen Ilana struggled in his grasp, but he held her fast. The second eternal stared over the balcony at Jenae's fallen body. His head hung low.

Melas attempted to run to Jenae, but Nidon seized him. "Stand fast!" he commanded. Melas fell to his knees, his mailed fists tearing at his helmet straps.

Nearby, two knights lifted Boradin between them. The king seemed barely able to raise his head to look up at the balcony. "I know your magic, Boradin," Gredoc shouted. "I'll kill her before you get close enough. You cannot save her. And even if you manage it, your son is inside. He will die."

Boradin said something to Nidon. "The kings asks that you let the hostages go. There will be no retribution. You may leave the Great Keep with your lives."

"And if we don't leave?" Gredoc laughed again. "We don't fear you. We fear only what will happen to the world if Akinos fails in his mission."

"Don't hurt her. Don't hurt my son." Boradin's voice was barely audible. Hadde heard fear in it.

"Lay down Forsvar and all go free," the eternal said. "Simply lay down your shield and this all ends."

Boradin looked at his shield and then toward the balcony. "I cannot. You ask the one thing I cannot surrender." He paused and glanced at the Knights of the House flanking him. "We'll withdraw. I'll call off my attack. A truce will give us time to negotiate."

"Not good enough. I'll give you leave to withdraw, but you must disarm the Knights of the House."

Boradin nodded. "It will be done. I'll have their arms sent in by noon."

"No. They will disarm now."

A rumble rose from the gathered knights.

"Now." The eternal pressed his blade against Ilana's neck.

"Disarm," Boradin shouted, waving his arms. "Plate coats, hauberks, and shields."

"And swords."

"And swords." Boradin's shoulders sagged. "Do it," he ordered. Slowly, the knights complied.

The eternal laughed. "Present yourself before me each morning, King.

If you do not, they both shall die. Now take your soldiers and be gone. I fear you not!" At the Eternal Knight's signal, his followers showered bolts, rocks, and spears upon the king's men.

"Fall back! Fall back from the keep!" Nidon shouted. He and another knight picked up Boradin and ran with him from the bailey. Six knights fell, struck down by missiles before they cleared the gate.

But one knight didn't follow the others. Heedless of his own safety, Melas ran to where Jenae lay on her back on the gravel. Rocks rained around him as he lifted Jenae's body from the ground.

He turned for the gate when a stone fell from above and struck him in the head. He toppled and landed motionless beside his fiancée.

Hadde rocked back and forth on her bed. They were all doomed. First to Akinos' conquering army and then to the Wasting. There was no good in the world left to fight it.

She realized now that Boradin had returned to save his family when he had received word that the Returnists had taken the Great Keep. But he had doomed the world to death in doing so. Akinos would get to King's Crossing and join his allies there. Morin's warnings would go unheeded. All would die.

But could she blame Boradin? Would she sacrifice her family to save others? To save hundreds? Thousands? The numbers didn't matter. Who wouldn't do everything possible to save their loved ones? Melas had even lost his life rescuing someone already dead.

Hadde pressed her palms against her eyes to stop the tears. She couldn't cry any more. She had cried too much already. But what else was there to do? She picked up her empty water jug and flung it against the wall, flinching as it shattered. Shards bounced across the moonlit floor.

Something bumped outside her cell. Hadde spun toward it as someone lifted the bar. She picked up her club and padded to the door, pressing herself against the wall as the door creaked open.

A shadowy, insubstantial figure slipped into the room. Hadde blinked her eyes, hoping to clear her vision. What trick of the light was it that she couldn't see clearly? The figure blurred and shifted in the darkness. It stopped in the center of the room, looking toward the bed.

Hadde hefted her club in both hands as the intruder turned toward her.

"Hadde, are you in here?"

"Maret?

The maiden squealed in fright and dropped the sack she carried. The shadow lifted from Hadde's vision and she saw the girl clearly. "Maret, how did you do that?" Hadde asked as she took the girl in her arms.

"Do what? I was so worried that I wouldn't find you."

"You were nearly invisible as you walked in."

"Well, it's dark."

"I know, but I see well in the dark. It was different." Hadde paused. "Like Orlos."

"What do you mean?"

"Twice Orlos surprised me. Once in the library and once in his chamber. The spiridus could make themselves invisible." Hadde stepped back, holding the maiden's shoulders. "I think... well, he did something to you. Maybe it really is his child in you."

"I just thought the Returists were ignoring me. One of the eternals said that I wasn't to be touched. He mentioned my father."

"I was afraid they would kill you like the others."

Maret shook her head. "The Messenger said that I was one of the select. When I asked what that meant, he said that my father was saved and that I would join him. He wouldn't say any more. Do you know what it means?"

Hadde opened her mouth and then paused. How much should she say? "Your father... he has gone over to Akinos."

"To Akinos? My father wouldn't follow him."

"He has, Maret. I spoke with him. He believes Akinos can stop the Wasting."

"You knew all this before, but you didn't tell me?" Anger flashed in Maret's eyes.

"I couldn't. Please, Maret, you suffered enough already." Hadde paused and considered telling Maret the rest of the story. What would she think if she knew that her father was eternal? That he was part of the Wasting?

"Why? Why would my father turn on the king?"

"Your father follows Akinos because he bears the Orb of Creation. And because Akinos isn't the monster he has been made out to be."

"But his followers killed Jenae. My father would never join people like them."

"I know, Maret, but they're not all that way. One of the eternals tried to stop Jenae's killer."

"Well, this Gredoc is evil. As are his followers. You have to help the maidens, Hadde. They'll all be killed. King Boradin will never give up Forsvar."

"I couldn't even free myself, Maret. What do you think I can do?"

"You can do it." Maret clutched Hadde's arm. "I saw you at the archery contest. And Prince Morin taught you how to use a sword."

Maret opened her sack and pulled out a bow. "I brought this from your room. There were two there, one like Hawkeye, and this one. I hope I brought the right one. The other was so big, and curved the wrong way."

"You did well, Maret." Hadde said as she took the bow. "The other was Belor's, and is too heavy for me. This was my spare. Did you bring arrows?"

"Yes, there was a quiver." She pulled Belor's bowcase from the sack. "I also brought some clothes, and this." She grasped a sheathed sword.

Hadde smiled as she took the bow. "How did you get these things?"

"The Returnists are all either guarding the walls or the maidens. Once I left her chambers it was easy to move around."

"Where were you held?"

"In Queen Ilana's chambers. If we escape the keep, we can get the king. He and his knights will save them."

"The king ran as soon as the queen was threatened. He will never do anything that risks her and Prince Handrin. Gredoc knows that he's safe as long as he holds the prince and keeps the king's magic at a distance. I don't even know if the king can make the rescue. He fell ill in the courtyard."

Hadde strung the bow as she thought aloud. "Boradin is trapped. If he departs Sal-Oras to fight Akinos, his family will die. But any rescue attempt will have the same result. The king won't attempt it, but we can." Hadde went to the window and stared at the barricade the Returnists had placed across the keep's entrance. Even if she failed and the hostages died, the king would be free to depart Sal-Oras and launch his attack on Akinos.

She paused a moment at the thought. Her shoulders sagged and she put her hand to her brow. What was she thinking? What had she become? Would she sacrifice Ilana, Handrin, and the maidens to see her task accomplished? An image of Morin flashed in her mind. *He* would do it. She felt a flash of guilt at the thought.

"Is there anyone who can help us?" Hadde asked.

"Most of the knights and soldiers who remained in the keep after the king departed were killed. Those who lived have gone over to the Returnists. Maybe some of them would help us."

"I don't think we can trust them. Is there anyone else?"

"Squire Melas, but he's wounded."

"Melas survived?"

"Yes, I helped tend him. They would have killed him, but I pleaded for his life. He's in the dungeon now."

"Badly wounded?"

"He's well enough to help."

"How many guards?"

"I don't know." Maret reached out and took Hadde's hand. "It doesn't matter, Hadde. I know you can do it. You can kill them and free Melas."

Hadde ignored the comment. She bowed her head and put her hand over her eyes as she thought. "You've been in the queen's chambers? What are they like?"

"There are two chambers. A bedroom and a parlor. You can only enter the bedroom from the parlor."

Hadde pulled her own clothes out of the sack and put them on. She couldn't wear the Rigarian dress for what she intended. "Is there a privy?"

"A privy? Yes. Why?"

Hadde picked up her sword. "Because I can't go in through the front door."

Chapter Twenty-six

"Down here?" Hadde asked.

"Yes, that's the dungeon." Maret wrinkled her nose as she nodded in the direction of an open door. "King Boradin held many prisoners there, but the Returnists emptied it."

Hadde pulled the maiden back into the alcove. "I need you to go to the stable and fetch fifty strides of rope. Do you think you can do it? Will anyone stop you?"

Maret shook her head. "I told you, they think I'm one of them because of my father. But why? What is the rope for?"

"We'll need it to save the Maidens. If anyone questions you, say that the Messenger sent for it. Once you have it, go to the bottom of the stairs near the Weapons Gymnasium. And bring a lantern back. It will be dark where we're going."

"I don't think I need one. I see fine now."

"Orlos has given you his sight, but Melas will need light. The maidens too."

As Maret set off, Hadde crept toward the dungeon door. There were no guards. Nocking an arrow, she eased down the stairs. She paused as she turned a corner. She expected a long corridor, as in the basement where Waltas pursued her. Instead she saw a large chamber with cells lining the walls. Most were open. Four large pillars obstructed her view of the debris-strewn room.

She continued down the stairs. A lantern lit the far corner of the chamber. She pulled some tension into her bow as she reached the floor. The bow was far weaker than Hawkeye, but it would do—especially against an unarmored enemy.

A Returnist guard leaned against the wall near a closed cell. He slumped as if asleep, his hood pulled up over his head. Only one guard. Hadde's heart raced.

She had a clear line to him. She raised her bow and then stopped. He was defenseless. Asleep. She remembered the young raider in the woods near her home. She had shot him in the back—he had had no chance. She closed her eyes for a moment. She could do it again. This man was a follower of the eternal who slit Jenae's throat. She hardened herself to the task. There was no room for mercy.

She drew her bow and let fly. The arrow struck the guard dead center in his chest. She pulled another arrow and nocked it, never taking her eyes from her target. He hadn't moved. He was already dead.

Something heavy clattered to the floor as strong arms seized her. Hadde kicked and tried to twist out of his grasp, but he held her tight. "Stop struggling! I'm Melas." He let her go and she turned to face him. Dried blood matted his hair and lay caked on the side of his face. A ragged bandage wound loosely around his head. His cold, hate-filled eyes met hers.

"How'd you escape?" Hadde asked.

"They left a half-wit to guard me," he said, his voice hard. "So I broke his neck. I was going to break yours next. What are you doing here?"

"I came to rescue you. I need your help."

"Help? Help with what?" He bent to the floor and picked up the cudgel he had dropped.

"We have to save the maidens."

"I couldn't save Jenae." For a moment his face softened and he looked like the young man she had once known.

"I know. I saw. But the others are still alive. We can help them."

He shook his head. "I don't care about them. I want revenge."

"After we save them—that's the time for revenge."

He took a deep breath and stared at her for a time. His eyes were moist with tears, but his jaw was set. "I want them to pay. They have to pay."

"They will. I promise. After."

"Hadde?" Maret whispered down the stairs. "Are you there?"

"You can come down," Hadde said. "It's safe," Hadde said.

Melas unshuttered the lantern they had taken from the Returnist guard. A shaft of light exposed the base of the stairwell. Maret appeared, a long coil of rope over her shoulder and a shuttered lantern in hand. Hadde went to her and relieved her of her burden. "Did you have any trouble?"

"No. They barely looked at me." She turned to Melas. "I'm glad Hadde saved you from the dungeon."

"I hardly saved him," Hadde said. "He was on his way out."

Melas turned to Maret. "I should have thanked you for helping me before, but I was in no condition to do so."

"I had to help you. I couldn't let both you and Jenae…"

253

"I'll join her soon enough," Melas said.

"No, you won't," Maret said. "We'll all escape here. And we'll save the other maidens as well. Right, Hadde?"

"We'll try our best. Let's not wait any longer." She motioned for them to follow her down the corridor.

"Aren't we going back upstairs?" Maret asked.

"We'd have to fight our way through too many guards. Melas and I will climb up through the privy shaft. We'll—"

"Privy? I'm not climbing up any privy." Melas glared at Hadde. "I said I would help you rescue them. But there's a limit to what a man will do. If I am going to die, I'm going to die with my honor intact—not in some sneak attack."

"Melas, please. We'll sneak into the queen's chambers and lower the maidens to safety. You want revenge, don't you? This will hurt the Returnists more than any suicidal assault. They need the hostages in order to hold the king here."

"How will we find our way?"

"I've been in the sewers before. I know——"

"You've what?"

"I didn't want to be there. Waltas chased me into them. We don't have time for the entire story. But I know enough for us to get around."

"Dromost take it! It won't be an honorable death, getting brained in a privy."

"I know you want revenge. I know you want to die. But this is about more than you. Think of the maidens. They have long lives ahead of them. If we cannot free King Boradin from this siege, we all die. You might want to die, Melas, but think of all those who don't. Think of all those the Wasting will take."

"We don't need to go through the privy," Melas said. "They won't expect an attack from within the keep. We'll surprise them just as much if we attack from the corridor outside the queen's chambers. And we won't be caught helpless in a privy shaft."

"But while we're fighting our way through, they will be killing hostages."

"I don't like it. I'm a Squire of the House. I don't crawl up filthy shafts to attack my enemy from behind."

"Melas, if we do it this way, all of the maidens will live. Your way, many are sure to die. Please, come with me. We must do this before dawn."

The squire glared at her.

"Please, Melas," Maret begged. "The Maidens need you."

"I despise this."

"But you'll come?" Hadde asked. He gave a grudging nod in reply.

She led them down the corridor where Waltas had pursued her. She ignored the fear that came with the memory. Or was it fear for what they were about to attempt? But there was nothing gained in thinking about it. The time for choices was past.

Hadde strode into the old privy chamber and pulled aside a few timbers to make the entrance larger. She heard the others follow her. All three stared down the shaft.

"It won't make a very heroic tale," Melas said.

Hadde squeezed his arm. "We'll make this work. The Maidens will come out alive and we'll come out alive."

Maret gagged and nearly retched. "This is awful," she said, turning from the pit.

"Stay by the door," Hadde said. "Help the maidens up into the room when we return." Maret only nodded in response, her hand held over her mouth.

Hadde handed her bow to Melas, climbed over the privy's edge, and lowered herself into the sewer. He passed her bow and a lantern to her. As she stepped off the piled rubble and onto the sewer path she heard talking from above.

"Come on, Melas," Hadde called. But instead of Melas, Maret was the next down the shaft. Hadde helped her onto the path. The maiden glanced at the stream flowing past and gagged. "It's wretched down here," she said.

"You don't have to come," Hadde said.

"I do. I have to help."

Melas reached down and handed Maret the second lantern before scrambling through the hole after them. He looked around. "You're certain the sewers lead out of the Great Keep?"

"All the way to the river." Hadde said. She thought for a moment, picturing in her mind the shit farmer's description of the sewers. "If we go this way, it will take us to where the queen's chambers are located."

"How do you know?" Melas demanded.

"Because the shit-farmer never stopped talking."

Maret moaned and grabbed Hadde's arm. "Ohh, the rats are everywhere."

Hadde squeezed her hand. "Go back up, Maret. Melas and I will do this."

"No." She swallowed and stood taller. "I'll be brave."

"Let's do this." Melas said.

Hadde led her companions down the path. After a short distance they came to a bend and she turned left. If she wasn't confused, they were under the back wall of the Great Keep. Alcoves in the opposite wall confirmed her suspicions. Most of the keep's privies were set into the outer wall. After passing a leftward branch, they came to another bend.

"Here," Hadde said. "One of these should be the one." She pointed across the sewer. "Maret, is the queen's chamber the last one on the corner of the keep?"

"Yes... I think so."

"So her privy should be the last?"

Maret nodded.

"No," Melas said. "There's another. In the guard tower at the corner."

"That faces to the back of the Keep," Maret said. "Not toward the Ost-Oras Gate."

"No, it doesn't."

"Well, which one?" Hadde asked.

"That one," Maret pointed at the second alcove in. "When I first arrived in Sal-Oras the queen's chamber was in another part of the castle. Her current room was an unused barracks. The privy is... well... a doubler, but one side is sealed up."

"You're certain?"

"I...um. I've been there."

"Melas?"

"She might be right."

Hadde gave her bow and quiver to Maret. Taking the rope from her shoulder, she crossed to the other side of the sewer. Melas joined her.

"You're going up unarmed? Take this back," he said as he unbelted her sword from around his waist.

"A sword would do me no good while I climb. Send it up on the rope when I reach the top." Hadde looked into the alcove. What she saw there confirmed Maret's description. One half of the privy had definitely seen more use than the other. "I'll climb up first and tie the rope off for you. If all is clear, I'll tug on the rope and you can follow me up."

"I should go first," Melas said.

Hadde tied one end of the rope around her waist. "No. Melas, you'll get your chance to fight. But right now we need stealth." She turned to Maret. "If all goes well, we'll lower them all down to you. Keep them calm and quiet until we're all together."

"I will."

Ducking under the lip of the shaft, Hadde peered upward into the darkness. The shaft was over a stride wide but narrower across. She entered the shaft, making sure not to step into the partially-filled sump to her right. Gagging, she eased to her left. She would be spared the worst of the foul mess. Bracing her back against one wall and her feet against the opposite, she started upward.

It didn't take long for her back to begin to burn with the effort. She ignored the pain and pushed rapidly upward. Breathing through her mouth, she avoided the worst of the stench. It was harder to close her mind against the occasional slick patches her boot—or worse, her hand—touched.

In the narrow confines of the shaft, the air was thick and cloying. She choked and had to stop. Her body convulsed with the urge to vomit. Fearing she might fall, she pressed herself even harder against the shaft's walls.

She had no choice, she had to keep going. She forced her legs back into motion, scrabbling higher. Sweat, or blood, dripped down her back. Her tunic must have been torn open by the rough walls. She had not gone far when the fire in her legs forced her to stop.

"What's wrong?" Melas called from below. Hadde closed her eyes. She had to do it. Just think of climbing. Nothing else. Breathing through her mouth, she started up the shaft again. The rough-cut walls dug painfully into her back. She glanced up and made out the shape of the privy hole above.

"Please, no one use it," she whispered to herself. She pushed herself faster, her thighs trembling with the effort. She stopped just below the cover and willed herself not to think about the forty-stride drop below her. Reaching out with one hand, she grasped the wooden privy hole. It seemed secure. She grabbed it with both hands and tried to pull herself through.

Too narrow. She cursed. Her right foot slipped and she uttered a startled cry. She clutched the privy lid as her feet scrambled for purchase, her hands sliding on the smooth lid. Pebbles and old masonry fell down the shaft beneath her. A chunk of stone followed. She pressed her foot into the gap it left. With all her strength, she braced herself against the wall.

Her head swam and her heart pounded. She took a deep breath, but nearly retched from the stench. Placing her hands on the wooden cover above, she lifted the privy's lid. Slowly, she slid it to one side. Climbing from the shaft, she surveyed the room. The only light came from one narrow, moonlit window. Hadde stepped to the door and bolted it.

Working quickly, she removed the toiletries resting on the other half of the privy and pulled the lid off. A single stout beam separated the two halves of the privy. After tying the rope to the beam, she gave it a stiff tug. Shadows moved in the lantern light at the base of the shaft.

Melas yanked the rope and Hadde quickly pulled it up. She untied the sheathed sword and dropped the rope back down the shaft. As Melas started up the rope, she crept to the door and pressed her ear against it. Nothing. From behind her she heard Melas climbing the shaft. She hoped she hadn't made as much noise as he was making. When he finally reached the top, she helped him from the shaft.

"Ugh," she said as she gave him the sword. "You look like... well, shit."

He glared at her. "I fell. You should see yourself."

"Some rescuers," she said. She nearly put her fingers to her lips to motion for quiet, but recoiled at the sight of them. She wiped them on her hose and motioned him toward the door. He nodded.

Beyond the door lay a short corridor. Melas tapped her shoulder and pointed to the next door. "That's it," he whispered. "We're in the right place."

"You're certain?"

"No guard tower has a privy like this. We must be in the Queen's chambers."

Hadde crept down the hall to the door and listened. The room beyond was silent. She worked the latch and pulled it open. She sucked in her breath as it creaked open. Sleeping figures lay curled under blankets on rugs surrounding a large bed. The maidens. Another figure slept in the bed. Hadde's gaze swept the room again. No guards. Or none she could see. Two doors led from the room.

Opening the door a little wider, she crept to the nearest sleeper and gently shook her awake. "Tira, it's me, Hadde," she whispered.

The maiden woke slowly at first and then choked and coughed. She looked at Hadde in confusion. "Oh, foul! What's that—"

"Shhh, don't say anything." Hadde glanced around the room to see if anyone else had awakened. "Are there any guards?"

Tira nodded and pointed toward one of the doors. "Hadde, what—"

"Quiet. We're getting you out of here. Wake the other maidens and lead them to the privy. Melas is here and will help you escape. You understand?" The maiden nodded and pulled herself from her blankets.

Hadde crept to the bed. The queen was deep asleep. She resisted Hadde's gentle attempt at getting her up. "Your Highness!" she whispered. Hadde glanced around the room. There were at most a dozen hostages. Queen Ilana yawned, looked at Hadde, and bolted upright in bed.

"What are you doing here?" she demanded, her voice a yell in the silent chamber.

Hadde clamped her hand over the queen's mouth, not caring how filthy it was. Ilana angrily grabbed it and tried to pull free, but Hadde shoved her back and pinned her to a pillow. Resisting the urge to choke the pampered royal, Hadde leaned close and whispered, "I'm helping you escape. Where is Prince Handrin?"

Hadde slowly pulled her hand from the queen's mouth. Ilana glared at her. "Where are the others? Where is Boradin?"

A whisper at least, Hadde thought. "The other rescuer is down the hall."

"One other? Just you and one other?"

"Your Highness, there's little time. We must escape before the guards are alerted. Where's your son?" The queen stared for a moment and then pointed. "In the next room," she said. "But there's one of those Messengers about. He was with Handrin earlier."

"Take the girls down the hall, Your Highness. A knight is waiting and he will help you escape. I'll get Prince Handrin and join you in a moment." As the queen nodded, Hadde walked to the door. The girls didn't speak, but they still made too much noise for Hadde to be able to hear anything behind the door. She put her hand on the latch when a thump behind her made her turn.

The maidens were getting dressed. "No!" Hadde hissed. You must go now. Your night shifts are enough." She took two of them by their arms and propelled them toward the door. "Put on shoes, but that's all. There's no time."

"They can't go out half-naked," Ilana objected.

"They'll go out half-naked or they'll die. Is modesty worth that price?"

Ilana aimed a glare at Hadde and then snapped, "Listen to her! Hurry, Maidens."

Hadde nodded her thanks to the queen. At least she had come to her senses. Hadde turned back to the door as the dozen girls shuffled down the hall. She had just put her hand on the handle when she heard a muffled shout from the privy. She pushed her way down the crowded hall.

"I'll not go down there," a maiden said to Melas. The others stared down the dark hole with horrified expressions, their hands crossed over their bosoms.

"You have to," Melas pleaded. "There's no other way."

"No!"

"Shhhh!" Hadde hissed as she entered the room.

"This is the rescue?" the queen demanded, entering the cramped room.

"It's this or nothing."

"I'm not going," one of the girls said, her voice too loud in the small room.

"There's no other rescue, Your Highness. This is your only chance."
Girls shook their heads as they backed away from the shaft. The queen
glared at Hadde.

Hadde took Ilana by the elbow and led her into the hall. "Your
Highness, please. If you go first, the maidens will follow your courage.
Please."

"I'm the Queen of Salador. Not some filthy commoner."

"The girls need you."

"Where are the Knights of the House? Where's my husband?"

"There's no time for this!" Hadde snapped. "You do this or you die.
You do this or your son dies!"

Ilana glared at Hadde. "I'll do it. But I'll not forget this."

"None of us will."

"Get my son!" Ilana snapped.

Hadde made her way through the queen's bedroom to the door to
Handrin's chamber. She listened, but heard nothing. Peering into the
chamber beyond, she saw the prince's small form lying on a sofa
wrapped in blankets. She quickly padded to him and shook him awake.

"Prince Handrin, it's me, Hadde of Landomere."

The boy looked at her in surprise. Hadde pulled his blanket from him.
"Come on, Prince, we're leaving."

"What? Why? You stink."

"I know. We're going to see your father, but we have to leave right
now."

"Sir Gredoc will be angry."

They both looked up at the sound of an opening door. Hadde found
herself staring into the silver face of Jenae's murderer. She stepped
between the prince and the eternal. "Handrin, run!"

Gredoc swept his sword from its sheath as he sprang forward. But
instead of attacking Hadde, he moved to cut off Handrin's flight. Hadde
snatched up a footstool and hurled it at Gredoc. The eternal struck it from
the air with his sword and leaped for Handrin.

"Wind!" the boy shouted. A blast of air caught his blanket and sent it
billowing over the knight's head.

"Hadde! Run!" Handrin yelled. She scrambled past the eternal and
followed the prince into the next room. Gredoc leapt after them. Hadde
ducked a slash at her head, but before she could recover, Gredoc
shouldered her aside and she tumbled to the floor. Rolling, she lashed out
with her foot and tripped the knight as he leapt past.

He crashed to the floor. "Dromost take you!" Gredoc cursed as he
rose.

"Handrin! Into the privy!" Hadde shouted. Gredoc raised his sword and turned toward Hadde. Before he could swing, a flash of fire engulfed his face. Crying out, he fell back.

"Go!" Hadde yelled. As the prince turned and fled Melas dashed into the room. Crying out, "Jenae!" he thrust his sword deep into Gredoc's chest. Melas yanked the blade free as the eternal toppled backwards. Silver blood coated the squire's blade.

White-clad Returnists rushed into the room. "Get out." Melas shouted, waving Hadde to the hall behind him. He struck down the first Returnist to charge him and parried another's blow. A vicious counter struck the Returnist's arm off at the elbow. Blood sprayed as the man stared at the stump in shock.

Hadde snatched up a pillow and threw it at a Returnist. It burst in a shower of white feathers as he chopped it in half. Hadde snatched Gredoc's sword from where it lay on the floor. A few strides away, the eternal struggled to his hands and knees. She couldn't help but stare for a moment. No mortal could have survived Melas' thrust.

More Returnists pushed into the room. "I'll hold them here," Melas said as he slashed at a Returnist.

"Not here. Hold them below!"

"You first."

Hadde ran from the room with Melas close behind. He slammed the hallway door closed and bolted it. A heavy blow crashed against the door as they ran to the privy. A second blow broke the bolt. Hadde glanced behind to see a Returnist stumble into the hall.

"Hold the door," Hadde said as they ran into the privy. "The bolt won't keep them out." Tira and Handrin stared at Hadde as she barged into the room, but she couldn't spare them more than a glance.

"Got it," Melas said. He bolted the door and then pressed his full weight against it.

"Why are they still here?" Hadde asked. "She added her weight to Melas'.

"There was no time to get them out," he replied. "I had to come and help you."

"Tira, tie the rope around the prince's chest," Hadde ordered. Rapid footfalls approached and the door shuddered in its hinges. "Hold on, Melas," she said as another blow struck the door.

"Wedge it shut with those boards," Melas said. "I can hold it."

"Are you done, Tira?" Hadde asked as she jammed the door shut.

"I'm done," Tira said. "I hope I tied it well enough."

Hadde checked the knot. "Good—good enough." She took the prince by the shoulders and stared him in the face. "We're going to lower you down. Your mother is waiting for you. Can you be brave?"

He glanced into the privy shaft. Hadde saw the fear in his eyes. But he nodded and said, "I can do it."

Hadde helped him to the edge and then lowered him into the pit. "Hurry, Hadde," Melas called. Tira yelped in fright as the door shuddered under an impact.

"I am—I am," Hadde replied. Her shoulders soon burned with the effort.

Wood splintered as an axe head appeared through the door. Melas lunged forward and thrust his sword through the gap. There was a surprised shout from outside and he quickly withdrew the blade.

The rope went slack. "He's down," Maret's voice echoed up the shaft. As fast as she could, Hadde drew the rope up.

"The Messenger," someone shouted from outside. A blow hit the door and it nearly shattered. Melas stepped back with his sword held ready.

Hadde looped the rope around the beam sitting across the open privy shaft before tying it around Tira. "Hurry, Hadde!" Tira said, clearly more terrified by the enemy at the door than the shaft blow.

"Go!" This time Hadde let the rope run through her hands, the loop around the beam slowing Tira's descent. Even so, the heat soon became unbearable, forcing Hadde to lower Tira hand over hand.

Boards flew into the room as the top of the door collapsed. Melas leapt forward, stabbing at the enemy outside.

"She's off!" Hadde called.

"Slide down. I'll follow," he said between thrusts.

Hadde shoved Gredoc's sword through her belt and slid down the shaft. The rope burned her as she descended, but she had no choice but to ignore the pain. Silhouettes moved in the darkness above and the rope jerked as Melas followed her. She hit the bottom and climbed onto the sewer path. The maidens, Ilana, and Handrin huddled together nearby. Maret stood near the shaft holding her lantern.

"Lead them that way, Maret," Hadde ordered. "I'll be with you soon."

"I don't know the way."

"Take the first right. I'll catch up." Hadde belted Belor's bow case around her waist. She took up Gredoc's sword and held it in both hands as Melas emerged from the shaft.

Slowly, too slowly, the queen and the maidens moved down the path. "Come quickly, Hadde." Maret said.

"We're with you," Hadde said.

The rope jerked and twitched behind Melas. "They're coming," he said.

"Let's go, Melas," Hadde said. "We have to protect the maidens."

"No. Your only hope is if I hold them here. If the Returnists get into the sewers, you'll never escape."

"I'll stay with you." Hadde said.

"Get out!" Melas shouted. "Shut up and get out!"

"I cannot leave you here." An image of Captain Palen being pulled from his horse by the Returnist mob flashed through her mind. She glanced at the retreating maidens.

"Leave me. This is my place. This is what I want." Torchlight grew brighter in the privy shaft. "Go!" He raised his sword as if to strike her.

Hadde pulled back at rage she saw in his eyes. "Flee if you get the chance," she said.

He turned to the alcove, his sword poised. "I couldn't save Jenae," he said over his shoulder. "I'll not fail these maidens. Farewell, Hadde."

Hadde led the escapees out of the sewer and onto the riverbank. The shit farmer's shed sat silent and dark nearby. All around them the city burned, the flames lighting the dawn sky. Here and there refugees fled, taking what few possessions they had saved from their homes. Others took the opportunity to pillage.

The maidens clung to one another; most cried. Ilana held Handrin close. A pall of dense smoke drifted over them. "What now?" Ilana demanded.

Hadde blinked her eyes against the bitter wind. "We have to get to your husband. His soldiers must surround the Great Keep."

"You're not certain where they are?"

"I was in a cell when this all happened. But I saw King Boradin and his men attack through the gate. I'm certain they're outside. He wouldn't have left. The eternal demanded he present himself each day."

"Well, lead on."

Hadde peered through the smoke. "I don't know the way."

"There is the downriver bridge." Ilana pointed. "The avenue above leads to the Great Keep."

"Come on, Maidens," Hadde called out. "Follow me." She glanced at the sewer entrance as she led them away. She wanted to believe that Melas still lived.

"Follow close, girls," Ilana said. The ragged band of maidens bunched close behind the queen. Hadde saw Maret at the back, hustling the slowest along.

No one paid the party any heed as they scurried along the river. The bridge over the Treteren stood high above them. Nearby a moored ship burned. Next to it, a battle raged as a warehouse was looted.

They had nearly made it to the base of the bridge when Hadde caught sight of a crowd running in their direction. A mass of Returnists, some armed, poured down the hill. She handed her sword to the startled Ilana and took her bow from its case as she looked for an escape. Hadde spied a narrow garbage-strewn alley a few strides away.

"Hide there," she shouted to the maidens. "Between those two buildings." Most heeded her call, but a few panicked. Ilana and Maret cajoled them toward the shelter. Hadde drew her bow as she backed into the alley. The crowd was nearly on them. But they hardly seemed to notice the maidens. Instead they looked over their shoulders. Hadde heard the rumble of hooves.

Behind her, Ilana shoved the last of the girls into hiding. Hadde leaped into the gap after them. Screams of pain and fear followed her from the street. A few dozen Returnists ran past, many splattered by blood and dirt. Red-clad knights charged behind them, cutting down the Returnists as they fled.

The Knights of the House showed no mercy. Swords and maces rose and fell relentlessly as the Returnists pled for their lives. The knights paid their cries no heed. Hadde pushed back further into the alley.

"There's no more room," Ilana said.

"No exit?"

"It's blocked. A gate."

A Returnist tumbled to the ground in front of their hiding place. He leapt into the alley as a knight wheeled to charge him. Hadde drew her bow and took aim. A maiden screamed behind her. Wide-eyed, the Returnist raised his hands and stumbled.

A knight appeared and clove the Returnists head in half. Panic engulfed the maidens as the blood-smeared knight stepped over the body and raised his sword. "Stop!" Hadde shouted. "We're not Returnists!" She held her bow at full draw. The knight paused mid-stride.

"Lay down your sword, Sir Knight!" Ilana demanded. She pushed Hadde aside. "Put down your sword!" She shook her finger as if scolding a child. She still held Hadde's sword in her other hand.

The knight lowered his sword and pulled his helm back on his head. "My queen?" His brow furrowed as he peered past them at the crying maidens.

"Get us out of here, Sir Gorwin," Ilana demanded. "Take us to the king."

"Yes, Your Majesty." The knight backed out and surveyed the avenue. He blocked the queen with his shield as she attempted to depart the alley. "It isn't yet safe, Your Majesty."

"Have you retaken the Great Keep? Where's my husband?"

"Returnists still hold the keep. We're retaking the city. Or what remains of it. How did you get here, Your Majesty?"

"Hadde and Squire Melas rescued us. They——"

Pushing past the queen, Hadde said, "Melas is in danger. He stayed behind to hold off our pursuers."

Gorwin stepped out of her way. "Where is he?"

"We came out through the sewers. He might still be alive. We have to go to him." Hadde glanced at the maidens sheltering in the alley. Could she leave them and run for Melas? Gorwin seemed to sense her anxiety.

"Knights, to me!" he shouted as he strode into the street. "To me!" Soon, nearly a dozen knights and soldiers crowded around him. Gorwin quickly counted off four of them. "Go with Hadde," he commanded. "She'll lead you to Squire Melas. He's in grave danger."

Hadde nodded her thanks to Gorwin and sprinted down the street. She heard the four knights following her, but they quickly fell behind. She didn't care, all that mattered was her race to Melas.

She slid down the muddy riverbank toward the sewer entrance, but halted for a moment before charging in. Pointing toward the shit farmer's shack she shouted back to the knights, "Torches! Torches in there!"

The lead knight, running as best he could in his coat-of-plates, waved in acknowledgement. She hoped he truly understood. "Torches!" she shouted again, and then dashed into the sewer.

After a few strides her eyes adjusted to the dark and her nose to the stench. She ran as fast as she dared, leaping gaps in the path without thinking. She thought she heard the sound of steel on steel echoing, but her own footfalls made it hard to tell.

Clutching her bow, she skidded around a corner. There was fighting ahead—and Ilana still held her sword. Hadde cursed her haste as she pushed forward. Men shouted. It had to be Melas.

Her breath rasping with the exertion, she sprinted down the tunnel. She saw him. Melas battled Gredoc on the sewer path ahead. Bodies lay sprawled around them. Two floated in the sewer.

The eternal bled argent blood from a dozen wounds.

Melas held his sword in two hands and rained blows upon Gredoc. But in the fury of his assault he was unaware of the Returnist who crawled from a sewer shaft behind him. "Watch out! Behind you, Melas!"

He made no sign that he heard her. "Behind you!" She drew her bow as she ran. The Returnist turned at Hadde's shout, but ignored her and charged Melas from behind.

The squire, unaware of the threat, parried a powerful blow from Gredoc, and with a lightning fast counter cut the eternal down. A gout of silver blood erupted from the eternal's neck as he toppled into the sewer.

As Melas wrenched his sword free, Hadde knelt and loosed her arrow. It flew wide. At the last moment Melas heard the approaching Returnist. He turned, raising his sword to parry, but was too late. The Returnist ran him through.

Hadde desperately loosed another arrow. It struck the Returnist in the hip, and with a cry of pain he staggered against the stone wall. The next arrow took him in the back. He spun toward Hadde, his teeth clenched in agony. She shot him one last time and he slid to the ground.

Melas lay unmoving on the sewer path. She ran and knelt at his side.

"Melas? Can you hear me?" She lifted his head.

His eyes fluttered open. "Did they make it?" he asked. Blood trickled from his mouth.

"They made it. You saved them."

The tension in his face eased. Heavy footfalls approached. Hadde grasped Melas' sword and glanced up to see approaching torchlight. The Knights of the House.

She looked back to Melas. His eyes were closed. "Melas? Stay with me."

He didn't reply. His face was utterly at peace. Hadde sobbed. He was so young.

Hadde followed the four knights as they bore Melas' body through the city. Fires raged all around them, but the fighting had ended. Some refugees filled the streets, while others watched their homes go up in flames. She wiped tears from her face. First Melas's fiancée and then his own life had been wrenched from him. All because of Akinos and his deluded mission.

A tremendous plume of smoke darkened the sky. A great fire raged ahead. More knights arrived and escorted the pallbearers. The Saladorans spoke with one another, but Hadde paid them no heed. Her name was mentioned, but she didn't lift her head to see who spoke.

She stopped at the entrance to the square before the Great Keep. The gatehouse and walls blocked her view of all but the castle's upper stories. Fire consumed all she could see. The Great Keep of Sal-Oras was doomed.

Activity drew her eyes to the gates. Soldiers poured through in both directions. Those entering were unburdened. Those leaving carried the bodies of the wounded and slain, or led prisoners at sword point. A third group carried some other burden. She squinted in their direction. Books.

Hadde sighed. King Boradin was saving his library. His city destroyed, his army exhausted, Akinos free, and the king chose to save his books. They were doomed.

A scream caught her attention. She glanced to the left of the gate and recoiled in horror. There, a forest of corpses had sprung up as the Returnist prisoners and dead were impaled upon spears and placed upright against the Great Keep's outer wall.

Thrashing furiously, a man attempted to free himself from the grip of two soldiers. Each grasped one of his legs. Hadde turned as another soldier rammed a spear through him. Turning away was little salvation. The sight that greeted her eyes wrenched her heart. She watched as the pallbearers lowered Melas' body to the ground next to a long line of his comrades.

A knight carefully crossed the squire's arms across his chest and stood silently over him. Two knights bearing another of the dead blocked her view. They placed their burden on the ground and stepped aside.

Suddenly Boradin was there, looking down at Melas. Nidon stood beside the king. Blood and ash covered the men, and their armor and tabards were gashed and rent. The king held Forsvar and his gilt mace, Nidon a great axe. Behind them stood a dozen knights, each as battered as the king and his champion.

Boradin held Forsvar in front of him and swept his mace up in a salute. Nidon and the knights behind him followed the king's example. They held their salute for a moment, and then as one swept their arms to their sides. Hadde found herself staring the king in his eyes. Neither dropped their gaze. She read grim determination in the set of his face.

As he strode in her direction, she stood her ground. He dared not accuse her of any wrongdoing. He would get worse than he gave. He had caused this. She remembered Morin's accusations against his brother. Boradin was no king. His idleness, his lack of leadership, his Dromost-damned library would give Akinos and the Wasting their victory.

"You're saving your books?" she said as he approached. "They will be no good to you when we're all dead! You've doomed us." The king strode toward her as if to knock her down. As she braced herself blue-white fire danced on Forsvar's rim.

She recoiled from the light, shielding her eyes with her hand. The attack never came. Boradin knelt before her, his head bowed low. Without a moment's hesitation, Nidon and the dozen escorts dropped to their knees. All around them, knights, soldiers, and servants turned to see what was happening.

Like ripples from a stone cast into a pond, all within the square fell to their knees facing Hadde. "I save the books," the king whispered, "because there is a future. There is a future because of you."

Boradin stood, but all others remained on their knees. "There are some, who if they were in my position, would claim infallibility." He didn't shout, but his voice carried clearly across the square and echoed off the walls. "I am not one of them."

From behind the gatehouse came a loud rumble. Hadde glanced up to see a corner of the Great Keep topple out of sight behind the outer wall. A ball of fire and embers rose high into the sky.

A grimace of a smile crossed the king's face. "My keep agrees with me," Boradin whispered.

Louder, he called out, "I've wronged this woman. This huntress. This warrior. Hadde of Landomere risked all to bring me tidings of great danger. And for her efforts, I locked her away. And how did she repay me? When my keep was taken, she again risked all to save the lives of my family and the Maidens in Waiting.

"I've made mistakes, but I'll not compound them. I shall redeem myself. And in my redemption Akinos shall be slain, the Orb of Creation recovered, and the Wasting ended. My redemption begins at this moment."

"Kneel, Hadde of Landomere," he said.

Swallowing her fear, she knelt before Boradin.

"I command that the Ladies in Waiting should cleanse the blood and filth from Hadde's body. She endured what few others would in pursuit of her cause. I command that the Maidens in Waiting shall sew for Hadde a tabard befitting her new station. On a green field they shall sew two argent arrows crossed. Above the arrow points shall rest Helna's golden Orb. I command that Champion Nidon and the Captains of the House shall arm Hadde in the best-forged mail and finest arms that can be found."

He paused. Hundreds of eyes upon her. She startled as the king's mace came to rest on her shoulder. Blue flames danced on the weapon's head.

"Lady Hadde of Landomere, I dub you a Knight of the House, Captain of Horse-Archers, Protector of the Crown Prince, Ambassador to the King, and a Baroness of Salador. In my name, Magus Elementar Rex, Boradin of Salador, so be it."

The mace passed from shoulder to shoulder as Boradin spoke, coming to rest on the top of her head.

"Rise, Lady Hadde." Boradin raised Forsvar as he turned to the expectant crowd. "Rise, Salador. Tomorrow we ride to war."

Chapter Twenty-seven

"You look like a knight," Maret said.

Hadde laughed. "I suppose I should. Thank you for the fine tabard." She let her gaze sweep across the gathered maidens. They stood shivering in front of one of the large mansions surrounding the Great Keep's square. Snow fell in fat wet flakes. A horn call echoed off the walls.

"We wanted to thank you before you departed," Tira said.

Hadde smiled, but shook her head. "I had help. Without Maret, I would still be in my cell. And think of Melas as well. He gave his life for us." The horn called again. Knights mounted their horses and formed into their companies. A squire led Lightfoot closer. Hadde nodded to him in thanks.

"The army rides, Lady Hadde," he said. The squire looked impatient to join his lance.

"I have to go," Hadde said. The girls surged forward and she hugged each in turn. It felt strange through her mail. Maret was the last.

"What shall I do?" she whispered in Hadde's ear. "My father rides with Akinos."

Hadde held her close. "If worse comes to worst I'll take you back to Landomere with me. But let's think of the best."

"You would really do that?"

"Of course. You're my friend, Maret. It's the Way of the Forest." Hadde let the maiden go and mounted Lightfoot. With a final wave, she rode off.

For three days the army marched north along the Treteren River toward King's Crossing. Blustery wet snow soaked and chilled them. Progress would have been impossibly slow if they had not abandoned most of the army's baggage train. Now they marched light, knowing they would have only one chance to defeat Akinos' host.

Each night they halted and found what shelter they could. Hadde fared better than most—years of hunting had prepared her well. She reached out from under her lean-to and pushed another stick onto her campfire. It burned brightly—not so those of others nearby. A few knights and squires had earlier approached and begged embers with which to coax their tinder to light. She happily obliged, but it hadn't done them much good.

One squire politely asked the use of her fire to cook his lance's meal. His pot of porridge bubbled as it hung from the iron tripod. The squire wasn't to be seen. Hadde smiled. They didn't know what to make of her. Boradin showed her great favor, but they were still Saladoran and she was still a woman.

Not for the first time, she thought of Belor and wished that he were alive. He probably would have looked forward to the coming battle. Even Melas would have gladly taken his ease by her fire. She looked toward the river. The dark water moved peacefully, heedless of the turbulence to come.

She leaned back under her shelter and pushed her armor aside. She sighed at the sight of the mail hauberk. Why polish the rust from it when it would only rain again tomorrow?

Someone approached. Hadde looked up, expecting the squire. She arched her brows at the sight of a short soldier trudging toward her. He wore an ill-fitting aketon and helm, and what appeared to be a ragged red and white striped horse blanket as a cloak. A shield banged awkwardly against his back. In one hand he carried a short thrusting spear. In the other he held a sack.

He stopped at the edge of the firelight. "Lady Hadde?" he asked in a high voice. "May I approach?"

"Of course." She thought she knew the voice, but couldn't place it for certain. He didn't look like any other Saladoran soldier she had ever seen. He jammed the butt of his spear into the ground and walked into the firelight. Grinning, he pushed the helm back on his head, exposing his face. "Do you recognize me?"

"Puddle? Is it you?" He beamed when she stood and embraced him. "What are you doing here?" she asked.

"I've been trying to find you. But I couldn't get away from my company. I wanted to give you this." He squirmed away from her and opened his sack. From it he withdrew Hawkeye.

"You found it? I thought it burned in the Great Keep!"

His smile widened as he handed her the bow. "I saved it when Lightfoot was brought into the stables after they arrested you. I kept it for you."

Hadde traced her hand along the bow's back. "Thank you. Thank you so much. But why are you in armor?"

He yanked his spear from the ground and hefted it. "The king needed soldiers to fight Akinos. And after what you did, saving the prince and such, I had to help."

"No, Puddle, you didn't have to do that." She stared at the boy. He looked barely able to stand under the weight of his equipment.

"I thought of you when they called for soldiers to join the ranks. I remembered what you said about being noble. And look, King Boradin made you one. I'll be a noble, too."

"You have to stay safe. Don't risk too much."

"I'm in the last rank." He frowned. "But if I'm lucky, I'll get my chance to be a hero like you."

"Don't try. It will get you killed."

Movement out of the corner of her eye caught Hadde's attention. Nidon emerged from the king's tent and, after a moment, he marched in her direction. Boradin had offered Hadde a large tent, but she settled for a quieter and more familiar lean-to set off on its own.

"May I join you?" Nidon asked as he approached. Puddle gasped and stood at attention at the sight of the champion.

"Please do." Hadde waved Nidon to a spot next to the fire.

"Take your ease, Puddle," Nidon said as he crouched. He raised his hands to the heat. "Not many fires like this one tonight."

"Years as a Huntress," she said. He nodded.

A wolf howled in the distance. No, not a wolf, Hadde realized. A man imitating a wolf. "The varcolac have returned," Nidon said.

"Akinos knows we're coming." Hadde stared into the fire. "I'm afraid that we might lose, Sir Nidon. I think the army was delayed too long. And it's too weak. Too tired."

"It doesn't matter," he said without looking up.

She looked up at him in surprise. His face was calm. "How can you say that? Of course it matters."

Nidon turned back to Hadde. "The army's size and fatigue don't matter, because the way of the warrior is death."

Hadde and Puddle stared at Nidon. "When the odds are even between life and death, the warrior chooses death." Nidon stared solemnly into each of their eyes in turn. "There is no need to think about it. There is no choice at all between a hero's death and a coward's life.

"I wouldn't care at all if Akinos rode at the head of an army of black-winged veden and I stood to face him alone. If it were my duty to fight him and die in doing so, I would do it without thought." Puddle gazed at Nidon, awestruck.

"I don't think I'm a warrior, then," Hadde said.

Nidon laughed and clasped her shoulder with his big hand. He leaned close. "You're a warrior. You may not think it. You may not want to be one. But you know what has to be done, and you do it. That's why you ride with us into the maw of death."

For two more days they marched north. Varcolac and Tyskmen dogged their movements, but no army blocked their path. Hadde rode at the head of the column with Boradin and the red-cloaked Knights of the House. Knights from all three Teren marched behind. More and more from the West Teren joined them each day. Behind the knights came vassal foot and guild mercenaries.

Hadde tapped Lightfoot's flanks and the little horse trotted to the left of the Knights of the House. She pulled her cloak closer about her and watched as Boradin's army deployed on the slope of a low hill on the bank of the Treteren River. A few flakes of snow drifted past. Ominous clouds promised more.

A stream ran across the front of the army, and beyond it rose a larger hill. There rested Akinos' army. A chill passed over her, but it wasn't from the cold. The army was bigger than she remembered.

She searched for any sign of Akinos or Morin amongst the soldiers of the opposing host, but saw none. A shout drew her attention. Below, where the stream fed into the river, lay a small town. Blue liveried Sal-Oras soldiers with pole-axes and crossbows cleared the town of the few Tysk who occupied it.

Ahead, along the stream bank, Saladoran footmen took up position. Crossbowmen to the front, spearmen in support. Soldiers from the West Teren held the left flank. Behind the spearmen rested two battles of knights in long lines. At the crest of the hill stood the Knights of the House.

Unlike Boradin's hill, the spur upon which Akinos' army stood had only been partially cleared of trees. At the edge of the woods Hadde saw movement, and from time to time Tyskmen emerged to jeer at the Saladorans. Hundreds more Tyskmen spread themselves in a ragged line across the floor of the valley between the two armies. The Tysk were well out of crossbow range and seemed content to crouch under their cloaks and observe the might of Salador deployed before them.

Lining the ridge behind them stood thousands of Akinos' Rigarian soldiers. Brightly colored banners and the hulking shapes of urias clearly defined each company. There were no varcolac or capcaun to be seen, nor any sign of Akinos. Dozens of mounted men rode amongst the Rigarians, but most wore the white cloaks of the Eternal Knights. None wore Morin's black.

She searched the enemy army, hoping for some sight of him. She feared for him in the coming struggle. Boradin might win the battle, but in doing so slay Morin. She wanted nothing more than an end to the Wasting, but what if it cost her Morin?

No. She shook off the fear. Morin would live and be restored to human form again. He was too strong—too smart to fall. He would escape and flee to Landomere with her.

The Tyskmen on the valley floor got to their feet and hefted their spears and javelins. As one, the voices of the Rigarians behind them rose in song. It started softly and increased in volume and intensity. As they sang, they crashed their spears against their shields. The words were indistinguishable, but the meaning of the music was clear. The song was one of victory, and she could hear the strength of the army in it.

A nearby trumpet blared a clarion call. Hadde looked to the herald. He rode with King Boradin and his escort in front of the Knights of the House. Three times the horn called, and then the Knights of the House raised their lances high and shouted.

"For the king, for the shield, for the land of Salador!"

More horns joined the herald's. As their call ended, the knights of the three Terens joined their voices with those of the House.

"For the king, for the shield, for the land of Salador!"

Soon the entire Saladoran army joined in and the valley echoed with their voices. All the while the Rigarians had kept up their own song and the hills reverberated with the noise. Hadde sat on Lightfoot's back, awed at the emotion and power of the music. Over the spur marched hundreds of Rigarian musicians. Trumpets and flutes joined the rumble of drums.

And then the music stopped.

From the opposite ridge rode three eternals—two entirely white-clad, the third in a tabard of yellow emblazoned with a black dragon. It was Maret's father, Earl Seremar. As they approached the valley floor, Hadde saw that each eternal carried a sword by its blade, hilt pointing skyward. They passed the line of Tyskmen and continued toward the Saladoran army.

"Come to me, Lady Hadde."

Hadde jolted in her saddle as Boradin's voice sounded in her ear. She looked to where he waited with Nidon in front of the Knights of the House and, putting her heels to Lightfoot, trotted up to them. "What are they doing, Your Majesty? Why do they hold their swords like that?"

"They wish to parlay. I'm going to speak with them and wish for you and Champion Nidon to join me. You've met Akinos and these Eternal Knights before. I wish for you to advise me if I have need of it."

"Yes, Your Majesty."

Boradin led Hadde and Nidon down the hill to the bank of the stream. Nidon held his sword in the same manner as the three eternals. The king held Forsvar, tendrils of blue fire circled the shield as if it anticipated battle. Across the stream, twenty strides away, the three eternals waited.

"My king," Seremar called out as he bowed his head toward Boradin.

"You call me your king? You, who march with my enemy's army."

"You are still my king. I am sent to seek peace between you and Akinos, wielder of the Orb of Creation. Akinos does not come as a conqueror, but as a redeemer. He does not wish your throne."

"He lays waste to my country. How can I befriend him?"

"All the harm that has been committed has been done in the name of our salvation," Seremar replied. "It was unavoidable."

"Unavoidable?" Boradin shook his fist at the eternal. "He could have delivered the Orb to me and all this suffering would have been avoided. He can still do so. Tell him to return what is rightfully mine."

Seremar shook his head. "Akinos has selected another path. Lay down your arms and join him in salvation."

"It isn't salvation he brings us, but destruction," Boradin said, anger rising in his voice. "I've been warned of the peril of the Orb. You eternals are the cause of our demise. You are the Wasting. You are our downfall."

"I know not of what you speak. We shall all become eternal, and in that find peace."

"Go back to Akinos and tell him I'll fight him. Tell him that I'll not let the Wasting take us all."

"Tell him yourself."

The Rigarian drummers sent a wave sound washing across the valley. Soon their horns joined in and the music swelled. Another battle line of Rigarians appeared over the crest of the distant spur and marched into the valley.

Hadde gaped as they appeared. The second wave was larger than the first. She turned her head as a murmur of dismay swept through the Saladoran army. Restless movement swept through the crossbowmen behind her.

"Look! Look to the woods!" one of them shouted. Hadde and others turned in the direction he pointed. Hundreds of Saladoran knights emerged from the trees on the Rigarian right. All wore some white emblem in addition to their East Teren yellow. A knight in black rode at their head. Hadde's heart lurched in her chest. Morin. No... she leaned forward in her saddle. This man rode a roan horse with white socks. Astor. The knights halted just outside the forest edge.

"Traitors," Nidon muttered.

For a moment the Rigarian army stood motionless. Then, to Hadde's surprise, the entire army about-faced and knelt toward the spur to their rear.

Over the hill appeared two companies of giant capcaun, each a score strong. All wore shining suits of gilded scale armor, and each had a huge two-headed axe resting on his shoulder.

Moments later two larger companies of varcolac appeared and flanked the giants. All wore mail of burnished steel and had cloaks of white fur draped over their shoulders. White bear-masks were drawn over their faces, and each bore two heavy javelins in his hands. Swords and short-hafted axes hung from their belts.

Between the two bands of giants appeared a huge wagon pulled by more capcaun. Three times the size of any ordinary wagon, it was painted in a rainbow of colors and inlaid with gold and silver. But despite the gay colors and ornaments, it was a machine of war. Long, polished blades curved out from the hubs of each wheel. Hadde shook her head in amazement. Each gleaming blade was as tall as a man. As long as the wagon was in motion it would be impossible to assail from either side.

Varcolac manned the wagon, each bearing a pole-axe. Forty Eternal Knights escorted the massive machine. Akinos sat on a richly decorated chair mounted high in the center of the wagon. He raised the Orb of Creation, and it flashed with brilliant golden light. As the Orb pulsed, the drums and cymbals of his army's band crashed into a frenzy of noise that washed against Hadde with a physical impact.

And then silence. The Rigarian army rose and turned to face Boradin. Akinos' host was far more powerful than Hadde had imagined.

"You've no hope of victory," Seremar said, echoing her thoughts. "Come with me, King Boradin. Speak with Akinos. He will tell you the truth. He will show you the glory of the Orb." Hadde glanced at Boradin. His gaze swept across the Rigarian army, she saw doubt in his eyes.

"Akinos will welcome you," Seremar continued. "Your son is our salvation. He shall wield the Orb. Come and speak with Akinos. He will respect the truce we have called."

Boradin nodded. He opened his mouth to speak, but Hadde cut him off.

"No! Your Majesty, you cannot. I've heard their arguments. I've touched the Orb. It feels like kindness, love, and goodness, but it's a lie. Akinos' efforts are the Wasting, and no matter how wonderful it feels or sounds, it is killing us."

"Be silent," Nidon said. "You may have been knighted, but it gives you no right to speak to the king in such a manner."

"But—"

"Who is she who rules your kingdom?" Seremar said. "Come with me, King Boradin, and all will be made clear." He raised his hand and offered it to Boradin. "With a single touch—mine, Akinos', or the Orb's—you'll feel Helna's grace. You'll feel the life-giving glory that will save us all."

"No!" Hadde grasped the King's forearm. "They can hold you powerless, drain the life from you. Morin——"

"Unhand him!" Nidon said.

Boradin yanked his arm from Hadde's grip. "Be silent, Lady Hadde."

"You cannot win," Seremar said. "Prince Morin marches to us as we speak. He brings his Teboran and Namiri allies with him. You'll be overwhelmed. Don't let it come to blows. Let there be peace."

"I've heard enough," Boradin said.

Hadde stared at the king, hoping he would reject Seremar, but fearing the worst. Nidon glared at her, daring her to speak again.

"Tell Akinos there will be no peace between us," Boradin said. "He will surrender the Orb to me or face the might of Salador." Hadde exhaled with relief as the king spoke the words. There was still some small hope that the Wasting would end.

The king took his mace from his belt. "Our parlay is ended. Return to your master or feel my wrath." Blue flames engulfed the mace's head.

Without a word, the three eternals turned their horses and rode toward Akinos' warwagon. Hadde wiped her hand across her sweaty brow. The fate of the world would be decided on the ground beneath her.

"Seek a place of shelter, Hadde," Boradin said. "But don't stray too far." The king thrust his mace into the sky. Brilliant light flashed from the golden head. He reared his horse around to face his army.

The assembled forces raised their weapons and cheered. Boradin saluted them, and with Nidon riding close behind, galloped across the face of the Saladoran host.

The first wisps of snow fell from a steel grey sky.

Chapter Twenty-eight

Hadde stared on as Tyskmen shouted war cries and sprinted forward. Massed Rigarians followed in close order. The battle had begun. The Knights of the House leaned forward in their saddles, clutching at their lances, eager to charge. Boradin and Nidon sat at their head.

Well below them, Saladoran crossbowmen aimed at the advancing Tyskmen and let fly a volley of deadly bolts. Dozens of Tyskmen fell, but hundreds more continued forward. Some of the Tysk were bow armed and stopped to loose arrows at the Saladorans. Most of the Tysk charged ahead, shields held high.

As the first Tyskmen reached the stream, they hurled their javelins at the Saladoran line. A few crossbowmen fell, but it was a rare Tyskman who lived to cast a second javelin.

Hadde wanted to block out the shouted orders, the snap of crossbows, the sick thuds of missiles striking home, and the cries of the wounded. The snow fell harder as more and more men from both sides died.

Akinos' Rigarians halted a hundred strides from the stream as their drums reached a crescendo. Two ranks of spearmen knelt in front of six ranks of archers.

They raised their bows and a thousand arrows flew into the snow-laced sky. The Saladorans quailed as the storm arched toward them, crying out in dismay as the arrows streaked downward. For a short time the Saladorans held on, but it wasn't an even contest. The Rigarian archers each wore an aketon and stood behind a shield wall of armored spearmen. The Saladoran crossbowmen fell back.

Hadde rode up to Boradin. "Why don't you raise a wind and blow their arrows away, Your Majesty?"

"I can only do so much. Would you've me waste my strength defending these crossbowmen? I must save myself for Akinos and the Orb of Creation."

"But—"

"If I spend myself now, I will have nothing later."

"Is that... is that what happened at the Great Keep?" Hadde asked.

"I was foolish," Boradin replied. "I wasted myself on the gate and that eternal. I nearly killed myself saving the maiden. I can't let that happen here."

"They're soldiers," Nidon said. "They do what they're told. Some will die, but that's war. And this snow hurts archery; Akinos will have to close with us. It favors us."

The Rigarians ceased their arrow storm and advanced to the stream bank. Once again the spearmen knelt and the archers loosed arrows over their heads. Only thirty strides separated the two armies. But unlike the fleeing crossbowmen, long kite shields, iron helms, and aketons protected the Saladoran spearmen who now stood before the Rigarian archers.

Horns blared and the Saladoran spearmen advanced into the stream.

The two armies crashed together. Men grunted and yelled as they thrust their spears. Some slipped and fell on the muddy ground to be trampled by their comrades or drowned in the stream. Hadde scanned the ranks of Sal-Oras spearmen for any sign of Puddle. It didn't take long to spot his striped cloak. The little stable hand struggled through the stream, his shield pressed against the back of the man in front of him.

A sudden burst of snow obscured the soldiers, and she lost him in the melee. Hadde wouldn't let Puddle die. "I cannot stand idly by and watch this."

"Have at them," Boradin said, waving her off. He didn't even look at her. She rode toward the fighting.

Saladoran spearmen struggled up the opposite bank. The Rigarians recoiled under the onslaught; for a moment Hadde thought they would break. But urias surged forward, and with massive strokes of their war clubs, they drove the Saladorans back. The spearmen scrambled up their own stream bank.

Hadde urged Lightfoot faster, passing impatient Sal-Oras knights as they readied themselves to charge. She drew to a halt fifty strides from the stream. There was no reason to go closer. There would be no missing the densely massed Rigarians.

She nocked an arrow and let fly. Hadde wasted no time watching the flight of the arrows, but nocked the next as quickly as its brother left the bow.

Not far from her stood a line of crossbowmen. Rigarian arrows still galled them. As the Saladorans gave ground Hadde found herself amongst them. Arrows whistled past. Lightfoot whinnied as one skimmed her flank. Two more thudded into the ground nearby.

"Let's move, Lightfoot," she said. "They've had enough of us." Her gaze swept across the melee in hopes of spotting Puddle.

"Hadde."

She turned. The voice was a whisper in her ear.

"Hadde..." The voice faded on the wind.

"Morin?" she said. He would know how to shift the balance of the battle. She peered to the hills to her left. Was that where his voice had come from?

"I'm coming. On...left flank with Teborans. Warn...."

"I cannot hear you," she said. Could he draw her voice to him? She looked to the hills but the wind whipped snow in her face.

"...Boradin my magic will... no harm. I cannot tell him... is shielding himself from magic. Tell him... fight eternals. Draw... into the battle. Akinos must be slain."

She held her hand to her ear. "Draw who into the battle? Akinos?"

"Wave if you heard me."

His voice was stronger now. Closer.

Hadde raised both her arms and waved. She thought she saw some movement on the hill in the distance. Men rushing through the trees. The snow made it too difficult to be certain.

"Good. ...see you. Tell Boradin not to waste his magic on me. Slay Akinos. I'll... no harm. Go!"

Hadde put her heels to Lightfoot's flanks and rode to where the king stood. Nidon and the Knights of the House cast wary eyes upon her as she approached. "Your Majesty, I've a message from Morin—"

He silenced her with a raised hand. "Meet them, West Teren," he said, looking off to the left.

Hadde felt the words pass her, carried on the wind by the king's magic. She turned in the direction of his gaze. A knight hundreds of strides away saluted Boradin.

Across the battlefield, Akinos' East Teren knights advanced down their hill. From the trees behind them emerged a horde of varcolac and Tyskmen.

The West Teren knights maneuvered to meet the threat. Both sides leveled their weapons and charged. The impact of the massed horsemen echoed from the hills. Lances shattered as knights were thrown from their horses. The West Teren force was larger, but the East Terens had more momentum as they charged downhill. Men and horses fell, but neither force broke through. They swirled in a chaotic melee.

"What do you want, Lady Hadde?" Boradin asked. She pulled her gaze from the fight. Both Nidon and Boradin were watching the struggling mass dispassionately. "Prince Morin sends you a message," she said.

"He did?" The king's gaze wandered across the battlefield. "He cast his voice to you?"

"Yes, Your Majesty. He sent a warning. He's approaching from our left leading the Teborans. He says that you don't have to fear his magic—he will do no harm. You must use your magic against the eternals. You must draw Akinos into the battle where he can be attacked."

"He would have me exhaust my magic while Akinos rests at his ease? How would I defeat him when he did enter the battle?"

Hadde shook her head. "I don't know, Your Majesty. Morin couldn't speak with you. He said you were too well shielded."

Boradin flipped his hand. "I've dropped my wind-guard. He may speak to me if he wishes."

"Prince Morin's plan has some merit, Your Majesty," Nidon said. "Akinos cannot ignore you if you enter the battle. He will have to respond. As it is, he will stand and watch as his army defeats us."

Boradin looked to the hills and then turned to the Knights of the South Teren standing in reserve on the hillside below. "Earl Crane," he casted. "Prepare the South Teren to hold the left flank. We'll be attacked there soon."

Nidon pointed down the slope. "Akinos looks to finish us."

Horns blared as the second line of Rigarians charged into the stream to assault the Saladoran line. "Sir Nidon, hold the House here. Attack Akinos at my command." Boradin raised Forsvar and shouted, "Sir Gorwin, ready the Knights of Sal-Oras! We charge!"

The snow let up as the king joined the knights of Sal-Oras. Hadde reached into her quiver as they prepared to charge. Only a dozen arrows remained to her. She would be through them in no time. Thousands littered the ground—so many they looked like the stalks of grain growing in a field. Following the charge, she would refill her quiver.

Hadde glanced up from the spent Rigarian arrows. Where was Puddle? She hadn't wanted to lose track of him. He wanted so much to be a hero that she was afraid he would do something foolish.

The ranks of Saladoran spearmen were thinner than before. The weight of the Rigarian advance bent the shield wall. In places it was in danger of breaking.

Hadde spotted Puddle still gamely pressing his shield against the man in front of him. To either side of him, taller men thrust their spears at the attacking Rigarians. From behind the Rigarian line, dozens of Eternal Knights leapt into the battle. One eternal sliced through the ranks near Puddle. Only one soldier stood between the stablehand and death. Unaware of his plight, Puddle pushed forward.

She couldn't let him come to harm. Hadde kicked Lightfoot's flanks and raced down the slope. But as she advanced, trumpets sounded and the Knights of Sal-Oras charged. The massed knights made it impossible for her to ride to Puddle. All around her, knights couched their lances, leveling their long shafts at the enemy. She caught a glimpse of Puddle confronting the eternal. The knights crashed into the fight.

Lances snapped and men and horses screamed. The knights cast down the broken shafts and drew their swords and axes. Rigarian arrows rattled off Saladoran shields and helms. Hadde glimpsed Puddle crawling on the ground. The eternal had been driven from him and stood fighting two knights. She pushed Lightfoot through a gap.

An urias clambered to the top of the bank next to the eternal. With a swing of his club, he struck a knight from his horse. Hadde loosed an arrow, taking the urias in the neck, but he didn't stop. He swung his club and drove back a spearman. Hadde put another arrow into the urias. The giant reeled backward and fell into the stream.

The eternal hacked deep into the neck of the remaining knight's horse. The animal reared and tumbled down the bank, taking its rider with it. Puddle, now on his knees, had taken up a spear and thrust it at the eternal. The knight knocked the feeble thrust aside and raised his sword.

Hadde's arrow struck the eternal in his chest, knocking him back. She spurred Lightfoot closer, loosing another arrow as she rode. Again and again, she shot the eternal, sending him stumbling into the masses behind him. He twisted and turned, fighting at those blocking his escape, but Hadde wouldn't relent. He collapsed into the stream as a final arrow struck him in the chest, his silver blood swirling with the muddy red water.

Another eternal leapt up the bank near Hadde. Her quiver empty, she drew her sword. He leapt at her and then suddenly collapsed. Before she could react, Boradin and Nidon were there. Nidon leapt from his horse, and as the eternal struggled to his hands and knees, the champion struck the eternal's head from his shoulders.

"What happened?" Boradin shouted. "Did you shoot him, Hadde?"

She held up her sword in answer. "He just fell. Nobody struck him. No missile hit him."

Boradin's escorting knight charged into the enemy soldiers nearby as Nidon remounted.

"It happened before, Your Majesty," Hadde said. "In the Great Keep. The eternal fell as he charged you."

"I struck him with my fire, that's why he fell."

"No, I saw Morin battle a dozen eternals. He burned them, but it didn't kill them."

"It's Forsvar," Boradin said, realization dawning on his face. "The Godshield protects me from magical harm. The eternals are creatures of magic." He laughed as he said the words.

"Then we must charge them!" Nidon shouted, joy clear on his face. "They fall as soon as Forsvar comes close!" He turned and pointed to another eternal fifty strides away. "Escort! To me!"

"Wait! King Boradin." Hadde called out, "Morin told me that the eternals gain all their strength from the Orb. Forsvar must cut them off from the Orb——"

"We know," Nidon shouted. "That's why we are charging. Stop wasting——"

"But what if Forsvar is brought close to the Orb itself?"

A smile crossed Boradin's face as the realization hit him. "That's it! We can win this."

"But first we must hold," Nidon said. "Now, Your Majesty!" Boradin's escort formed up around him, and with a command from the king they charged down the line.

For a moment Hadde thought of riding with them, but it was not her kind of fight. She sheathed her sword and rode for Puddle. She didn't slow Lightfoot, but reached down from her saddle and grabbed his collar. The sudden weight nearly dragged her from the saddle, but she held on and pulled the boy from danger.

When they were clear, she dropped him and jumped from the saddle. "Puddle, are you hurt?" He sat on the ground, shaking with fear. Blood streaked his face. "Puddle?"

"I'm not hurt." He glanced toward the battle line. Saladoran Knights and Rigarians battled where the eternal had stood, but the death of the urias and eternal had halted the enemy advance.

"I need you to do something for me, Puddle," Hadde said, turning back to the boy. She reached down and forced him to look at her. "Gather arrows for me. As many as you can."

"But I should…" He looked toward the whirling mayhem, fear in his eyes.

"I need you to do this, Puddle. I can do more harm to them with Hawkeye than you can with your spear." She stood and pulled him to his feet. "Will you do it?"

"I will, Lady Hadde."

Hadde leapt into her saddle. Despite the king's efforts, the Saladorans fell back. Boradin retired behind the line with an escort of just two Knights of the House. He removed his helm; Hadde could see the exhaustion in his face.

Horns and shouts of alarm sounded from the left. Hundreds of warriors in boldly striped tunics charged from the wooded hills. Some wore mail, but most were unarmored. They carried bows and short spears, axes and round shields, and wore their light hair in long braids.

"The Teborans attack!" someone shouted.

The Knights of the South Teren wheeled and charged. They drove the Teborans back, but not far. The rough terrain and steepness of the slope soon stole the advantage from the horsemen. The knights had saved the flank. But for how long? Hadde saw more and more Teboran warriors rush from the hills.

Fire erupted amongst the South Terens and they were thrown into disarray. Hadde glanced at Boradin and saw the tight look in his eyes. He rode toward her. "It's Morin. You told me he would do no harm."

Hadde looked back to the battle. She saw Morin amongst a group of horsemen at the edge of the trees. "I don't think he's hurting them, Your Majesty," she said. "It's just a show of flame."

"They've broken through!" someone cried out. Hadde turned toward the shout. Varcolac poured through the Saladoran line. Earl Ciros drew his West Teren command into a tight ring, assailed on all sides.

"Nidon," Boradin called. "Bring the House. Restore the line."

As the king spoke, a flash of light drew Hadde's attention away from the battle. Across the stream, Akinos' war-wagon rolled ominously forward, shrouded by snow. Eternal Knights rode before it, with varcolac and capcaun marching on both flanks.

"No!" Hadde shouted, pointing to the wagon. "Look!"

"Wait, Nidon!" the king called out. "Wait for me. We'll charge Akinos. This is our chance!"

The king rode off. The din of battle assailed Hadde, but she felt strangely alone. Fifty strides to her left and right men hewed at one another in a savage melee. Few ran, and no group broke or routed. She sat in the gap that had opened in the battle line, seemingly invisible, ignored by all.

Her gaze wandered over the dead who clogged the stream and turned its water red. The snow fell heavier, frosting those long dead. A horseman appeared on the far side of the stream. A horseman in black on a black steed.

Morin.

"Here, Lady Hadde." Puddle ran up to her, clutching two handfuls of arrows.

"In my saddle quiver." She barely looked at him.

"Hadde," Morin said. *"Come to me. For good or ill, the final stroke falls. Come to me and I'll see that you are safe."*

With a roar, Akinos' escort of bear-masked varcolac charged through the stream, throwing themselves against the Saladoran shield wall. Behind them, the war-wagon advanced with its escorting capcaun and

Eternal Knights. The Orb of Creation flashed in Akinos' hand.

It was too much. The men of the South Teren could take no more and with cries of fear and anguish, they broke under the onslaught. Hadde caught her breath and looked for Boradin.

A trumpet sounded, clear above the rout. And as its last note faded came the cry, "For the king, for the shield, for the land of Salador!"

The Knights of the House spurred their mounts forward and charged for Akinos. Boradin and Nidon rode at their head, Forsvar blazing with blue-white light.

"Come, Hadde, now!" Morin urged.

"Run, Puddle, you have to escape," Hadde said. "The knights will do the rest."

Hadde watched him run off. If all else went wrong, at least he might survive. Hadde spurred her horse forward. The gap in the battle line wasn't wide, but no one blocked her path. Lightfoot splashed across the stream. Hadde reined in next to Morin, but he stood transfixed by the battle and didn't glance at her.

"Charge, brother!" Morin cried out.

The crimson wedge of Saladoran knights cut through the chaos of battle. Varcolac, fighting to the last, were smashed aside as the warhorses rode them down. Lances snapped and swords plunged as the Knights of the House scattered all who stood in their way.

"Let's go." Morin said, finally turning to face Hadde. "I have to be close when he falls."

"Who?"

Astor's horse skidded to a halt next to them. Mud and blood covered man and horse. In his right hand he held a yellow lance streaked red. "Morin, what are you doing?" He shoved his helm back on his head, exposing his sweat-soaked face. "Akinos needs you."

"Return to your command, Astor. I'm riding to him now."

Astor turned to Hadde and his eyes widened. "What—what is she doing here?"

"She's with me. Under my protection. Return to your command." Morin urged his horse forward and Hadde followed. Astor sat unmoving as they rode off.

Ahead, the Knights of the House broke through the last of the varcolac and charged for the war-wagon. Akinos' Eternal Knights stood impassively as the Saladoran knights approached.

Cheering, the Knights of the House formed up around their king and charged Akinos. The eternals leveled their lances and counter-charged.

Forsvar blazed even brighter and, at the same moment, the Orb of Creation, which until then had burned with a golden fire, suddenly

284

dimmed. As the light faded, the Eternal Knights slumped in their saddles. Some dropped their lances while others fell from their horses altogether.

The Knights of the House smashed into the defenseless eternals. Lance tips punched through armor and swords slashed without mercy as the silver knights were cut down.

Akinos' war-wagon surged forward as the capcaun pulling it strained against their harnesses. The great scything blades flashed in Forsvar's light as they swept through their deadly arcs. The nearest of Boradin's knights pulled up short of the wicked scimitars.

The blades cut down three knights, hemmed in by the press of the battle. From behind the wagon's high walls, varcolac aimed heavy crossbows at the Saladorans.

The capcaun, Akinos' last reserve, roared with fury as they waded into the struggle. Boradin raised his mace and fire exploded at the front of the war-wagon. The vehicle listed sharply and stopped. Hadde's attention was pulled away as Morin toppled from his horse in front of her. Lightfoot veered to the right and only narrowly avoided trampling him.

Hadde leaped from her saddle and crouched beside Morin. She pulled his helm from his head and gasped when she saw his face. His silver skin turned dull gray and faded toward black. "What's happening to you?" She hugged him close to her. He sagged in her grasp. "Don't die!"

His eyes fluttered open.

"He's using it all," Morin groaned, "to keep himself alive. He's not sharing... life with the eternals. Forsvar is shielding the Orb. Limiting it." His skin was nearly black. "I didn't see this."

"What can we do?"

"Slay him, Hadde." Morin's eyes closed and he sagged to the ground.

Hadde turned from him and stared through the snow at the war-wagon. It had stopped moving and tilted forward at an awkward angle. Atop it, varcolac raged as they fought off the attacking knights. Akinos was there, but the Orb had lost its fire, and he sagged on his throne. Capcaun surged into the attacking knights, driving them back.

Leaping into the saddle, Hadde drew Hawkeye from its sheath. "Go, Lightfoot!" Ahead of her, Squires of the House, unable to close in melee, sent crossbow bolts flying at Akinos. No magic shielded him, but two varcolac did so with their bodies. One fell, struck by three bolts. Another leapt in his place. No one shielded Akinos from behind.

Four capcaun crashed into the attacking knights. Their huge axes swept through great arcs, taking down three mounted knights and knocking more from the wagon's walls. The Knights of the House fell back. Hadde reigned in Lightfoot. Drawing Hawkeye, she took aim at

Akinos' back.

Her arm trembled and she paused. She remembered his face, his healing touch, the goodness that radiated through him and the Orb of Creation. But she remembered also what Morin had told her. It didn't matter what was in Akinos' heart. He was the Wasting. As long as he lived, the Wasting would grow worse. As long as he lived, Morin would remain a creature of the Orb.

Hadde released her thumb and let the arrow fly. Her aim was true, but Akinos moved as she loosed it and it stuck one of his shielding varcolac. The injured berserker staggered but didn't fall. She nocked another arrow and drew it to her ear.

Hooves thudded in the snow behind her as a horse galloped closer. She turned to see a black knight charging her, his yellow lance leveled at her. She drew and loosed her arrow in a single motion. Lightfoot screamed as the horses collided. Hadde was thrown. Her head struck the ground and stars shot across her vision.

She blinked into the cloud-filled sky. Had she blacked out? Gentle snowflakes settled on her face. Grimacing in pain, she tried to rise, but a great weight pinned her to the ground. She turned her head. Lightfoot rested on her right leg.

"Lightfoot?" Hadde said. The horse didn't move. The broken shaft of a lance pierced her flank. Hadde gasped in pain as she slid her leg from under the horse. As she lifted her head, she spotted Astor lying on the ground nearby. His dead eyes wide open and staring, a grimace frozen on his face, her arrow in his neck.

She choked back a sob and lay atop her horse. For a time she didn't move, caught in a deep well of grief. Lightfoot. Her constant friend. Another death. The sound of the battle drew her back. She hadn't completed her task.

She glanced over her shoulder to where she had last seen Morin. His still form lay on the ground where she had left him, his horse standing loyally beside him. Morin was dying. She wanted to help him, to ease his suffering. She considered going to him, but the tumult of the battle dissuaded her. There was only one way to save him.

Kill Akinos.

Fighting still raged near the war-wagon, but the tide of battle had turned. Capcaun and varcolac surrounded the Knights of the House, mercilessly hewing down the beleaguered warriors.

Ignoring the pain, Hadde struggled to her feet. Her right leg burned with the effort. She glanced to the ground for Hawkeye, and found it broken at her feet. "Dromost burn you, Akinos. You take everything from me."

286

A flash of blue-white light drew her gaze to Forsvar. The Godshield's fire still burned, but something was wrong. It was Nidon who held the shield. His helm had been knocked off and his mail coif had been pulled back, exposing his bare head. Blood streamed from a cut on his scalp, but it couldn't mask the fury in his eyes.

The champion held Forsvar, and it blazed with the same fire as when the king held it. With blow after blow, he stuck at varcolac and capcaun alike, only to have each slain opponent replaced by another.

Then she saw Boradin. Two knights supported the king. Blood covered his face and his head sagged to one side. He was the army's only hope. Without his magic, all was lost. Not far from him, Hadde saw the crippled war-wagon. The back gate had been let down and two capcaun struggled to remove Akinos' chair.

Here was the cause of all of her misery. Akinos' deluded mission of saving the world was the force behind all the destruction and death surrounding her. All his good intentions meant nothing.

"Why couldn't you listen to Morin?" she shouted, but nobody heard her over the din of the battle. Hadde limped toward the war-wagon, scanning the ground as she walked. She soon found a bow in the hands of a dead Tyskman and took it.

"This is for Belor and Melas. For Jenae, Lightfoot, and the king. This is for them and all the others, Akinos."

She took aim and let fly. The arrow dropped short. But now she knew its range. She pulled a handful of arrows from the dead man's quiver and struggled forward.

A wounded Rigarian limped past Hadde using his broken spear as a cane. Neither of them paid the other any attention. The capcaun had managed to lift Akinos' litter, but were having difficulty getting through the press of varcolac surrounding them.

Hadde stuck her arrows in the ground and nocked one. She loosed it at Akinos, but it glanced off of the armor of one of the capcaun bearing him. He didn't even notice.

"Bastard!"

The capcaun abandoned his efforts at removing the litter and lifted Akinos in his arms. Hadde loosed another arrow. The giant turned in Hadde's direction and both Akinos and the capcaun saw her at the same moment. Too late.

The arrow flew true.

Akinos' body jerked as the arrow pierced his chest. Hadde watched the last of the golden fire die within the Orb. The capcaun stared as Akinos' arm slowly lowered and the Orb slipped from his grasp. It struck the wagon bed and tolled like a massive gong, the sound echoing across the battlefield.

A shudder passed through Akinos' host, as if all the creatures of the Orb were suddenly aware of his passing. All stared in the direction of the war-wagon and their dead creator. "The archer's offspring shall slay the sun." Hadde mumbled the words. She could still see her arrow in his heart.

Chaos erupted. The second capcaun atop the wagon lunged into the one bearing Akinos, throwing both over the side. The capcaun dove to the floor of the wagon and came up triumphantly holding the Orb of Creation in his hand. His grin disappeared in a shower of blood as a varcolac cut off his arm with a savage blow from his halberd.

All thought of the battle disappeared as the desperate struggle for possession of the Orb began. Another capcaun grabbed the varcolac from behind and lifted him screaming from the wagon bed. Other varcolac hewed at each other with pole-axes and swords as they scrambled for the Orb.

Hadde turned from the melee and limped to Morin. Rigarians and varcolac fled past her as Akinos' army crumbled. She ignored them. As she reached Morin, an anguished cry caused her to turn to the war-wagon. A varcolac, Orb in hand, jumped from the wagon to a horse's back. Others rushed him, but the horse leaped forward and evaded them. Nidon and a few Knights of the House battled their way onto the wagon but were too late to stop the escape.

Hadde knelt by Morin and cradled his head in her arms. His face was black; only a shadow of silver still remained. She brushed his brow. "Morin!"

His eyes opened. Dull silver. He opened his mouth but no words escaped.

"Morin, I slew him. Why haven't you healed? Why aren't you human again?"

"Where?" Morin gasped. "Where is the Orb?"

Hadde searched the slope beyond Akinos' fleeing army. The varcolac with the Orb rode hard, leaving his foot pursuers behind. The Orb had flared back to life, Forsvar's aura no longer quenching its fire.

"A varcolac has it," she said. "He's escaping." She turned back to Morin. Silver veins cut through the iron black of his skin.

"My brother? The Godshield?" His voice strengthened as the silver spread over him.

"Morin, what's happening?"

He ignored her questions and stared up the hill at the fleeing army. "Where's my brother? Where's Forsvar?"

"Boradin fell in the battle. Nidon has the shield."

"Good... good."

"Good? What are you saying?"

Morin's tarnished silver face stared back at her.

"Why are you still eternal?" she asked.

He struggled to his feet. "Get my horse, Hadde, before someone steals him."

"No! Tell me what's happening!"

"I must leave. I must catch the varcolac before he learns to control the Orb. And before any Saladoran thinks to slay me. Go home to Landomere, Hadde," he said over his shoulder as he fetched his horse. "Go home to your family. Your mission is accomplished. So many eternals have been massacred this day that you can be assured that the Wasting has ended. And with Akinos dead, there will be no more of them. You've saved us all. Go back to Landomere and live out your life."

His skin gleamed bright silver. He was about to mount his horse when she grabbed him by his arm. "No! What about you? What about us? Why aren't you restored?"

"I'll never heal, Hadde. I'm an Eternal Knight. I shall be one forever."

"But you said you'd heal once Akinos was slain."

"I lied." He jerked his arm free and leaped upon his horse. Any sign of weakness was gone.

She felt her throat tighten. "Why would you lie to me?"

"Because I needed you to have hope. Without hope, I was afraid you wouldn't accomplish your mission."

"What mission?"

"To escape Akinos' camp and ride to my brother. To tell him to slay Akinos."

"I would have done that anyway. Once you told me Akinos wouldn't listen to you... after you told him that he and his eternals were the cause of the Wasting."

He sat on his horse and looked down at her. "I couldn't take the risk."

"What do you mean?"

"I never told Akinos that the eternals are the cause of the Wasting."

She stared mutely at him.

"Hadde, if I had told him, he might have done something about it. And then I never could have taken the Orb. I couldn't take that risk. I needed my brother to slay Akinos and I needed to be here to take the Orb when Akinos fell. My only mistake wasn't realizing Forsvar's power. I didn't know it would fell me when its magic contacted the Orb of Creation."

He looked back up the hill. "I've wasted enough time. Good-bye,

Hadde. Good luck." He turned his horse and spurred it forward.

"I thought you loved me!" she shouted at his retreating back.

The horse stopped and Morin faced her. "I did, Hadde. But now you must forget about me. I'm dead and my love died with me. It died the moment I became an Eternal Knight."

Wheeling his horse, Morin charged up the hill in pursuit of the Orb of Creation. Without thinking, Hadde ran after him. She had only gone a few strides when her injured leg gave out and she fell to the ground.

"Dromost take you, Morin," Hadde muttered as she stared up at his retreating back.

She struggled to her feet and took two more steps after him before stopping. Nearby a horse snorted and pawed the ground. Astor's horse. She could take him and pursue Morin. He might be eternal, but his horse wasn't. She was certain she could outride him. But what was the point? Morin had made his choice. He was gone.

No, she would take the horse and ride for home. She'd been gone far too long.

Epilogue

Hadde turned Astor's horse from the path and rode into the woods. She heard Maret follow on Quickstep.

"Where are we going?" Maret asked. "Is this the way to Landomere?"

"I just want to stop a moment," Hadde replied.

"But we haven't been riding that long."

Hadde halted her horse by a neat pile of stones under a young tree. She dismounted and knelt on the soft ground.

"What's this?" Maret asked.

"It's a cairn. It's the resting place of my friend Belor."

"Oh... your friend from Landomere. I... I will give you a moment."

"Thank you," Hadde replied as the girl withdrew. *Young woman*, Hadde thought. Maret was no longer the silly young maiden she had been.

Hadde lowered her head and touched one of the stones. "We did it, Belor. The Wasting has ended."

It had ended. In this, at least, Morin hadn't lied. Hadde saw it in the green grass and the signs of wildlife as she and Maret journeyed through Salador. Spring had arrived. A true spring full of life. Landomere would be even more alive, Hadde was certain.

The pleasant thought vanished at the memory of the dream-Belor rising from his grave. She yanked her hand back and stared at the mound, expecting the rocks to tumble aside at any moment. A *nightmare of regret*, Akinos had called it.

She grimaced. Couldn't she have a moment's peace? Would the memories of the last month never leave her?

A gentle breeze brought a honey scent to her nose. Hadde smiled in recognition. She perked up and glanced around for the source. She saw them at the head of the cairn. Tiny, luminescent white flowers growing amongst the stones. Everbloom had come to Salador.

Days later they entered the Great Forest itself. Bogs no longer broke the Spiridus Road and trees no longer wept sap from open wounds. It was as if a great weight, a shadow of despair, had been lifted from Landomere, and everyone and everything could breathe easier.

But her dark thoughts still followed her. She frowned at the memory of Morin riding off after the varcolac and the Orb of Creation. He had never glanced back. Had he forgotten her already? She sighed. Morin was eternal and she was nothing. No, not nothing. She was the dagger he had used and then discarded.

"You're thinking of him again," Maret said.

"No, I'm just—"

"You told me to stop you if I saw you thinking of him. And it's easy to see when you are."

Hadde halted Astor's warhorse and stared at the great expanse of trees before her. Maret reined in Quickstep just ahead.

"Let him go, Hadde. Let him go, and look around you. Landomere lives again. The world lives again." Maret smiled. She absently placed a hand on her belly. "I feel it. I feel life."

A silverjay alighted on a tree branch and some of the weight lifted from Hadde's shoulders. It had been years since she had seen one of the reclusive birds. Life returned. "A new beginning," Hadde said. "Let Morin chase his Orb. I'm done with him."

They rode farther into the forest. Hadde fiddled with her horse's reins. Less than a day's journey remained. "You know, Hadde," Maret said, "I'm a little afraid. Will your people truly accept me?"

"It's the Way of the Forest, Maret. They'll treat you as one of their own."

"Will I have to dress like you?"

"Only if you want to." She smiled at the girl. "Let's not dally, we're almost there."

The journey had been hard, especially on Maret. But she had borne it well and had already begun her transformation from pampered maiden to hardened traveler. She sat easily on her saddle now, and no longer complained about sleeping on the ground, curled close to Hadde for warmth. There would be trying times ahead. Life in Landomere was a world away from Saladoran court. But Maret was young, and she would adapt. And in Landomere she would not be an outcast.

Maret stopped and Hadde halted next to her. "Look," Maret whispered. Hadde stared in the direction the girl pointed. There stood the stag Hadde had pursued ages ago. A shiver rolled down her spine.

"It's beautiful," Maret said. The stag stared at them and then pawed the ground. It nodded its massive rack in their direction before turning and trotting away. "No, he's leaving." Maret's voice was crestfallen.

"Come on," Hadde said as she started after the animal. This time it was no pell-mell pursuit through Landomere. The stag repeatedly stopped, looking back to check their progress.

"Where are we going, Hadde? Why are we following it?"

"You'll see." The stag leaped over a bush and disappeared from view. Hadde heard the tinkling of falling water. Smiling, she led Maret around the bush and into the Spiridus Glade.

A gentle breeze blew through the vibrant green forest canopy. Hundreds of leaves swirled and danced as they fell, the last of those killed by the Wasting. Most came to rest on a carpet of fern, while others floated on the pond's surface. The waterfall splashed down the face of a hill completely shrouded by white flowers. Hadde's heart stirred at the sight of their blooms.

"This place is..." Maret's voice trailed off as she stared, awestruck, at the glade.

Hadde put her hand over her Spiridus Token. Dismounting, she said, "Come on, Maret, I have something to show you."

They made their way to the hill and climbed its steep slope. Hadde couldn't help smiling as the flowers' scent overwhelmed her. Behind her, Maret giggled.

"I've never seen anything so wonderful," Maret said as they reached the peak. Hadde nodded as she stepped toward the water-filled basin. The music of the water as it rushed from the spring made her want to sing. Slowly, she pulled the Spiridus Token over her head.

Thank you.

"What?" She turned to Maret.

"I didn't say anything."

Thank you.

Hadde frowned. Maret's lips hadn't moved. The chill Hadde had felt before spread to her arms and legs and up her neck. She followed Maret's gaze. A whirlwind of leaves spun and danced under the arching branches of a great oak.

You brought him home. The voice echoed in Hadde's mind. *Away too long.*

"Who?" Hadde asked.

"Orlos," Maret replied, her voice distant. She held her hand to her abdomen.

Your task is done.

The world spun and Hadde nearly swooned. She clutched the Token. "That was my task? To bring Orlos home? That's why you gave me this?"

You saved me. Thank you. Peace....

"That's all you wanted? For me to bring him home?"

I live again. The spiridus has returned.

"But why? Why didn't you tell me before?"

The leaves settled to the ground as the wind died. No reply came. Hadde stared at the Token in her hands—identical to the one Maret wore. Orlos' token. If only Hadde had known her task. She could have... she could have what? If things had gone differently, Akinos might have won and the Wasting would have taken them all.

Hadde reached out and placed her Spiridus Token on the flat stone in front of her.

"Why are you doing that?" Maret asked.

"This is where I found it. And I don't want it any more. I want to forget it."

"Should I leave mine as well?"

Hadde glanced at Maret and then back to the pool. "Keep it for your child."

They camped in the Spiridus Glade that night and rode for Long Meadow in the morning. The day was bright and warm. Birds sang in the forest as everywhere life re-emerged. Hadde's thoughts turned to Morin. During the night she had discovered another of his lies. He had told her that he could no longer love. That love had been taken from him. But what of Seremar? He was eternal, and yet he still loved Maret.

Maybe Morin still loved her. He just loved the Orb more. He had cast her off so he could pursue his true love. And he had freed her from a life of playing second to Helna's gift. Maybe that was his kindest deed.

Hadde halted her horse. The setting sun cast long shadows through the trees. She knew this land. They were close. "Why have we——" Maret started, but Hadde raised her hand.

"Calen," Hadde called out. "You can come out from behind that log."

"Hadde?" Her apprentice appeared from his hiding place.

"It's me."

He ran to them. "I knew you'd return! The Wasting has ended!"

Hadde laughed for the first time in many days. "I know it." She dismounted and embraced him.

"How did you know I was there?"

She smiled. "Because I'm a Huntress and you're my apprentice."

"We missed you."

"My parents? Are they well?"

"They are." He stared up at Maret. "Who is this?"

"This is Maret. She's going to stay with us."

He grinned up at the maiden. "Welcome to Long Meadow."

Hadde smiled as she put her hand on his shoulder. "Calen, run for the village. Tell them I am home."

Acknowledgments

This project never would have seen the light of day without the help of some wonderful people. First and foremost I'd like to thank the critique group of Ann Emery, Sally Stotter, Lena Pinto, and Lisa Hollis McCulley. They displayed incredible patience taking in a novice writer, tearing him down, and building him back up. It was sort of like boot camp, only with cookies.

I cannot thank enough my friend Mike Shultz for his help and advice. His chapter by chapter critique of the novel was invaluable. He is always willing to help, whether it is grammar questions, plot advice, or computer issues. This novel couldn't have happened without him. Another friend, Kemp Brinson, came to the project late, but his advice truly added depth to the novel. Any writer would benefit from his wisdom.

Christian Cameron saved *Eternal Knight* very early in the process when he reminded me that bad guys see good guys when they look in the mirror. His example as an author has been an inspiration to me.

Joan Shal earns my praise for her copy-editing efforts. It was a lot of work and she accomplished it quickly and expertly. Don't blame her if you find any errors, I had to go and fiddle with things even after her "final" copy edit. All errors are mine!

Ken Hendrix gets the credit for the wonderful cover he designed. Steve Sandford is responsible for the fantastic map. Both men are terrific artists.

I'd like to thank my mother for getting all of this rolling many years ago when she put that copy of *The Hobbit* into my hands. She never stopped feeding me novels and I credit her with giving me my love of reading. My father, who left teaching to become a businessman, devoured motivational, self-help, and goal-setting books. He passed each to me at a very impressionable age, and they made a lasting impact.

My thanks to Sensei Marchand and Joshu Billings of TSMMA for instilling in me the focus, attitude, and non-quitting spirit necessary to take this project to completion.

Finally, I'd like to thank my wife, Helen, for displaying incredible patience as I poured hundreds of hours into this project. I promise the next one won't take as long.

About the Author

Matt Heppe lives in suburban Philadelphia with his wife and daughter. He teaches economics and military history, and in his free time does mixed martial arts. He is a United States Army veteran, having served in Germany and the Middle East as a UH-60 pilot. He is currently writing the sequel to *Eternal Knight*. You can visit him on the web at: http://mattheppe.blogspot.com